'Let me go, and the gods will love you.' Not the Gods of Ys, Gratillonius thought. In a moment's confusion: But I in my heart give Them no honour any longer. Why should I do this thing?

Iron answered: Because I will destroy myself, my Kingship, everything that is left me to care about, if I openly flout Their will.

Hornach wailed and half turned to run. Get it over with! thought Gratillonius, and advanced. His opponent twisted around, raised sword, chopped wildly. Gratillonius caught the feeble blow on his shield. The other throat was open to him. He smote.

The trouble then was that Hornach did not die. He flopped on the ground, spouting blood and screams. When Gratillonius bent down to give a mercy stroke, hands tried to wave it off . . .

I *am* no knacker! he cried into the nothingness and the cold. I am a soldier. Threefold Gods Who robbed the world of Dahilis, will You not send me honest enemies? If you make sport of me, why should I pour out blood for You? Taranis, Lir, Belisama, be warned. I am calling on Mithras to come end Your day, Mithras, Lord of Light.

Thus did the King pay homage to the senile gods of Ys.

Also by Poul Anderson

POUL AND KAREN ANDERSON

The King of Ys 2: Gallicenae

GRAFTON BOOKS

A Division of the Collins Publishing Group

LONDON GLASGOW
TORONTO SYDNEY AUCKLAND

Grafton Books
A Division of the Collins Publishing Group
8 Grafton Street, London W1X 3LA

A Grafton UK Paperback Original 1988

Copyright © Poul and Karen Anderson 1987
Maps © Karen Anderson 1987

ISBN 0-586-07342-6

Printed and bound in Great Britain by
Collins, Glasgow

Set in Times

ROMA OCCIDENTALIS

... Antonine Wall
--- Hadrian's Wall
-.- Boundary of Empire
-x- East/West Boundary
Corvorum Insulae—Channel Islands
Eburacum—York
Dubris—Dover
Gesoriacum—Boulogne
Condate Redonum—Rennes
Lutetia Parisiorum—Paris
Caesarodunum Turonum—Tours
Augusta Treverorum—Trier
Lugdunum—Lyon
Vienna—Vienne
Vindobona—Vienna
Mediolanum—Milan
Burdigala—Bordeaux
Narbo Martius—Narbonne
Massilia—Marseilles
Caesaraugusta—Saragossa
Tarraco—Tarragona
Chersonesus—near Sevastopol
Sequana—Seine
Liger—Loire
Garumna—Garonne
Rhenus—Rhine
Albis—Elbe
Rhodanus—Rhone
Iberus—Ebro

Luguvalium–Carlisle
Isurium–Aldborough
Eburacum–York
Mona (1)–Man
Mona (2)–Anglesey
Deva–Chester
Viroconium–Wroxeter
Lindum–Lincoln
Glevum–Gloucester
Isca Silurum–Caerleon
Segontium–Carnarvon
Abonae–Sea Mills
Aquae Sulis–Bath
Borcovicum–Housesteads

Isca Dumnoniorum–Exeter
Vectis–Wight
Venta Icenorum–Caister St. Edmunds
Venta Belgarum–Winchester
Anderida–Pevensey
Rutupiae–Richborough
Dubris–Dover
Durnovaria–Dorchester
Camulodunum–Colchester
Calleva Atrebatum–Silchester
Corstopitum–Corbridge
Sabrina–Severn
Tamesis–Thames

CALEDONI
Scoti
Picti
DAMNONII
Antonine Wall
VOTADINI
MARE GERMANUM
SELGOVAE
HIVERNIA
NOVANTAE
Borcovicum   Hadrian's Wall
Luguvalium   Corstopitum
BRIGANTES
Mona (1)
Isurium Brigantum   Eburacum
OCEANUS HIVERNICUS
Mona (2)
Segontium   Deva   CORNOVII
Lindum
ORDOVICES
CORITANI
ICENI
Venta Icenorum
Viroconium
TRINOVANTES
CATUVELLAUNI
DEMETAE
Camulodunum
SILURES
Isca Silurum   Glevum
Tamesis   Londinium
Abonae
Rutupiae
CANTI
Sabrina   Aquae Sulis   Calleva Atrebatum
Dubris
BELGAE   Venta Belgarum   REGNI
DUMNONII
Isca Dumnoniorum   Durnovaria   Anderida
Vectis
OCEANUS BRITANNICUS
KA 86
BRITANNIA

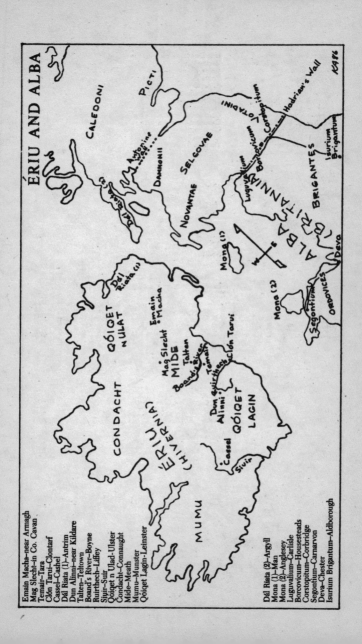

ÉRIU AND ALBA

Emain Macha—near Armagh
Mag Slecht—in Co. Cavan
Temair—Tara
Clón Tarui—Clontarf
Cassel—Cashel
Dál Riata (1)—Antrim
Dun Ailinni—near Kildare
Talten—Teltown
Boand's River—Boyne
Ruirthech—Liffey
Siuir—Suir
Qóiqet n Ulad—Ulster
Condacht—Connaught
Mide—Meath
Mumu—Munster
Qóiqet Lagin—Leinster

Dál Riata (2)—Argyll
Mona (1)—Man
Mona (2)—Anglesey
Luguvalium—Carlisle
Borcovicum—Housesteads
Corstopitum—Corbridge
Segontium—Carnarvon
Deva—Chester
Isurium Brigantum—Aldborough

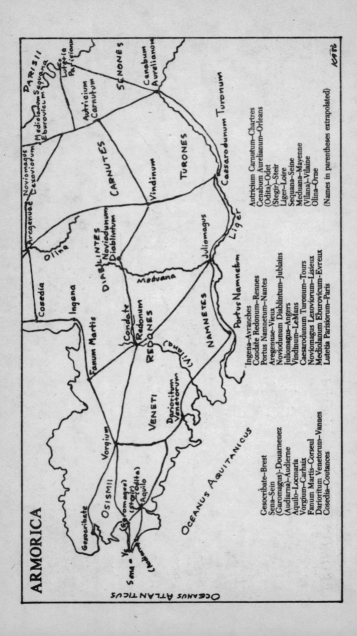

ARMORICA

OCEANUS ATLANTICUS

OCEANUS AQUITANICUS

Gesoribate—Brest
Sena—Sein
(Garomagus)—Douarnenez
(Audiarna)—Audierne
Aquilo—Locmaria
Vorgium—Carhaix
Fanum Martis—Corseul
Darioritum Venetorum—Vannes
Cosedia—Coutances

Ingena—Avranches
Condate Redonum—Rennes
Portus Namnetum—Nantes
Aregenuae—Vieux
Noviodunum Diablintum—Jublains
Juliomagus—Angers
Vindinum—LeMans
Caesarodunum Turonum—Tours
Noviomagus Lexoviorum—Lisieux
Mediolanum Eburovicum—Evreux
Lutetia Parisiorum—Paris

Autricium Carnutum—Chartres
Cenabum Aurelianum—Orleans
(Odita)—Odet
(Stegir)—Steir
Liger—Loire
Sequana—Seine
Meduana—Mayenne
(Vilana)—Vilaine
Olina—Orne

(Names in parentheses extrapolated)

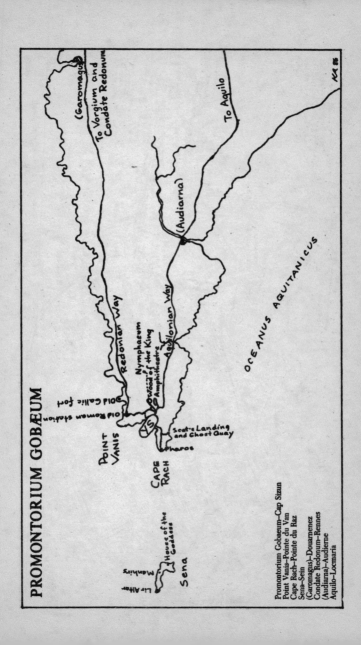

PROMONTORIUM GOBÆUM

(Garomagus)

To Vorgium and
Condate Redonum

To Aquilo

(Audiarna)

Redonian Way

Aquilonian Way

Old Celtic fort

Old Roman station

Nymphaeum
Oracle of the King
Amphitheatre

POINT
VANIS

Scot's Landing
and Ghost Quay

CAPE
RACH

Pharos

OCEANUS AQUITANICUS

House of the
Goddess

Menhirs

Lia Altar

Sena

KR 86

Promontorium Gobaeum—Cap Sizun
Point Vanis—Pointe du Van
Cape Rach—Pointe du Raz
Sena—Sein
(Garomagus)—Douarnenez
Condate Redonum—Rennes
(Audiarna)—Audierne
Aquilo—Locmaria

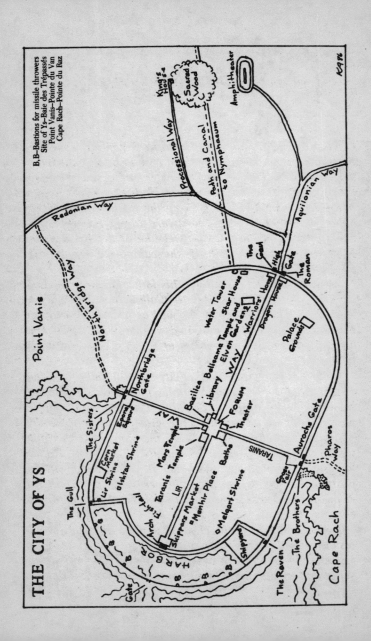

THE CITY OF YS

B.B-Bastions for missile throwers
Site of Ys-Baie des Trépassés
Point Vanis-Pointe du Van
Cape Rach-Pointe du Raz

Point Vanis

Northbridge Way

Redonian Way

Aquilonian Way

King's House

Sacred Wood

Amphitheater

Processional Way

Path and Canal
to Nymphaeum

The Gaul

High Gate

The Roman

Water Tower

Star House and
Warriors' House

Belisama Temple

Dragon House

Library

Elven Gardens

WAY

Palace Grounds

Basilica

FORUM

Theater

Northbridge Gate

Epona Square

WAY

Mars Temple

Taranis Temple

Baths

TARANIS

The Sisters

The Gull

Corn Market

Ishtar Shrine

Lir Shrine

Arch

Fish Market

LIR

Skippers Market

Menhir Place

Melqart Shrine

Aurochs Gate

Goose Fair

Pharos Way

Gate

HARBOR

Shipyards

B

B

B

B

B

The Brothers

The Raven

Cape Rach

K496

Synopsis

Gaius Valerius Gratillonius, born in Britannia, joined the Roman army at an early age and rose to be a centurion in the Second Legion Augusta. After some years he was called with a detachment north to Hadrian's Wall. A great barbarian onslaught was striking the frontier, native Picti allied with Scoti from the westward island Hivernia. Led by Magnus Clemens Maximus, Duke of the Britains, the Romans cast them back. In the campaign, Gratillonius distinguished himself.

As a boy he had sailed with his father, then a merchant captain, on several voyages to Gallia, and especially to Armorica. This familiarity, as well as his war record, led Maximus to give him a unique assignment. He was to lead a small band of his legionaries to Ys, at the far end of the peninsula.

Little was known about that city-state. It had drawn into virtual isolation from the troubles that beset the Empire. However, since the days of Julius Caesar, four centuries past, it had been technically a foederate, a subordinate ally, of Rome. Gratillonius was to go there and take the long-vacant office of prefect: essentially, a resident Roman 'adviser' whose advice had better be followed. From this position he was to use his influence to keep as much of Armorica as possible peaceful in a difficult period soon to come.

It was unspoken but clear that the difficulties would result from Maximus's crossing the Channel with troops at his back, in an effort to overthrow the co-Emperors of the West and make himself supreme. Gratillonius did not disapprove. Corruption, ineptitude, and weakness were rife; barbarians ravaged Imperial lands; Rome herself, the mother city he had never seen, was no longer the seat of power, even in the Western half of the divided realm. Gratillonius believed a strong hand was needed and Maximus could provide it. His admiration for the leader and his receiving the assignment were in spite of religion. True to his family tradition, Gratillonius was a Mithraist, in an era when Christianity was triumphing and his faith dying out, its few adherents often persecuted.

Having taken ship to the Continent, he and his men made a long march west to Ys, on which they found countless instances of oppression by the state and devastation by the barbarians. The coasts were hardest hit, repeated victims of Saxon and Scotic pirates.

On their island Hivernia, which they called Ériu, the Scoti were divided into tuaths, not quite the same thing as tribes or clans, each with its king. Such a king was usually subordinate, together with others like himself, to a stronger lord. The island as a whole held five Fifths, not truly kingdoms though as a rule one man dominated each. They were Mumu in the south, Condacht in the west, Qóiqet Lagini in the east, Qóiqet nUlat in the north – and Mide, which an upstart dynasty had carved out of Condacht and Qóiqet Lagini. The great Kings of Mide centred their reigns, if not their residences, on the holy hill Temir. Niall maqq Echach now held that position, a mighty warlord and the mastermind behind the joint attack on north Britannia that Maximus had turned back. Smarting from this, he plotted fresh ventures against the Romans.

Approaching Ys, Gratillonius was stunned by its beauty. Then suddenly he found himself in single, mortal combat.

Battles of this kind, held in a sacred grove, determined who would be King of Ys, or remain so if he won. He was required to answer all challenges, and to spend the three

12

days and nights around full moon at the Red Lodge in the Wood. A new winner was immediately married to the nine Gallicenae, the Queens. These were chosen whenever a regnant Queen died, from among children and grand-children of her Sisterhood. Such a girl must serve as a vestal virgin until age eighteen – unless first the Sign, a tiny red crescent, appeared between her breasts. If it did, she was consecrated and married to the King. A Queen had the gift of conceiving children only when she desired, and bore only daughters. Most in the past had possessed strong magical powers, but in later generations these had been increasingly fading away.

It was as if the ancient Gods of Ys were losing strength, Taranis of the heavens, inhuman Lir of the sea, and triune female Belisama. These were the Three, the patrons of the city. Persons who wished to also paid homage to various lesser deities, mostly of Gallic origin. On the fringe of a Roman Empire now officially Christian, Ys remained altogether pagan. Under Imperial pressure, it maintained a single Christian minister for a handful of believers. At present this was one Eucherius.

The bloodshed of the ritual combat replaced ancient human sacrifices. Otherwise Ys was highly civilized and the cruel Roman games were unknown there. Over the centuries, Kings had been of widely differing character and lengths of reign. For the past five years the post had belonged to brutal Colconor. At last the Nine could endure him no longer. They cast a curse upon him and a spell to bring yet another challenger.

This they did on the small island Sena, out among the rocks and reefs beyond the headlands. It was reserved to them alone. Except on certain annual occasions or in emergency, one of them must always be on it, holding Vigil to honour the Gods. Usually they did this by daily turns. Sometimes one might be weatherbound for days on end.

13

Foreknowing when Gratillonius would appear, the Queens conspired to get Colconor drunk and pique his quick temper, so that he gave the Roman a deadly insult. Nevertheless Gratillonius should not have responded with a challenge. Afterwards he wondered what had possessed him. But by then he had slain Colconor and, to his astonishment, been crowned King.

Rather, at the ceremony he refused to put on the crown, which would have violated his religious vows. However, he could serve other Gods, if he did not exalt them above Mithras. King of Ys as well as prefect of Rome, he hoped to be the more effective in his mission.

Truly bewildering was his instant marriage to nine strange women. They were aged Quinipilis; ageing Fennalis; Lanarvilis, who took the most interest in statecraft; stern Vindilis; gentle Innilis; lazy Maldunilis; scholarly Bodilis; Forsquilis, young but with witchy knowledge and powers such as no other of the Sisterhood did any longer; and youthful Dahilis. Gratillonius did not consider the rite binding on him, but would make the best of it for the time being. Dahilis came first to his bed. He and she promptly fell in love, and he postponed relations with the rest.

Quinipilis and Fennalis he could lawfully let be, for they were past childbearing age. That was fortunate, since as a Mithraist he could not join with the latter when another wife of his, Lanarvilis, was her daughter.

He learned some of the history of Ys. Originally a Carthaginian colony, it acquired Egyptian and Babylonian elements. Still more did it interbreed with the Celts, who were then entering the country. With their immediate Gallic neighbours, the Osismii, the Ysans enjoyed friendship, but others they must occasionally fight. They assisted Julius Caesar in his conquest of the Veneti, and he visited the city and made alliance with it.

This he never mentioned in his writings, apparently

14

because that was part of the largely secret treaty. Records of Ys were always sparse and had a way of becoming lost in the course of time. The Ysans attributed this to magic, the Veil of Brennilis. She had been first among the Queens in Caesar's day. Later she got Augustus to send engineers to raise a wall around Ys. Else the sea, its level slowly rising, would at last have covered the site. According to Brennilis, the wall must be of dry-laid stone, so that the city would always be hostage to its Gods. After their own construction methods repeatedly failed, the Roman builders conformed.

They devised a great gate on the seaward side, operated by the tides themselves. At ebb it opened to let ships through, at flow it closed to keep the city dry. Its ultimate security was a huge, counterweighted bar secured by a lock. Of the two keys, the Gallicenae kept one in a secret place. The other was an emblem of royalty, borne always by the King unless he travelled out of Ys and its small hinterland. Except at such times, his was the ceremonial duty of locking and unlocking the gate.

Moreover, he presided at the Council of Suffetes and various rituals throughout the year, and in case of war was expected to take the lead. The Council met at the quarter days, and whenever else the King summoned it, to make policy decisions. It comprised representatives of the thirteen aristocratic clans, the Suffetes; of the city's industries and occupations; of the Temples of Lir and Taranis; and the Gallicenae. The King, regarded as an incarnation of Taranis, was the high priest of that God; but a magnate, the Speaker for Taranis, handled most of that Temple's affairs. Lir Captain headed the cult of the sea God, while the Nine served Belisama.

Many Kings had been content to be figureheads, living well until they were cut down in the Wood or came to some different death. (In the latter case, there were special provisions for getting a successor.) Other monarchs had used their authority vigorously, for good or ill. On the whole, Ys flourished, living off the sea, its manufactories, and its far-ranging merchantmen. Yet as Rome declined, Ys suffered too, and became ever more self-isolated. Gratillonius was determined to remedy this.

There was considerable opposition to the measures he proposed. Among its leaders were Hannon Baltisi, Lir Captain, and, to a lesser extent, Soren Cartagi, Speaker for Taranis. Soren and Lanarvilis had when young intended to marry; but before her vestalhood ended, she was Chosen. They remained secretly in love.

At the urging of Dahilis – who, without jealousy, felt deep affection for her eight Sisters – Gratillonius finally sought them too, except for Quinipilis and Fennalis. The King of Ys was always potent with the Nine, although impotent with any other woman; such was the will of Belisama. Vindilis frankly disliked his attentions, and he ceased, but they became reasonably friendly.

Meanwhile his legionaries settled down to life in Ys. Young Budic, a devout Christian, visited the minister Eucherius, and found him in conversation with the learned, though pagan, Bodilis. Cynan and Adminius went out on the town and encountered the fisher captain Maeloch. The latter was among those who lived in tiny Scot's Landing below the sea cliffs. They were, by inheritance, the Ferriers of the Dead, an awesome duty, though otherwise they were as rough and gusty as all their kind.

Meanwhile, too, Niall maqq Echach planned a great seaborne raid. He would steer wide of Ys, for it was said that its Queens could command the weather, and attack Gallia to the south. He expected to make vast inroads, for civil war once again racked the Empire as Maximus strove against his rivals and drove them before him. Niall's son

16

Breccan, young but his eldest and most beloved, persuaded the King of Mide to take him along.

Gratillonius feared that sort of danger. Forsquilis sent her spirit forth in the form of an owl to spy widely around, and so learned of Niall's intent. Gratillonius was unsure whether to believe in her magic or not, but made his preparations according to her word; for he knew what a deadly wound such an assault would inflict on his civilization.

The Nine called up a storm when the fleet was at sea. Blown east, most of the Scoti perished among the rocks around the promontory. Some made desperate landings but were killed or beaten off. Among the latter was Niall. As his ship sailed by the city, a bolt from its artillery slew Breccan. Grief-stricken, measurelessly angry at Ys for its witchcraft against him when he had intended it no harm, Niall vowed revenge. He and his few surviving followers beat their way home to Ériu.

The Ysans and Romans had also suffered. Among the fallen legionaries was Gratillonius's deputy and fellow Mithraist Eppillus. An uncanny vision on the battlefield had raised religious awe in all who were there, no matter how they interpreted it afterwards. Gratillonius swore Eppillus would rest on the headland he had defended. Burial above the sea had long been forbidden, as being offensive to Lir; the old necropolis lay crumbled and abandoned near the lighthouse. Despite the antagonism it caused, Gratillonius forced the Council to let him hold the Mithraic funeral.

Cynan requested initiation into that faith, and Gratillonius instructed him. The centurion-King was now a happy man; not only had he won a major victory, his dear Dahilis was expecting her child by him.

They went together to the Nymphaeum in the hills at the eastern frontier of Ys. There vestals served by turns, and Dahilis asked for a blessing on the unborn babe. Gratillon-

ius took the opportunity to conduct the initiation of Cynan at a nearby spring. Dahilis came upon the rite and was horrified. This water, sacred to Belisama, was being used in the service of a God Who allowed no women in His cult. Gratillonius soothed her somewhat.

Calling upon Innilis in Ys, she found that Queen in bed with Vindilis. The two had become lovers during the ghastly years with Colconor, though Ysans generally abhorred such acts. Shocked, sorrowful at having to keep a secret from her beloved husband, Dahilis nevertheless promised help, and got Innilis to seek counsel from Quinipilis. The old Queen saw no harm in the relationship, but said it should be made known to the rest of the Sisters. However, Gratillonius's affronts to the Gods of Ys boded ill.

He himself was appalled to learn how Vindilis, Forsquilis, and Maldunilis had betrayed Colconor to his death, foul though the man had been. He decided to shun all the Nine save Dahilis. This worsened the friction between him and the magnates, despite his popularity among the common people. Finally those same three women sought him out in the Wood and, by the power of the Goddess, made him be again their lover. Afterwards he was shaken to think how he had been possessed. Still, his relationship with the Nine grew more harmonious, and gradually he gained support among the city's leading men.

Nonetheless the conflict between him and the Gods seemed ineluctable. He would not make amends to Them. Instead, he planned a long journey around Armorica, to confer with the Roman authorities and get them to stay neutral in the civil war while strengthening defences against the barbarians. By so absenting himself from a number of important rites, Gratillonius again defied the Three.

Under Dahilis's irenic influence, Innilis willingly became pregnant by him. In fact, all the Queens were concerned

18

for his well-being. Forsquilis conjured up an oracular dream that seemed to say his sins could be expiated by certain painful acts on the part of the Nine, and by one who awaited a child standing Vigil on Sena at midwinter, when ordinarily all would be ashore for the Council. Since Dahilis would be nearly at term then, the choice naturally fell on Innilis.

Eucherius, the Christian pastor, died. Gratillonius, who had grown fond of the old man, first promised to arrange for a replacement. Soon after that, he departed on his mission.

Innilis suffered a terrible pregnancy. Gratillonius was barely back when she had a miscarriage. The Nine decided that Dahilis must take her place at midwinter on Sena. Gratillonius learned of their intent and tried to stop it, but they refused. To carry her away by force would destroy everything he had accomplished here or ever hoped to. Moreover, it was her own desire to do the thing for his sake.

He insisted on accompanying her. It was forbidden a man to set foot on the island above high-water mark, but he could at least wait at the dock, ready to help her if need arose. The sacred barge left them alone out there.

A storm blew up while Dahilis was going about her religious duties. When at night she had not returned to the house of the Queens, Gratillonius broke the prohibition and went in search. After hours he found her, crippled by a fall, unconscious, freezing to death, and in labour. He carried her back to the house but could not save her. Immediately after she died, he cut their child from her womb.

Forsquilis had knowledge. She got Maeloch, who had long cherished 'little Queen Dahilis', to take her out to Sena in the morning. They bore home the body, the infant, and Gratillonius.

The mother being gone, the King must name the new princess at a ceremony in the Temple of Belisama. Against custom, in memory of his beloved he called her Dahut. Then at once, still stunned by grief, he was married to the next Chosen Queen. This was Sasai, a homely, dull-witted girl who picked the royal name Guilvilis. She was almost as bewildered and unhappy as he; but the power of the Goddess united them whether they would or no.

It seemed to the Gallicenae and the Suffetes that by her death Dahilis had given the Gods a sacrifice that healed the breach between Them and the King. After the sea burial the magnates, led by Soren, pledged him their support, as long as he abided by the ancient laws.

On a later night the knock of an invisible hand called forth the Ferriers of the Dead, as had happened throughout the centuries, to bring the souls of the recently departed out to Sena for the judgement of the Gods. None knew what came thereafter. It was widely believed that some of the dead, Queens especially, returned for a while in the form of seals to watch over those they had loved in life. For this reason, the seal was an animal sacred and inviolable to the people of Ys.

I

1

The child knew only that she was upon the sea. It was enough to overwhelm her with wonder. That this was the Blessing of the Fleet lay outside her understanding as yet, like nearly all those sounds her father made: ' – And how would you like to come along, little one?' What spoke to her was the strength of his arms and the laughter rumbling in his breast as he took her up and held her close.

Already fading out of her were the marvellous things that happened at the docks, people in bright robes, deep-chanted words followed by music that sang, chimed, whistled, quivered, twanged, boomed, as the procession went from hull to hull. The grey-bearded man in the lead was frightening to see, with his long pole and its three sharp spikes that he held on high, but behind him came the Mamas – nine of them, though she was too small to have the use of numbers. Some carried green branches that they dipped into pots that others bore, and then sprinkled oil on the prows. The first had a bowl that swung from gold chains and gave off smoke. When the wind shifted and brought the smoke to the child, it smelled sweet. She and her father stood aside, watching. He was very splendid in his own robe, a great sledge hammer at his side, on his breast the Key that usually hung inside his clothes; but she had no words for any of these things.

Afterwards he picked her up again and carried her on board a ship that led the rest forth. The water in the harbour basin was lively, for the gate stood wide and a fresh breeze blew yonder. As her father's yacht passed through, the deck started to roll beneath her. Keeping her feet became a delightful game. The air was shrill and cold. It flung salt spray that tingled on her lips. The planks she stood on were still sun-warmed, giving off a fragrance of new pitch.

Everybody was jolly, men and women and such children as they had with them, none of those as young as the girl. From aft resounded the coxswain's drum, setting time for the rowers, whose oars cracked against the holes. Between strokes they often tossed words back and forth that made them grin. The ship creaked too, stays thrummed, a ruddy pennon at the masthead went *snap! snap!* Gulls mewed, hundreds of them, a snowstorm of wings, dipping and soaring. Other birds were likewise out in their darker throngs, aloft or afloat, and sometimes their cries also cut through the wind.

The craft that followed spread formation into a half-moon. Many were bigger than this, whether low and lean or high and round-bellied. Many more were smaller, duller-painted, and the men in them weren't so finely dressed. Some had raised sails, the rest continued under sweeps. Behind them rose the city wall, sheer, murky red save for the frieze under its battlements, and its towers, and the still taller spires, inside whose copper and glass and gilt flung light blindingly back at the sun. The headlands bulked rugged on either side, surf tumultuous underneath. The valley and hills beyond were turning green.

But it was the sea that captured the girl child, the sea. At first she clapped her hands together and shouted. Later she stood silent, aware of nothing else, for this was everything, this was the forever changing boundlessness that she had not known was within herself.

22

The sky reached pale and clear, only a few clouds scurrying at the edge of the world. Waves rushed and rumbled, long, maned, foam-swirled, wrinkles dancing in webs across their backs. Colours played over them, through them, grey-blue, grass-green, purple-black. Where they broke on the rocks and reefs that lay everywhere about, they bellowed hollowly and sent milkiness fountaining. Torn-off strands of kelp moved snakishly in their troughs. Creatures swam, tumbled, darted, at one with the waves, not only fowl but the sleekness of seals, a few times the silver leap of a fish or the frolicsome grace that was a porpoise. The child did not recognize a piece of driftwood as being off a wreck.

Time was no more, nothing was except the miracle that had taken her unto itself. She did not come back to anything else until the helmsmen put their steering oars over and the yacht turned again landward. The parade was done.

Most vessels headed the same way, wanting their berths prior to commencing the season's farings. A few bore southeasterly, towards fisher hamlets along the coast. The child realized that her adventure neared an end. She did not weep, such was not her nature, but she made her way to the side, the better to watch while she still could.

This was on the foredeck, above and forward over the rowers' benches. The bulwark was too high for her to lean over. When a seal drew alongside, she had just a tantalizing glimpse. Nearby squatted a bollard, the anchor rode coiled around it, the hook leaning massive against it. An active creature since her birth, she got a purchase on the hemp and climbed on the top. There she glanced widely around.

Aft she spied a streak of land low in the water, from which rose a single building, dark, foursquare, sur-

23

mounted by a turret. But she had already seen that. What she wanted to do was look at the seal.

It swam close, easily matching the speed of the oarsmen. The amber-brown of its coat was warm amidst the brilliance of the waves. It did not move like its fellows, intent on prey or whatever else they sought. Rather, as much as possible, it kept gazing upward. Its eyes were big, beautiful, as soft as sleep. Enchanted, the child stared back into them.

A grown-up noticed her on her precarious perch, exclaimed, and hastened to pluck her off it. He was too late. The yacht rolled heavily. It was nobody's fault — these were notoriously treacherous waters — and had happened several times today. The girl was pitched loose and went overboard.

As she fell, the yells from above reached her faintly, unreal, lost in the welcoming noise of the sea. It received her with a single enormous caress. Her thick garments drew her under. A lucent yellow-green blindness enfolded her. She felt neither chill nor fear, merely surprise, a sense of homecoming. The sea tossed her about much like her father bouncing her in his arms. A humming began to fill her head.

Before she could gasp a breath, solidity struck, gripped, whirred her away. Held between the front flippers of the seal, she drank wind and salt scud. And then her father was there, threshing clumsily but mightily through the billows. Somehow it became he that clutched her, kept her face in the air, roared for a line. Scrambling and confusion overran them; and they were back on deck. She released her shock and bereavement in a wail.

He hugged her close to him. She felt his heart slugging behind the iron Key. His voice shuddered. 'Are you well, darling? Are you all right, my little Dahut?'

24

The summons came to Gaius Valerius Gratillonius in the third year during which he had been Roman prefect and King of Ys. Having read it, he told his majordomo to arrange accommodation for the courier, because he would need a few days to find out precisely what his reply must be. Thereafter he sent for Bodilis and Lanarvilis.

Bodilis arrived first. It was raining. In the upstairs conference room where he received her, a brazier did somewhat to relieve cold, but a couple of lamps mainly cast unrestful shadows that made the pastoral frescos on the wall dim and unreal, like memories of the summer that was waning. She had left her cloak with the palace doorkeeper. Though it had a cowl, drops of water sparkled in the dark-brown waves of her hair and misted the strong-boned countenance. Two graceful strides brought her to him. He took both her hands – they were warm beneath the dampness – and smiled down into the deep-blue eyes – not very far down.

'It's good to see you again,' he said, and brushed his lips across hers, a kiss quick and cool but aquiver. 'How have you been, and the girls?' He spoke Latin, and she replied in the same tongue. They ordinarily did when by themselves; she wanted to maintain proficiency in it.

'Oh, Kerna is all agog, planning a feast to celebrate when she finishes her vestalhood, and Semuramat is wild with envy and insists the eight years still ahead of her might as well be eternity,' she laughed. Of the three children she had by Hoel, Talavair had completed Temple service and was married, with one of her own on the way.

'Una was sound asleep when your messenger came.' That was the daughter Bodilis had given Gratillonius last year.

He sighed. 'If only I could spend more time in your household.'

'No,' she said earnestly, 'don't think like that.'

He nodded. Had Dahilis been less beloved by her Sisters than she was, his lavishing of attention on her would have created stresses he could ill afford. Since her death, he divided his nights as evenly as feasible among the seven Queens with whom he slept, and his days among all the Nine – or, rather, what remained of his nights and days after royal duties and masculine recreations. 'Well, we'll have tomorrow, you and I, if the moon be willing. Keep it clear for me.'

She smiled. 'I've been preparing. But why have you called me here today?'

'Best we wait for Lanarvilis . . . No, you may as well read this at once.' He pointed to a papyrus sheet on the table. It was curled from having been carried as a sealed-up roll. She spread it between her hands and brought it close to a lamp. As she lowered her head, nearsightedly, to scan the writing, she murmured, 'Lanarvilis too, and none other? Are we to compare notes on your youngsters? Then why not Guilvilis?'

The jape fluttered forlorn. She had spied the grimness upon him. 'It's not that you two – well, you three – among the Gallicenae have happened to bear me offspring this soon,' he explained in his methodical fashion. 'Although I well know it's not chance pure and simple. You and Lanarvilis took most thought for the future. You both saw that after what . . . happened with Dahilis, my fathering of more princesses would strengthen my shaken standing in Ys.'

'Also,' Bodilis said, 'we are neither of us young women. Time is at our heels.'

26

'Well, because you are what you are – yourself learned and wise, she versed and shrewd in the politics of the city – I want your counsel before I tell anybody else about this matter.'

'Whereas you think poor Guilvilis is neither,' remarked Bodilis sadly. 'She has nothing to offer you but her utter love.'

He bit back a retort that any dog could do as much. It would have been unkind, and not quite true. He must not blame the newest of the Nine for supplanting Dahilis; that had been no wish of her own. Guilvilis was dull, true, but she was humble and sweet and helpful; the first infant she had brought forth, Sasai, was healthy and seemed bright enough; she was carrying a second. 'Read,' he said.

While Bodilis did, Lanarvilis came in. Blue gown and tall white headdress showed that she had been taking her turn as high priestess at the Temple of Belisama. Nothing less than the wish of the King would call such a one away, and it had better be business vital to the city or the Gods.

Gratillonius greeted the big blond woman courteously, as was his wont. Between them was little of the warmth he had with Bodilis or the wildfire with Forsquilis. Even when they coupled, she held back her inmost self. But they had become friends, and partners valuable to each other in the governance of Ys. 'What betokens this?' she aksed briskly in her native language.

'A moment,' he requested in the same speech. 'How fares Julia?' Her sixth and most likely last living child, the babe was frail, often ill. Sometimes, when it fell out that the King visited Lanarvilis while she was keeping Dahut, the beauty, vitality, and wilfulness of Dahilis's daughter seemed almost inhuman by contrast, elflike – no, catlike.

'Her fever grew so fierce yesterday that I sent for Innilis, who laid on hands and gave her medicine,' replied the mother. 'Today she's much better.'

27

'Ah, good. Will you be seated?' Gratillonius gestured at a chair. After two and a half years in Ys, he had come to take that article of furniture for granted, well-nigh forgetting that it was not commonplace elsewhere.

Lanarvilis settled down. He joined her. Bodilis finished reading, passed the letter to her Sister, and likewise sat. For a while, silence took over the room, apart from the susurrus of rain outside.

Then Lanarvilis, whose lips had been moving and forefinger tracing, lowered the papyrus and said with a rueful smile, 'I find my Latin worse rusted than I knew. It seems the Augustus commands you to report. But you've been sending him news of your stewardship whenever he required it.'

'He wants me to come in person,' Gratillonius said.

She drew a sharp breath. 'Where?'

'Augusta Treverorum. You may remember hearing how he entered it in triumph early this year' – after he, Magnus Clemens Maximus, scattered the army of co-Emperor Gratianus, who was presently murdered; and Valentinianus made a peace that gave Maximus lordship over Britannia, Gallia, and Hispania, while Valentinianus retained sovereignty over Italy, Africa, and part of Illyricum. The Eastern half of the Empire stayed under Theodosius in Constantinople.

''Tis understandable,' Gratillonius went on. 'The issues are settled, the weapons fallen silent, the task no longer to seize power but to wield it. He can learn more, and better, of Ys in interviews with me than from any amount of clumsy writing.'

'And what will he do with the knowledge?' Bodilis wondered.

Gratillonius shrugged. 'We shall see. Yet I have ever maintained that Maximus Augustus is the stern physician whom sick Rome needs. He'll heed my advice, if it be sound. This is among the things I'd fain discuss with you two, what my recommendations ought to be.'

'He may forbid you to return here,' Lanarvilis fretted.

'I doubt that. True, he need no more fear a hostile Armorica at his back. But you know how much is left to do, putting down piracy and banditry, reviving trade, weaving the whole peninsula back together. I'm in the best position to lead that work, and I've proved my loyalty to him.'

'You may be gone for a long while, however.'

Gratillonius nodded. 'Belike so. Even on Roman roads, 'twill be more than half a month's journey, unless I kill horses. And though the conference should not fill many days, I want afterwards . . . to use the opportunity.'

'They'll not like it – Suffetes, votaries, commoners, all folk in Ys – having the King take leave of them.'

'I've been away erenow. Granted, this may prove a lengthier absence. But no military leader will be called for, and our interior affairs prosper. As for my ceremonial and sacral tasks, they can either await my return or be delegated. I want your thoughts on all this.'

Bodilis's gaze grew intent. 'What else have you in mind to do?' she asked.

'Well,' he said uncomfortably, 'you remember that when the Christian minister Eucherius lay dying, we promised him a successor in his church. That's two years gone, and the pledge still unfulfilled, as busy as we've been. I'll seek a man we can get along with.'

'That's a small matter, to Ys and in your own head,' she responded. 'I've come to know you, my dear. What is your true intent?'

'Very well!' he blurted. 'You know how I've wished to found a Mithraeum, for the worship of the God Who is mine. I cannot, unless first I've won the rank of Father in

29

the Mystery. My hope is to find a temple where this can be done.'

Lanarvilis looked shocked. Bodilis remained calm: 'You may search through a vast territory, if I've heard aright about the persecution of that faith.'

'Oh, I wouldn't. Mithras is a soldier. First and foremost. He expects a man to do his duty. But if I went as far south as, say, Lugdunum – I'd need permission, but I suppose I can get it – I should at least learn whether any such congregation is left within my reach.'

'Would your elevation take long?'

'I trust not. Once, aye, years; but there are so few of us these days, and our needs are so urgent. I promise I'll not seek consecration if it demands more time than Ys can spare.'

'I see.' She glanced away, thoughtful.

'This is unwise,' said Lanarvilis nervously. 'Your breaking of traditions has already caused discord in abundance. If now the King, high priest and Incarnation of Taranis, openly gives allegiance to a foreign God – '

'I've made no secret of my prayers,' Gratillonius answered. 'Never in aught that matters have I failed to give the Gods of Ys Their due. Nor will I.' He felt an emptiness as he said that. In his soul he had forsworn Them. 'Have we become Christians here, to deny respect to everything divine other than the Lord of our narrow sect?' He forced a grin. 'Or sects, rather. They might as well have a dozen different Christs, the way they quarrel about His nature.'

Dubious, she yielded. 'Well, we can be tactful.'

'Aye.' Bodilis leaned across the table and laid her hand over his. 'Dear, if you are going to Lugdunum, and not terribly belated, would it be too much farther for you to come home through Burdigala?'

'What?' he asked, startled.

Her smile was wistful. 'You remember how for years I've been in correspondence with Magnus Ausonius, the poet and rhetor. He's retired to his estate there. If you could bring him my greetings, and carry back an account of him as a person, it would be – almost like meeting him myself.'

Pity touched Gratillonius. Her life was not impoverished. More than the perquisites of a Queen, she had the riches of her spirit. But she had never travelled beyond the island of Sena in the west and the frontier of the Ysan hinterland in the east, a few leagues away. The glories of Greece, Rome, all the great civilizations of the Mediterranean and the Orient, existed for her only in books, letters, and the conversation of an occasional visitor. Bound by Imperial law and military discipline, he nonetheless had freedoms she could but dream of. 'Why, indeed,' sprang from him, 'if I can, indeed I will.'

3

Again the King stood on the dais in the council chamber of the basilica, at his back the twenty-four legionaries remaining to him, behind them the eidolons of the Triad, and before him the Gallicenae and magnates of Ys. He wore a robe inwoven with gold-threaded tapestry figures to represent the eagle and thunderbolts of Taranis. In sight upon his breast hung the Key, and to his right, deputy Adminius had received the Hammer.

The garb was a part of his message, for at the quarterly meetings he had not dressed quite this grandly, and in everyday life he picked clothing simple and serviceable. It told the assembly that today he was not the blunt-spoken soldier with whom they handled the affairs of the city; he was embodied Power, secular and sacred. Several of the councillors must have anticipated this, for they too were attired in antique vestures or in Roman togas.

Still, after the invocations, Gratillonius used plain language. Oratory was not among his gifts, and while he had become fluent in Ysan, a number of its subtleties would always elude him. First he summarized the situation in the Western Empire and the reasons why he hoped for a better future, at least in those parts where Maximus had control.

'What are the Augustus's plans for us?' growled Soren Cartagi.

'That we shall learn,' Gratillonius told them. 'I am bidden to his presence.'

The news drew the storm of protest he had expected. He let Lanarvilis and Bodilis do most of his arguing for him. Although unprepared, a few joined in on their side, such as Sea Lord Adruval Tyri and Mariner Councillor Bomatin Kusuri. Their grounds were practical. 'In Roman eyes, our King is an officer of the army and the state,' Adruval reminded. 'If he goes not when ordered, that's insubordination. D'ye want a legion coming to winkle him out of here?'

Vindilis's lean features whitened. 'Let them dare!' she cried.

'Nay, now, be wise, my Sister,' Quinipilis urged. Her voice was unsteady; in the past year or so she had much weakened. 'How could we stand them off?'

'The Gods – '

Forsquilis the seeress interrupted in a tone low and carrying: 'I think the Gallicenae may no longer be able to raise the Gods in aid; and They Themselves are troubled. For the heavens have moved from the Sign of the Ram to the Sign of the Fish, and the old Age dies as the new comes to birth.' Her gaze dropped and her hand passed across her robe, under which a life swelled towards its own forthcoming.

'Will the Emperor let our King return?' asked Innilis. She sounded terrified.

'Why not?' said Bomatin. 'He's been doing a masterly job here.'

'Doing it for Rome,' Hannon Baltisi, Lir Captain, snarled. He raised his arm. 'Oh, I agree he's served us well. I don't believe he'd willingly do us an evil turn. But what will he have to say about things?'

'Aye.' Soren nodded his massive head. 'When Rome was caught up in its tribulations and forgot Ys, we stayed free. Now there's a strong Emperor, the kind who always wants more power – and more cash – and he's become aware of us. What's next?'

Gratillonius decided he had better assert himself. 'Hold!' he boomed. 'Hear me!' Having got silence, he adopted an easy manner:

'My Queens and worthies, bethink you. What's to fear? I served under Maximus when we cast the wild men back from the Wall. I know him for a man able and well-intentioned. He'll listen to me.

'Consider what Ys has done for him. We kept Armorica quiet. We saved Gallia from what would have been a ruinous barbarian attack. We have taken the lead in rebuilding defences throughout the peninsula. Commerce begins to revive as the risks diminish. Folk should soon start reconstructing what's been destroyed. Maximus must be a madman to wish this changed; and he is not. That's the more so when he still has to reckon with the untamed Germani and Alani and, it may be, his fellow Emperors in the South and East. Far from helpless, Ys is in an excellent bargaining position.

'I'd liefer not brag, but this and more we have done

under my guidance. And I have been not only your King, but also the prefect of Rome.

'Then be glad if we can renew our ties to Rome the Mother!'

There was some discreet applause, some reservation, several faces that stayed troubled. Hannon Baltisi scowled, cleared his throat, and rasped:

'Well and good, O King, save for this, that Rome has long since become whore to Christ. Need I recall to you how they mock the Gods there, violate temples, smash images, hound worshippers? Will Christ dwell in peace with the Gods of Ys, those Gods who alone hold Ocean at bay?'

Mumbles and whispers passed among the forty-two. The legionaries who formed Gratillonius's honour guard kept still, but he could virtually feel resentment radiate from most of them at such a denunciation of their faith. He weighed his reply carefully. The old man's travels, in his days as a sea captain, had if anything reinforced his fanatical hatred of the Church; but persons more moderate were uneasy, and for cause.

'This is a question among many that I hope to take up with the Augustus,' Gratillonius said. 'It touches me too, not only in my royal office but in my heart.' He congratulated himself on the subtlety of this reminder that he was a Mithraist. Before ground could be broken for the temple of his dreams, foundations must be laid in the minds of men. 'But I'm unafraid. The fact is that the Empire continues full of people who are not Christians, a number of them in high positions. Maximus knew my beliefs when he appointed me your prefect.

'Clergy are few and far between in these parts. The Augustus should be satisfied with a new minister here for the Christians among us, just as we had before. That was a harmless man. Fate willing, I'll have a voice in choosing his successor. Rest assured, 'twill be no Ambrosius!'

Bodilis and three or four others recognized the name of the forceful bishop of Italian Mediolanum, and smiled. Relief spread visibly through the rest.

Gratillonius pursued his advantage. 'To that end, I may have to search a while,' he warned. 'Also, 'twould be well that I make myself familiar with conditions throughout Lugdunensis, aye, and in Aquitania – ' he saw Bodilis kindle, and tipped her a wink – 'so that we'll be ready to cope. This will keep me away for a period of months. I'll be absent at the equinox and mayhap at the winter solstice, as well as other occasions. Yet I'll leave the city in order, fully able to steer itself that long. Surely the Gods will take no offence, when this is for the well-being of Their people.'

He knew himself for a hypocrite. But his ultimate purpose was honest, and as a soldier he had never objected to ruses. He sat down on the throne, resigned to a theological dispute. Bodilis and Lanarvilis were primed to conduct it for him. Afterwards would come practical topics. What should he say and seek in Treverorum? He sincerely wanted suggestions. If need be, let discussion go on for a few days.

Only a few, however. He must not keep the Emperor waiting.

4

It chanced that this was his night to spend with Innilis. Knowing how he felt, and remembering the mother, his wives tried to shift custody of Dahut so that he could see her when he visited each of them. The effort failed more often than not, since strict rotation was impossible. He might be preoccupied, perhaps out of the city altogether, in the hinterland or on the water or standing his monthly Watch at the Wood. He might have been working hard or late, and in sheer weariness bedded down alone at the royal palace. For her part, a Queen might likewise be overbusied, or having her courses, or sick. Pregnancies and childbirths had been intervening too, and bade fair to increase. Forsquilis was now fruitful, Guilvilis was again, and Maldunilis had finally decided to trouble herself about it. Moreover, the two Gallicenae with whom he did not sleep, aged Quinipilis and ageing Fennalis, claimed a share in the upbringing of Dahilis's daughter, which for the sake of harmony could not be denied them.

Fortune did have Dahut at Innilis's house when King and Queen arrived on that evening. 'Oh, my lord, my lady, how good you're back!' exclaimed the maidservant Evar as they entered. 'The little one's been that fretful. She threw such a tantrum I feared she'd hurt herself, I did, and restrained her.'

Dread struck. 'Is she ill?' Gratillonius demanded.

'Nay, lord, I think not. Like a crazed ferret she's been, for dashing about and throwing things – oh, my, ferrets don't throw things, but my lord knows what I mean – 'Tis but that kids are troublous in their third year. Well, she's not quite in that yet, is she? But ever so far ahead of her age, already speaking, and so much alive. With my lady gone all day – Does my lord want to see her?'

'I do.' He brushed past the woman and strode to the room that had been designated a nursery.

When he opened the door, he saw the debris of small destructions strewn about, a broken toy chariot, stuffing ripped out of a rag doll, general chaos. The chamber pot stayed upright; in certain things, Dahut had a feline neatness. The child was curled on the bed, brooding over

36

her wrongs. She had stripped off her clothes. Sunset light, striking through the windowpane, turned her skin to ivory, hair to gold, eyes to lapis lazuli. O Mithras, how she recalled Dahilis!

She gathered her limbs beneath her, again like a cat. 'Father,' she hissed.

'Ah,' he blustered, 'we've been having a mutiny, have we? What for? Why have you been such a bad girl?'

She struggled for words. 'I wos . . . wos . . . *me*.'

Did she mean 'all alone'? How could he tell? He hunkered down and spread his arms. 'Well, well, little rebel, let's make it right again, hey?'

She uncoiled and sped to him. He hugged her withy-slimness. How sweet she smelled! 'You mustn't do this, you know,' he said into the warmth between her throat and shoulder. 'It's not kind to your Mamas, or their poor servants who have to look after you.'

'You di'n' come,' she gasped; but she shed no tears, she hardly ever did.

'Oh, you were awaiting me? I'm sorry. Your Papa had work to do. Let's get you nicely dressed, and then before Evar brings you dinner we'll play horse and I'll sing you a song – because you're the single human being who does not flinch when I sing, and too soon will that end.'

– Innilis ate lightly and simply. Gratillonius liked the fare her kitchen offered, after the frequently elaborate meals he got in Ys. She had learned to give him portions of adequate size. Ordinarily they made small talk over the table and retired early, for although she often showed him affection, they had few interests in common. This evening she spoke earnestly. The glow of beeswax candles lay over the delicate features and in the big eyes.

'Sometimes I fear for Dahut,' she said. He could barely hear. 'There is something about her.'

He harked back to a night on Sena, and a day when a

seal had saved the child from drowning, and incidents more fugitive. It took courage to reply, 'Mayhap we see the beginnings of a destiny. Or mayhap not. Who can say? I've scant faith in astrologers or fortune tellers. Let's take each day as it comes. We must anyhow.'

'Oh, I thought not of the occult. I meant only – well, I've fretted about this, and talked with Vindilis – Vindilis and others – Do we do right, shunting her from household to household, with never a den where she can snuggle down? Is this why she's wild?'

He frowned. 'I know not. How could I? She's my first-born.' Unless he was the casual begetter of a brat or two in Britannia, of which transgression he hoped Mithras had absolved him. 'And the King of Ys can't be a real paterfamilias. Has not the Sisterhood always shared in the raising of a princess whose mother died?'

'Aye, but I think never like this. You are different. And Dahut is. I cannot put it in words, I'm too weak and stupid to understand it, but Vindilis says – You *are* the bringer of a new Age, and you did father Dahut.'

Different, he thought, indeed different. The daughter of Dahilis is so spirited, so intelligent and beautiful.

– After Innilis miscarried, he had agreed with Vindilis that henceforward she should use the Herb. The next stillbirth could kill her, or the next live birth give another pitiful Audris. Six fertile Queens were ample.

She had not asked him to refrain from making love to her. He had found his way to what was best: much kissing and caressing, then much gentleness, for a single time. About half such joinings seemed to give her pleasure, and the rest no distress. At least, she cuddled close afterwards.

This night she stayed awake a while, which was unusual. He could feel how she tensed and faintly shivered against him. 'What vexes you?' he asked. When she grew evasive, he pressed the query. In the end she confessed:

'Oh, you, Grallon, fear about you.' She seldom gave him his proper name any more but, like an increasing number of Ysans and Osismii, softened it. 'You're bound away.'

'I'll return,' he said.

She drew a ragged breath. 'Aye, since you've promised it. But how long will you stay? You surely yearn back to your homeland.'

He lay for a spell, unspeaking. The question haunted him too, but nobody else had raised it. He was astounded that this meek person should. And what in Ahriman's name was the answer?

Of course there was a great deal yet to do in Ys, and he hated leaving a task unfinished. The challenge here called him beyond himself. The making of a useful thing in statecraft was muddled and never really complete, unlike the making of a thing in woodcraft. Just the same, the satisfactions bore no comparison to each other. He had shaped history and law, he had raised bulwarks for the lives of people . . . What would come of it all? A barbarian wave had broken itself against Ys, but the tide of barbarism was still at the flow, over land as well as sea. Could he abandon the defences he had been building?

And yet, never to have a son, if it was true what chronicles and belief said. To abide among aliens until the last death-fight in the Wood made an end of him –

And meanwhile, would those duties truly have been so important? Once the rule of Maximus was firm, his peace would soon reach this far. Likewise, in due course, would his law. What then would be left for the King of Ys? Ceremonies; routines; judgements that made a difference to the parties concerned but were yawnfully tedious for the judge, and as readily rendered by somebody else.

Even now, calm was descending. Though northern Britannia seemed again troubled, the rest of that diocese lay secure. Communications had redeveloped to the point where Gratillonius had had three letters from his father, and sent back replies. To visit the villa once more! Not that he'd accept the wretched curial existence of his free will; but he shouldn't have to. Given the tiniest hint, Maximus Augustus ought to confer senatorial rank on a man who had served him well. And mighty work remained to do in the outer world, reform of the state, subjugation of the barbarians, binding of wounds upon Mother Rome, winning of fame immortal.

Was that his wish?

If not, why not? Ys would never consentingly let its King depart for good. In the past he had wondered about cutting his way free, he and his legionaries or a rescue expedition from outside. But that thought was obsolete – which gladdened him, because he recoiled from any idea of killing his subjects. Come the time, he need merely make a pretext for another journey, and fail to return. It wouldn't hurt the city's institutions too badly. Precedents existed; not every king had died in the Wood. The Suffetes would get somebody – until, no doubt, the Christians came to power here also, and made an end of those bloody successions.

Three years hence, let us say, what reason would Gratillonius have to dwell in Ys?

Well, status, friends, his wives, or certain among them, and Dahut, whom he could smuggle out but would that be the best thing for her?

Innilis nestled against him, weeping most quietly. 'Nay, I will abide,' he said, and wondered how much of a liar he was, 'as long as the Gods allow.'

II

1

'Again the tuba, the tuba calling:
"Come, legionary, get off your duff!"
The hobnails rising, the hobnails falling,
We're bound for glory, or some such stuff.
Farewell, dear wenches! There's time to kiss you
And gulp a beaker before we go.
The Lord on high knows how we will miss you,
So give us memories that will glow.'

It was one of the old, interminable, nonsensical songs that men had sung as they marched from Pontus to Hispania, from Egypt to Caledonia, and beyond, in the service of Rome. Footfalls crashed rhythmically beneath its beat. Words rang into the woodlands bordering the highway, until they lost themselves among trees and shadows. This was mostly second-growth forest, beech, elm, hornbeam, though here and there gloomed a huge oak, hallowed perhaps since before the first Caesar, until cultivation died away a hundred or more years ago. Leaves were still thick, full of greenish-gold light, but some had begun to turn colour. The air below was windless, cool, scented by damp earth. Overhead were fewer wings than last month; many birds had, by now, departed south.

Riding at the front of his two dozen infantrymen and their pack animals, Gratillonius saw stone pavement run straight before him until, at a dim distance, it went from sight in one of those curves that had been the engineers' reluctant concession to terrain. Behind him lay turbulent Condate Redonum, where soldiers of his had nearly got into a fight with members of the Frankish garrison. Ahead, he had been informed, was the Liger valley, rich and well populated as of yore. At Juliomagus he would swing east and follow the great river for a while. His route was not the shortest possible, but almost entirely, it followed roads like this. Spared slogging through mud in the wet season, and most often spared the toil of preparing a walled and ditched camp – because well-secured official hostels stood along the way, near which they could simply pitch their tents – the men should make their best time to Augusta Treverorum.

They were eager too. While they had all become fond of Ys, and several had formed strong ties, the hankering to be back among things Roman was only natural. That had been a large part of his reason for taking the whole twenty-four as his escort, and nobody else. As for the rest of his reason, he wasn't quite sure, but he had a notion that Magnus Maximus would not take kindly to a spokesman native to witchy Ys.

Otherwise his feelings were happy. He also was bound home to his people.

> 'I'm getting old and my joints are creaky,
> The lentils grumble within my gut,
> My tentmates snore and the tent is leaky,
> And come a combat, I might get cut.
> But never mind, we have got our orders.
> So cheer up, fellows, for I do think
> When we have crossed over foreign borders
> There will be wenches, and lots to drink!'

''*O-old!*' Adminius cried. The deputy could bring a surprising volume out of his narrow chest. 'Battle ranks!'

Gratillonius heard clatter and scramble. He drew rein.

Gravel scrunched to silence on the shoulder where he rode. Glancing back, he saw the vexillation quickly bring the animals together and themselves in position either to protect or attack. He'd kept them in crack training.

Adminius trotted over to him. 'Being cautious, sir,' he said. 'Wot does the centurion want we should do?'

Gratillonius peered ahead. No danger was obvious in the mounted man who had come around the curve and was galloping their way. As he spied them, he waved and shouted frantically, and kicked his horse to go faster. The beast was sweaty but not yet lathered; it hadn't carried him far. The man was portly, with black hair cut short and a close-cropped fringe of beard in the Roman style, but tunic and trousers showed him to be a Gaul. Soon Gratillonius made out a dull-red splotch on his left thigh, from which edges of cloth flapped back. A flesh wound. That went with the condition of the horse.

'No pursuit,' Adminius deemed. "E's escaped. Didn't seem worth chasing, I s'pose.' He squirted a gob of spit from a gap between teeth. His thin, sandy-stubbled face crinkled in a grin. 'Well, they didn't know anybody like us was anywhere near, eh, sir?'

Beneath Gratillonius's calm went an ugly thrill. 'We'll wait and hear what he's got to say.'

The Gaul halted in front of them. For a moment the only sounds were the whickering breath of the horse and the man's gasps. His eyes rolled. At length he got out, 'Romans! Legionaries! God be praised! Quick, and you may yet save us!'

The Latin was fairly good, with an accent that Gratillonius recognized as that of the Namnetes. He had come as far south as their seaport two years ago, when he was trying to link the cities of the littoral in cooperation against barbarians and neutrality in the civil war. 'The sooner you make sense and tell me what the matter is, the sooner we may be able to do something about it,' he snapped.

'Bacaudae – ' The man groaned.

'That's no news. Let's have facts.'

The stranger gulped, shuddered, mastered himself in some degree. 'My wagon train . . . goods out of Armorica and Britannia . . . left Redonum . . . Bishop Arator and his attendants joined us there, bound for a conference in Portus Namnetum. We'd been told the route was safe. I b-b-brought guards anyway, of course. But now, in th-th-this forsaken stretch . . . suddenly, there they were, scores of the vilest robbers springing out of the woods and – ' He plucked at Gratillonius's wrist. 'God aided me to flee, because I found you. Don't delay! It's only two or three leagues. The guards will fight. You can get there in good time. God calls you!'

The centurion spent a flash considering. His mission took primacy. However, his squadron should be a match for any plausible number of outlaws; banditry required suppression; and if word got about that he had been less than zealous in the cause of a prelate, he might as well turn land pirate himself. Worse could be the consequences to Ys.

'On the move!' he barked. Adminius shouted commands. Metal gleamed as the formation reshaped itself and started off.

The Gaul kept his horse alongside Gratillonius's. 'Can't you go faster?' he pleaded.

The centurion shook his head. 'Three or four miles at a dead run in full armour wouldn't leave the boys fit for much. We'll do what we can. I promise nothing. We may find everybody in your convoy lying throat-cut, and your merchandise gone with your animals. In that case, I can't pursue. We're on urgent business of the state. I can only

44

ask the garrison commander in Juliomagus to try for vengeance.'

He felt no great excitement. If he could save yonder folk and kill marauders, that was fine. It depended on how long the guards could hold out. The steady, relentless tramp at his back had carried Rome's eagles across the world.

'Tell me what to expect,' he said. 'First, what strength did you have?'

The merchant swung his hands and sometimes keened over the loss he might suffer, but piece by piece, the tale came forth. He was one Florus, a dealer in fabrics. With money what it was these days, he most commonly traded rather than bought and sold, which meant he handled a variety, not just cloths but leathers, furs, raw materials. 'This trip my best acquisition was a consignment of those wonderful weavings they do in Ys, that have scarcely been seen for many years, oh, priceless . . .' The train consisted of four mule-drawn wagons; their drivers; the reverend bishop with two priests and four deacons; Florus himself; and six guards, toughs who hired out for this kind of duty despite the law frowning on it. Two were Gauls, three were Frankish laeti, and one was a brown-skinned person who said nothing about himself but might well be a deserter from the army. 'We take what we can get, right, centurion? We make do.' The guards had sword or axe, plus a few spears. Their armour amounted to boiled leather jackets, cheap kettle helmets, shields of barbarian type. Then, to be sure, the muledrivers possessed knives, cudgels, whips. And three of the deacons were young and sturdy, equipped with stout walking staffs. 'They should be able to fend off the evildoers a while, don't you think? But hurry, hurry!'

'How did you get away?' Gratillonius inquired.

'Oh, I was mounted, by the mercy of God, and when

they swarmed out it was clear what they intended, and by God's grace they didn't close a line across the road to the north before I'd gone past. They almost did. You can see where a spear hurt me. Do you have a surgeon with you? Or at least poultices? This kind of injury inflames so readily. It hurts me abominably.'

'We're not stopping for anything just yet, friend. Why did you flee? One more *man* defending might make all the difference.'

'But I had to get help. God saw to it that I could get help.' Florus's voice sank to a mutter. 'That means the goods will be safe, doesn't it, O Lord? You'd not let Your faithful servant be ruined, almighty God Who delivers us from evil.'

Gratillonius snorted and sent his horse a little ahead.

Slowly the tumult became visible from afar. Noise drifted thin. Gratillonius signalled for double time. He was tempted to speed in advance for a better look. It was getting hard to see any distance as the sun declined and dusk began to seep out of the earth. He resisted the impulse. He had no right to take unnecessary risks. Solitary heroics were for barbarians and fools.

Yonder they grew aware of his approaching force. He saw the struggle die down, like a wave that smashed itself on the reef outside Ys, recoiled in foam, and dwindled away. The next wave was coming . . .

He reined in and jumped to the ground. The men saw his intention and needed but a minute to tether the horses. 'You, keep out of the way!' he told Florus. He unslung his shield from the harness, slipped the retaining strap over his neck, gripped the handle, drew blade, and took his place as leader. The squadron advanced.

Nearing, he saw that the battle was almost done. The travellers had given a good account of themselves. Somehow they'd got three wagons on the sides of a square, cutting loose the mules, which might well panic. There hadn't been time to bring the fourth around, it stood off where the robbers must have led it, but a crude little fort existed. While three guards held fast at the open side, their comrades and certain of the other men repelled foes who sought to climb over the vehicles or crawl underneath.

Yet they could not long keep off assailants whom Gratillonius estimated to number thirty. As he guessed at once, they were still alive – some of them – only because the bandits lacked proper training and discipline. After being cast back with losses, the outlaws milled around, none wanting to be the first to meet that steel again. They tried to bargain. Gratillonius learned afterwards that the bishop had strengthened the will to resist, calling on divine help, while he cleverly strung the talk out. At length the brigands lost patience and made a fresh charge. It failed likewise, though at heavy cost to the defenders.

After that, the attackers resorted to slings. Kept up, the bombardment would have done its job. The travellers took wounds and a couple more deaths. However, they had enough protection to be difficult targets, and eventually the supply of missiles was exhausted. Yet the defence was now so weakened that the bandit leader could egg his men on to a third assault. It broke through and was in among the wagons when the legionaries arrived.

Gratillonius took his troop towards chaos. The outlaws were Gauls, in ragged, filthy garb, pieced out with hides or old blankets or whatever else came to hand. Hair and beards were matted, greasy manes, out of which glared faces gaunt, scarred, weatherbeaten. Shoes were agape, rudely mended, or mere bags of skin stuffed with grass. The barbarians who raided Britannia were better off. Weapons were spears, knives, pruning hooks, firewood axes, a few swords acquired somehow. The wielders screamed hatred and defiance at the Romans. At the same time, those on the fringe were pulling back, making for the trees, in disorderly fashion. They knew that if they stood their ground they'd be butcher's meat.

Which was exactly what they ought to be. 'Right and left!' Gratillonius called. 'Circle them!' He leading a detachment, Adminius its mate, his men hastened to bag as many as they could.

Those inside the laager could not readily disengage from opponents who, heartened, fought furiously. It had never been a proper battle at all, but more like a riot. It pushed combatants apart, flung them against their fellows, sent them tripping over each other. Somebody fallen but alive might grab at an ankle or cling to a spearshaft. Wrestlers on the ground further impeded everyone.

First from the soldiers went the terrible flight of javelins. Meant for use against shields, here they struck unprotected flesh. Men fell, writhed, shrieked. Those who tried to help them to safety were themselves delayed. And then the legionaries were upon them.

A fair-haired youth with downy whiskers attempted to dodge past Gratillonius. The centurion gave him the sword between rib cage and pelvis, forcing the blade right and left to make sure of the liver. Flesh resisted softly, heavily, helplessly. The lad went down. Before Gratillonius could pull his weapon free, a full-grown man was at him, weeping, howling, belly wide open as he swung his arms back for an axe blow. Gratillonius rammed the boss of his shield into the solar plexus. Breath whooped from the Gaul. He dropped his axe and fell to his knees. Gratillonius crashed the bottom rim of his shield against the man's temple. The Gaul crumpled.

Gratillonius had delivered a knockout blow he hoped wasn't fatal. He wanted prisoners to bring to Juliomagus for beheading, or whatever the judgement would be –

examples. He withdrew his sword. Blood pumped forth. A stump end of gut protruded past the tattered shirt. 'Mother,' the youth wailed, over and over. Gratillonius went on. The whole episode had taken just a minute or two, scarcely interruptng the rhythm of onslaught.

He saw a cluster of men pass under the trees, disappearing amidst boles and brush. They bore along a figure robed and struggling. He had no chance to think about it. He only had a fleeting perception of one who seemed in charge, slender, swift of motion, uniquely well-clad. After that, Gratillonius was busy finishing the engagement.

– The legionaries had suffered no harm worth mentioning. Of the travellers, besides Florus, there survived, slashed and battered but reasonably hale, two Frankish men-at-arms, three drivers, a priest, and a deacon. The rest lay stretched out on the roadside, blood wiped off as best might be, dead or dying. The clergyman had already prayed over them.

And Bishop Arator was missing.

As for the robbers, a full twelve had fallen in battle or, hopelessly wounded, received the mercy stroke. Their bodies were stacked on the opposite side of the road. Nobody had cleansed them, closed staring eyes or tied up fallen jaws, but the kindly shadows were well on the way to covering them. Six captives sat bound to the wagons.

Nobody said much. Most of the survivors were still too stunned. Now and then pain made somebody moan. Otherwise they huddled, shivered, looked emptily before them, clutched the bread and wine that had been passed out. The soldiers were in full self-possession but occupied with making a safe camp, since they would spend the night here. An occasional sentence, grunt, oath sounded beneath the thud of axes, the sucking noise as spades turned wet humus.

Gratillonius and Florus had drawn aside at the latter's

request, away from the dead, wounded, captured, the thickening blood puddles. As yet, the sky and the crowns of trees were bright overhead. A few rays slanted golden through the westside gloom. Only a hint of chill was in the air. Crows cawed.

'But the bishop is gone,' Florus wailed. 'A holy man, a lord of the Church, borne off by a gang of sacrilegious murderers! I'll never live down the scandal, never. And my mules, my well-trained carters, lost! Why could you not make better speed?'

'I told you,' Gratillonius said wearily. 'If you mean to complain at the garrison, spare your breath. Any competent officer will understand. Be glad we saved what we did and can help you finish your journey.'

His command would have to do that. The chances of some other group coming along, whom he could dump the chore on to, were slight, as feeble as traffic had become. He couldn't leave these people without escort when a dozen outlaws were still at large. The delay in his own progress would be excused him. Though the Christians would be aghast at what had happened to a veritable bishop –

'*Hs-s-s*,' whispered from the brush. 'Roman, listen.'

Gratillonius spun about. He saw nothing but tangled green, murk behind it. Helmetless in the aftermath of battle, the breeze cool upon his brow, did he hear a rustling?

'Hs-s-s,' went the voice again. 'Hark'ee.'

'What's this?' yelped Florus. 'Are the murderers back? Help! To arms!'

Gratillonius caught him by the nape and squeezed till he whimpered. 'Be still,' the centurion said, never looking away from the forest. 'Go back to your wagons and say nothing. I'll handle this.'

'But – you can't – '

50

'Begone and shut up, or I'll have you flogged.'

He let go. Florus stumbled off, half sobbing. Gratillonius spoke softly: 'Who are you?'

'The Bacauda chief. Make no move, if you want your bishop back alive.'

Something eased in Gratillonius. He heard himself chuckle. 'Very well,' he said. 'Now how shall we go about bargaining?'

2

The centurion's tent was large enough for two men to sit in, on its floor which kept out the dampness of the soil. Its walls likewise withstood autumnal cold. Outside, a wind had arisen after nightfall, to rush through branches, whirl dead leaves away, rattle the leather of the tent and make its poles tremble. Within, a lantern threw dull highlights on to faces, against monstrous shadows.

'Your price is high,' Gratillonius said.

Rufinus shrugged and grinned. 'One bishop for six Bacaudae. Take it or leave it. Myself, I think I'm being swindled.'

Gratillonius peered at him. His invited visitor was young, about nineteen or twenty he guessed, though the spirit behind the green eyes seemed as old as the night wind. Rufinus was of medium height, much of it in his legs, and wirily built. Features otherwise sharp and regular were marred by the scar of a cut, poorly treated, puckering his right cheek and giving his mouth the hint of a perpetual sneer. Though his beard was still scanty, he kept it trimmed in an unconventional fork. His black hair was also short, and reasonably clean, as were the rest of his person and his clothes. Faded, many times patched or darned, shirt and breeches were of stout material. A deerskin jerkin gave additional protection, and he had doffed a cowled cloak. His footgear was clearly from no shoemaker's shop, but just as clearly made to his measure with a degree of skill. At his belt were a pouch, a knife, and a Roman sword.

'You put me in a cleft stick,' Gratillonius said. 'Unless I let dangerous bandits go free, what will become of the bishop?'

'He'll be butchered like a hog,' Rufinus answered coolly. 'Before then, maybe some of the boys will use him.'

'What?'

'Well, we seldom see a woman, you know. Though in this case, it'd be revenge more than lust. *I* wouldn't want that withered prune.'

Fury thickened in Gratillonius's throat. He could barely stay where he was, and not assail the other. 'You rotten snake!'

Rufinus lifted a palm. 'Hold on,' he said. 'I'm only warning, not threatening. I'd forbid such a thing if I could. But I'm no army officer. We're free men, we Bacaudae. We choose our leaders ourselves, and follow their orders if and when we want to. My gang is enraged. If they don't get their friends back – if, instead, those fellows go off to death, maybe first to torture – I can't stand in the way of their justice. They'd kick me aside.'

He leaned forward. His Latin flowed easily despite rough accent, sloppy grammar, and idioms strange to Gratillonius. 'As is,' he said, 'I'll hear curses aplenty when they learn they won't get a ransom besides the exchange. I wonder how you dare hold back stuff that could make you sure of your holy man.'

Gratillonius returned a grim smile. 'He's not my holy man. I'll have to answer for whatever happens. Leave me this much to show. If you won't, well, I need just report that no meeting took place.' He didn't know if he could bring himself to that. Certainly he could not if put under oath. However, he needn't reveal his vulnerability. 'Besides, think. You'll have to go far and fast, before the garrison comes after you. This wood isn't too big for them to beat. Four of our prisoners are too hurt to walk much. They'll encumber you enough, without adding boxes of goods.'

Rufinus laughed. 'Right! That's how come I gave in on that point. I did hope for some solidi, but you win.'

He grew serious, with an underlying liveliness that never seemed to leave him. 'How's this sound? We meet at sunrise. You keep your men in camp. We're woodsrunners; we'll know whether you're honest about that. We'll show up half a mile south with the bishop. One of us'll stand by him – me – ready to kill if anything goes sour. You release our four disabled buddies and give time for us to carry them well away. Then two of you bring our two hale down the road. You can have their hands tied and leashes on them, and you can have swords, but no javelins. We stop a few yards apart and let our hostages go, both sides. The bishop's slow on his feet, so I'll release him first, but you've got to release ours while he's still near enough for me to dash up and stab him. Naturally, you can pay us back in kind if I play you false. We scamper off into the woods and you return to camp. Satisfied?'

Gratillonius pondered. This was a quick intelligence he dealt with. 'The leashes will be long, so your fellows can't bolt off after we let go,' he decided. 'When they reach you, you can cut the cords.'

Again Rufinus laughed. 'Done! You're a workman, Gratillonius. Be damned if I don't like you.'

In his relief, the centurion couldn't help smiling back. 'Aren't you damned already?'

Mercurially, the Gaul turned sombre. 'No doubt, if it's true what the Christians say. But then I expect the fire for me won't be so hot as what they keep for the great landowners and senators. Do you really know the masters you serve?'

Memories crowded on Gratillonius. He scowled. 'Better them than outright banditry. I've seen enough places looted and burnt, women who'd been raped over and over, children and oldsters killed for fun, that I've lost no sleep after striking down what reavers I could – be they barbarians or Romans.'

Rufinus gave him a long look before murmuring, 'You aren't from hereabouts, are you?'

'N-no, I'm a Briton. But these past two years and more I've been in Armorica. Osismiic country, that is.'

'I don't believe there're any Bacaudae that far west.'

'There aren't. Most of it's been picked too clean. Ys alone has stayed well off, because it's got ways to keep the wolves out.'

Rufinus sat straight. His eyes caught the lantern light as they widened. 'Ys,' he breathed. 'You've *been* there?'

'I've operated in the area.' Gratillonius's instinct was to reveal no more to an enemy than was unavoidable. 'Now I'm on a different mission. I planned no fight with you. Nor did those wayfarers you attacked. For whatever you've suffered, blame yourselves.'

'Ys, the city of fable – ' Rufinus broke off, shook himself, spoke sharply. 'I've never been yon way, of course, but I can guess what kind of "wolves" you're thinking of. Saxons and Scoti for the most part, hey? And some Gauls who took the chance to go looting around after everything was wreckage – though I'll bet a lot of those were driven to it by hunger. Where was the Roman

54

state that taxed them and ordered them about, where was it when they needed it? But anyhow, they were not Bacaudae.'

'Do you mean you're something else than marauders?'

'I do.' With bitterness: 'You wouldn't care to listen. I'll go now. See you in the morning.'

'No, wait!' Gratillonius thought for a moment. 'If you'll stay a while, I'll hear you out.'

'How's that?' Rufinus asked, surprised. He had got up. His movements were apt to be quick, nervous, but deft.

'Well, you see,' Gratillonius explained, 'I am a Briton, and my time in Gallia has all been at the far western end, except for a march there from Gesoriacum. But I may be, well, in future I may be having business elsewhere. I can handle it better if I know how things are. All I know of the Bacaudae is that they're vagabond gangs of runaway serfs, slaves, every sort of riffraff. I mean, that's all I've heard. Is there more to it?'

Rufinus stared down at the big, blunt-featured, auburn-haired man. 'You're a deeper one than you make out,' he said low. 'I'd give a bit to learn what your business really is. But – Look here. What I've got to tell won't please you. It'll be the truth, but the truth about Rome. I'm not after another fight.'

'I don't want any either. Say what you will, and if I get angry, I'll hold it in. I may or may not believe you, but . . . I've had worse foes than you.'

Rufinus's smile glistened forth, bad though his teeth were. 'The same right back at you, Gratillonius! Let's.' He lowered himself.

The centurion rose in turn. 'How about some wine to help our tongues along?'

– The tale came out in shards. Sometimes Rufinus japed, sometimes he struggled not to weep. Gratillonius plied him with drink and questions, and meanwhile tried to fit events together in his mind. Later he would try to understand.

Rufinus was born to a smallholder near the latifundium of Maedraeacum in the canton of the Redones, about twenty miles northwest of Condate Redonum. Albeit impoverished, the family was close-knit and had its joys. Rufinus, the youngest, especially liked herding swine in the woods, where he taught himself trapping and the use of the sling. Yet even before his birth, the vice was closing. The best of the land had been engulfed by the manors. Imperial regulation made needed goods costly when they were available at all. Such transactions were generally furtive, while farmers had no choice but to sell their produce openly, under strict price control. Meanwhile taxes climbed out of sight. Rufinus's father more and more sought refuge in the cup. Finally, his health destroyed, he coughed himself to death one winter.

Rather than let children of hers be sold into slavery for back taxes, the widow conveyed the farm to Sicorus, owner of Maedraeacum, and the family became his coloni – serfs. They were bound to the soil, compelled to deference and obedience, required to do labour for their lord and, after working for themselves, pay more than half the crop over to him. Their grain they must have ground at his mill and at his price. There were no more forest days for Rufinus. Thirteen years old, he was now a field hand, his knees each evening ashake with weariness.

The following year his pretty older sister Ita became the concubine of Sicorus. She could not be forced, under the law. However, he could offer easements for her kin – such as not assigning her brothers to the most brutal tasks – and for her it was a way out of the kennel. Rufinus, who adored her, stormed to the manor house to protest. The slaves there drove him off with blows. He ran away. Sicorus coursed him down with hounds, brought him

56

back, and had him flogged. The law permitted chastisement of contumacious coloni.

For another year, he bided his time. Whispers went along the hedges and in the woodlots; men slipped from their hovels to meet by twilight; news seeped across this narrow horizon. It came oftenest on the lips of wanderers who had made their lifework the preaching of sedition. The Empire had rotted to worthlessness, they said; Frankish laeti at Redonum sacrificed human beings to heathen Gods; raiders harried the coasts, while war bands afoot struck deep in from the East. Meanwhile the fat grew fatter, the powerful grew ever more overbearing. Had not Christ Himself denounced the rich? Was not the hour overpast to humble them and take back what they had wrung from the working poor? The Last Day drew nigh, Antichrist walked the world; your sacred duty was to resist him. Righteous men had sworn themselves to a brotherhood, the Bacaudae, the Valiant . . .

Ita's death in childbed was the last thing Rufinus endured. After that, he planned his next escape carefully, and found his way to the nearest Bacauda encampment.

– 'We're no saints, oh, no, no,' he hiccoughed. By then he was fairly drunk. 'I learned that soon enough. Some amongst us are beasts of prey. The rest're rough. I give you that. But the most of us, the most of us, we only wanted to live in peace. We only wanted to till our plots of ground, and keep the fruits of our work, and have our honour under the law.'

'How do you live?' Gratillonius asked. He had matched the Gaul stoup for stoup, but he was larger and not half starved.

'Oh, we hunt. What a pleasure that is, when we know we're poaching! We raise a little garden truck in the wilds. We rob when we can, from the rich, like that futtering smug trader today, but we swap the loot in honest wise

57

for what we need. And merchants who pass through sections, regular-like, where we are, they pay toll. They're not s'posed to, but they do, undercover, and save 'emselves trouble. And our own people, serfs who've not fled and what few small freehold farmers are left, they help us out, for love.'

'For love. Indeed.' Gratillonius made his voice heavy with sarcasm. 'I'm a farm boy myself. I know farmers. What you say sounds exactly like them.'

'Well, we're fighting their war,' Rufinus declared. 'It's only right for them to pay their share. Food, clothes, that sort of thing. Besides, we protect 'em against bandits.'

Gratillonius shrugged. He could well imagine what their protection consisted of. Cotters who declined it were apt to find their roofs ablaze or their throats slit.

Rufinus read his thought and said defensively, 'It *can* be for love. How d'you think I got this outfit of mine?'

By charm, Gratillonius imagined. This young man had an abundance of that. Let him enter the drabness that was the life of some isolated, poverty-stricken wife – in and out of it, like bursts of sunshine when wind drove clouds across heaven, like an elf by moonlight – If every Bacauda were as glib, the band today would have looked a great deal less scruffy.

Still, said Gratillonius's stubborn mind, Rufinus was in fact as neat and clean as possible in his kind of existence: which revealed something about him.

The centurion shifted the subject towards matters of more immediate interest. 'Well, then, have you Bacaudae a secret kingdom that considers itself at war with Rome, the way the Persians usually are? That doesn't square with what I've heard. But tell me.'

'M-m, no, not really,' Rufinus admitted. 'We do have emperors – an emperor for each region – but he doesn't do much except lead his own group and be at the head of the gatherings, when several groups meet. We call the head of any other band its duke.' His sardonic tone implied that the title didn't mean 'leader' but was a deliberate parody of Roman organization. 'I'm the duke of mine.'

'A bit young for that, aren't you?'

'There are no old Bacaudae,' Rufinus said quietly. Gratillonius remembered Alexander of Macedon. For that matter, he himself was twenty-five when he became King of Ys.

'We do make our deals,' the Gaul went on in a rush, as the wine sent another tide through his head. 'I've heard of bargains struck with Scotian or Saxon. Our folk'd guide 'em to a manor, they'd sack it but in return let the serfs be. And I got friendly with a Scotian – fled his homeland, he did, on account of a feud, and came to us – he told me 'bout Hivernia, where Rome never ruled, where they've always been free – '

Rufinus started, stiffened, once more shook himself. 'I'd better not go on,' he said. 'I might let too much slip out. You're a good fellow, Gra – Gra – Gradlon. But I can't let you in on any secrets of the brothers, could I, now?' He picked up his cloak and lurched to his feet. 'G'night. I wish we could be friends.'

'I'll take you past the sentries,' the soldier offered, rising too. He would have liked to continue the conversation, but it verged on questions that might suddenly make this two-legged wildcat lash out, and his duty was to get the bishop back unharmed.

They walked together into the windy dark, mute. As they parted, they clasped hand to arm.

III

1

About fifteen miles west of Augusta Treverorum there was an official hostel where Gratillonius decided to spend the night, even though sundown was still a couple of hours off. This was doubtless the last such place till he reached the city. Starting at dawn, with nothing to do except swallow breakfast and strike tents, the soldiers should reach their destination early enough next day that he would have no trouble getting them settled in and word of his arrival borne to the Emperor. Besides, he might find no suitable campground between here and there. The hills roundabout were largely given over to vineyards, with scant room between rows. Hazed and dreamy under the declining sun, this country seemed to lie in a different world from Armorica, as did most of what he had passed through. It was as if wars, brigands, and wild men had never been, save in nightmares.

As was common, the hostel maintained an open space for military parties. Having seen his established and supper cooking, Gratillonius sought the house. The dignity of his mission required that he avail himself of it, whether or not it was the kind of fleabag he had found too often along the way.

A man stood outside. He had come forth when the legionaries arrived and watched them set up. As Gratillonius neared, he lifted a hand and said, 'Greeting, my son. Peace be with you.' His Latin had an odd accent; he could not be a native Gaul, though it shortly turned out that he used Gallic idioms with ease.

Gratillonius halted. Dignity also required he return courtesy, no matter how poor and unkempt the person was who offered it. This one didn't cringe or whine, either. He stood straight, spoke levelly, and looked you square in the eye. 'Greeting, uncle.' – what soldiers usually called an elderly man who had a bit of respect due him but not too much.

The stranger smiled. 'Ah, that takes me far back. I was in the army once. Let me compliment you on the smartness of your squadron. Sadly rare these days. Not many units of old-fashioned regulars left, are there?'

'Thank you.' Gratillonius looked closer.

The other carried his years well. While slenderness had become gauntness, the shoulders were wide and unbowed, and if his gait was no longer lithe it remained firm. A snub nose marked a face pallid, lined, and gap-toothed, which you barely noticed after meeting its brilliant blue gaze.

Puzzlement rose in Gratillonius. Why should somebody like that, clearly well-educated, go in a coarse dark robe, hardly fit for a slave, belted with a rope underneath a camel-hair cloak – when his footgear was stout though well-worn, bespeaking many leagues of use? Had he fallen into poverty? Then he should at least have had the pride left to keep himself clean. Streams, ponds, and public baths weren't that scarce. He had in fact laved hands and feet, but Gratillonius could smell him. Pungent rather than sour, declaring that he spent much time in the open, the odour nevertheless demeaned him . . . did it not? He shaved, but probably seldom, for white stubble covered jaws and cheeks. Likewise it bristled over the front half of his pate. Behind, hair rose wildly; it would have waved in the breeze if he had washed it.

61

'Well, you'll want to inspect your quarters before we eat,' he said. 'Shall we go in?'

Gratillonius stared. 'You're lodging here?'

The old man smiled. 'I'd rather sleep under God's stars or the roofs of His poor, but – ' he shrugged – 'a bishop travelling a main highway isn't allowed that.'

Gratillonius stood a moment in his neat Roman outfit, confronting the beggarly figure, and wondered whether he had heard aright. Arator had been bedraggled when the Bacaudae released him, but his clothes were of the best, and it didn't take him long after reaching Juliomagus to reappear bathed, barbered, and resplendent. 'A bishop?'

'Unworthy though I be. Martinus of Caesarodunum Turonum, at your service. May I ask your name, my son?'

Gratillonius stammered it forth, together with his rank and his legion, scarcely hearing himself. His head was awhirl.

'You are a long way from your home base, eh? I think we shall have considerable to talk about. Come.' Martinus took him by the elbow and led him inside.

While he changed clothes in his room, Gratillonius tried to put his thoughts in order. Only recently had he first heard of yonder person, but what he had heard was extraordinary.

Passing through the Liger valley, he had observed that the small pagan temples that elsewhere dotted the landscape were absent, or made into heaps of stone and charred timber. Occasionally he went by the stump of a tree that had been huge and ancient; occasionally he spied, afar, a hut raised by a spring or on a hilltop which must have been a sacred site, where now a single man dwelt. Curious, the centurion had inquired among people he met when he stopped for a night. He learned that the bishop of Turonum and a troop of monks had been going about for years, not only preaching their Christ to the rural population but destroying the halidoms of the old Gods and rededicating these to the new.

'A great and wonderful work!' cried devout young Budic. At last his faith was marching out of the cities.

'Hm,' said Gratillonius. 'The wonder is that the people stand for it.'

Well, he reflected, this Martinus did have the Imperium at his back. Gratillonius himself was technically violating the law when he worshipped Mithras. Had the heathens killed the churchmen, they would have risked terrible punishment. Still, they might have resisted in other ways. Gratillonius well knew how stubborn and sly rustics could be.

It seemed as if Martinus overwhelmed them, simply by being what he was. Gratillonius was unsure how much belief to give stories of miracles wrought by the holy man. They said he healed the sick, the lame, and the blind by his touch and his prayers, that he had even recalled a dead boy to life. They said that once, demanding a hallowed oak be cut down, he had accepted a challenge to stand, bound, where it would fall; as it toppled, he lifted his hand and it spun about and crashed in the opposite direction, narrowly missing and instantly converting the clustered tribesfolk. Maybe so. Gratillonius had seen strange things wrought by his Gallicenae.

He thought, though, most of the force must lie in Martinus himself. The bishop was humble as well as strong. He dwelt outside the city, in a community of like-minded men whom his reputation had drawn to him. Mainly they devoted themselves to worship and meditation. When they went forth evangelizing, Martinus never ranted or threatened. People told Gratillonius that he spoke to them in their own kind of words, quiet, friendly, sometimes humorous. They told of an incident: he and

63

his followers had torched a Celtic temple, but when the flames were about to spread to the landowner's adjoining house, the bishop led the firefighting effort.

He had never desired his office. When it fell vacant, a trick brought him from his peaceful monastery elsewhere, and a crowd fell upon him and carried him off, willy-nilly, to be consecrated. That was the second time he had been conscripted. The first was long before, he a lad in Pannonia who only wanted to enter the Church, borne away at the instigation of his pagan father and enrolled in the army. Not until the twenty-five-year hitch was up could he give his oath to his God. Thereafter he had been clergyman, hermit, monk – Had that God chosen this means of training him for his mission?

Or was it only, or also, that the Gods of the land were failing, that in some secret way folk knew they had no more reason to honour Them? Gratillonius remembered what Forsquilis had said in Ys . . .

He re-entered the main room as the kitchen help were bringing out supper. Martinus's entourage sat at table. They amounted to four men, younger than their leader but tonsured and dressed like him. The bishop sat offside, on a three-legged milking stool he had evidently taken along, and ate from a bowl on his lap. The food he had ordered for them consisted of vegetables, herbs, and a few scraps of dried fish stewed together. Prayers preceded the repast. A reading from the Gospels, by a brother who fasted that evening, accompanied it. Gratillonius ate his robust fare in silence.

Afterwards Martinus beckoned him over, proffered a bench, and said cordially, 'Now, centurion, do you care to tell us what you've been doing? You must have many curious adventures under your belt.'

Gratillonius dug in his heels against liking the man, found himself dragged towards it anyhow, and settled down. 'I am . . . on business of the state, reporting to the Emperor,' he said.

'I thought so. And we are bound home after business with him. Maybe we can help each other, you and I.'

'Sir?'

'I can give you an idea of what to expect. There's been trouble at court, a most cruel strife. God willing, it nears its end, but you'll do best to avoid certain topics. For my part, I'd be very interested to learn more about how things are in Armorica . . . and Ys.'

Martinus laughed at Gratillonius's startlement. 'Obvious!' he continued. 'In Treverorum I heard incidental mention that Maximum Augustus's prefect at the mysterious city was coming. Who else would you be, you who identified yourself as belonging to a Britannic legion? Take your ease, have a fresh cup of the excellent local wine, and yarn to us.'

He and his companions did not join in, sipping merely water, but Gratillonius got from them a sense of cheer, the sort that men feel when they have completed a hard task. He used his own call for more drink to buy time for thought.

How much dared he relate? He had shaded his dispatches to the Emperor, omitting details of religious and magical practices. He had spent hours on the road rehearsing in his mind how he should reply to various possible questions. He would not give his commandant any falsehood. But if he provoked outrage and cancellation of his commission, what then?

'Well,' he said, 'you must be aware that we're getting matters under control in our part of the country. We'd like to help with that over a wider range.' The tale of his brush with the Bacaudae and the deliverance of Bishop Arator, augmented by the exclamations and thanksgivings of the monks, took a usefully long while. He went on to remarks about the revival of trade that was beginning, and finished quickly:

'But it'll soon be dark, and I want to start off at daybreak. You mentioned things I might need to know. Will you tell me?'

Martinus frowned. 'The full story would take longer than till bedtime, my son.'

'I'm a simple roadpounder. Can't you explain enough in a few words?'

The ghost of a smile crossed Martinus's lips. 'You ask for a miracle. But I'll try.' He pondered before he started talking.

Nonetheless Gratillonius was bewildered. He could only gather that one Priscillianus, bishop of Avela in Hispania, was accused of heresy and worse. The centurion knew that 'heresy' meant an incorrect Christian doctrine, though it was not clear to him who decided what was correct and how. In a vague fashion he was conscious of the division between Catholics, who held that God and Christ were somehow identical, and Arians, who held that They were somehow different. Mithraism was an easier faith, its paradoxes a part of the very Mystery and in any event nothing that directly concerned mortals.

This Priscillianus preached a canon of perfectionism which Martinus felt went too far; fallen man was incapable of it without divine grace. Yet Martinus also felt that this was no more than an excess of zeal. Certainly it spoke against those charges of fornication and sorcery that the enemies of Priscillianus brought. There might have been no large stir had not people by the hundreds and perhaps thousands, despairing of this world, flocked to the austere new creed. As was, Bishop Ambrosius of Mediolanum got the then co-Emperor Gratianus to issue a rescript banning its adherents. They scattered and concealed themselves.

Priscillianus himself and a few followers went to Rome to appeal to the Pope. Among them were women, including two friends of the consul Ausonius. This gave rise to nasty gossip.

The Church had adopted a rule that when internal disputes arose, the final appeal would be to the bishop of Rome. Pope Damasus refused to see Priscillianus. The accused proceeded to Mediolanum, where through an official who was an enemy of Ambrosius they got a rescript restoring them to their churches.

Then they took the offensive, getting charges of calumny levelled against their principal persecutor, Bishop Ithacius of Ossanuba. He fled to Treverorum and found an ally in the praetorian prefect. Intrigues seethed. Maximus revolted and overthrew Gratianus. Ambrosius travelled north to help negotiate the treaty that divided the West.

Ithacius brought his allegations against Priscillianus before the new Augustus. Maximus ordered a synod convened at Burdigala to settle the matter. Much ugliness ensued, rumours of immorality, a noblewoman stoned by a rabble. In the end, Priscillianus refused to accept the jurisdiction of the synod and appealed to the Emperor in Treverorum.

Prelates flocked to the scene, Martinus among them. While he did not say so, Gratillonius got the impression, which later conversations confirmed, that he alone did not fawn on Maximus. Rather, he argued stiffly for what he held to be justice. When the Augustus had him at table and ordered the communal wine cup brought first to him, Martinus did not pass it on to Maximus, but to the priest who was with him; and the Augustus accepted this as a righteous act.

Ithacius saw his religious accusation of heresy faltering, and against Priscillianus pressed the secular, criminal charges of sorcery and Manicheanism. Martinus took the lead in disputing these.

He won from Emperor Maximus a promise that there would be no death penalties. However much the Priscillianists might be in error, it was honest error and deserved no worse than exile to some place where they could meditate untroubled and find their way back to the truth. Gladdened, Martinus started home. The whole wretched business had caused him to neglect his own flock far too long.

– '"Wretched" is the right word,' Gratillonius muttered.

'What?' asked Martinus.

'Oh, nothing.' Gratillonius's glance went to a window. Deep yellow, the light that came through it told him that it was time for his sunset prayer to the Lord Mithras. Besides, after what he had heard, he needed a few lungfuls of clean air. 'Excuse me if I leave,' he said, rising. 'I've duties to see to before nightfall.'

The monks took that at face value, but Martinus gave him a look that held him in place like a fishhook before murmuring, 'Duties, my son, or devotions?'

Gratillonius felt his belly muscles tighten. 'Is there a difference?'

'Enough,' said Martinus. Was the motion of his hand a blessing? 'Go in peace.'

2

The squadron entered Augusta Treverorum by one of two paved ways passing through a gate in the city wall. That gate was a colossus of iron-bound sandstone blocks, more than a hundred feet wide and nearly as high, with twin towers flanking two levels of windows. Behind it, structures well-nigh as impressive showed above roofs closer to hand, basilica, Imperial palace, principal church; and approaching, the men had noticed an amphitheatre just outside that was like a shoulder of the hill into which it was built.

Façades reared grandly over streets, porticos gleamed around marketplaces, where people in the multiple thousands walked, rode, drove, jostled, chattered, chaffered, exhorted, quarrelled, postured, pleaded, vowed, were together, were alone. Feet clattered, hoofs thudded, wheels groaned, hammers rang. The noises were a veritable presence, an atmosphere, filled with odours of smoke, food, spice, dung, perfume, wool, humanity. Litters bore a senator in purple-bordered toga and a lady – or a courtesan? – in silk past a Treverian farmer in tunic and trousers, a housewife in coarse linen carrying a basket, an artisan with his tools and leather apron, a porter under his yoke, a guardsman on horseback, slaves in livery and slaves in rags, a pair of strolling entertainers whose fantastical garb was an extra defiance of the law that said they must remain in that station to which they were born –

Gratillonius had seen Londinium, but it could not compare with this. Abruptly Ys seemed tiny and very dear. He got directions and led his soldiers in formation, giving way to nobody. Before their armour the crowds surged aside in bow waves and eddies.

Space was available at the metropolitan barracks. Maximus kept a large household troop and a substantial standing army. Their cores were legionary regulars, drawn from border garrisons as well as from Britannia. However, more men, auxiliaries among them, had departed for the South with Valentinianus. Thus total Roman strength in Gallia was much reduced. Echoing rooms and empty parade grounds, in the midst of civilian wealth and bustle, roused forebodings in Gratillonius. The Mosella had only about a hundred miles to flow from here before it met the Rhenus, and east of that great river laired the barbarians. Many were already west of it.

He made arrangements for his men. Several whooped joyously when they recognized acquaintances from Britannia, and everybody was chaffing to be off into town. 'Keeping them taut won't be easy,' Gratillonius warned Adminius. 'Temptations right and left, starting with booze and broads, leading on towards brawls.'

The deputy grinned. 'Don't you worry, sir,' he answered. 'I'll let 'em 'ave their fun, but they'll know there's a 'and on the tether.' He cocked his head. 'If I'm not being overbold, maybe the centurion'd like 'is own bit o' fun? I'll soon find out where that's to be 'ad.'

'Never mind,' Gratillonius snapped. 'Remember, I want you reporting to me regularly at my lodging.'

He proceeded alone to the government inn where he would stay. Temptation – aye, he thought, it simmered in him too; and he realized he had been thinking in Ysan, while certain of his wives stood before him, unclad and reaching out, more vivid than the walls and traffic around.

The room he took was clean and well-furnished, if a little time-faded. He unpacked and got busy. First he must notify the palace of his arrival. He had already prepared a note to that effect – writing never came easily to him – and now tied it together with a commendation that Bishop Arator had given him. That letter was embarrassingly fulsome, but explained his not coming sooner and, well, should do his career no harm. Escape from the curial trap –

After he was finished in Ys, if ever he was –

He didn't want to pursue that vision. Hastily, he sought

the manager of the house, who dispatched a messenger boy for him.

As Gratillonius then stood wondering what to do, a uniformed centurion entered from the street, stopped, gaped, and shouted his name. 'Drusus!' he roared back at the stocky form – Publius Flavius Drusus of the Sixth, whose unit had side by side with his fought its way out of a Pictic ambush. They fell into each other's arms, pounded each other's backs, and exchanged mighty oaths.

'I'm staying here too,' Drusus explained, 'waiting to deliver a report. Since we won his throne for the Augustus, my vexillation's been stationed at Bonna. Reinforcement for the Fifth Minervia. The war whittled that legion pretty badly, not so much through casualties as because most of it stuck with Valentinianus. The Germani got so uppity that at last we made a punitive expedition. I've been sent to tell how that went; pretty good. Come, we've daylight left, let's go out on the town.'

'I'm supposed to report, like you,' Gratillonius demurred. 'I'd better be here when they call me.'

Laughter rattled from Drusus. 'Your heels will freeze if you just sit waiting, old buddy. I thought today I'd finally got my summons, but no, they told me there the Emperor was suddenly too busy again. You'll be lucky if you're called inside this month. And if the word happens to come when you're out, no sweat. Everything's scheduled hours and hours in advance, because whenever some backlog of state business can get handled, there's so much of it. Enjoy while you've got the chance. I'll go change clothes and be right with you.'

Gratillonius sat worrying till his friend returned, and asked as they went forth: 'What's happened? Maximus didn't allow this kind of shilly-shallying in Britannia.'

'Not entirely his fault,' Drusus replied. 'You remember how he always oversaw as much as possible personally.

Well, he's the same now that he wears the purple. And it worked for a while. Name of Christ, how we sliced through Gratianus's ranks! But being Emperor is different, I guess. He keeps getting interrupted by new problems.'

'Why does he want a direct account of a border clash?' Gratillonius wondered.

'M-m, don't quote me. I could get in trouble.'

'I wouldn't do that to you, Drusus. D'you imagine I've forgotten that day in the rain? All the puddles were red.'

Hand squeezed shoulder. 'I remember too. Well, nobody's told me anything officially, understand, but when a smell comes downwind I can usually tell whether it's from a rose or a fart. After Gratianus died – and he was murdered, make no doubt of that, murdered when he'd been promised safety at a feast with an oath on the Gospels – ' Drusus glanced about. They were anonymous in a throng of people intent on their own lives. 'Maximus put the blame on his cavalry commander, but never punished the man . . . Anyway. While negotiations were going on afterwards, Maximus got the Juthungi to invade Raetia. He had connections to them. Pressure on Theodosius to make a settlement. Valentinianus is only a kid, under the thumb of his mother. But her Frankish general in his turn got the Huns and Alani to harry the Alemanni so close to the Rhenus that Maximus had to move troops to that frontier.

'Which is why I'm still posted yonder, and the Augustus is anxious about whatever the barbarians may be up to, and why. They've got a taste of playing us Romans off against each other.'

Gratillonius raised a dam against the words that rose in his throat. What was this fellow saying about their Duke, the man who rolled midnight back from the Wall?

Gratillonius told himself that a commander could not

72

always control what his subordinates did, and statecraft unavoidably had its dirty side, and Drusus was a solid sort who might be misled but who should be heard out before any arguments began. 'Well, however that is,' he said, 'why aren't things better organized here? It doesn't sound a bit like Maximus. Can't he get competent officers any longer?'

'It's the Priscillianus mess,' Drusus answered. 'Before then, we had a pretty smooth mill running. But since that rift spread this far – '

He paused before he sighed and added, 'I don't understand any miserable part of it. This town's full of jabber about the First Cause, the Sons of God and the sons of Darkness, Spiritual Man, mystical numbers, and I don't know what else, except I was there when a man got knifed in a tavern ruckus that started over whether or not the age of prophecy is over. I think Priscillianus has to be wrong when he says men and women should stay apart, never get together. If that is what he says. I don't know. But why all these fights about it? I wonder if Christ in Heaven isn't weeping at what they're doing in His name. Sometimes I almost envy infidels like you.'

They had wandered down towards the river. Through an open portal they saw the bridge across it, and vineyards and villas beyond. A fresh dampness blew off it. Leaves blazed with autumn. Gratillonius remembered Bodilis reading to him a poem Ausonius had written in praise of this stream: the author had sent her a copy. *Like a girl-child playing with her hair before a mirror, fisher lads sport with shadowy shapes underwater.* Suddenly laughter welled up in him and he pitched away the cares of the world. They'd climb back on to him soon enough. 'Not our department,' he said. 'How about we find us a place where we can have a drink and swap brags?'

3

Four days later he was in the presence of Maximus Augustus, but as a prisoner.

News had exploded through the city. The Emperor, who had promised clemency for the Priscillianists, was rehearing the entire case. Bishop Ithacius withdrew as prosecutor. It was said that he feared the wrath of such powerful colleagues as Martinus and Ambrosius.

Earlier, the bishop of Mediolanum had come back this far north, ostensibly to see the bones of Gratianus returned to Italy for burial, actually to attend the first trial. Maximus refused him a private audience but received him in consistory, where he in his turn declined the Emperor's proffered kiss of peace and accused the latter of being a lawless usurper. Maximus responded in the course of proceedings with a denial that Valentinianus was his equal; if nothing else, the boy-Emperor and his mother were known to have strong Arian leanings.

Though Ambrosius had since gone home, the qualms of Ithacius were natural. In his place, Maximus appointed Patricius, an advocate for the treasury. Did the Augustus want the property of the heretics?

Gratillonius found a military tribune who was a reliable conduit of information, rather than rumours. What he learned about the goings-on within the Church perturbed him less than what he learned about Maximus. How long must he hang around this cursed city? Most of his time he spent sightseeing, or talking with chance-met men. They were a varied lot, many of them trading up and down the rivers or overland. There grew before him a vision, clearer than ever, of the Empire, how vast it was and how troubled.

The detachment came for him towards evening, when he had lately returned to the hostel after a day's ride in the hinterland. A vintner had hailed him and invited him home for a cup and a gab; there the pretty daughter of the house smiled upon him. Now he sat in the common room prior to supper, more content than he had been, thinking back over the small experience. The door opened. Four soldiers in combat gear tramped through, and at their head a centurion.

'We seek Gaius Valerius Gratillonius, of the Second Legion Augusta,' that man announced.

'Here he is.' Gratillonius's heart leapt up as fast as his body.

'In the name of the Augustus, come.'

'At once. I'll just outfit myself – '

'No. Immediately.'

Gratillonius stared into faces gone hard. A prickling went over his scalp. 'Is something wrong?' he asked.

The centurion clapped hand to sword. 'Silence! Come!'

Household staff gaped, shrank aside, and saw their guest depart surrounded by armed men. Folk outside likewise fell silent as the group strode down the streets to the basilica.

Guarded gates led to a cloistered courtyard where dusk was rising: for the sun had gone below the outer walls. Light still glowed on the upper courses of brick and red sandstone that made up the great building within, and flared off glass in its windows. Numb, Gratillonius accompanied his escort into this citadel of his hopes, past several checkpoints and thus at last to the audience hall where the Emperor was.

The soldiers clanked to a halt and saluted. Gratillonius did too. That was his old commandant there on the throne, the same Hispanic hatchet features and lean body though purple be wrapped around and a golden wreath set above. He hardly noticed the splendour of the room or the several councillors who sat or stood beneath their master.

The officer waited for the Imperial nod before reporting that he brought the person required. 'Ah, Gratillonius,' Maximus said low. 'Step forward. Let us look at you.'

The King of Ys posed for what seemed a long while, until he heard: 'Know that we have been told such evil of you that we have ordered your arrest. What have you to say for yourself?'

Despite foreknowing he was somehow in danger, Gratillonius felt as if clubbed. 'Sir?' Breath sobbed into him. He braced his knees, gave Maximus eye for eye, and declared, 'My lord, I have served you and Rome to the best of my ability. Who's spoken ill of me?'

Maximus straightened and clipped, 'Your own men, centurion, your own men. Do you call them liars? Do you deny having trafficked with Satan?'

'What? Sir – my lord – I don't understand. My men – '

'Silence.' Maximus nodded at a pinch-lipped person in a drab tunic. 'Calvinus, read the report.'

That one took up a set of papers and began what soon became a singsong, like a chant to his God. It developed that he was high in the Imperial secret service. His agents were everywhere, in every walk of life, with instructions to keep alert for anything the least suspicious and follow it up until they had sufficient clues to warrant full investigation. As if across a sea, Gratillonius heard how his legionaries, innocently talking in barracks and around town, had spoken of him. There was no need to interrogate any of them; all were ready to boast about their leader and about the wonders of Ys.

Gratillonius heard how he, in a pagan ceremony where the images of devils were brought forth, had wedded nine women who were avowed witches. He heard how he had accepted and openly borne the emblems of a sea demon and a demon of the air. He had sent forth a spirit in the form of a bird to spy upon his enemies. He had ordered magic to raise a storm. He had betrodden an island that was from time immemorial the site of the blackest sorcery –

Courtiers shivered and made signs against malevolence. Lips moved in whispered prayer. The squad that had taken Gratillonius kept martial stiffness, but sweat came forth; he saw it, he smelled it.

At the end, Maximus leaned forward. 'You have heard the charges,' he said. 'You must realize their gravity, and the necessity we are under of finding the truth. Sorcery is a capital offence. The powers of darkness have reached into the very Church; and you are a defiant unbeliever, who bears upon himself the mark of it.'

What mark? He had left the Key of the gate behind in Ys, as being too vital to risk anywhere else. He'd grown a beard there, but it was close-cropped like a Roman's. He did wear his hair in Ysan male style, long, caught at the nape to fall down in a tail . . . He clawed out of his bewilderment and thought Maximus must refer to the brand of Mithraic initiation on his brow, though it had faded close to invisibility and – and Mithraists were loyal Romans.

'You may speak,' the Emperor said.

Gratillonius squared his shoulders. 'Sir, I've practised no wizardry. Why, I wouldn't know how. The Duke – the Augustus always knew what my religion is, and it doesn't deal in magic. They believe differently in Ys, true. Well, given my job, how could I keep from showing respect to their Gods? I did – I did ask help from whatever powers they might have, but that was against barbarians who

menaced Rome. As for that time on Sena, the island
Sena, I wasn't supposed to set foot on it, but my wife – a
wife of mine was dying there – ' His throat locked on him.
His eyes blurred and stung.

'You may be honest.' Maximus's tone was steady; and
did it hold a slight note of regret? 'We had cause for
confidence in you, and therefore entrusted you with your
mission. But if nothing else, you may have been seduced
by the Evil One. We must find out. God be praised, now
that the Priscillianus matter nears an end, we have had a
chance to hear this news of you. And we have given it
prompt consideration as much for your sake –
Gratillonius, who did serve valiantly on the Wall – as for
Rome's. We will pray that you be purged of sin, led to
the Light, saved from perdition.' Abruptly the old military
voice rang forth. 'If you remain a soldier, obey your
orders!'

He issued instructions. The squad led Gratillonius
away.

4

In the early morning he was brought from the cell where
he had spent a sleepless night. On the way down the
gloom of a corridor, he met a procession under heavy
guard. At its front walked a grey-haired man, skeletal,
eyes fixed luminous upon another world. Four men came
after, and a middle-aged woman and a younger who held
hands. All were in coarse and dirty garb. They moved
stumblingly, because they had not only been half starved
but severely tortured. They stank. Lanterns burned
smoky in the dank air around them. Hoarsely, they tried
to sing a hymn.

'The heresiarch and those followers of his who've been condemned,' said one of Gratillonius's guards to him. 'They're off to the chopping block. Have a care, fellow, or you'll be next.'

– Light was dim also in the interrogation chamber. Gratillonius could just identify scenes of the Christian hell painted on its plaster. How neatly the instruments and tools sat arranged. This could have been an artisan's workshop. Nothing felt quite real, except the chill. Two men ·waited, the first skinny and wearing a robe, the second muscular and in a brief tunic, ready for action. They studied the prisoner impersonally. He heard through a buzzing in his head:

' – by command of the Augustus. Cooperate, and this may be the only session we'll need. Otherwise we will be forced to take strict measures. Do you understand? We're coping with none less than Satan – '

Surprised at his meekness (but resistance would have been of no avail, when he was so alone), Gratillonius undressed. His nudity made him feel twice helpless. The torturer secured him in a frame so that he stood spread-eagled and took a lead ball off a shelf. It dangled at the end of a thong. Meanwhile the questioner continued talking, in an amicable voice. ' – your duty to help lay bare the work of Satan. We do not wish to harm you. Simply as a warning – '

Snapped by an expert hand, the ball smote Gratillonius's elbow. Agony went jagged up that arm. He strangled a scream. He *would* not scream.

' – now tell me, in your own words – '

Whenever he resisted or equivocated, not that he meant to play games but often he wasn't sure how to respond, the blow landed, on joints, belly, the small of the back, until he was a single slab of pain; the worst was that the next attack might come between his sprangled thighs.

Weirdest was that, from time to time, the proceedings would stop, they would bring him water, the torturer would sponge the sweat off him while the questioner chatted about everyday things.

Mithras, Who hates a liar, give me to cling to the truth! ' – I did n-n-no such deed, ever. Others may have, I don't know about that, I'm just a soldier, but it was for Rome, everything I did was for Rome.'

'He might want a taste of the hook,' said the torturer thoughtfully.

The questioner considered. 'Once.'

When the barbs went into his thigh and out again, Gratillonius knew what it was like to be raped.

'But I cannot tell you more!'

'You've said a good deal already, boy.'

'All I could. All.' And never screamed, Gratillonius thought blurrily. Never screamed. That much pride is left me. But I don't know if I can keep it after my arms and legs crack out of their sockets on yonder rack, or when he starts hitting me in my manhood.

'Well,' said the questioner with a smile, 'that will do for today. Please remember how much the state needs your cooperation, you, a soldier; and think what it means to your salvation.' The torturer fetched salves and bandages and set about dressing open wounds. 'You haven't suffered any permanent damage, you realize. I pray God you don't, dear soul.' The questioner stroked the prisoner's wet hair. 'But that depends on you.'

He called the guards to bring Gratillonius back to his cell.

5

After two days and nights, wherein nothing happened except diminishing soreness and horrible expectations, suddenly he was brought forth. The person in charge was unctuous though uncommunicative. Gratillonius would see the Emperor! First he must needs be bathed, groomed, properly attired . . .

This time Maximus sat in a room small and plainly furnished, himself simply clad, behind a table littered with papers and wax writing tablets. Apart from two soldiers at the door and the two that led Gratillonius in, he was unattended. Gratillonius gave him a salute, noticing with faint annoyance how awkward it was in his condition. 'Sit down,' the Emperor directed. Gratillonius lowered his weariness on to a stool.

Maximus observed him closely before saying, 'Well, centurion, how are you today?'

Something grinned within Gratillonius. Aloud he answered, 'All right, thank you, sir.'

'Good.' Maximus ruffled the beard over his craggy chin, stared into space, and proceeded: 'You came through interrogation rather well. We've no reason to doubt you were innocent of any criminal intent. Your rescue of Bishop Arator argues in your favour, too. Not being of the Faith, you failed to see the wiles of Satan before you. Meditate on that! But your intentions were patriotic. I expected they'd prove to be. You understand we had to make certain.'

Gratillonius spared himself a reply. It would have been too much effort, for no clear purpose.

'Now.' Maximus's gaze swung back to stab at him. 'Let us hear what you have to relate about Ys.'

Surprised, Gratillonius stammered, 'The Augustus . . . has my dispatches – '

'If those sufficed, I needn't have brought you here.' Maximus barked a laugh. 'Since time is lacking, and you're in no shape to take the initiative, I must. Listen well and answer clearly.'

His questions were shrewd. At the end, he nodded and said, slow-toned: 'Aside from your mistakes – and we pray you've learned your lesson – aside from those, you've done a creditable job. We're minded to keep you at your post. But.' He raised a finger. 'But we set restrictions on you. You will not further abet the practice of sorcery in Ys. Do you hear? You will not. Instead, you, as the prefect of Rome, will do everything in your power to suppress what is diabolical.'

A smile quirked his lips. 'I know that won't be easy. You're set among pagans, and they seem to be especially obstinate. I'm not sure any Christian could handle them at all, and certainly I've no Christian officer available with anything like your capabilities.' He sighed. 'I must use whatever God sees fit to send me.'

He grew stern: 'We shall not let witches live. Once the last of this Priscillianist obscenity is behind us – we'll be sending agents to Hispania to root it out, down to bedrock – once that's done and the West is secure, look for us to enter Ys and inquire into your stewardship. Therefore be zealous. To drive the lesson home, you'll be led from here to receive five strong lashes, one for each wound that Our Lord suffered upon the Cross. No more, and with an unweighted whip. We are disposed to be merciful.'

Gratillonius mustered strength to say, 'I thank the Augustus.'

'Good,' replied Maximus. 'Thereafter you may return

to your quarters and recuperate. Use the time well. Think about your errors, seek counsel, pray for the grace of the Holy Spirit. Then, whenever you are fit to travel, you may do so.'

Dulled though Gratillonius's mind was, a flickering went through it. He dared not wonder if he was being wise before he said, 'Augustus,' – how weakly his voice resounded in his skull – 'you tell me to get advice – from learned men. Well, may I search for it elsewhere than here?'

'What? Where else?' Maximus scowled. 'No, do not linger in Caesarodunum Turonum. They're devout there, but you might become confused about certain things.'

'I meant farther south, sir. To Lugdunum, Burdigala, places where . . . where many sages live.'

'Are you quite right in your head? You're no student, to sit at the feet of philosophers.'

'The Augustus knows . . . we need a new Christian minister in Ys. That calls for searching. Not just anyone will do.'

Maximus fell into thought. 'His appointment is not yours to make,' he said at length, 'but the Church will take your recommendation into account, I suppose. You may prove mistaken. Still, the idea is to your credit.' Again he paused. 'And as for your personal request – well, why not? It should do your soul good to see more of the Empire, of Christendom, than this Northern fringe. And clergymen who were not involved in the affair here, they may appeal better to your heart.' Decision came. 'You may travel freely, provided you stay within Gallia, conduct yourself properly, and take no longer than, oh, six months until you return to duty. My secretary will prepare a written authorization.'

Wistfulness brushed him. 'After all,' he said, 'we were

soldiers together, you and I, soldiers on the Wall. Go with God.'

'Thank you, sir,' Gratillonius made himself utter.

Maximus's glance went back to the documents before him. 'Dismissed.'

Gratillonius's guards led him off to the whipping post.

6

Four-and-twenty legionaries, fully encountered, marched out of the rain into the common room of the hostel. They shooed the help away and came to attention, ranked, before the couch where Gratillonius lay on his side to spare his back. Lamplight made their metal gleam against the shadows that had stolen in with eventide. As one, they saluted. 'Hail, centurion!' rolled forth.

He sat up. The blanket fell off him. 'What's this?' he demanded.

'By your leave, sir,' Adminius replied, 'we're 'ere for yer judgement.'

'What do you mean?'

The deputy must wrench the words out: 'We 'eard wot 'appened, and 'ow it was our stupid fault. Word's got around, you see. Sir, w-w-we wants ter make it good, if we can. Only tell us wot ter do.'

Budic's lip quivered. Uncontrollable tears ran down his cheeks. 'That *I* should have betrayed my centurion!' he nearly screamed.

'Quiet, you,' Adminius snapped. 'Bear yerself like a soldier. Sir, we await yer orders. If you can't tell nobody ter flog us, we'll do it ter each other. Or anything you want.'

'We haven't yet found out who hurt you,' said Cynan starkly, 'but when we do, they're dead men.'

Shocked, Gratillonius got to his feet. 'Are you a Roman?' he exclaimed. 'I'll have none of that. They did their duty, under orders, as Rome expects you will. If anything rates punishment, that notion of yours does. Kill it.'

A part of him noticed that he hadn't got dizzy this time, rising. Anger was a strong tonic. But he was recovering pretty fast, too. That knowledge went through him in a warm wave. He looked upon his men in their misery, and suddenly had to blink back tears of his own.

'Boys,' he said with much carefulness, 'you're not to blame. I never instructed you to keep silence, because I never expected trouble myself. Who would have? And let me say, this show of loyalty damn near makes me glad of what happened. It hasn't done me any real damage anyway, aside maybe from a few extra scars. Give me three or four days more, and I'll be ready for the road.'

'To Ys, sir?' Adminius blurted.

Gratillonius shook his head. 'Not at once.'

'Well, wherever the centurion goes, all 'e'll need is ter whistle us up. Eh, lads?'

The squadron rumbled agreement.

'I'm not likely to require much of a troop in the South, where I'm bound,' Gratillonius said, 'and as for Ys – Shut in here, I've had time to think. Some of you are very likely homesick, after all your while in foreign parts. I can probably dispense with a Roman cadre, the way things are now set up in Armorica. Before leaving Treverorum, I can try to arrange reassignments for you, to your proper units in Britannia.'

'Wot, sir? No!' – 'Not me.' – 'Please, I want to stay.' – 'We're *your* men, sir.'

'You're Rome's men,' Gratillonius reminded them

85

sharply. Behind his mask of an officer, he wondered. Barbarian warriors gave allegiance not to any state but to their chieftains. Was the Empire breeding its own barbarians? He thrust the chilling question aside. He could not penalize love.

Also, he could not be entirely sure that there would be no further use in Ys for these roadpounders of his.

'Well, think it over, and quickly,' he said. 'I told you, I'm starting off soon, and whoever comes with me will be gone a long time.' He drew breath. 'Thank you for your faithfulness. Dismissed.'

''Bout face!' Adminius barked. 'Off ter barracks. I'll follow shortly. Want a private word with the centurion first.'

When the rest had tramped out the door, Gratillonius reseated himself and looked up at the thin face. He saw brashness abashed. 'Well, deputy, what do you want?' he asked.

'Um, sir, I don't mean ter get above myself, but – could I speak freely, like? Man ter man.'

Warmth rose afresh in Gratillonius. He smiled. 'Go right ahead. If you overstep, I'll simply tell you.'

'Well, um – ' Adminius wrung his hands and stared downward. 'Well, sir,' he said in a rush, 'the centurion *is* a man, very much a man, but 'e's been through a 'ard time, after driving 'imself so 'ard, and now means ter begin again, sooner than wot a medic might call wise. It's not for me ter tell yer 'ow ter be'ave. But we in the troop do worry about yer. You're getting your strength back, seems. But where's any pleasure? A man can't go on forever with no fun, no little rewards ter 'imself. Not unless 'e's a flinking saint, 'e can't. Could I, or anybody, 'elp the centurion to a bit of re-cre-ation? I'd be that glad, I would.'

'You're kind,' Gratillonius said, 'but the food and drink

86

are tolerable in this place, and – I am a marked man, who'd better watch his step. Enough.'

'No, not enough! Listen, sir. I know it wouldn't do ter bring a woman in 'ere, or anything like that. But if you go out, would a spy follow? I don't think so.'

Gratillonius chuckled. 'I haven't made your acquaintance with the sort of house you have in mind.'

'No, sir, you're a very serious-minded man. But listen, if you would like a bit of sport, let me recommend the Lion's Den inn at the end of Janus Way. Can't miss it. It's safe, draws a nice class of customer, the drinks and the games are honest, the girls are clean, and right now they've got the damnedest band of musicians you ever 'eard. That's if you want, of course. I've said my piece. If the centurion 'as nothing else for me, goodnight, sir, and do be good to yerself.' Adminius saluted and bolted.

Gratillonius laughed. He hadn't done that since his arrest. It was a grand feeling. What a dear bunch of mother hens he led!

At that, he thought, the deputy had a point. Before setting off on what was, after all, business of the most serious, he'd be well-advised to refresh his spirit, get out of this dull dwelling, to where winds could blow the lingering horrors from his head. A vintner who'd been hospitable, and his pretty daughter –

The girl was doubtless chaste –

Gratillonius felt the stirring in his loins. And that had not happened either, following his imprisonment, until now. Fear about it had begun to nag him . . .

By Hercules, but he'd been long deprived! And he'd spend additional months before coming back to his wives. Into his wives. The visions flamed up. Oh, he'd been told that some or other spell made it impossible for the King of Ys to possess any but the Gallicenae. That was in Ys, though, hundreds of leagues away at the far, lonely end of Armorica, Ys Whose Gods he had in his heart forsworn and Who were fading away into myth. What power had They left Them? As he recalled the comfort that lay in a woman's arms and breasts, the forgetfulness of self that lay between her legs, his rod lifted fully. When he regained his feet, it stayed firm.

He cast hesitation aside, fetched his cloak, and went forth into a fine rain that he thought really should steam off his flesh.

– She was a big young blonde whose guttural accent somehow excited him the more. He didn't quite make out her name, but she told him she was from east of the border. Hard pressed these days, many half-civilized Germani drifted across the Rhenus in search of employment, and often women trailed along. Roman authorities usually looked the other way, what with a labour shortage acute and worsening. While she talked and her right hand raised the cup of mead he had bought her, her left began to explore his person.

He paid the fee for two turns and they went upstairs. None of his Queens would ever know if he could help it, but if perchance they found out, surely most would understand that a man has needs.

A couple of tallow candles burned in the cubicle where her bed was. Their rankness was exciting too, like animals in rut. His member throbbed. She pulled off her gown and stood smiling at him. Her bosom was heavy above a rounded white belly and a patch that the wan light shaded but that gave off brass glints. He scrambled out of his clothes.

Then he felt the coldness and the shrivelling. His knees shook, his pulse rattled.

They lay down and she tried this and that. Nothing availed. Finally she said, 'Vell, too bad, but I got to go vork, you know?' He sighed and nodded. There was no mention of a refund.

– He groped his way through night, back towards the hostel. It had been foolish not to carry a lantern. The rain fell heavier than before, with a wind to dash it into his eyes and hoot between the walls. Chill sneaked under his cloak.

So, he thought. I am once for all the King of Ys. Anywhere I may be, as long as we both shall live.

Despite himself, he smiled a bit. Then maybe they're not mistaken about other things in Ys, he thought. Maybe the soul of Dahilis is still somewhere thereabouts, waiting for me.

He could almost believe that something of hers had watched over him. He was in search of the highest consecration of Mithras. His hypocrisy before Maximus still tasted nasty in his mouth, necessary though it had seemed. At least now he was, like it or not, free of any further impurity.

IV

1

Even without the need to make fortifications each afternoon and demolish them next morning, the march to
Lugdunum took half a month. It might have gone faster,
but Gratillonius wanted to assure himself of complete
recovery. He had seen what could happen when men
overtaxed their healing bodies. Also, he had been unable
to obtain sufficient rations for his squadron in
Treverorum, but must needs get them piecemeal at way
stations. Several were out of commission, which meant
delay while soldiers searched and dickered. Maximus's
war had caused some of the damage. More was due to
incursions of Franks and Alemanni. The Romans had
succeeded in driving those barbarians out ten years ago,
then lacked funds and labour for complete restoration.

The countryside was beautiful, but autumn travelled
south with the troop, bearing downpours and shivery
winds. Journey's end and roofs overhead felt good indeed.
Gratillonius gave his soldiers and himself a few days to
rest, see the great city, and take what pleasures were
available. He knew they would be close-mouthed, and in
any event he had not confided his real purpose to them,
except for Adminius. The deputy's Christianity was nom-
inal, and his boyhood in the Londinium slums had taught
him how to learn much while revealing nothing.

Gratillonius felt it best to keep his own inquiries about
Mithras worship incidental to those about possible clergy
for Ys. The latter questions were the merest token. He

knew full well that such an appointment could only be made in the North. However, if secret agents demanded a report on him, this should satisfy them.

Whatever guilt he felt had left him as he sat hour by hour in the saddle or lay alone in his tent at night. It was Maximus who was the betrayer. He had not strengthened the Empire, he had split it asunder as Roman slew Roman. He had not given it peace and prosperity, he had raised persecution and fear. He had broken pledge after pledge, to Gratianus, to Martinus, to poor old Priscillianus, to the Senate and the People of Rome; how long would he keep his to Valentinianus? He proposed to violate the ancient compact with Ys. Gratillonius disliked practising deception, but such knowledge about his commandant had eaten away his resistance to it.

Seeking a better mood, he wandered around Lugdunum and found marvels, stately public buildings, baths, theatre, and, outside its walls, sculptured tombs, magnificent aqueducts, an artificial lake for mimic sea battles. While many warehouses stood hollow, commerce still flowed along rivers and roads. Though poverty lurked in tenements and alleys, joviality flourished in taverns, foodstalls, bawdyhouses, odeions, the homes of the well-to-do. Few folk seem to worry about much besides their private lives, unless they be devout Christians intent on the afterworld.

No Mithraeum survived here, but presently Adminius heard that one was left in Vienna, some twenty miles south. Gratillonius's spirits lifted. He ordered departure the following day. None of the twenty-four asked why, or what else he had in mind.

A considerably lesser city on the left bank of the Rhodanus, Vienna nevertheless possessed its splendours, including a large circus and a temple that Claudius Caesar had erected four hundred years ago. More to the point, military accommodations and civilian amenities were adequate. The troop might be staying for some time.

Adminius had ferreted out the name and location of Lucas Orgetuorig Syrus, a wine merchant. Walking thither the day after his arrival, Gratillonius found a house with a moderately prosperous shop. Syrus proved to be an old man whose features, despite generations of intermingling, bore traces of his family's Asiatic origin. When Gratillonius gave him the initiate's grip, his dim eyes widened, then filled with tears, and he came near collapse. Rallying, he took the newcomer to a private room, where Gratillonius made the signs of reverence before speaking those secret words that identified his rank in the Mysteries as Persian.

'Be welcome, oh, very welcome, my son,' Syrus quavered. 'It's been so long since any of the faithful appeared who were young and strong. Are there more like you?'

Gratillonius nodded. 'Three, Father, men of my company. Two have the rank of Occult. The third joined us a couple of years ago. He's only a Raven, of course.'

'He has not been advanced? Why not? Advancement should be swift, when we are so few, so few – ' The voice trailed off.

'How can it be, Father, with none superior to me where we've been? That's why I've sought you, that, and the hope of your blessing.'

'The blessing you have, my son, but . . . but let us be seated. I'll call for refreshment and we'll talk. Or am I being selfish? Should I first send for Cotta? He's our Runner of the Sun, he deserves to hear. Oh, I must share these glad tidings with him.'

'Later, Father, I beg.' Gratillonius assisted the frail form to a bench. 'Did you wish drink? Permit me to call a servant.'

Conversation went haltingly. Syrus had not lost his wits, but they were apt to wander, and twice he dozed off for a few minutes as he sat. Gratillonius learned this congregation existed on sufferance, provided it stay discreet and refrain from any hint of proselytization. It might have been banned altogether, as the Imperial decree required; but Syrus's family had money and his son carried weight in civil affairs. Although himself a Christian, the younger man did not care to see his father's heart broken. Death would close down the Mysteries soon enough.

Gratillonius explained his desire as best he could. 'I know it's a great deal to ask, such a promotion, especially when I can't stay here long. It may be impossible. If so, I ask forgiveness for presuming. But if it can be done – if I can be raised to your rank, Father – why, Ys will have a temple of the God, and full celebration of His rites, proper instruction for the young, elevation of worshippers. The faith will live!'

'A wonderful vision, my son,' Syrus whispered. 'Foredoomed, I fear, but wonderful. Mithras, sentry at the frontier of the dark – ' His head drooped, snapped back up; he gulped air. 'I must think, study, pray. It *is* irregular. But, but I wish – how I wish – Can you come to services tomorrow sundown? Bring your fellow believers. It will be a common rite, they too may take part, and welcome, welcome – '

Gratillonius gave him an arm and upbore half his weight when he shuffled off to bed.

– Mithraeums had never been large. The one in Vienna consisted of a single room in Syrus's house. Its windows had been boarded up and plastered over to simulate a cave. Benches along the walls left just a strip of aisle between. A cord at the entrance end marked off the vestibule. Neither font nor image of lion-headed Time stood there, only a basin for holy water. At the sacrificial end, the Bullslaying and the Torchbearers were merely painted above a table that did duty for an altar. Nothing was squalid; wax candles gave light, incense sweetened the air. But of the handful of regular attenders, every head was grey or white.

Yet after the feverish chatter beforehand had stopped and men entered this sanctuary, solemnity brooded over it. The lesser members took stance behind the cord and made reverence as the higher – two Lions, two Persians (Gratillonius the second), the Runner of the Sun, and the Father, all in minimal vestments – passed by. The offering was simply wine raised before the Tauroctony. The re-enactment by the two seniors – of Mithras overcoming the Sun, then crowning Him to be forever after the Unconquered – was bare-bones simple. The liturgy was brief. Subsequently those forward reclined on the benches while Ravens, Occults, and Soldiers brought the sacred meal and served them. That food, at least, was of the best, within the limits of prescribed austerity. Gratillonius savoured it, as being like a sign unto him of the soul's ascent Heavenward . . . when he had tasted nothing holy but prayers for nigh on three years.

Thoughts tumbled through him. Why was he doing this, why was he feeling this? He knew he was not a deeply religious person – no spiritual kin to, say, Martinus of Turonum. Well, but what else had he to cleave to? The Gods of Achilles, Aeneas, Vercingetorix were dead: phantoms at most, haunting glens and graveyards and the dusty pages of books. The Gods of Ys were inhuman. Christ was a pallid stranger. Rome the Mother was a widow, her husband the Republic and their tall sons long since dead in battle, herself the booty of every bandit who came by. Mithras alone stood fast, Mithras all alone.

When they consecrated Gratillonius a Father, he felt
weariness drop off him like a cloak of lead unclasped, and
himself momentarily victorious.

There had been too much he must learn, in too brief a
span. He had no gift for acquiring doctrine, words,
gestures, arcana; he must hammer them into his head,
toiling till dawn grizzled his window and he fell into a few
hours of sleep wherein his dreams gibbered. Meanwhile
he must ever strive to keep chaste and pious. That was
not hard for the body, requiring little more than exercise,
cleanliness, and temperance. But his mind was a maniple
of barbarian recruits, raw, rebellious, slouching off every
which way the instant that the drill-master's glance strayed
off them. He should have had years for his undertaking
and done it openly, while the rest of his life went on in
everyday wise. Instead, he rammed his way through the
teachings, hoped for godliness, and took precautions
against the authorities.

Probably no one would ever denounce him. He had
entered Vienna quietly, stayed inconspicuous, responded
to questions with evasive phrases about a confidential
assignment. His men knew nothing and were content to
enjoy themselves – aside from Maclavius, Verica, and
Cynan, his fellow Mithraists, and Adminius. Those would
not give him away. Syrus's congregation had learned
silence. However, somebody else might notice how often
Gratillonius visited that particular house.

No matter! he told himself. By the time such gossip
reached Treverorum, if it did, he'd be back in Ys.
Maximus would look upon his establishment of a Mith-

raeum there as an act of rebellion, which it was, but could scarcely do anything about it for another two or three years, during which anything might happen. Live each day as it comes, like a soldier in the field.

They raised him to Runner of the Sun and he concelebrated the Mystery with Syrus. In his exhaustion, he felt only that he had passed a mark on an endless uphill road.

But when Syrus and Cotta together had finished the rite that made him Father, and for the first time he – with his own hands, farmer's, soldier's, woodworker's hands – lifted the chalice before the Tauroctony, and drank the blessed wine – then abruptly, blindingly, the sacredness of it came upon him. Did the Sun lift out of the night in his spirit, to blaze in terrible majesty from his heart? He knew not. As he spoke the words, he wept.

Everyone embraced him. 'The grace of Mithras be with you always, beloved brother,' Syrus wished.

That was impossible, of course. After he left the sanctum, he was merely Gratillonius. What had happened within, he could barely remember.

Maybe You will reveal Yourself to me again, God of my fathers, he thought. Or maybe not. I am unworthy of this much. But I will serve You as steadfastly as lies in the power of mortal flesh and grimy soul.

– The Birthday was not far off. Syrus asked Gratillonius to join him in honouring it. The old man cried a little when he heard that that would be unwise. The legionaries had lingered suspiciously long as it was and must be off straightaway. Gratillonius gave him the kiss of peace, and received it.

In the morning the squadron started west towards Burdigala. Gratillonius had another promise to redeem.

3

Decimus Magnus Ausonius smiled. 'You show me the lady Bodilis as still more fascinating in person than in correspondence,' he said. 'You see, she's had so many questions for me that I failed to question my own assumptions. Thus I came to regard her as a brilliant human being, but one condemned to existence in a stagnant backwater. My mistake. What you have had to tell makes me wonder if Ys may not hold the world's highest civilization. Were I capable of the journey, I would accompany you there, Gratillonius, and explore it. "Oh, that Jupiter might restore to me the years that are fled!"' His quotation and the sigh that followed were rueful, though quite without self-pity.

'But I talk too much,' he went on. 'Better to listen. In a sense, Ys is more distant than the farthest land we know of. That mysterious force which has worked for centuries to erase its name from our chronicles – You can remain a while, can't you? Please.'

'I should be returning soon, sir,' Gratillonius answered.

'You are restless. You hunger for achievement. Well, let us work some energy off you before we dine.' Ausonius guided his guest to the door.

Gratillonius went along gladly. Inclement weather had kept people indoors these past two days, during which he – after getting his men barracked in the city – had stayed with the poet. Not that he hadn't enjoyed himself. Ausonius was delightful company. Still erect and lively in his mid-seventies, he had been more than a famous teacher of rhetoric; he had been tutor to ill-fated Emperor-to-be Gratianus in Treverorum, afterwards prefect of Gallia, Libya, and Italy, eventually consul. In retirement since Maximus took the throne, he remained active among colleagues, students, civic leaders, a large household and its neighbourhood, while from his pen streamed verses and epistles to friends throughout the Empire.

Nevertheless it was a special pleasure to step forth on the portico of the rural mansion, flush lungs with fresh air, and look widely around. Rain and sleet had yielded to sunshine which, although slanted from the south, gave January a pledge of springtime. Grounds swept darkling with moisture down to the bank of the Garumna; mist smoked off the river, roiled by a breeze, half obscuring the vineyards beyond. On a paved path that the men took, doves moved aside from the sapphire arrogance of a peacock.

'A slave told me you have several scrolls in your baggage,' Ausonius said. 'May I ask what the texts are?'

Gratillonius hesitated. They were from Syrus, aids to his memory of doctrine and rites that a Father must know, and none of lesser rank. When he had no more need of them in Ys, he was to destroy them by fire, with certain prayers. 'I'm sorry. It's forbidden me to tell.'

Ausonius gave him a close regard before murmuring, 'You're not a Christian, are you?'

'I follow the Lord Mithras.'

'I suspected as much. Well, I'm Christian myself, but hold that to be no grounds for scorning the ancients or any upright contemporaries who believe otherwise. Surely God is too great to be comprehended in a single creed, and we mortals do best simply to pay our due respects and cultivate our gardens.'

Gratillonius recalled poems of Ausonius that Bodilis had shown him. They were concerned with everyday matters, sometimes humorous, sometimes grave, sometimes – as when he mourned the death of his wife or a child – moving, in a stoic fashion. *'Gather you roses, girl, whilst they and you are in flower, remembering how meanwhile time flies from you . . .'*

Hoofbeats drummed. The men turned to look. Up from the riverside galloped a mud-splashed horse, upon it a boy of eight or nine years. 'Why, yonder comes Paulinus,' the rhetor exclaimed happily.

Gratillonius had met the lad, Ausonius's grandson, born in Macedonia but now here to get the finest possible education. Being shut in by the rain had made him miserable, despite the elder's unfailing kindliness. The ride had evidently refreshed him, for he drew rein at his grandfather's hail and greeted the men in seemly wise. 'Are you ready to go back to your books?' Ausonius asked, smiling.

'Please, can't I ride some more first?' Paulinus begged. His Latin was heavily Greek-accented. 'Bucephalus, he's just getting his second wind.'

'Discipline, discipline, you must break yourself to harness before you dare call yourself a man . . . But in indulging you I indulge myself. Go as you will. "Good speed is to your young valour, boy! So shall you mount to the stars!"' Ausonius quoted with a chuckle. 'Meditate upon that line. It should make Vergilius more interesting to you.'

'Thanks!' Paulinus cried, and was off in a spatter of wet earth.

Ausonius clicked his tongue and shook his head. 'I really must become stricter with him,' he said. 'Else a rhetorician of considerable potential could go to waste. But it isn't easy when I remember his father at that age.'

Gratillonius thought of Dahilis and Dahut. 'No, it isn't easy,' he said through sudden, unexpected pain. Hastily:

'Still, he ought to keep in shape. He may well find need for a set of muscles.'

'Oh? Why? We moderns don't revere athletes like the Greeks in their glory. His career should resemble mine, writing, teaching, public office.'

Gratillonius's gaze went eastward, towards the Duranius valley through which he had come on his way to Burdigala. Those thickly wooded steeps and hollows lay not great distance hence. Yet little traffic moved there any more, for fear of the robbers who haunted them. 'How long do you suppose that sort of life will stay possible?' he asked harshly. 'Why, already – when was it? – about twenty-five years ago, the barbarians cut the aqueducts of Lugdunum itself.'

Ausonius nodded. 'I remember. It caused the taxes to fail that year.'

'Didn't it mean any more to you than that?'

'Oh, these are troublous times, admittedly.' The furrows of the old countenance turned downward in sorrow. 'My friend Delphinus was fortunate in passing away before his wife and daughter met their fate at the hands of the tyrant Maximus.' Ausonius gripped the arm of Gratillonius. 'You've intimated that you were a witness to the evil done in Augusta. If you've spoken no more about it, I can understand. But the martyrs are safe in heaven – we must believe – and a measure of justice has since prevailed.'

'Really?' asked the centurion, surprised. 'How?'

'You have not heard? . . . Well, I suppose you scarcely could have, on the road as you were.' (Or immured in Vienna, Gratillonius did not add.) 'I have received letters, including one from a colleague who is in correspondence with Martinus, the bishop of Caesarodunum.'

Gratillonius's pulse quickened. 'I've met that man. Tell me what happened.'

'Why, Martinus was on his way home when he learned of the executions of the Priscillianists, a breach of Maximus's promise to show them mercy. He burned up the road back to Augusta and demanded to see the Emperor. That was denied him. But Maximus's wife, a pious lady, grew terrified, begged Martinus to dine alone with her and discuss it. They say he had never done that with a woman, but consented, and she laved his feet with her tears and dried them with her hair. The upshot was that Maximus did hear Martinus out, a thunderous denunciation, and agreed not to send inquisitors to Hispania, heretic-hunting, as he had planned. In exchange, Martinus celebrated Communion with the bishops who had been active in the prosecution. So you see, civilization, tolerance, common decency won in the end.'

A glow awoke in Gratillonius. 'By Hercules,' he exclaimed, 'that Martinus is a soldier yet!'

At the back of his mind went the thought that this boded better for Ys, and for the hopes he cherished, than hitherto.

'Be less pessimistic,' Ausonius urged. He gestured. 'Look about you. The foundations hold firm. Broad, fertile, well-cultivated acres; flourishing cities; law and order, which reach into the very place of the usurper. True, the Empire has its difficulties. But the life of the mind goes on, and that is what matters. That is what is eternal.'

The mood of the younger man changed as he listened. He wanted to be away, immediately, back into action. He curbed himself. Best he abide a few days more, for his own sake as well as Bodilis's, maybe also for the sake of Ys and Dahut. Let him gather what roses he could and bring them home. If ever he returned here, the flowerbeds might well lie trampled by the hoofs of warriors' horses.

V

1

Ever was there something strange about Mumu, something apart from the rest of Ériu. To this southernmost of the Fifths, it was said, the Children of Danu withdrew after their defeat by the Children of Ír and Éber; now their King dwelt within the Mountain of Fair Women, the síd beyond the plain of Femen. Folk gave more sacrifices to Goddesses than to Gods, and believed that by mortal men certain of These had become ancestresses of their royal houses. Female druids, poets, and witches practised their arts as often as did males, or oftener. Here above all it was terrible to be out after dark on the eves of Beltene and Samain, when the doors between the worlds stood open – so swarmed the dead and every other kind of uncanny being.

Highlands walled Mumu off. Traffic did go back and forth, but less than elsewhere, and war with men of Condacht. Qóiqet Lagini, or Mide seldom became more than a season of skirmishes. The Ulati were far in the north; one scarcely even heard of them. The men of Mumu bore ample spears against each other. At the same time, safe harbours brought about overseas trade in a measure unknown to the neighbour realms. Roman goods arrived from as far as Aquitania: wine, oil, glass, earthenware, in exchange for gold, honey, beeswax, furs, hides. Likewise did the sumptuous fabrics of Ys. Scot's Landing, below that city, took its name not from pirates out of Ériu but from the frequent, peaceful visits of Mumach fishers.

The Christian faith got its first foothold on the island among their kinfolk, who claimed that some of the Lord's own apostles had been there.

Missionaries had not yet reached the rugged country about the Mountain of Fair Women when Lugthach maqq Aillelo was king over its allied tuaths. Afterwards poets told how Fedelmm, daughter of Moethaire of the Corco Óchae, fought him. Not only did she have warriors at her beck, she was a mighty witch. The story went that she had a friend in the female warrior Bolce Ben-bretnach from Alba. Perhaps as a way to making peace, Bolce sought out Lugthach and laid upon him the demand that he bed her. He could not refuse one with her powers, and thus Conual maqq Lugthaci was begotten. At the birth, the father was away but Fedelmm was present, and to her the mother gave Conual for fostering.

Fedelmm took the infant home. The next night a coven was to meet in her house. Lest harm befall him, she hid Conual in a hole beneath the hearthstone. One of the witches sniffed him and said, 'I do not destroy anything save what is under the cauldron.' At that, the fire flashed downward and burned the ear of the boy.

From this, some say, came his nickname Corcc, the Red; but others say that was the colour of his hair. He also became known as Conual maqq Lárech, because his foster mother bore the nickname Láir Derg, the Red Mare.

To her came a seer, who read the child's hand and told him: 'Always set free any captives you meet, if you are able. Do this, and your race will grow great and your fame endure.' Conual could scarcely have understood, then, but throughout his life he strove to obey the commandment.

So went the stories. They did not say why Fedelmm soon gave the fostering over to Torna Éces. She may have wished the lad to be free of the dark forces around herself.

Torna was the foremost poet of his day, a man who saw deeply into things and knew promise when he found it. Already he was raising Niall maqq Echach, son of the King of Mide. He had rescued the child from the murderous spite of the King's new wife, Mongfind, the witch-queen out of Mumu.

Conual was only three or four years old when Torna deemed Niall of an age to return to Temir, show that he was not dead as everybody there believed, and claim his rights. Mongfind could wreak no further harm upon him. However, after his father died, she succeeded in having her brother Craumthan maqq Fidaci hailed King.

A better person than his sister, on the whole he reigned well. His grief was that he was childless. When he heard about Conual, who was his cousin, he sent for the boy, meaning to make him an adoptive son. Torna let Conual go, counselling him to remember the kindly duty given him.

The newcomer was soon a worshipful friend of the older Niall and, when big enough, accompanied him to war. Fighting in Qóiqet Lagini, they took a prisoner who proved to be a learned man. On that ground, Conual persuaded Niall he should be released without ransom.

The closeness between the princes aroused all of Mongfind's malignancy. Niall was by then too strong, with too many handfast men, for her to seek his overthrow. It would take very little to break the uneasy peace and let him avenge the wrongs she had done him and his mother Carenn. But she could poison Craumthan's mind against Conual, word by sly word. At last, sick of soul, the king decided he must be rid of the youth.

He could not well have his fosterling slain at home. Instead, Mongfind whispered, he should entrust Conual with a message for a Pictish chieftain in Alba who was tributary to him. As a leavetaking gift, Craumthan gave Conual a shield whereon stood words engraved in ogamm. Conual took them for a good luck charm.

Having crossed the North Channel and being wearied, he made camp on the beach. Who should chance by but the scholar he had set free? Conual welcomed him, and presently fell asleep. The guest read what was on the shield, as the Pictish lord would also be able to do. The bearer was to be killed. The scholar changed the inscription. Hence, when Conual reached his destination, he was lavishly received, and soon got a daughter of the chieftain in marriage.

Thus the story, and few men would be so rash as to gainsay a poet. Yet naked truth may be garbed in many different words. This tale might be a profound way of relating that Conual Corcc got in trouble at Temir and perforce departed with what small following he could muster, but won high standing in his exile.

Of Niall, the poets told that he became King in Mide after Craumthan and Mongfind destroyed each other with an envenomed drink. Erelong he was warring abroad as well as in Ériu and gaining a mighty name.

Conual Corcc dwelt four years with his wife among her people. He gathered men sworn to him and led them in battle through the great onslaught Niall masterminded and Magnus Maximus repelled. Afterwards he brought them and their women down to the country of the Ordovices and Silures. A good many Scoti had settled there as Roman power ebbed out of the hills.

Slowly that tide turned. Before leaving the Wall, Maximus had sent an ally, Cunedag of the Votadini, to take charge in that part of Britannia. Between him and the Second Legion, stationed at Isca Silurum, the Scoti found that they could no longer seize land as their numbers increased, but must fight to keep what they had. Conual Corcc became a leading war chieftain of theirs, who often raided deep into regions the Romans had supposed were safe. Loot made him wealthy.

Yet he was, in his way, a thoughtful man. Torna may have put that into him. Wherever he went, he looked keenly at things, and he turned the memories of them over and over in his head. He considered the farms, manors, towns, fortresses – the tools, machines, books, laws, the sense of a dominion and a history vaster than they could imagine in Ériu. Captives whom he let go spoke well of him upon returning home. In the course of time, truce and trade with Conual became just as possible as war. When he visited a Roman centre, he asked endless questions; and to Romans who ventured into his purlieu on peaceful business, he gave hospitality and protection.

It was not that he had any wish to become a subject of their Empire. He understood too well what it was doing to itself. Besides, more and more he yearned for his homeland. But the riches and the knowledge he was gaining here would let him return in strength.

2

It was noon when the legionaries again saw Ys. Sun and sky stood winter-wan, but light gleamed off the few clouds and many wings aloft. Grass on the headlands was, as yet, sere above their stern cliffs. Glimpsed from these heights, the water below ran in amethyst, beryl, flint, silver. Its noise growled through a shrillness of wind, air alive with salt, kelp, and frost. And there between the steeps rose turreted ruddy walls, soaring and flashing towers. At high tide the sea gate was closed, surf battering under the battlements, and that too was utterly right, a part of coming home.

The soldiers raised a cheer. Riding in front of them, Gratillonius signalled for double time. Hobnails crashed on paving. Westbound along Aquilonian Way, the men saw ahead to the end of Cape Rach, where the pharos loomed beyond clustered tombs. But soon their road swung north and downward, into the valley. Folk began to spy them and flock forth shouting from homes, farms, orchards nestled in the hills. Sentinels observed afar and sounded their trumpets. Aquilonian Way turned west again at the amphitheatre, whose walls barred sight of the sacred grove. Thence the track ran straight between smithies, tanneries, carpenter shops, all the industries required to be where people did not live, until it entered High Gate.

'The King, the King!' Crowds jubilated. Gratillonius's eyes stung. He swallowed hard. Did they truly love him like this? He recognized an occasional face among those that swirled around, Herun the navy man, Maeloch the fisher, several marines who'd been escorts of his or fighters against the Scoti, a wineseller for whom he had once got restitution from a swindling wholesaler in Condate Redonum, a woman whom he had once given a judgement against an abusive husband, lesser Suffetes – the magnates would seek the palace for a more formal reception – 'Company dismissed!' he rapped. His men broke formation and flung themselves into the throng, searching for comrades and sweethearts.

Gratillonius rode on. An impromptu guard formed, burly commoners who cleared his way for him, genially if not always gently. The press eased off as he turned from Lir Way into the crookedly rising streets along which the wealthy had their houses. Nobody was forbidden to go there, but most Ysans had a feel for what was becoming, an ancient dignity he had never encountered elsewhere.

At the main entrance to the palace he dismounted, gave his horse over to the excited servants, and strode in his armour through the garden – winter-bare, but trees and shrubs awhisper in the wind – to the modest-sized building. Up its staircase he went, between the sculptured boar and bear, under the gilt eagle on the dome, the creatures of Taranis. Bronze doors, intricately figured, were flung wide for him, and he passed the entryroom and came into the atrium.

There they stood, his Queens and their daughters – and Dahut, next to Quinipilis. O Mithras, how the child had grown, and how solemnly she stared from under a golden mane! Also present were the men of the Council, attendants hovering in the background. He halted with a military stamp and clang, raised his palm, intoned, 'Greetings, my ladies and worthies,' while his heart thuttered and he forced his eyes to swing around, away from the girl who looked so much like Dahilis.

The male grandees didn't matter. Not yet. But what of the Gallicenae? Bodilis smiled at him in unchanged serenity. Tears shimmered on the thin cheeks of Innilis, who huddled close to expressionlessly saluting Vindilis. Lanarvilis's ceremonial gesture showed more warmth. Maldunilis squealed in delight; she was very pregnant. The gaze of Forsquilis smouldered out of her Athene countenance above the infant she bore, whose age must be about two months. How Quinipilis had grown old, the hands trembling that clutched the staff on which she leaned, flesh dried away from the knotted, painful bones, though her grin crinkled wicked as ever. Fennalis too seemed less plump than erstwhile, like an apple that has begun to wither. Guilvilis stood timidly to the rear, her own newest babe clutched to her bosom, her older daughter by Gratillonius clinging to her skirt.

Three stepped forward and confronted him: Soren Cartagi, Speaker for Taranis; Hannon Baltisi, Lir Captain; Forsquilis, whom the Nine serving Belisama must have chosen to be their voice today. 'Welcome, King, thrice welcome to Ys, your city,' they said together. 'May you henceforth long abide in our midst.'

'I thank you,' said Gratillonius out of an unreasonably dry throat. Seeking to lighten the atmosphere: 'And I so intend. You seem well prepared for my arrival.'

Forsquilis nodded. Her glance caught his. He nodded back. On the previous three nights, when his band made camp for lack of other accommodation, a great owl had ghosted by.

'How have you and the city fared?' he asked.

Soren shrugged. 'There's little to tell, save that – No matter now, no large matter at all.'

'What mean you?' Gratillonius demanded.

'Ah, we'd not spoil this hour,' Hannon said. He was seldom that cordial. 'It can wait. You're the one with the real news, whatever it be.'

'News indeed.' Gratillonius drew breath. 'Too much for telling at once. When I do, I think you'll agree my journey's borne fruit we had need of, knowledge, though some of it be bitter on the tongue. Bodilis, I did visit Ausonius.' She grew radiant. 'As for the rest of what I have to convey, it will require much time and thought of us. Best we wait until tomorrow or the day after.'

Soren opened his mouth as if in protest, but Forsquilis cut him off. 'We understand,' she said. 'With no immediate danger, 'twould be foolish to rush into complexities. Come, let's proceed to the banquet we've prepared for our King.'

3

When the others departed after the festivities, she stayed.

In his secret self, Gratillonius had hoped for that. After celibate months, the Bull ramped through his blood. A phantom went there as well, memory of failure in Treverorum, fear of new punishment for his sin. Forsquilis was both the most passionate and the most artful of the Nine.

In a candlelit bedchamber, he invested a few moments of extravagant admiration, bent over the cradle of little Nemeta. (After all, he had been unable to keep from hugging Dahut.) The mother ended that herself, pouncing and clutching, purring and mewing.

They well-nigh ripped the clothes off each other. Her beauty flamed at him. He never knew whether he cast her down or she pulled him down. He entered her with a roar, and her hips surged beneath him like the sea.

After the second time they were satisfied to lie talking while strength regathered itself. He half sat, propped on pillows against the headboard that was usual on Ysan beds. She lay curled in the curve of his left arm, her hair spilling amber-brown across his chest. The odour of her was warm and wild.

'Ah,' she crooned, 'I've missed you, Grallon.'

'And I you.' His free hand strayed over her breasts. Milkful, they jutted proudly from her slenderness. How golden the light was upon that white skin.

'I'm sure you did,' she answered, 'especially after – ' The words turned into a laugh. Appalled, he felt her fingers on his lips. 'Nay, we need speak naught of that.

Stallions will be stallions, for which I thank our Lady of the Lovetime.'

'Is there aught you don't know, you witch?' he gusted in his relief.

She sobered. 'Much. The politics of men and their Gods – ' Her look sought a shuttered window . . . and the night wind beyond? 'You have returned a sadder man than you went, my darling. Why?'

Strangely, it was not strange to blurt to this cat-female, as if she were a man or wise Bodilis: 'Maximus, Emperor Maximus, I misjudged him. He lives not for Rome but for power, and for power not only over bodies but souls.'

From him stumbled the story of what he had seen and endured. Forsquilis held him close.

'So you see Ys is in danger,' he ended. '*You* are, your whole Sisterhood. He means to destroy what he calls witchcraft, rip it out by the roots and cast it on the fire.'

'And you're to do his weeding for him, eh?' she said low, again looking elsewhere.

'I won't. I am the King of Ys, as . . . I finally, truly discovered on this faring . . . But I cannot rise against Rome!' he yelled.

That roused Nemeta, who began to cry. Forsquilis flowed from the bed, took up the babe, soothed and nursed her, the eidolon of young motherhood, while she asked coolly, 'What then do you propose to do?'

'I know not.' Gratillonius smote fist into palm. 'I've thought and thought. I suppose we have two or three years' grace. Maximus must secure his frontier along the Rhenus and make a lasting settlement with Valentinianus – aye, still more with Theodosius in Constantinople.'

'And meanwhile,' she said, smiling down at her child, 'much can happen.'

He nodded violently. ''Tis my hope. Already Ys is central to the defence of Armorica. If we can weave such

111

a net of alliances that we are vital, with so many powerful friends in the Empire that he must keep his hands off us – '

'I was thinking of what might happen to Magnus Maximus,' she said.

A shiver went through him.

Forsquilis straightened and gave him a level regard. Her tone turned brisk. 'Well, these things can await the morrow. We've a third celebration to carry out, I trust, you and I. It should be soon, for you'll need a good night's sleep.'

Her words roused fresh lust and gladness. 'Oh, we can lie abed late.'

She shook her head. 'Nay, that would not be meet. You must be up betimes, O King. Too long has your duty been undone.'

'What's this?'

'Ah, no large task. 'Tis only that postponing it further would dishonour Taranis.' The Queen frowned. 'Hm, I'd forgotten, we never told you. Well, soon after you departed, a challenger arrived at the Wood. We've perforce housed him there, fed him, supplied him with harlots and amusements and whatever else befits one who might become King, these past months. High time to end the farce.'

Gratillonius sat upright. His muscles tautened. 'A fight to the death?'

Forsquilis laughed anew. 'Nay, merely a chore, albeit a sacral one. This is a pitiful shrimp of an Osismian. Clear 'tis, he heard the King would be long away, and knew what a challenger is entitled to, and came to take advantage, with the intent of sneaking off ere you returned. But I divined as much and warned Soren, who ordered a surreptitious watch kept on him. When news of your advent blossomed today, he tried to flee, but was promptly seized. Tomorrow morning you'll kill him, and there's an end of the business, aside from the rites that follow.'

She tenderly laid her babe, now drowsy, back in the cradle; turned about; glided towards the bed, arms wide. 'I believe you are ready now,' she whispered. 'Come, let's make love. A long, long love.'

4

Rain blew up during the night. By dawn its chill drizzle engulfed sky, sea, hills. At the Wood of the King, it dripped off bare oak branches and runnelled down trunks and made soggy last year's leaves on the earth. The blood-coloured house at the border of the grove was dulled, as if the blood were starting to clot.

There waited Soren in his sacerdotal robes, together with six marines, their horses and hounds. They were the guards over Hornach, who had dared strike the Hammer to the brazen Shield that hung in the yard outside.

His centurion's battle gear moved easily on Gratillon-ius's frame as he mounted the steps to the portico. Grotesque idol-shaped columns grinned at him. Underneath the roof lay shadowiness through which he peered at his opponent. Hornach was not quite the weakling of Forsquilis's contempt, but he was scrawny; the mail into which they had stuffed him draped limp over knocking knees, the helmet threatened to slide down his nose. Even in this cold, his fear stank.

'Hail!' boomed from the seven men and the household staff to the King.

Hornach reached out. 'Oh, please,' he croaked, 'please,

I've made a horrible mistake, I'll surrender, abase myself, do anything – '

'Shall we accompany you, sir?' asked a marine. 'Wouldn't do to make you chase him. Heh!' he snickered.

'Nay, that were unseemly. 'Tis never been done thus,' Soren declared. 'We'll put a leash around his waist for you to hold, my lord.' A snarl: 'Unless you, you wretch, can find the manhood to die as Taranis wills.'

'I have an old mother, sir, I've been sending her coins from here, she'll starve without me,' blubbered the Osismian. A trouser leg darkened and clung to the shin; he was dribbling piss.

Gratillonius had expected a straightforward fight against somebody like a Bacauda – had deceived himself into expecting it, he suddenly understood. His gullet thickened. 'This is no combat, 'tis butchery,' he got out. 'Unworthy of the God. I accept his surrender.'

Hornach went on his knees, weeping, and scrabbled to hug the King's. His guards yanked him back. 'That may not be, lord,' said Soren, shock clear to see beneath his implacability. 'This creature issued the challenge. Worse, he did so in falsehood. Strike him down, in the name of the God.'

Gratillonius remembered Priscillianus.

But he was the King of Ys, and here was a rogue who had taken an impudent gamble. 'Well,' he said, 'let it at least be quick.'

After praying to Taranis, they hitched a cord around the waist of Hornach. Gratillonius led him on his wabbling way through the brush, until they stood alone in a glade. Rain mumbled in the trees around, washed away tears, sought past armour. Dead leaves squashed underfoot. Gratillonius undid the leash, stepped back, drew sword and brought up shield. 'Make ready,' he said.

Hornach shuddered, once. His blade jerked forth. It

was of the long Germanic sort, and either he had refused a shield – unlikely – or no one had thought to offer him it, or he in his terror to voice the request.

'Have at me,' Gratillonius invited. Do! screamed within him. 'You might win, you know. You might become the next King of Ys.' He gagged on his lie.

'Let me go,' Hornach pleaded. 'I meant no harm. I never did. Let me go, and the Gods will love you.'

Not the Gods of Ys, Gratillonius thought. In a moment's confusion: But I in my heart give Them no honour any longer. Why should I do this thing?

Iron answered: Because I will destroy myself, my Kingship, everything that is left me to care about, if I openly flout Their will.

Hornach wailed and half turned to run. Get it over with! thought Gratillonius, and advanced. His opponent twisted around, raised sword, chopped wildly. Gratillonius caught the feeble blow on his shield. The other throat was open to him. He smote.

The trouble then was that Hornach did not die. He flopped on the ground, spouting blood and screams. When Gratillonius bent down to give a mercy stroke, hands tried to wave it off.

Abruptly Gratillonius must vomit.

When he had finished, Hornach lay still.

Gratillonius stood in the rain, plunging his blade into the earth, over and over, to cleanse it. The image of Ausonius said: *'What you have had to tell makes me wonder if Ys may not hold the world's highest civilization.'*

I *am* no knacker! he cried into the nothingness and the cold. I am a soldier. Threefold Gods Who robbed the world of Dahilis, will You not send me honest enemies? If You make sport of me, why should I pour out blood for You? Taranis, Lir, Belisama, be warned. I am calling on Mithras to come end Your day, Mithras, Lord of Light.

VI

1

Up from the South wandered spring, and as she breathed upon naked boughs and wet earth there leapt forth blossoms, leaves, new grass, tender herbs, across the length of Armorica. Sunbeams and cloud shadows pursued each other, with rainsqualls and rainbows, till the wind lay down to rest and whiteness brooded huge in the blue. Lambs, calves, foals explored meadows, amazed by brilliance. Wives reopened their homes to air while they scrubbed away winter's grime; farmers hitched ox to plough, mariners bent sail to yard.

Little of the day had entered the house of Queen Vindilis, unless it be a certain bleak freshness. When Fennalis arrived, she gave her brief greeting and led her straight through the austerely ornamented atrium to the private room. Refreshments did wait on its table, nothing more than wine, bread, cheese, and, to be sure, oysters in their opened shells.

Having closed the door, the women made reverence before the image that occupied a niche, Belisama in Her aspect of the Wild Huntress. 'Be seated,' said Vindilis then. 'Avail yourself. How fare you?'

'Oh, you know my rheumatism plagues me in change-able weather, and we get so many bad colds among people at this season that I've scarce had time to think.' Fennalis was much in demand as a healer, second only to Innilis. She lacked the Touch that sometimes came to the latter, but she had the sympathy, together with more practical skill. She lowered her dumpy form to the couch, reached for a bite and a sip, chuckled. '*I* know you've not asked me here to put polite questions.'

Humour died away as she looked up at the one who stood over her. As usual, Vindilis was plainly clad for a person of rank in Ys: today a gown of pearl-hued wool bordered with a procession in blue of the Goddess's cats and doves, a massive garnet brooch at her throat. Hair drawn back in tight, coiled braids made doubly vivid the white streak through its blackness and emphasized the aquilinity of her features. In the greenish light from the window, her eyes seemed enormous, full of night.

'I thank you for coming,' she said, with no softening of her tone. 'I believe you'll agree 'tis on a matter of moment.'

Fennalis's pugnosed countenance registered puzzlement. She ran fingers through the snowy mane that bristled out of the pins and comb wherewith she sought to control it. 'Why me? I'm not wise or strong or, or anything. Oh, if I can help you, dear, of course I'll try.'

'I am with child,' Vindilis told her.

Fennalis half rose, slopping wine from cup. 'What? Why, wonderful!'

'That remains to be seen. Yesterday Innilis examined me and confirmed what the signs had said. The birth should come about winter solstice.'

Fennalis sank back and was quiet a while before replying low, 'Why are you troubled? 'Twas your choice to leave off using the Herb. Aye, you're not youthful, but you've kept yourself as fit as a lynx. Fear not.'

Vindilis snapped forth a laugh. 'Does the smith who is forging a sword fear it will cut him down? Nay, what frets him is that it may prove weak in the wielder's hand.'

'What mean you?' Fennalis asked, not quite steadily.

Vindilis began pacing, to and fro before the couch. Her skirts whispered. She stared before her as she said: 'I confide in you because you are the only one I can. And you are neither weak nor foolish, Fennalis, underneath those flustery ways of yours. Six children have you borne to three different Kings, and all are still alive. Under Colconor, you could have drawn yourself into the background – he had little yen for you – but instead you stood up to him, again and again, took his abuse, fended the worst of his cruelties off Dahilis as well as your own daughters. And in the end, if you were not the first, neither were you the last who dared call on us to curse him. Since then – '

Fennalis waved her hands. 'I am not hostile to King Grallon.'

Vindilis laughed anew. 'Nor intimate of his, either. You made no secret of your displeasure when he would not truly take you for his wife, and in Council you've opposed more than one proposal of his.'

Fennalis sighed. 'That's past. He's true to his faith, and so meant me no insult. Whatever dreams had stirred in me have quietly gone away. I am content.'

'Are you?' Vindilis swung about and stood confronting her. 'The rest are, more or less, aye. Think them over. Bodilis is his favourite, his . . . his friend. Lanarvilis has her disagreements with him, but not very often any more. To her, he is Rome, the Roman virtue and the Roman peace she imagines once existed. Quinipilis surely has her doubts, but she enjoys his company and is, anyhow, too old and weary for dispute. To Maldunilis, he has a big cock and is kindly. Guilvilis is his adoring brood mare. Forsquilis – who can ever tell what Forsquilis thinks? I dare not yet be frank with her. That leaves you.'

'And Innilis.'

'Innilis . . . will follow my lead.' Suddenly the voice of Vindilis had a lullaby sound. 'But what shall it be? She also looks on him as a good man, and . . . sometimes his attentions give her pleasure. The Lady forbid that I ever put Innilis in danger or distress.' She signed herself.

'If you are embittered, why are you bearing his child?' Fennalis asked as softly.

Vindilis smiled slightly. 'I am not aggrieved. He slew horrible Colconor. He does his best for Ys and for his Queens, and his best is generally excellent.' She drew breath. ''Tis not his fault that Innilis and I can snatch only stolen, secret moments. 'Tis not his fault, even, that that aborted get of his almost killed her. Nay, we could be far worse off. I doubt we could be better off.'

'But still you oppose him.'

'Because he *is* what he is!' Vindilis cried. 'I've not come lightly to this. I've watched, questioned, listened, pondered. I've prayed to the Mother of Stars for guidance. No clear answer came to me, but – what dreams I had, what signs I read in the sea-foam and heard in the sea-wind, all seemed to call me forward.'

Fennalis occupied herself as prosaically as might be with slicing the cheese. 'At last you decided to have his child,' she said.

Vindilis nodded. 'What other hold on him can be mine?'

She went to the window and stood staring into it, as if able to see clearly through the small, leaded panes, out beyond the city and across the Ocean. ''Twas no easy decision,' she said to the woman at her back. 'A wish for this was never vouchsafed me. In my vestalhood I meant to renew my vows and become a minor, virgin priestess. What hopes I cherished ran towards things like founding a gymnasium for girls. Understand, Fennalis, I do not hate the minds or the deeds of men. 'Tis their sweaty, hairy bodies that repel me – that, and their supposition that because of what's between my legs, I should forever stay within walls.'

Fennalis forbore to mention the freedom that most Ysan women enjoyed. 'I remember,' she said. 'The Sign came upon you and – You were lucky that Hoel was King then. He too was decent.'

'Just the same – did you know? – 'twas Quinipilis, my mother, who forced me to open my womb to him. Forced me, I say, by endless arguments and browbeatings and – ' Vindilis shrugged, grinned. 'She was a formidable character in her day, she was. At last I gave in and produced the grandchild she wanted. One. You know well I never paid Runa more heed than I absolutely must. Poor little brat. I hope I'm shrewder these days, more in control of myself.'

There was a silence, apart from a *whoo-oo* of spring-time wind under the eaves.

'Why do you tell me this?' Fennalis asked at length.

Vindilis turned about. 'Is it not clear? I want your counsel, your help. For Ys and its Gods.'

The older woman put aside the food with which she had toyed and took up her wine instead. It was more fitting. 'You want influence on Grallon beyond your mere persuasions.'

'Aye. I need it. We all do.'

Vindilis resumed her caged pacing. 'Think,' she said. 'Because he has done so well, authority flows more and more to him. Now he's put the final seal on his Kingship, his halidom, by slaying a challenger in the Wood. That wipes out, from the minds of the people, any last fear that he may not yet have settled his account with the Gods. And he's young, strong, skilled. Surely he'll make short work of any future contestants.'

'But he is a Roman!'

'What about this new Emperor Maximus, who sent him to us?'

'Grallon explained he won't let Maximus in,' Fennalis ventured.

'So he says. Belike he means it. But can he, can Ys hold off the Romans without the help of our Gods? And in spite of the outcome of that fight, I do not believe he is friends with Them. Why, he intends building a temple to his Bullslayer. What will Taranis feel when His priest and avatar bows down to Mithras?'

'That may – I know not – '

Vindilis pressed on, like a hunter towards wounded quarry: 'Also, what may happen, what will he do, when next the Sign descends? Have you never lain awake wondering, you whom he refused because Lanarvilis is your daughter? Quinipilis has few years left her – mayhap only hours. Which of the vestals will the Gods then choose?'

'It could be any.'

'Are you so hopeful?' Vindilis compressed her lips. 'Myself, I doubt They will make the matter easy for him. I think They will give him a daughter of one of us. And not your Amair. Not when They have Lanarvilis's Miraine and Boia. Or . . . soon Innilis's sad, weak-witted Audris will be of marriageable age; and not long after that, Bodilis's Semuramat or my Runa. The Gods have Their sport with us, don't They, Fennalis? You're old too, after all. Or any of us could die unexpectedly. What *then*?

'I say to you, whatever peace is between Grallon and the Gods is as uneasy as peace between Rome and Ys; and it will erelong be put to the test. We Gallicenae must make ready for that, as best we are able. Therefore I am bearing the King a child. A lure, a hostage, a talisman? I know not. Help me, my Sister.'

The energy seemed to go from Vindilis. She lowered herself to a chair opposite the couch, lifted a wine cup, drank, and stared into emptiness.

'I see,' Fennalis breathed. 'Yours is a noble soul.'

'Nay,' Vindilis mumbled. 'Only one that would fain stay free.'

'Belike that's the same thing . . . Well, you're right. We must seek to steer the King away from what he might otherwise do. I mean all the Nine, once you and I have found the ways to explain this to them. And, yea, motherhood does confer power, if used wisely.'

Vindilis nodded. 'As small a touch as proposing a name.'

'What?' Fennalis asked. She considered, and nodded in her turn. 'Aye. Though 'twas he who wanted the three Roman tags we have.'

'Our Sisters were clever enough not to speak against it.'

What they thought of were not Maldunilis's Zisa, Guilvilis's Sasai, or Forsquilis's Nemeta. The custom was that the first-born of a Queen should carry her mother's vestal name onward. But Guilvilis now had Antonia, called after a sister of Gratillonius afar in Britannia; and Lanarvilis had borne Julia, honouring his mother; and Bodilis had Una, though whom that commemorated had not been declared.

'I expect he'll like my suggestion,' Vindilis said.

'What is it?'

'Augustina. From the legion that was his.'

2

In the two years following his disaster at Ys, Niall maqq Echach waged war over and over in his own land of Mide. Tuaths that thought him weakened, or in disfavour with the Gods, would refuse him his due, and take arms when he fared to demand it. The first several such battles were desperate, for he had indeed suffered heavy loss, the finest of his warriors. Yet he blazed his way through, won victory, made stern terms of peace, brought heads and hostages back to Temir. As word got around, rebelliousness slacked off, while a new crop of young men began dreaming of glory and booty to be gained in the host of this lord.

It was Éndae Qennsalach, King over the Lagini, who had egged on much of this revolt. Bad blood was ancient between his folk and Niall's. Some three hundred years before, Tóthual the Desired had founded Mide, carving the largest part of it out of Laginach territory. Nevertheless, the King of the latter wedded a daughter of Tóthual – but, wearying of her, confined her in a secret place, gave out that she was dead, and got her sister's hand. When the second wife chanced to discover the first, both died of the shame this incest had put on them. Tóthual thereupon raged through Qóiqet Lagini, slaying, plundering, burning, till he got abject surrender. His price was the paying, every second year, of that tribute which came to be called the Bóruma.

So vast was the sum of cows, pigs, cloaks, bronzeware, and silver that it would have beggared the Lagini. Hence the time was not long until they refused. Since then, those Condachtach and Mide Kings who had the claim seldom got it satisfied, and only by collecting it at sword's point after a bitter war. Thus did hatred build up over many lifetimes.

Éndae, always a maker of trouble for Temir, took what he thought was a chance to bring ruin on his enemy. In the third summer, Niall came looking for revenge.

The armies met south of the River Ruirthech. That was a day when clouds blew like smoke, low above the valley, underneath a sky the hue of lead. Rainshowers rushed out of them, drenched men, washed their wounds and their dead, passed away on the keening wind. All colours were dulled except those of blood and gold. Shouts, horn calls, hoofbeats, footfalls, clamorous wheels, clash and rattle of weapons, were somehow muffled. But blows fell as heavy and sharp as always.

Niall's chariot boomed ahead. Grass was thick but slippery beneath its iron-shod fellies; it took all the skill Cathual the driver owned to keep onwards full tilt. Behind him the King stood cat-balanced against the rocking and jouncing. Niall roared, stabbed with his spear, smote with his blade, lifted their reddened points on high for a sign to his followers. He himself was a banner, a guiding comet. Above the height of him, hair and beard fell primrose-yellow from the helmet, seven-coloured cloak fluttered back from the wide shoulders, gold and amber shone upon the saffron tunic. The handsomeness of his face was twisted into battle fury, wherein eyes glinted lightning-blue, teeth bone-white. Hounds ran alongside, to leap, bay, slash, tear, howl. He seemed as much beast as they, as much war-god as Lúg come to earth. Many a brave man saw what approached and fled, casting his arms from him, wailing the same blind panic into his comrades.

Withal, Niall remained a leader, a part of him watchful and aware. He kept track of the other chariots in his van, right and left. Nearest was that of Domnuald, son by the second of his Queens. This was the lad's first combat, he no more than fifteen summers of age. Hard practice rewarded itself; Domnuald poised easily and struck keenly. Hair like his father's hung wet down cheeks still girlish. O Brigit, Mother of Love, how he recalled Breccan, who died in Niall's arms outside the wall of Ys!

Older sons drove in the wings, themselves already blooded men, restless as stallions, toplofty as eagles.

Several nobles had chariots too. More chose to come behind afoot, leading their tenants, with swords, spears, axes, bills, slings, while bows twanged and arrows hissed. The din cut through wind and rain, on up to the hasty clouds. There cruised scaldcrows and ravens, birds of the Mórrigu, gathering at Her feast.

Before Niall, and soon around him, the Lagini fought back. They were equipped and marshalled like his men, and maybe numbered the same. Most of them battled wolfishly well. But they could not make headway. They could not even hold fast. Day had not much dwindled when they were all fled, or captive, or sprawled and emptily staring corpses.

3

Éndae sent a herald to ask for truce. Niall received him as was fitting for one whose person was sacred, and sent him back with word of agreement.

The meeting place they set was near the battleground, a house of the king of the tuath that lived thereabouts. While they waited, Niall and his chieftains took it over and made merry. Dark as the afternoon was, they burned lamps and links without stint. Breaths smoked white athwart shadows crouching, dancing, changing shape, filling every corner and the smoky spaces under the roof. Highlights gleamed, an eye, a smile, a lifted beaker. This was no mead hall, with benches along the walls and a flock of servants. The highest ranking men sat on stools, the rest on the clay floor, and drink passed from hand to hand. Nonetheless, merriment rang.

'Have you a song for us, Laidchenn, dear?' Niall called.

'I have that,' answered the poet. As was the custom, he

had accompanied the army to watch what happened and afterwards put it in words. That was as honourable as to fight, or more so; for what was the use of mighty deeds, did they not live in memory and the fame of them travel afar? 'But I ask leave to wait a while.'

'How is this?' wondered Niall. The buzz of talk died away until rain sounded loud on the thatch overhead.

Laidchenn gestured. He was a burly man with fiery, bushy hair and beard, carelessly dressed, but a man to command awe – chief singer to the King, former pupil of Torna Éces in Mumu. 'You know that I, like you, have brought a young son of mine along for the experiencing of his first war, though Domnuald is to become a valiant fighter whereas Tigernach is studying art under myself. Would you be so kind as to hear the lad's piece? A maiden effort, but burning within him it is, and I think not unworthy of you.'

'He is very welcome,' said Niall graciously.

Tigernach stood up. He was about the same age as Domnuald, and growing towards his father's body form. Brown-haired, his countenance was plain, somewhat marred by skin eruptions beneath a fuzz of whiskers. He did not shake a chiming rod, for he was, after all, a novice in the craft. Yet melody rippled clear and true from his harp, and boldness – brashness, almost – rose in his tones.

'Lord who harried Lagini,
Star-brilliant in the battle – '

His verse lacked subtlety, the tropes were sparse, and older men winced a bit at its fulsomeness. However, it was properly composed and showed high promise, as spirited as it was. Niall thanked him and gave him a silver brooch. Tigernach blushed so it could be seen in the dimness, mumbled his own thanks, and sat down. Laidchenn glowed with pride.

Of course, there was no comparison to the father's

words. They soared, they cried, they sent ghosts shivering up and down backbones. Tears rolled over leathery visages, fists clenched, eyes stared outward beyond the world, as Laidchenn wove his magic.

Meanwhile King Éndae drove up with a dozen well-born attendants. Guards made them wait until the chant was finished and the reward given. A youth at Éndae's side protested. 'Hush,' said the King. 'This is meet and right. Never show disrespect to a druid or an ollam poet. That is a gess upon all men.'

He stared glumly into the gloomy day. Rain and mist made vague the encampment of the invaders, though he heard their boisterousness loudly enough. Closer by, servants of the dispossessed laboured at the cookhouse to prepare a magnificent meal, or at the pens to feed cattle that would doubtless be herded away.

At last the guards let the newcomers in. When Éndae's champion announced him, and the Laginach King himself entered, Niall did not rise, nor even lift a knee. However, he did in seemly words offer a few seats he had reserved, and call for full cups that the guests be refreshed. Attendants bore off their overgarments and brought dry cloaks for them to wrap themselves in against the chill.

'Well,' said Niall presently, 'shall there be peace between us or shall there not?'

'That we must see,' answered Éndae. He was a lean man, grey of hair and beard.

'Let us begin by knowing each the other,' Niall said, and beckoned Laidchenn to name the Mide men on hand, with their honours.

'No such show have I this mournful day,' Éndae said, 'but myself I will tell you who accompanies me.' He gestured. 'Here are my sons – '

He came to one about the same age as Domnuald and Tigernach, also clearly a war-virgin until now: slim, comely, intensely black of hair, white of skin, blue of eye. 'Eochaid, youngest who has followed me; but younger still are brothers he has at home, and they growing.'

'Why, that is the name my father bore,' Niall said with a smile. 'Well met, Eochaid, I hope.'

He got back a glower. Cruel it was that defeat make rank a lad's first taste of battle.

Éndae hastened on with the introductions. 'Now, then,' he concluded, 'the Gods this day have seen fit to grant you victory, Niall maqq Echach; but you will be acknowledging that it was dearly bought, and the valour of the Lagini abides. What offer do you make us, that we swear peace with you?'

Niall tossed back his bright locks. 'No offer, Éndae Qennsalach. Why should I pay for that which I have won? Henceforward you shall keep your spoon out of my stewpot; and, obedient at last to oaths given long ago, you shall deliver the Bóruma.'

Breath hissed between teeth, but men sat still, not altogether surprised – save young Eochaid, who leapt to his feet and howled, 'What, would you gnaw us bare, you maggots? Never!' His voice cracked across, which enraged him the more. 'We'll pull you from our flesh and stamp you flat!'

'Quiet,' Éndae commanded. He reached to pluck at his son's sleeve. 'You disobey.'

Eochaid was unaware. 'Maggots, blowflies, beetles you are!' he raved. 'Wait, only wait, and we'll seek your nests and smoke you out!'

Laidchenn surged erect. The bulk of him loomed huge in the flickering gloom, a touch of flame in his beard. He rang his poet's chimes. Men shrank into silence. 'Have a care, boy,' he warned. 'Overwrought or no, you slander honourable foes, like some mad crone in a ditch. Behave yourself.'

Eochaid wept. His arms flailed. 'Crone, am I? Go back to your sheepfold, old ewe, and let the rams tup you again!'

Horror ran around the room. Before anyone else could rally the wit to speak, Laidchenn's son Tigernach was up also. In him, fury was a winter storm.

'You fling filth like that at my father, at a poet?' he hissed. 'Go down in the dung yourself.' He made a twin spike of the first two fingers on his left hand and thrust it towards Eochaid. As if something inside him had foreseen, brooded, prepared, the verses snarled from him:

> 'Listen, you light-witted youth!
> For that you thus dared speaking
> Words unwise and without truth,
> We shall soon hear you shrieking.
>
> 'Bellowing your bluster out
> As if you'd gnawed a nettle,
> You'd be shrewder not to shout
> But kick an empty kettle.
>
> 'Shame there shall be on your face.
> It is of your own earning.
> Curs will cringe when in disgrace.
> May likewise you be learning!'

Eochaid screamed, stumbled backwards, fell to his knees, clutched at his head. On cheeks and brow three great blisters were springing forth, blood-red, sleet-white, mould-black. He groaned in his pain.

4

Towards sundown the rains blew over and the wind lay down to rest. Laidchenn and his son walked from the house, away from others who likewise came forth, off towards the river.

Clouds still towered in deepening blue. Light, pouring level through the valley, reached to a rainbow. Grass drank those rays and gave them back in glitter and green glow. They made treetops smoulder, water glimmer. The air was cold and quiet, save as shoes scuffed and slithered over wetness or voices came faint across distance. Most of those cries were sounded by carrion birds, scared into darkling clouds by men who searched the battlefield for kin and comrade.

'You should not have done it,' said Laidchenn softly. 'I did not reproach you then, for that would further have undermined King Niall; but now I tell you, a satire is a weapon more fearsome than knife or poison.'

Stubbornness made Tigernach thrust out his lower lip, though it quivered. 'How did it harm our King, if one who behaved thus in his presence suffered punishment?'

Laidchenn sighed. 'It was too harsh for a grieving, bewildered boy. His insults diminished none but himself. Surely his father was about to send him outdoors with a heavy penance to do. Now – The blisters will heal. They may or may not leave disfiguring scars. But the wound in the soul will fester for aye. Niall saw this – I could tell – and softened his demands. Else the damaged, unappeased honour of the Lagini would have forced them into war to the death. After Ys he can, as yet, ill afford that. You have cost him dearly, my son.'

Tigernach's will broke. He shuddered, covered his eyes, wavered on his feet. 'If the King wants my head for that,' he choked, 'here it is.'

'Not so.' Laidchenn squeezed the shoulder beside him, and kept his hand on it as the two walked along. 'We understand each other, himself and I. His feelings were clear to me from his glances my way and the words he used. Folk should certainly avenge injuries done their darlings. He is not angry because of your anger on my behalf. He is only . . . rueful. After all, he did win the day; he did exact good terms; the Bóruma was really too much to hope for, unless in some later year.'

Still Tigernach sorrowed. 'Indeed, my heart,' Laidchenn went on after a moment, 'none was more surprised than me at what happened. Who would have thought that you, as far as you are from being an ollam poet, that you could already cast a destructive satire? Did a God seize you, or do you have it in you to become at last as powerful as Torna? Whichever, clear is to see that you have been marked for a fate that will touch many lives.'

Tigernach drew an uneven breath and straightened.

Laidchenn gazed towards the river. Mysterious flittings and rustlings went through the reeds along the bank. 'Beware,' he said. 'Henceforward be always careful, and never use your art but on those occasions when you feel sure you must. This day you have made us an unforgiving enemy. Do not do it again without sore need. Your fate will be famous, but perhaps it will not be happy.'

VII

1

At high summer, the rain sometimes fell nearly warm through unmoving air. It was heavy upon the day when Queen Lanarvilis received Lir Captain and the Speaker for Taranis. Sight quickly lost itself in that iron-coloured cataract; it found no more sky, no more sea, only dim walls along streets where water rushed and gurgled. What filled the world was the noise of the downpour on roofs and paving, and below this, remote and eternal, waves a-crash against the rampart of Ys.

The men gave their hooded cloaks over to the servant who admitted them and proceeded directly to the room where the priestess waited. For them, its numerous candles did not truly fend off gloom, nor its red-blue-ivory-crystal sumptuousness offer comfort. She had attired herself in a loosely cut dress of white silk whose folds and drapes joined with a silver headband to make a timeless dignity. The visitors were in plain civil tunic, trousers, half-boots. Besides the weather being unsuited for robes, they had not wanted to draw notice on their way here.

'Welcome,' she said, touching her breast in the salutation between equals. The gaze of Soren Cartagi followed that hand. 'Be seated, pray. I've naught set out but wine and water, for your message asked I receive you on grave business. Gladly, though, will I call for better fare, and afterwards have you be my guests at supper.'

Taking the couch that faced her chair, Hannon Baltisi shook his craggy head. 'I thank you, my lady, but best we

132

not linger, the Speaker and me,' he said. 'Folk might wonder why, and this needs to be secret.'

Soren joined his companion. For a moment, play of light tricked the eye, and Soren's hair and beard seemed as grey as Hannon's. As he settled down, they regained their darkness around his broad, beak-nosed visage. It was just the scattered white in them, more of it all the time. He and Lanarvilis regarded each other, forgetting that a third party was present, until she said slowly: 'This concerns the King, does it not?'

'Who else?' Soren growled.

Her voice wavered a little. 'What's wrong? I read trouble, anger on you, but – but he's done naught that he shouldn't.' Flushing, compelling herself to look steadily into the faces, both the faces: 'It happens he spent last night with me. After three years wedded to him, I'd have known if aught was awry. Did it touch the city, he'd have told me.'

'What had he to say, then?' Soren asked impulsively.

The colour mounted in her cheeks. 'No affair of anyone else!' She regained self-possession; she had had much practice at that. 'Oh, mainly small talk. We played a while with Julia, and he babbled about the latest wonderful thing Dahut has accomplished, and we went on to discuss his journey in autumn. Naught new. His plans remain the same that he set forth at the Solstice Council.'

Hannon nodded. Tension gathered in his lank frame. At that meeting he had led the opposition to the King's proposal to make yet another circuit about western Armorica and down to Portus Namnetum, weaving tighter his web of alliances. Gratillonius had been far too much away, neglecting his sacral duties to the point of contumely before the Gods. In the end, a compromise had been reached. Gratillonius would go, but not until after

133

the equinox, and he pledged himself to have returned by winter solstice.

Before Hannon could speak, Soren did: 'I beg my lady's pardon. No intrusion – no discourtesy intended. The more so when we are here to seek your counsel and help.'

Lanarvilis leaned back in her chair and let her hands lie quietly crossed on her lap. 'Say on.'

''Tis this, this temple of his foreign God Mithras he means to build.' Soren choked and coughed.

'Why, I thought that was agreed on. Reluctantly by a number of Suffetes, aye. But when we, the Gallicenae, having searched our hearts, our books, and our dreams, could find naught forbidding it, as long as he stays dutiful towards the Gods of Ys – '

'How long will that be? At the combat in the Wood – ' Soren curbed himself. 'No matter that. 'Tis Lir Captain who bears the word today. I simply came along to give my support, my own plea for yours. You and I have worked together often over the years, Lanarvilis.' He hunched where he sat.

The older man's voice rolled forth as if once again he trod the deck of a ship. His look commanded, too.

'Forgive me if I'm curt, my lady. You know 'tis my way.

'Ill did Grallon's wish strike me. Bad enough having a Christian priest mewling amongst us again. The King can't help that, I give you, and no true man or woman 'ull pay any heed. But this Mithras, now – well, in my seafaring days I learned somewhat about Mithras. Mind you, he's no bad God like yon Christ. He stands for uprightness, manliness, and He'll let other Gods abide. But He *is* the Bullslayer, the Comrade of the Sun. He sets Himself above the rest and lays a law of His own on His worshippers. Remember how Grallon must needs refuse the crown after he won Kingship. Not a great thing in itself, maybe, but a sign of . . . what else?

'In storm, in fog, in dead calm and sea-blink through endless silences: I have known the Dread of Lir, my lady. Ys lives on His sufferance. No disrespect to Belisama or Taranis, nay, nay. We live by Them too. But the Pact of Brennilis made Ys forever hostage to Lir, did it nay?'

Quietness deepened until the rainfall sounded torrential. Lanarvilis nodded and signed herself. Soren knotted his fists.

'And Lir wears no human face,' Hannon said.

After a heartbeat, he went on: 'Well, Grallon aims to take a warehouse down by the harbour, unused since trade went to hell ere we were born, he'll take that and make it into a temple of Mithras. You remember this was after the Council wouldn't let him buy land and dig a cave out in the hinterland.'

They could barely hear Lanarvilis: 'The earth is Belisama's. And Mithras will have no women devotees.'

'Taranis makes fruitful the earth,' rumbled from Soren.

'Therefore Grallon needs a house in town,' Hannon said. 'Now that arrangement seemed to me just as wrong. What gave it Lir for His honour, Lir Who's so quick to wrath?' He paused, filled his lungs, stared past the Queen. 'Well,' he said, 'people don't pray to Lir, you know. We sacrifice, we obey, but He'll have none of our cries, none of our tears. His sea is already salt enough.

'And yet – well, sometimes He does make His will known, 'stead of whelming those who go against it. He did for Brennilis, long ago. If now we're at the end of the Age she birthed, might He again? I went forth by myself, in a boat, beyond sight of land. I fasted, I thirsted, I held myself sleepless, till – '

He surged to his feet. 'Nay, no vision, no voice, only a remembrance. But when I uttered it aloud, soon there

135

came a breeze blowing me back home, and seals and dolphins gambolled all about under the moon.'

He placed the big, scarred sailor's hands on his hips, stood astraddle next to the second servant of Taranis, looking down at the high priestess of Belisama, and said: 'This is my simple thought. That Lir be honoured, let the temple of Mithras also be hostage to Him. When the Romans built our wall, the waters didn't come so high as they do today. In the seaward towers are rooms which're below the waves, abandoned on that account. I've been to see, and one at the bottom of the Raven Tower would do fine. 'Twas never meant for more than a storage cellar; no windows. Dripping wet, but that can be fixed. 'Tis lower than anything he could dig ashore, so 'tis a cave, better than trickery with a warehouse. And – I met Mithras folk when I was young, abroad – the raven is a holy bird to them. What happier sign could Grallon ask for? Or we?'

Again silence, but for the rain. Air slithered, candle flames guttered.

'I see,' Lanarvilis finally murmured. Her head was bowed; Soren could no longer read her face.

'You understand, don't you?' the Speaker asked eagerly. 'If Gratillonius will accept this, every faction should be satisfied. We'll have interior peace, and peace with the Gods.'

She lifted her glance to confront his. 'You want my help,' she said, flat-voiced, 'because you know he is no fool. He'll know that this means placing Mithras under Lir.'

'Nay, not really. A gesture of respect, and should there not be respect between Gods? Lir gives Mithras this fine site. Mithras, in turn, acknowledges that Lir, that the Three are the patrons of Ys.'

Soren leaned forward. Impetuously, he reached across

the table between couch and chair. Blindly, Lanarvilis did likewise. Their hands met and clung. Hannon sat back down, folded his arms, rested like a reef outside Sena.

'You want me to . . . persuade the King,' Lanarvilis said.

'First, we suppose, persuade your Sisters,' replied Soren. 'Make the Gallicenae work together on Gratillonius till he agrees.'

'I expect we can,' Lanarvilis said.

'You can do so much with him, you Nine,' rushed from Soren. 'The power that lies in women!'

She withdrew her hands, sat straight, and told him, 'Most of that power comes from patience, Soren, from endurance.'

He snatched a cup and half emptied it in a gulp, though the wine had not been watered.

2

Some thirty miles east of Ys lay the head of navigation on the River Odita. Thence the stream flowed south for about ten miles to the sea. These were birdflight distances; it was longer for a man, whether he went by land or water through the winding valleys of Armorica. There a Roman veteran had taken the lead in founding a colony, three hundred years ago. It was actually a little below the farthest north a ship could reach when tide was high; that point was just above the confluence of the Odita with the lesser Stegir. He chose the site because of its handiness to a Gallic settlement and hill fort on the heights behind. Those had long since been abandoned, levelled by man and nature until only traces remained. Houses and small farms replaced them, though for the most part Mons

Ferruginus was unpeopled, a woodland through which a few trails wound.

The Roman named the colony Aquilo, from the Aquilonian district of Apuleia in Italy whence he hailed. Sufficiently inland not to fear surprise attack by pirates, it became a minor seaport. Here entered wares of metal and glass, olives, oil, textiles. Out went mainly products of the heavily forested hinterland, hides, furs, nuts, pigskin, preserved meat, tallow, honey, beeswax, timber – but also salt, beneficiated iron ore, preserved fish, garum sauce, and the marvellous things they wrought in gold, silver, ivory, shell, and fabric in Ys.

The fortunes of Aquilo waxed and waned with those of the Empire. However, its leadership stayed in the hands of the founder's descendants. These Apuleii intermarried with their Osismiic neighbours and folk of other cantons until by blood they were almost purely Armorican. In their lives they stayed Roman, even claiming that their ancestor had been kin to the famous writer. They sent their elder sons to be educated at such centres of learning as Durocotorum, Treverorum, and Lugdunum. Eventually they won elevation to senatorial rank. As such, they were no longer supposed to engage in trade; but they had ample relatives to serve as their agents while they devoted themselves to civic and – increasingly of recent decades – military affairs.

Gratillonius had passed through three years before, on his mission of keeping the western end of the peninsula quiescent while Maximus warred. Now, when he returned, Apuleius Vero made him heartily welcome. They had struck it off at once, in spite of the host being a devoted Christian.

After all, the centurion served Rome too; he had fascinating things to tell of the city in his charge; he was making possible a revival of commerce. For his part,

Apuleius was well-travelled, well-read, experienced in the ways of the world. After his student days in the South he had dreamed of a public career, and begun by becoming a confidential amanuensis to the govenor of Aquitania. But the death of his father laid on him the duty of coming back and taking over a post in which Gratillonius considered him wasted. Likely Apuleius would have agreed, save that Roman virtue and Christian piety both forbade him to complain against fate.

'You wish to strengthen further the ties between Ys and the Gauls?' he asked when they were alone. 'Why? Not that the resumption of dealings hasn't profited everybody. It has, and nowhere more than in my poor Aquilo. However, the Empire is again tranquil, and the barbarians have drawn in their horns since that disaster the Scoti suffered. Can trade not grow of itself?'

He was a slender man in his mid-thirties, of medium height, dark-haired, straight-nosed, clean-shaven, with large hazel eyes whose nearsightedness caused him to wear an appearance of intense concentration. Somehow he seemed to Gratillonius more Hellenic than Roman, perhaps because in his quiet fashion he took pride in a bloodline going back to Magna Graecia. As the man sat, his wife Rovinda came softly in and replenished the wine and nuts they had been enjoying. She was young, comely, the daughter of an Osismiic headman. Since their marriage two years ago, Apuleius had been teaching her the manners of a senatorial matron; but she had never lacked inborn gentility. They had a single child thus far, a girl, and another swelled within her.

Gratillonius weighed his reply. He had rehearsed it in his mind, for he would need it repeatedly, but this was the first time.

'I'm afraid that tranquillity is only on the surface, and

can't last much longer,' he said. 'You've heard of the Priscillianist business last year?'

Apuleius grimaced. 'Ugly, from what little I know. Unworthy of the Faith. But it's behind us now, praise God. Isn't it?'

'I'm not sure.' Gratillonius frowned into a lampflame. The floor of the house was warm from a hypocaust, but the air kept a chill, and outside the shuttered windows an autumn wind wuthered. 'The Church stays divided, and it and the Empire are woven together. Maximus accuses Valentinianus of heresy. It may be just a pretext. But what a dangerous pretext! No, I don't think we've seen the end of civil war.'

'God help us,' Apuleius said sorrowfully. 'But what can we do, you and I? We're nothing but minor officers of the state. How can you bypass the Duke of the Armorican Tract?'

Gratillonius smiled. 'You think I might take too much on myself? Well, I am the prefect of Rome, not of Maximus Augustus but of Rome, in Ys, which is not a province but a sovereign ally and has made me its King. I read that as meaning I've got discretion to act in the public interest as I see it, and answer for my actions afterwards . . . to the proper authority.'

'That would be the Duke, wouldn't it? How will he feel about you making his policies for him?'

'I may be cocky, Apuleius, but I'm not crazy. I wrote and got his leave to, m-m, "do what seems best to develop further those good relations between Ys and the Roman communities on which a start has lately been made." The Duke's no dunderhead either. He recognizes the facts, no matter how he has to gloss them over. First, he's necessarily most concerned with the eastern and inland parts of the peninsula. I can do in the west what he cannot, and he knows it. Second, he never was happy about Maxi-

140

mus's rebellion. He hinted pretty strongly, in writing to me, that my aims please him.'

'I see . . . But what are they?'

'This: that western Armorica, and as much else of it as I can reach, not get embroiled in any new fighting. That we refuse demands on us to come help kill our fellow Romans, in anybody's cause.'

'Which means the cause of Maximus, you know.'

Gratillonius nodded. 'I think, if we do stand together in this resolution, I think he'll know better than to order us to break it. Later, if he prevails – well, at least we Armoricans will be strong enough to have some say in what happens to us. And he might not prevail.'

'Valentinianus is weak,' Apuleius mused, 'but if Theodosius should take a hand – '

A tingle went through Gratillonius. 'It could be. Who knows? In which case Armorica might expect quite favourable treatment. A daydream, maybe. I don't tell myself any nursery tales about us making the difference in what happens. I just think our chances will be better, and Rome will be better served, if Armorica looks after its own, unitedly.'

'Under Ysan leadership.'

Gratillonius shrugged. 'Who else is taking the initiative? Besides, Ys is the natural leader of this whole region.' He grew earnest. 'Believe me, though – I give you my word of honour – I've no ambitions for myself.'

Inwardly, fugitively, he wondered. The world groaned in its need for a man who could set things right. Why could nobody else see what must be done? It was so simple. Government firm, just, obedient to its own laws; military reforms and the taming of the barbarians; honest currency; reduction of taxes, of every burden that was destroying the productive classes; liberation of the individual man from bondage to the estate to which he was born; religious toleration – nothing else, really, than what he had hoped Maximus would enact.

But Gratillonius had no legions to hail him Emperor. He would do well if he could save Ys for Mithras and Dahut. If he was very fortunate, he might save Armorica. Give him that and he would lie down contentedly on his deathbed, knowing he had been a good son of Rome.

Apuleius considered him a while before saying, 'I think I'll believe you. To be frank, I also think you talk too vauntingly. What do you and I really know – ' a hint of bitterness – 'in these backwaters where we sit?'

'I've been out,' Gratillonius replied. 'Last year, for months, over much of Gallia. I spoke with men as various as Maximus himself in Treverorum and Ausonius – well, an old, learned man in Burdigala.'

Apuleius sat straight. 'What?' he exclaimed. 'Ausonius? Why, I studied under him. How is he?'

Gratillonius gladly let conversation go in that direction. Apuleius's admiration for Ausonius was not unalloyed. Arriving in Burdigala while Julianus the Apostate still reigned, himself at the vulnerable, combative age of twelve, he had – as he wryly admitted – changed from an indifferent to a prayerful Christian largely in reaction against the coolness or outright paganism he encountered everywhere around him. Ausonius, he felt, was a man of antiquity, born out of his time, who accepted Christ with the same impersonal politeness he would earlier have accorded Jupiter. And yet, and yet, Ausonius had such riches to give . . .

The evening ended a trifle drunkenly and altogether cheerily.

Morning was lucent. Gratillonius made it an excuse for staying another day. He would take advantage of the weather to do what he had not had time to do on his previous visit, ride around the countryside and get a little familiarity with it – for purposes of military planning if that need should arise, he told Apuleius.

His host smiled, and declined to accompany him. Apuleius was no outdoorsman. He kept fit with methodical exercises, as a duty, but gave his leisure to his books, correspondence, religious observances, family, and whatever intelligent conversation came his way. He offered to assign Gratillonius a guide, but the latter refused in his turn and rode off alone.

The fact was that he wanted solitude, as a man does now and then. It was hard to find when he must always be either the King of Ys, the prefect of Rome, or a centurion of the Second. Therefore he likewise left behind the legionaries who were escorting him, to take their ease with the Aquilo garrison. This consisted of some infantry recruited mostly among the local Osismii and a few horsemen. Younger men of the civil population formed a reserve that would augment it in times of emergency. The Duke had never felt that more strength was needed here. True, pirates often ravaged the estuary – a few years ago they wrecked the lovely villa of the Pulcher family – and occasionally rowed upstream; but to date they had always been driven off short of the city. Ruinous though Vorgium was, the main force in these parts continued to be stationed there.

Gratillonius was soon out of Aquilo. On the left bank

of the Odita, it amounted to a few hundred homes – cob, timber, brick, the elegant but small town house of the Apuleii – together with such establishments as a church, a smithy, a marketplace, and a couple of warehouses down by the harbour. Smoke seeped from thatch roofs or curled out of holes in tile coverings; wives went about their tasks with pauses to gossip; wheels creaked; an anvil rang. This late in the year, no merchant vessels lay docked, and Gratillonius did not go out that gate and over the bridge to the west. Instead, he took the eastern portal. The walls around the city were of the old Gallic sort, earth over interlocked logs reinforced with rubble, wooden blockhouses at the corners.

On his right, as he followed a dirt road upstream, was a narrow strip of lowland, behind which rose that long, high hill called Mons Ferruginus. Dwellings dotted it, well-nigh lost to view among the reds, bronzes, golds of autumnal woods. Most migratory birds had departed but heaven was bewinged by crows, sparrows, robins, a falcon afar.

After a short distance, he saw the lesser Stegir flow from the north and join the Odita on the opposite side. Past that was a bridge to cross, whose planks boomed underhoof. On the farther shore the land rolled gently. He left behind him the Odita, which here ran from the east before it bent south, and took a rutted road parallel-ing the Stegir. It led him through cultivated land, the estate of the Apuleii. He saw the cottages of three tenant families. Beyond them he passed the manor house. Its owner used it mostly as a retreat. Sere weeds and bram-bles filled much former ploughland, with saplings as outrunners of the mildwood in the offing. Lack of mar-kets, lack of labour – how much of this had he come upon!

His spirits revived after the road, becoming scarcely

more than a path, took him into the forest. That began about where the channel of the Stegir shifted west. It walled in the farmland on two sides. Mainly it was oak, though beech, maple, ash, and other trees made it at this season a storm of colour. There was scant underbrush; deer kept that down, as well as the swine that boys herded. The ground was a softness of soil and old leaves, with fallen boles on which moss grew smaragdine. Squirrels frisked about, small red meteors. Vision faded off into sun-spattered shadows. The air was cool, moist, smelling like mushrooms.

He rode on for a timeless time, letting his thoughts drift. And then, abruptly, a stag stepped into view ahead of him, a glorious beast with a mighty rack of antlers. He reined in. It stopped and stared down the path at him. He had brought a bow along in case of such luck. His hand stole down to unsling it, take an arrow, nock, aim. The stag bounded off. The shaft missed. 'Harroo!' Gratillonius shouted, and urged his mount into gallop.

A while the chase thundered over the ruts. Gratillonius's big gelding narrowed the gap. The stag veered and went off among the trees. Gratillonius followed.

Of course it was in vain. He dared not keep on at full unheeding speed where a root or a burrow might cause his horse to snap a leg. The quarry soared now right, now left, until presently the splendid sight glimmered away. Gratillonius halted and swore. His mount whickered, breathed hard, stood sweating.

The man's oath was good-natured. He hadn't really expected to take the prey. The challenge had merely been irresistible, and he'd got a grand run. Best he return to his route. He wanted to reach cleared country on the far side of the woods and survey it before he must start back.

He had ridden for a spell when it came to him that he should already have been on the road. How could he have

145

missed it? Every direction looked the same, and a haze had drawn over the sky to obscure the sun. What he sought was no spear-straight Roman highway but a track that twisted to and fro like the ancient game trail that doubtless underlay it. He could cast about for hours, randomly seeking a random goal.

He swore with more feeling. The anger was at himself. He had imagined that in the past few years he had learned to control a quick temper, an impulsiveness, that used to get him into unnecessary embroilments. Well, apparently that thing was not dead in him; it had been lying low, biding its chance to spring forth.

'Gone astray, lured off by a deer, like a chieftain in a folk tale,' he muttered. 'I'll never hear the end of this.'

To be sure, if he could get back before dark, he needn't confess . . . When he studied the sky carefully, bearing in mind the time of day and year, he established which way was south. The Stegir was certain to be somewhere yonder. Having reached it, he could follow it till it met the Odita.

The quest proved long. The forest floor was only partly clear. Often he must work through or around brush, logs, or pools. When at last he found the stream, the going along it was no better.

The sun went out of sight. Murk and chill welled from the earth. He realized that night would overtake him. To struggle on would be foolhardy. Best he halt soon and make himself as little uncomfortable as possible while he waited for dawn. He had taken with him just a piece of bread and cheese, long since eaten. His belly growled.

The Stegir gurgled around a thicket. Having passed this, he suddenly came upon a hut. A trail, narrow but clear, went thence, doubtless towards the road. Gladness jumped within him. He would still have to spend the night, but here was shelter, and a quick journey come

146

morning. He drew rein and dismounted. His horse's head drooped, as exhausted as the poor beast was.

The hut was tiny, a cylinder of wicker and clay, moss-chinked, under a conical thatch roof. A hide hung from a stick in place of a proper door. He had seen better housing among the Picti. However, the oak whose boughs arched above was magnificent. 'Hail,' he called. 'Is anybody home?' The gloomy depths around blotted up his voice.

The hide crackled aside and a man stepped out. He was tall, powerfully built in spite of gauntness. A crag of nose and headland of chin jutted from a long, hollow-cheeked face; the black eyes were set deep under shaggy brows; the stiff black hair and beard, roughly haggled, were shot with white. He wore a coarse linsey-woolsey robe, belted with a rope. The bare feet were calloused and begrimed. Clearly he had not bathed at any recent time, if ever, although an outdoor life made his odour pungent, a bit smoky, rather than sour.

'Peace be with you,' he said in Latin. His voice was rather harsh. 'Are you lost?' He smiled, showing large teeth. 'You seem to be a stranger to these parts, and at this hour I doubt you've come for counsel.'

'I am Gratillonius, a soldier, and I have certainly missed my way. Is Aquilo very far?'

'No, but too much for you to reach before nightfall, my son. May I offer you my humble hospitality? I am Corentinus, a hermit.' The man looked up between boughs to grey-purple heaven, sniffed the air, and nodded. 'We'll have rain in a while. At least my roof is tight.'

'Thank you.' Gratillonius hesitated. He didn't want to impose on poverty. 'Could I, in return, help or – or make a donation?'

'You may make an offering to the Church if you wish.

I myself have no needs that God and these two hands cannot fill.' Corentinus regarded him. 'You must be famished. It's not my habit to eat more than once a day, but I'll prepare you something and – ' the laugh rang – 'he would be a rude host who didn't share with his guest.'

Gratillonius led his horse to drink, unsaddled and rubbed it down, tethered it nearby to graze on some herbage that kept a few withered leaves. Meanwhile he cast mind back over what he knew about hermits. That was hearsay. A practice, said to have originated in Egypt, was spreading northward through Europe, devout Christians going off to be alone with their God, away from the temptations of the world and even the distractions of the Church. Believers, including otherwise pagan country-folk, often sought out such holy men, who must surely have wisdom and powers beyond the ordinary.

This Corentinus didn't seem quite to fit the picture. If nothing else, he looked too robust; and he must once have been fairly well educated.

Turning from his chores, Gratillonius saw him, robe hiked over knobbly knees, squatting in the burn. Its iciness made no visible difference to him. He murmured – a prayer? – and reached underwater. After a moment he rose. A large trout lay in his hands. Lay! Eeriness touched Gratillonius. The fish was alive; its sheen in the fading light showed it to be healthy; but it did not flop, and it had come straight into that grasp.

'God provides, you see,' said Corentinus calmly. He waded ashore and went into his hut. Half stunned, Gratillonius followed. The interior was dark, save for a small, banked fire on the dirt floor, which gave just enough light to work by if you knew where everything was. Corentinus took a knife that rested on a slab with a few other objects. 'Be you blessed, little brother,' he said, 'and be God thanked for His manifold mercies.'

With a deft motion he sliced the flesh from one side of the trout and tossed the piece down. Gratillonius sucked in a breath of astounded outrage. He had never condoned cruelty to animals, and this was wanton. Yet the fish only waved its tail. Before Gratillonius could speak, Corentinus had gone back out. Gratillonius came after, automatically. The hermit cast the half filleted creature into the stream and signed the air with the Cross. Gratillonius gasped again. The trout was swimming off as if unharmed – and was it in fact whole, healed?

He grew aware that Corentinus had laid a hand on his shoulder and was speaking in a low tone: 'Fear not, my son. What you beheld is no sorcery. It happens daily, unless I am fasting. Thus God keeps me fed. Why He should vouchsafe such grace to me, a wretched sinner, I know not, but He surely has His purpose. Now let's go settle ourselves and talk. You look like a man with good stories in him, and I must admit that in my weakness I can grow weary of seeing nobody except an occasional rustic.'

Gratillonius mustered will. He had witnessed things stranger than this, in and around Ys, and some of them had been malignant, whereas Corentinus seemed wholly benign. 'Remarkable,' he heard himself say.

'A miracle.' Corentinus waved. 'And yet is not all Creation a miracle? Look around you, my son, and think.' He led the way inside and urged his guest to take the stool that was his single item of furniture.

In quite everyday fashion he laid the piece of fish across a mesh of green twigs and hunkered down to roast it above the coals. 'It's better baked,' he said, 'but as hungry as you must be, I won't make you wait for that. You'll find hardtack in yonder box. Dried peas and things too, but again, I don't want you to endure the time it would take to cook them. No wine or ale available, I fear.' He grinned. 'Who dines with a hermit must take short commons.'

'You are . . . very kind.' The fire, poked up into sputtering flames, picked sights out of shadow. He saw a towel, a spare robe, a blanket hung from pegs in the sooty wall. No bed. Well, he had his horse blanket and cloak, with the saddle for a pillow. The implements he glimpsed were of the crudest, except for that excellent sharp knife. (Corentinus must not want his wondrous fish to feel pain at being carved.) A stone pot, an earthen jug, a grass basket, a couple of wooden bowls and spoons – No, wait. As far as possible from the hearth was a second slab. Upon it, wrapped in fine linen, rested what Gratillonius recognized as a book, doubtless a Christian Gospel.

Through the smoke-tang he began to smell cooking meat. His mouth watered. Corentinus looked across at him and grinned anew. Highlights traced the big bones of his face, ruddy amidst murk, and the whiteness of his teeth. 'Brace up, lad,' he said. 'We'll soon have some cargo down your hatch.' The Latin had turned accented and ungrammatical, commoner speech.

'How long have you lived here?' the centurion asked.

Corentinus shrugged. 'Time ceases to have meaning after a few seasons of seeking eternity.' Again he talked like a schooled man. 'Um-m . . . five years?'

'I hadn't heard of you, though I visited Aquilo three years ago.'

'Why should you? I'm nobody. You must be far more interesting, Gratillonius.'

'What, when you can do magic like this?'

Corentinus scowled. 'Please! I said it is no sorcery, no pagan trick. *I* don't do the thing. When I had first fled my sinfulness, an angel of the Lord appeared to me in a dream and told me of the divine favour I was given. I didn't know what it meant, I was bewildered and frightened. After all, the Devil had come in the same guise, no, in the guise of the very Christ, to my holy father Martinus, and tried to deceive him.' His tone softened. 'Oh, I had to rally my nerve, I can tell you. But what could I do except obey? And behold, my little brother swam quietly into my hands, just as you saw; and I understood that God's mercy is infinite.'

Gratillonius wrestled with his honour and lost. He cleared his throat. 'I'd better be frank with you,' he said. 'I'm no Christian myself.'

'Oh?' Corentinus seemed no more than mildly surprised. 'You, an officer who goes around on what must be important missions?'

'Well, I – All right, sir. I follow the Lord Mithras.'

Corentinus looked long at him. 'It's well for you that you didn't dissemble, my son. I don't matter, but God doesn't like false pretences.'

'No. My God doesn't . . . either.'

'You may wish to reconsider, after what you've seen this evening.'

Gratillonius shook his head. 'I don't deny your God has powers. But I will not deny mine.'

Corentinus nodded. 'I'd begun to suspect you were not of the Faith. Your behaviour, your stance, everything. I knocked around in the world before coming here.'

'If you don't want me under your roof, I'll go.'

'Oh, no, no!' Corentinus raised his free hand. 'God forbid! You're a guest. A most welcome one, I might add.' He smiled a bit wistfully. 'I've no hopes of converting you in a single night, and know better than to try. Let's just swap yarns. But . . . you spoke of making me some return for hospitality. If you really mean it, then what you shall do is think. Look around you at God's world and ask yourself how could it have come to be and what this life of ours is all about. Think.' He paused. 'No,

I'll not ask that you pray for guidance. You couldn't, if you're as true a worshipper of Mithras as you seem to be. I do ask that you open your mind. Listen. Think.'

After a brief silence: 'Well, I believe supper is ready; and you haven't yet got out the flatbread!'

He insisted Gratillonius take nearly the whole of the food. His share was only a token of friendliness. There was nothing but water to drink. Regardless, the two men soon fell into talk that lasted through the rain till the sunrise.

Corentinus took fire at what Gratillonius told about Ys. He had been there once, as a crewman on one of the few outside ships that called; he had toured its wonders and, he admitted without breast-beating, its resorts of sin. That Ys was coming back into the Roman sphere struck him as a happy portent.

Indeed, despite his isolation, he was astonishingly well-informed. Mention of Priscillianus grieved but did not surprise him; he had known. It turned out that he still got occasional letters from his mentor Martinus.

As for his past, he was the son of a Britannic immigrant to Osismia, born on the fundus of a well-to-do, thoroughly Romanized family. There he received a good basic schooling, though he was more interested in ranging the woodlands or galloping the horses. (He and Gratillonius found kindred memories to chuckle at.) But meanwhile his father's fortune was declining: between the general ill health of commerce, the depredations of the barbarians, and the grinding down of the curials. (Now the two could be grim together.) At the age of fifteen, Corentinus got out from under the ruin and went off on his own. Through what connections remained to him he obtained a berth on a ship, the law being winked at, and spent the next several years as a sailor, a rough man in a rough life.

Finally a storm blew his vessel so far out to sea that the

crew despaired of winning back. Most perished miserably in the attempt, in spite of forgetting whatever Christianity was theirs and making horrid sacrifices to other Gods. Corentinus saw visions in his delirium. When at last he reached the Liger mouth, once he had regained strength he made his way to Pictavum, where Martinus then was, Martinus of whom Corentinus had never before heard from any human mouth.

This man gave him instruction while he settled into the monastic community. Its books added to his learning. In time he grew restless, and was delighted to accompany Martinus when the latter went to Turonum; to take baptism at the hands of Martinus after Martinus became the bishop; to aid in the effort to evangelize the countryside – until he fell from grace with a heathen woman. Aghast at himself, he asked leave to seek forgiveness through penance, and returned to Osismia to become an anchorite. There it was revealed that, despite everything, God had not cast him off.

– Gratillonius re-entered Aquilo full of thought.

4

As closely as it followed winter solstice, the Birthday of Mithras at Ys gave a glimmer of daylight, barely more than six hours, in a cavern of night. Before sunrise, walls on either side made the pomoerium brim with darkness. Air was bitterly cold. Beyond the rampart growled the sea, and above it skirled the wind. Yet Gratillonius dared hope he saw a good omen in the stars flickering overhead.

Lanterns bobbed, brought faces half out of shadow, made grotesqueries flutter across stone. Buskins clicked, raiment rustled, men kept mute as he led his procession up the stairway. The Raven Tower bulked four-square out into the surf, its battlements like shields raised against heaven. Sentries, who had been told what to expect, saluted and stepped aside. Lantern-glimmer showed awe on one countenance, misgiving on another, stiffness on the third and fourth. The door stood open. Gratillonius and his followers entered the turret. A stairwell gaped before them. They mounted, came forth on top, looked across the parapet to the dawn.

It whitened above inland hills, turned their ridges hoar, crept down the valley, while stars went out. The towers of Ys caught in a flash of copper, gold, and glass. The roofs of Ys rose from murk like whales from the sea. Beyond them Point Vanis reared and brightened. Closer by, Cape Rach thrust ruggedly forth. Shifting illumination made it seem as if the old dead were stealing back to their sleep in the necropolis. The pharos smoked briefly – its keeper had snuffed the flame – then gleamed of itself. Ocean sheened, wrinkled, spouted off reefs, out to Sena and on across the curve of the world. Drifts of kelp darkened it here and there; seals tumbled about in the waves.

There were a few minutes to wait. Men stood contemplative or talked in low voices. Gratillonius and his father drew aside, until they looked down on the finger of sea that reached between headland and city wall, east towards Aurochs Gate. Thus confined, the water dashed noisily against stone and a strip of beach. Gloom still dwelt in that gap, but glints went like fire.

'The moment draws near,' said Marcus Valerius Gratillonius.

'At last,' answered Gaius his son.

Marcus smiled one-sidedly. 'I never believed those historians who put ringing periods in the mouths of

154

leaders when a great event is about to happen. Real people mumble words worn smooth of meaning.'

'Well, we can keep silence.' Gaius's gaze strayed west towards the seals and Sena. Did the shade of Dahilis really linger somewhere yonder? Did she watch him now?

Marcus summoned resolution. 'Except for this. It's not too late to turn back. Not quite.'

Gaius sighed. 'It always was. I'm sorry, father.'

Since a delegation of Ysan marines, and the legionary Cynan for spokesman, sought him out at the villa in Britannia this past summer and brought him here in the royal yacht, Marcus had questioned the wisdom of establishing a Mithraeum – so lavish, too – in this of all cities. True, the King had overcome opposition, but he had not quelled it in many hearts, and those were only the hearts of men.

Nonetheless Marcus had accepted the instruction and ultimately the consecration that raised him to Runner of the Sun. How strange it felt to Gaius, to be the guiding Father over this man who had brought him into being.

'I understand,' Marcus said, almost meekly. He had aged much in the past few years. 'Forget my croakings. We'll build Him His fortress.'

On the frontier of the night – Day was advancing.

'Good for you, sir!' Gaius blurted.

Marcus plucked at the sleeve of the hierophantic robe. 'Afterwards we'll have time for ourselves, won't we?' he whispered.

Gaius squeezed the bowed shoulder. 'Of course. I promise.'

Between royal and Roman duties, the King had had small opportunity thus far to be with his palace guest, and then it had mostly gone to preparing the latter for his role this morning. Fortunately, Marcus had been glad to explore the city and enjoy his grandchildren, Dahut the foremost.

Come spring, he must return home, lest that home crumble from the hands of the family. He and his son did not suppose they would ever meet again. But first they could lighten the Black Months for each other. That was why Gaius had sent for Marcus.

He could more readily have elevated somebody else. Soon he must do so. By issuing invitations during the year, he had gained a congregation for the hallowing of his temple: three Ravens, two Occults, a Lion, two Persians. Additionally, he had seen Cynan through to the rank of Soldier, Verica and Maclavius to Lion. That was all he had.

Light flared. The sun rose over the hills. Gaius Valerius Gratillonius led his men in hymn and prayer.

Before they went below, he raised a hand in salute to Point Vanis, where rested the bones of Eppillus.

Candles in holders of gilt bronze waited inside the tower. With these the party descended. The uppermost room was a watchpost and rain shelter, the next pair were given over to storage. Farther on they echoed empty; those times were past when the treasures of Ys had overflowed into them. Walls sweated, air grew dank, flames streamed smoky, as the stairs went down below the surf.

Finally came a space refurbished. Hidden ducts ventilated the fires of a hypocaust that kept it warm and dry. Statues of the Torchbearers flanked a doorway. A mosaic floor in black and white showed emblems of the first three degrees in the Mysteries. On plastered walls glowed frescos of the tree that nourished infant Mithras and of His reconciliation with the Sun. Benches stood beneath, and a table bearing food, drink, and utensils for the sacred meal. A new wall with its own door shut off the

156

sanctum. With holy water sprinkled off pine boughs, with incense of pine cones, with wine and honey upon each tongue, the Gratillonii led the dedication.

Thereafter it was time to go back above and hymn the noonday sun. It glimmered wan, low in the south. Clouds were gathering, wind shrilled, seas ran white-crested.

The men returned to the Cave of Mithras. Only Father Runner, Persians, and Lions passed through to the sanctuary; the rest had their lesser devotions to perform in the pronaos.

The King of Ys could well honour the God from the East. Here the Dadophori were sculptured again, in their faces, eyes, postures something not quite Greek or Roman, fluid and sleek, like a wave or a seal. Lion-headed Time stood stern in His own marble, serpent-enwrapped. The font was the carven calyx of a flower. The four emblems in the floor led the gaze onward, past benches above which glistened symbols of the planets, to the twin altars at the far end, where Mithras arose from the Rock, and to the high relief of the Bullslaying that filled yonder wall. The ceiling was deep blue, with golden stars. Candles stood ready in sconces, lamps in niches, to give brightness once they were lit. Soon here, too, resin sweetened the air, along with incense.

Pater and Heliodromos trod forward. Together they led the rites.

Afterwards came the Sacrifice, for all initiates. On this unique occasion it began with blood. Cynan, having been duly purified, brought in a caged dove which he had gone to fetch in the course of exercises outside. Marcus Gratillonius took it forth and held it tight while Gaius cut its head off with a clean slash and let it bleed into a golden bowl. Cynan bore this and the remains into the pronaos. Tomorrow he, the Occults, and the Ravens would immolate them. Meanwhile the Gratillonii enacted the subjugation and coronation of the Sun by Mithras.

Finally they officiated over the divine meal which the lower ranks served the higher, a foretaste of the soul's ascent after death. Upon this great occasion it was fare less frugal than was customary: beef, subtle seasonings on the vegetables, honeycakes, the best of wines drunk from silver cups. When it was finished, Gaius Valerius Gratillonius gave benediction, and the men departed for the upper earth.

Weather hid the sunset. Nevertheless they said their prayers atop the Raven Tower before they bade one another farewell.

Gratillonius made his voice hearty as he did. Inwardly there remained a wistfulness. He had seen the Spirit enter certain worshippers; from Cynan it had fairly flamed. Nothing had touched him akin to the divine fire that lighted his consecration.

Or had it? The God revealed Himself in forms as infinitely various as the forms and signs of love. Was the feeling of completion, of rightness, that Gratillonius did have – was it Mithras's 'Well done' to His soldier, while also reminding him that the establishment of a lonely outpost was not in itself any victory?

Night fell upon son and father as they made their way back to the palace. Wind yelled, drove rain and scud before it, filled streets with chill. Under the sea wall, tide ramped and snarled.

VIII

1

The equinoctial gales blew out of Ocean like longings, to wake the soul from winter drowse. When a milder air had borne Marcus off, Gaius Gratillonius felt a redoubled need to be away himself, in action. Luckily – perhaps – there was a call upon him that neither Gallicenae nor Suffetes could deny was urgent. A letter from Maximus had scathingly denounced him for founding a new temple of Antichrist; it had been inevitable that word of that would eventually reach Treverorum. Were it not for pressing demands on his attention, the Augustus wrote, he would recall his prefect, occupy Ys, and extirpate demon worship. As it was, he must content himself with requiring the prompt installation of a new Christian pastor.

The centurion had an idea of what those demands were. Indeed he had better mend fences, both temporal and ghostly. Writing to the Duke of the Armorican Tract, he requested a conference. The reply was that that high official would be in Caesarodunum Turonum for the next several months, and receive him there. It was the civil if not military capital of Lugdunensis Tertia; the Duke doubtless had fence mending of his own to do.

With a few soldiers at his back, all mounted, Gratillonius set forth. He allowed himself and them two days' rest at Aquilo. Otherwise they pushed hard, down to Portus Namnetum and up the Liger valley.

That was lovely country, freshly green and blossomful.

Riding through, he felt cheer reborn in him. Why yearn for the barracks in Britannia or hope for a precarious prominence in the Empire? Ys was his home. Its people had become his people. He could see his work on their behalf grow beneath his hands. If he could have no woman besides his Queens, weren't they sufficient and then some? If none of them could bear him a son, did he not have Dahut? The little darling was so bright, so headstrong. She might very well grow up to be another Semiramis, Dido, Cartimandua, Zenobia, but happier fated; her father would lay the foundation for that! And, of course, his other daughters were sweet.

Danger prowled around Ys, but so it did everywhere in the world. As Quinipilis was fond of saying, to borrow trouble was stupid, considering the interest rate on it.

Crossing a bridge from the military highway to the left bank, his party passed through the gate of Turonum and found quarters. He was both relieved and perturbed to discover that the civil governor was absent, summoned to the Emperor along with his counterparts throughout Gallia. At least now he could confer straightforwardly with the Duke.

They got along well at their first meeting. It was privately agreed that neither would send forces to any internecine conflict. They would explain that defence against the barbarians must take precedence. It was true.

As for Gratillonius's need of a clergyman, the Duke recommended him to Bishop Martinus. 'He comes into town once a week, usually, from that monastery of his, to lead services at the main church. M-m-m, I know what you are, but it'd be wise of you to attend them then.'

Always scout ahead if you can. Gratillonius went for a preliminary look, and was shocked. The church was larger than most, and rather handsome for a building erected in recent decades. However, it was filled with madmen – the

160

sick of mind and feeble of mind, ragged, filthy, some roaring, some shivering, some posturing, some taking attitudes absurd or obscene, while mutters went through the dimness. 'San, san, san . . . I am Jupiter, but they have me locked in hell . . . Fintharingly and no, no . . .'

A deacon explained upon being asked that this was at the order of the bishop. Elsewhere energumens, as such persons were called, wandered starveling, shunned for fear of the demons supposed to possess them, when they were not whipped off with curses, beaten, tormented, sometimes raped or killed. Martinus decreed that they be fed and sheltered in the house of God. Each Saturday he came in among them, clad in sackcloth and smeared with ashes; he lay full length on the floor in their midst, and hour after hour implored mercy for them or wrestled with the Fiend who afflicted them. His touch and his prayers had seemingly freed a number to return to the human world. The rest adored him in their various weird fashions.

Gratillonius thought of his Gallicenae. They too, Innilis especially, had had a measure of luck in coping with insanity. But when they failed, the law of Ys was that the sufferers must be expelled. 'It's well done of the bishop,' he said.

'Oh, his is a loving soul, sir, underneath the strictness,' replied the deacon. 'He served in the army, did you know? Conscripted, and spent twenty-five years before he could have the baptism he longed for, but never did his charity falter. When he was stationed at Samarobriva, I've heard – not from him – how one freezing day he saw a near-naked beggar. He'd already given away most of what clothes he had, but he drew sword, cut his cloak across, and let this man have half. No wonder he has power to heal. Of course, he had been a military physician.'

Gratillonius decided it would be politic to absent himself until Sunday. Besides, the idea of a man grovelling among the crazy repelled him. He hired a boat and went fishing.

On the Lord's day, after sunrise prayers to his own Lord, he was early at the church. This would be far from the first Christian ceremony he had watched, but he wanted to observe everything he could. The energumens were gently but firmly guided out on to the porch, where a couple of priests with the rank of exorcist took them in charge. Trained by now, they gave no trouble. Meanwhile the interior was cleaned and made ready. The congregation arrived piecemeal. A comparative few went inside, most of them middle-aged or elderly, the baptized. Catechumens occupied the porch; of these, a majority were women. There was no objection to those excommunicated for sin or to unbelievers like Gratillonius, if they behaved themselves. Who knew but what the scales might fall from their eyes?

Solemnly, the bishop led his priests and deacons in. Martinus had changed little in a year and a half, save that he was freshly barbered, his sallow face smooth aside from the many furrows, his hair standing white – unkempt still – behind the ear-to-ear frontal tonsure which made his brow seem cliff-high. He wore the same slave-like garb, and went barefoot. His attendants were as humbly clad, and for the most part equally gaunt.

Folk knelt while the ordained led a prayer. There followed a reading from the Prophets. ' – *Shall not the land tremble for this, and those who dwell in it mourn, while it rises up like a flood of Egypt and is cast back and drowned?* – ' The people joined in singing a short response: ' – *Glory unto God omnipotent* – ' Standing, they heard the bishop read from an Epistle: ' – *The natural man does not receive what the Spirit of God*

162

teaches; to him this is foolishness; he cannot know it, because it is only knowable by the spirit. – ' A choir sang a psalm. Martinus preached the Gospel. He was no orator. In terse soldierly words, he discoursed on the centurion whose servant Jesus had healed. ' *– Lord, I am not worthy for You to come under my roof. –* ' Gratillonius wondered about that text. For all his devotions and meditations, yonder fellow kept uncommonly aware of what went on around him.

'Silence,' enjoined a deacon. While bishop and priests prayed, the offerings of the faithful were brought forth in processional, goods and money. Some were earmarked – for the poor, the ill, a family member in need – and the deacon read aloud the names of those beneficiaries, and Martinus included them in his prayer.

It was the dismissal. Those in the porch left at its end. The doors behind them drew shut. What came next was the Communion service, for the baptized only. Well, Gratillonius thought, we bar our lower ranks from the highest Mysteries of Mithras.

He sought an exorcist, who was helping shepherd the energumens. 'I have to see the bishop,' he said, and gave his name. 'Will you tell him? I'll be at the Imperial hostel.'

'He receives supplicants – '

'No, this has to be a private talk. Tell him it's with the King of Ys.'

The priest gaped and gulped. However, the man before him, big, healthy, well-clad, was not obviously a lunatic. To be sure, standing aside as a spectator, he had revealed himself a pagan. But Martinus dealt with many a heathen chieftain in the hinterland. 'I can't approach him for some hours yet, sir, not till he's finished his Church business, and afterwards his charities and austerities. Expect word about sunset.'

Briefly, Gratillonius bristled; then he eased off and laughed. Maybe Martinus washed the feet of the poor, but be damned if he toadied to the mighty!

The message that evening, carried by an awestruck boy who had memorized it, was: 'The bishop will return to the monastery immediately after worship tomorrow sunrise. He will be glad to meet you at the western city gate and have you accompany him. It will be afoot.'

– On this side of the river, the road was unpaved. Rain had fallen during the night, and morning was cold and damp, though warming as the sun climbed. Mist smoked above the water. Dew glittered on grass and young leaves. The hills reached silvery with it. Birds twittered; high and high, a lark chanted its '*bi-bi-bi*'. Few people were abroad. While Martinus needed a staff, he strode along without asking Gratillonius to slow down. A few monks who had come with him followed at a respectful distance.

For a time conversation went lively between the leaders. Martinus was ardent to learn everything Gratillonius had done, seen, heard, planned, since their last encounter. But when talk turned to the future, his mood darkened.

' – And so I've got to have a minister of your faith for Ys, soon.' Gratillonius finished. 'Please don't look on it as a political move. I am what I am. From your viewpoint, too, wouldn't it be best we get a reasonable man like old Eucherius?'

Martinus peered afar. Somehow his thin, snubnosed countenance came to resemble a Caesar's. 'God rest Eucherius.' His tone was steely. 'From what I've heard, he did his pious best. He was weak, though. We require an evangelist there, who will take up arms against Satan.'

'But not one who'll, well, antagonize the city. How would that help your cause? Give me somebody I can work with.'

164

'Despite your own paganism.' Martinus gentled. 'Oh, I understand. Yours is a sore dilemma.'

'Never mind me. I'm thinking of Ys. And Rome. What good will it do Rome if your man provokes the people into throwing him out? Maximus would – Well, remember what the Priscillianus business cost.'

Martinus's knuckles whitened above his staff. 'I can never forget,' he said low.

Presently: 'Let me confess to you.' He wrenched the words out. 'For we must indeed try to understand each other, you and I, for the sake of the souls in your worldly care, and – and Rome.

'Maximus did agree to call off his inquisitors, and to give the surviving Priscillianists in his dungeons light sentences. However, on this he put a price. As a sign of blessing, I must help celebrate the consecration of Felix as bishop of Treverorum.

'Now Felix was, is, a fine man.' Martinus caught his breath. 'But to share the Eucharist with Ithacius, the persecutor – Well, in the end, perforce, I did.

'On the way home, I walked through midnight of the soul. It seemed to me that whatever powers of well-doing had been granted me by God must be gone, because of this covenant with evil. Then an angel of the Lord appeared to me and said I had done what I must and was forgiven.' He said that almost matter-of-factly, before he grew stark again: 'Nevertheless, I have seen Satan at work within the Church itself. I will never attend another synod of bishops.'

They trudged on in silence until Gratillonius had marshalled words: 'So you realize how careful we need to be, choosing . . . a trustworthy servant of God for Ys.'

Martinus had recovered calm. 'I do. A man devout, learned, civilized, but also virile, familiar with the common folk yet wise enough to cooperate with you for the general welfare and . . . resistance to tyranny.' He gusted a sigh. 'Do you know any such paragon? I wish I did!'

Gratillonius's heart leap. He had spent a great many hours thinking about this. 'Maybe I do.'

By then they had nearly reached their goal, about three miles downstream from Turonum. Sheer hillsides, honey-combed with caves and burrows, curved backwards to wall in a broad, grassy flatland. Primitive huts covered the low area, wattle-fenced gardens among them. Although the community was said to number well over a thousand, most dwelling in the caves, few were in sight, nor did smoke rise from any but two or three shacks.

This was the Greater Monastery that Martinus had founded, to which men flocked who had despaired of the world and would seek salvation beyond it. Women came too, but were housed in the city; the bishop clove husband from wife as ruthlessly as he split away fleshliness from himself. Mostly the monks subsisted on donations, or on the proceeds of possessions they had turned entirely over to the Church when they enrolled. What food they grew, what fish they caught, were mere concessions to the body's need of some recreation. They shared a single meal a day, of the simplest kind. Nearly all their waking hours they passed in prayer, contemplation, mortification, reading of Scripture, attendance on the preaching of their master.

Gratillonius could not comprehend how any human being would seek such an existence. Yet as he beheld it, the power of it sent a chill through him.

'Whom have you in mind?' Martinus asked.

The centurion hauled his mind back to realities. 'You know him. One Corentinus. We met last year, he and I, when I blundered on to his hermitage, and hit it off. On this trip, I stopped at Aquilo mainly so I could go back there and talk with him again. It went even better. I think

166

he's right for Ys – since we must have somebody – and I hope you'll agree.'

'Corentinus . . . Hm-m.' The bishop pondered, while his feet and staff ate the distance to sanctuary. 'It may be. It may be. An old seaman, posted to a seafaring folk . . . I must think. It's clear God has marked Corentinus for some high mission. You know about the miracle of the fish, don't you? Well, then – ' More silence, apart from the scrunch of sandals, the song of birds. 'I must think, and pray for guidance. But it does seem as though – He'll have to return here, get instructed, be consecrated chorepiscopus. That may take months. However, I could write to Maximus that it's in train.'

'I'm afraid he won't be willing, Corentinus,' Gratillonius warned. 'What he wants to do is sit in the woods and beg forgiveness.'

Also, those woods had been full of flowers, fragrances, peace.

Martinus laughed. 'He'll take his marching orders if they're issued him. Stay a while, you. Let's talk this over at length. You're a soldier; you can survive our hospitality. If my decision is positive – and I suspect it will be – I'll give you a letter you'll convey to Corentinus on your way back.'

Gratillonius bridled. 'Sir, I *am* the prefect of Rome and the King of Ys.'

Martinus laughed louder. 'Why should you not also be God's messenger boy?'

2

Early summer brought a spell of calm, light, warmth. It had prevailed for days when Quinipilis's turn to have Dahut came, and she took the girl out on the water.

'I promised her this, the first chance we'd get,' she snapped when her manservant expressed qualms. 'Would you have a high priestess break her word? A promise to a little kid is the most sacred kind there is. And nay, we'll not want the royal yacht or any such cluttered-up thing. What you can do is carry my word to Scot's Landing. So get off your arse!'

As he left, the man grinned to himself. The old lady had a rasp for a tongue and a lump of butter for a heart.

Maeloch was quick to arrive from the fisher hamlet under Cape Rach. His *Osprey* was under repair after storm damage. Meanwhile he welcomed extra earnings, and this would be a pleasant job. When he entered the Queen's house he found woman and child on the floor playing with little animals that King Grallon had carved in wood. 'Here he is, sweetling,' Quinipilis said to her charge. 'We can go now.'

'Oh, go, go, go!' sang Dahut, and soared to her feet. She was taller than most three-year-olds, wand-slim, wind-swift. Beneath flaxen billows of hair, her eyes were huge, deep blue, in an exquisitely sculptured face. 'We go sail!'

'The airs willing, princess,' Maeloch said. 'Else must I row.' His coarsely clad, burly form, black mane and beard, rumbling voice, caused her no alarm. It did not seem that anything had ever frightened Dahut.

'Well, help me up, oaf,' Quinipilis ordered with a nearly toothless smile. As he did, she caught a sharp breath.

'Does something hurt, my lady?' he asked.

'Of course something does. What d'you think 'twould do, in this wreck of a body? Like always having feet in a boiling kettle, if you must know. Let's begone.'

'Uh, better if my lady stays home. I'll take good care of the princess, believe me. How I do remember her mother.'

'Nonsense! Should I deny me a pleasure because of some verminous twinges? Fetch me my staff. 'Tis in yon corner; are you blind or only drunk? Give me your arm.' Quinipilis leered. 'I want all Ys to see I can yet snare a lusty young man for escort.'

Dahut skipped with them down the winding street. Folk they met, mostly servants in livery, gave deferential salutation. Many recognized Maeloch as well as the Queen. He was not only a fisher captain, frequenter of taverns and sometimes joyhouses like most sailors; he was a Ferrier of the Dead.

'Why d'ye go in this wise?' he wondered.

'On Dahut's account,' Quinipilis explained. 'She's ever been wild about the sea. Can't get close to it, or out on it, enough.'

A grimness crossed Maeloch's weathered countenance. He knew where and how the child had been born. Should that not have left a dread of the realm of Lir within her? Instead, it was as if He had touched her then, and was forever after calling her.

'Her dad takes her when he can,' Quinipilis went on, 'but he has scant free time, poor fellow. And then 'tis in his yacht. The notion came to me 'twould pleasure her to fare in a small boat.'

Maeloch could not keep his forebodings while the bright small presence who already looked so much like

Dahilis skipped beside him. 'We could land on a skerry I know and spend a while,' he suggested. 'Might get hungry, though.'

'I'm not quite in my dotage! We'll have provisions aboard.'

Thereafter Quinipilis must save her breath for walking. 'Wan' a' hear a song?' Dahut asked the man. Her hand lay tiny in his. She pointed at the woman, who smiled as if receiving an honour. 'Ol' Mama taught me.' She lifted a voice clear and true:

> 'Starfish, starfish, what have you seen
> Deep in the water, deep in the green?
> "I saw the darkness, far from the day,
> Where the seals go to hunt and play."'

From the Forum, broad and busy Lir Way brought them through Lowtown to Skippers' Market and the triumphal arch. Beyond was the harbour. At early ebb, tide had drawn the sea gate open; but on this mild day, the basin curved almost waveless beneath the city wall. Shallops cruised back and forth, a merchant ship was standing out, more vessels lay docked, bustle went over the stone arc of the quay. Trade was reviving under the reign of Grallon.

A well-stocked boat waited at a slip as Quinipilis had ordered. They went aboard. Maeloch cast off, put oars in tholes, rowed powerfully. They passed between the awesome doors of the gate. He found sufficient breeze that he could step and stay the mast, set sail, pole it out for a broad reach, and merely steer.

It whispered, the breeze, cooling the brilliance that flooded from above and dusted diamond-sparkle across the sea. It stirred, the sea, in low waves that somehow moved as one, like a single huge being gently breathing in its sleep. Today whiteness did not shatter on the cliffs or the strewn reefs, only swirled and murmured. Otherwise

Ocean was a million shifting shades of blue, save where a kelp bed rocked, or a swimming gull or cormorant. Such birds wheeled aloft in their multitudes, seldom crying. Dahut's gaze winged out among them, on past the dim streak that was Sena, to the line where vision met worldedge and lost itself in sky.

Her heed returned when a seal drew near. There were always many of the beasts around Ys, they being protected. Most were plunging through the water or basking on rocks. This one met the boat and swam alongside, a few feet away. Often it looked at Dahut, and she looked back, losing her earlier excitement, becoming mute and motionless though appearing very happy.

'That's strange,' Maeloch said after a while. His voice, which could outshout storms, was hushed. 'Dolphins'll play thus with a craft, but scarce ever a seal.'

Quinipilis nodded. 'I think I ken it,' she answered as low. Clear sight remained to her. 'Yon particularly beautiful coat, a kind of gold under the brown, and those big eyes. Could be the same as was there when the babe went overside. You've heard? I glimpsed it. And a few times since on the beach – '

'A seal saved me and my crew once. Guided us home through a fog, when else we'd sure have run aground.'

Quinipilis nodded. 'We're both wont to signs of the Otherworld, nay? As close as we are to it, in our different ways.' She glanced at Dahut. 'Sea child.'

The girl returned to playfulness when Maeloch dropped sail and rowed to that skerry he had mentioned. It was large of its kind, an islet, bare rock but strewn with weed, shells, bleached and contorted sticks of driftwood. Tidepools gleamed on its lower ledges. She clapped her hands and carolled. Maeloch lay to, hung out rope bumpers, jumped ashore with the painter and made fast to an upright thumb of stone. 'Come ye, sweetling,' he called.

'Nay, first put sandals back on. 'Twouldn't do having the barnacles cut those wee feet.'

He assisted Quinipilis, then brought a chair and parasol carried along for her, then set out luncheon, while Dahut scampered round and round, shouting at each new marvel she discovered. After they had all refreshed themselves he led her by the hand, explaining things as best he could. Quinipilis watched, smiled, sometimes talked in an undertone to nobody he saw. At last he said, 'Well, Princess, best we be starting home.'

Dahut's face clouded. 'Nay,' she answered.

'We must. The tide's turning. That'll help your poor old Uncle Maeloch, for the wind's down and he'll have to row a lot. But if we wait too long, the tide'll close the gate, and we'll have to make for Scot's Landing, and your poor old Aunt Quinipilis can't get up the cliffs there.'

The child stuck out her lower lip, clenched fists, stamped foot. 'Nay. I *b'long* here.'

'Not the way the sun's putting a flush in that white skin of yours, ye don't. No mutiny, now. Ye can play till I've stowed our gear.'

Dahut whirled and sped from him.

When Maeloch returned to Quinipilis he found she had dozed off in her chair, as the aged do. He left her alone while he loaded the boat. Always he kept half an eye in Dahut's direction. She had gone down to the water and become quiet. The rock sloped in such wise that could see merely the fair top of her head.

Having finished his task, he gave Quinipilis a slight shake. She drew a rattling breath and blinked confusedly. 'Dahilis – ' she mumbled. Her senses steadied. 'Oh, my, such eldritch dreams I was having.' Painfully, she hobbled to the boat and got in with Maeloch's assistance.

The sailor went after Dahut. 'Time to go,' he said, and stopped and stared.

On the ledge beneath him, the girl was side by side with the seal. Maeloch saw that the animal was female. Her narrow, earless head (how much the head of a seal called to mind a human corpse) had brought muzzle against cheek, through a tumble of tresses. The fishy breath seemed to give no offence. Did a murmur, a hum or a tone, resound from the long throat?

'Dahut!' Maeloch bellowed. 'What the thunder?'

The two started, rolled apart, exchanged a look. The seal slithered into the water and dived below. Dahut leapt up. The wet body had soaked her gown so that it clung to the curves of her, which were not yet a woman's curves but slender as if to cleave waves. Calming, she walked towards him without protest.

Maeloch squatted to inspect her. 'Ye're not hurt?' he grated. 'Damnation, whatever happened? Don't do that sort o' thing! A big beast like yon could tear ye in shreds. Saw ye nay its teeth?'

'She came and sang to me,' Dahut answered like a sleepwalker.

'Sang? Huh? Seals don't sing. They bark.'

'She did so.' Sheer wilfulness brought the girl back to herself. 'She sang 'bout the sea 'cos I wan'ed she should.' Turning, she called across the luminous, moving miles: 'I'll come again! I'll al'ays come again!'

The mood flitted from her. She gave Maeloch an impudent grin, a wink, and her hand to hold. What could he do but lead the daughter of Dahilis to the boat and take her home to her father?

He knew he would never understand what he had seen; but he, who dealt with the dead as his forebears had done before him, need not be daunted by a mystery as tender as this. 'She sang, did she?' he asked.

'She did, she did.' Dahut nodded violently. 'She tol' me 'bout my sea.'

'What did she tell you?'

'I 'member. You wan' a' hear?' The treble that lifted towards the gulls was childish, but the words no longer were, and the melody ebbed and flowed. It was not a song that had ever been heard in Ys.

> 'Deep, deep, where the waters sleep
> And the great fish come and go,
> What do they dream in the twilight gleam?
> The seals will always know.

> 'Far, far, from the evening star
> Comes the storm when the wind runs free
> And the cloud that lours with the rain that pours.
> The seals will always see.

> 'High, high is the evening sky,
> Deep is the Ocean swell.
> Where foam is white in the changing light,
> The seals will always dwell.'

3

For the past three years, except when it was impossible, Gratillonius had given a day every month to open court. Anybody was free to enter the basilica during those hours, to watch the proceedings or to lay before him a trouble – dispute, complaint, need – that lower authorities had failed to resolve. Turn by turn, he heard them out, and rendered judgement with military briskness. He had neither time nor patience for subtleties, though he strove to be fair. In doubtful cases he generally found for the humble. They had less to fall back on than the well-off.

The setting was impressive. Tiered benches looked down towards a dais on which the King sat enthroned, the

Wheel embroidered in gold on his crimson robe, the Key hanging out in view upon his breast, the Hammer across his knees. At a table to his left sat a recorder whose pen ran as fast as words were uttered, on his right a jurist with scrolls containing the laws of Ys before him. Behind the seats four legionaries in full battle gear stood at attention; and behind them loomed the eidolons of the Three, Taranis the Father, Belisama the Mother, kraken that represented inhuman Lir.

On that day, a rainstorm made dim the light from the glazed windows and laved the chamber with its susurrus. Candles in wall sconces and lamps on the desks cast their small glows, uneasy in the draughts. More people than usual had come to observe, for a notorious case was to be heard. The smell of wet wool garments gave sharpness to the air.

Gratillonius heard pleaders in order of arrival. Nagon Demari registered outrage, but Donnerch the wagoner guffawed, when they must wait for several of the lower classes. An elderly woman stated that she did not want the charity of the Gallicenae, for her son's widow could perfectly well pay her support as the son himself had done; having obtained the figures, Gratillonius so ordered. A man found guilty of theft brought friends, whom the magistrate had ruled unreliable, to declare he had been with them on the night of the crime; Gratillonius released him on grounds of reasonable doubt, but warned that this would be taken into account if there was another accusation. A sailor declared that his captain did wrong to make him suffer six lashes for a minor infraction, and ought to pay compensation for the injustice; after several of the crew had testified, Gratillonius said, 'You were lucky. I'd have given you nine.'

Thereupon it was time for Nagon Demari, Labour Councillor among the Suffetes, and Donnerch, son of

Arel, carter. Nagon spoke at length about his beneficence in organizing the longshoremen of Ys into a guild, now that trade was improving, thanks to wise King Grallon. He made a mouth as he said that: a stocky, cold-eyed man who despite aristocratic blood had been born poor and scrabbled his way up in the world till he sat in the Council. 'Spare me this and get to the point,' Gratillonius snapped.

Nagon looked indignant but explained that handling cargo obviously involved carrying it inland, wherefore carters should belong to the guild, pay its dues, require its fixed charges for their work, and perform such services for the guild as its leadership needed. Donnerch had not only refused these requests, made for his own good, and done so in unseemly language, he had brutally assailed two of the brotherhood who sought to persuade him.

Three newcomers entered the hall. Gratillonius drew a quick breath and raised his hand. 'A moment,' he interrupted. Louder: 'Thrice welcome, honoured sir!' with the same repeated in Latin.

Corentinus made salutation. A letter had declared he was coming, but Gratillonius had not looked for him quite this soon. He must have ridden hard, he and the two strong young men who must be deacons assigned him. The new chorepiscopus of Ys had shed much of the forest hermit. Nose, chin, cheekbones still jutted, deep-set eyes still smouldered under tangled brows, but hair and beard were neatly clipped and he had evidently bathed at hostels where he overnighted. His head was bare, the tonsured locks drenched and matted; but the paenula hanging from his shoulders to his knees, off which water dripped, was of good quality, and beneath it the long shanks displayed Gallic breeches tucked into boots.

'We shall hear you out tomorrow – ' Gratillonius started to tell those who stood before him.

'Nay,' said Corentinus. He used Osismian, but already

176

he could throw in enough Ysan words that he was intelligible to every listener. How had he learned them? 'We have arrived early, and God forbid it be in pride. Let us abide your leisure.' He folded his height down on a rear bench. Stiffly, the deacons joined him.

Donnerch answered the question in Gratillonius's mind. 'Why, I know that fellow,' he exclaimed. 'Hoy-ah, Corentinus!' He waved. The clergyman smiled and made a responding gesture. 'I got as far as Turonum, trek before last,' the wagoner said, 'and he heard about me being from Ys and paid me for a few days of language teaching. I earned it, lord. How he worked me!' He was a big young man, yellow-haired, freckle-faced, ordinarily cheerful.

'*May* we get on with our business, O King?' Nagon demanded.

'If you'll be quick about it,' Gratillonius replied.

Presently Donnerch said: 'By Epona, but he lies, him! Hark'ee, lord. I'd no reason for paying into his mucky guild and doing his mucky will, did I? And so I told my fellow independent carters. Then this pair of toughs came to call on me. When they started talking about two broken arms, I snatched my mule whip off the wall. I have the cudgels they dropped on their way out, if the King wants to see 'em. Aye, they had me hauled up on charges of assault, but the magistrate didn't believe 'em, though he dared not call 'em perjurers either. So here we are.'

'*Perjurers?*' shouted Nagon. 'Lord, I've come on their behalf because their injuries are too cruel, too grievous, after that barbaric attack –'

'Silence!' Gratillonius commanded. 'Think you the King is blind and deaf? I've stayed my hand erenow, Nagon Demari, for there's been much else for me to do, and it did seem you'd bettered the lot of your workers

177

somewhat. But darker stories have grown too many of late. This is only the newest of them.'

'Two honest men swear, against this known drunkard and brawler, that he fell on them with a dangerous weapon, unprovoked. Poor Jonan lost an eye. Cudgels? Donnerch could find two cudgels anywhere.'

'Getting hurt is a hazard of building empires,' Gratillonius said, 'and I warn you to stop trying to build yours any bigger. Free carters are not longshoremen. Henceforth, leave them alone. And . . . Donnerch, mayhap you were needlessly rough. Tell your friends that next time something like this happens, there will be a full inquiry; and whoever has taken arms against a man without real need, he'll know the scourge or the axe. Dismissed.'

Donnerch barely suppressed a whoop, Nagon did not conceal a glower. Gratillonius wondered whether he, the King, had won or lost today. He needed all the support he could call on, when he must protect not a mild Eucherius but a forceful Corentinus.

Luckily, just two more cases were left, and those minor. He adjourned before any further petitioners could arrive. In a rear chamber he exchanged his robe for everyday tunic, trousers, hooded cloak. The Key felt momentarily chill against his skin.

Returning, he ignored everybody else that lingered, to greet the chorepiscopus properly and have the deacons introduced to him. Those seemed like vigorous and dedicated men, but well under control of their leader. 'It's good to see you again,' Gratillonius said in Latin, quite sincerely in spite of awaiting difficulties. 'I hope you'll like Ys.'

'I do,' the minister answered. 'Too much. As I rode in, what memories came back.' He squared his shoulders. 'My friend, I don't know whether you've done me the greatest service or the scurviest trick; but Bishop Martinus said this is God's will, and that must suffice me. Will you show us to the church?'

'Why, you're here too soon. Nothing's properly ready. I'll quarter you in the palace till then.'

Corentinus shook his head. 'No, thanks. The fewer fleshly comforts and temptations, the better. To tell the truth, a reason I pushed hard on the road was fear that you, in mistaken kindness, would outfit our dwelling luxuriously.'

'Well, come look, but I warn you, the place has lain neglected since Eucherius died.'

'The more merit to us,' Corentinus said almost merrily, 'as we make it into a fortress of God.'

Gratillonius thought of his Mithraeum, also an outpost lonely and beleaguered. Let Corentinus settle in, get some rest, begin to find out for himself what Ys was – not only a seaport with the usual gaiety, unruliness, swindlings, sorrows, vices, ghosts, dreams . . . though in Ys they were stronger and stranger than elsewhere – not only a city of wealth, power, beauty, industry, corruption, vanity, arrogance, like others . . . though in Ys these flourished as they had not done elsewhere since the high days of Rome – but a whole society with its own ways and Gods which were not akin to those of any other, ancient, pervasive, and enduring. He, Gratillonius, had not yet fully come to terms with Ys, and he was no Christian. He hoped Corentinus would not break his heart, battering against what the evangelist must needs perceive as wickedness.

They went out into the Forum and the rain. Wind sent the water at a slant, silver that glinted cold across the mosaics of dolphins and sea horses, and downward from basin to basin of the Fire Fountain at the centre. The wind hooted and plucked at clothes. It bore a sound and a smell of Ocean. Hardly a soul was in sight. Gratillonius led the way across to the former temple of Mars.

'Sir – lord King – ' He stopped and looked towards the voice. The speaker was young Budic, who as a legionary of his had today taken a turn in the honour guard at the palace. 'Sir, an Imperial courier brought this. I thought I'd better get it to you right away, and you'd be hereabouts.'

'Well done,' said the centurion of the Second, and took a scroll wrapped in oiled cloth. He kept impassive, though his heart slugged and his throat tightened. Budic stood staring as he walked on.

In the portico of the church he said to Corentinus: 'Let me read this at once. I suspect it's something you should know about too.'

The chorepiscopus traced a cross in the wet air. 'You're probably right,' he replied.

The letter was clearly one sent in many copies through Gallia, Hispania, and perhaps beyond.

– *Magnus Clemens Maximus, Augustus, to the Senate and the People of Rome, and to all others whom it may concern, charging them most solemnly and under the severest penalties to carry out those duties laid upon them by Almighty God and the state . . .*

– *After four years of patient negotiation, it has become clear that accommodation with Flavius Valentinianus, styled Emperor, is unattainable . . . Intransigence and repeated violations . . . The abominable heresy of Arius . . . The cleansing of the state, even as Our Saviour drove out money changers and demons . . .*

– *Therefore we most strictly enjoin the people and those in whose care the people are, that they remain loyal and orderly, obedient to those whom God has set above them, while we lead our armies into Italy and wherever else may prove needful, to the end that the Western Empire, harmo-*

niously with our brother Theodosius of the East, again
have tranquillity under a single and righteous ruler.

4

An autumn storm roared, whistled, flung rain and hail,
throughout one night. It made doubly comforting the
warmth of Bodilis's bed and body. By morning the
weather was dry but the gale still ramped. Man and
woman woke about the same time, smiled drowsily at
each other through the dimness, shared a kiss. Desire
came back. He laughed, low in his throat. 'There's no call
on me today,' he said, drawing her closer.

That was not true. There was always something to
clamour for the attention of the centurion, the prefect,
the King. Only the day before, news had arrived from
beyond the Alps, via the Duke of the Armorican Tract:
Maximus was firmly in possession of Mediolanum and
Valentinianus had fled eastward out of Italy. Gratillonius
then made an excuse to visit the wisest of his Queens, out
of turn, for her counsel and afterwards her solace.

Nevertheless – 'Just you and me,' he said in the Latin
she wanted to maintain for herself. 'Later, let's breakfast
with Una, hm?'

'M-m-m,' she responded, and in other ways as well.

He often thought that if he could have his wish, she
would be his sole wife. She had not the raw ardour of
Forsquilis, good-natured sensuality of Maldunilis, dumb
eagerness to please of Guilvilis; somehow, in her enough
of each was alloyed. She was handsome rather than
beautiful, and the years were putting grey into the wavy
brown hair, crow's-feet around the blue nearsighted eyes,
wrinkliness under the throat, sag in the breasts. But she

181

was no crone, and good bones would endure. Though her monthly courses had not ended, it did not seem she would bear him more children, ever. Well, he had plenty now, and Una was a darling second only to Dahut. Before all else was the *wholeness* of her. She knew things, thought about them, gave him her judgements, submitted to nothing save the truth as she saw it. She was his friend, such as he had not had since Parnesius on the Wall; and she was his lover.

They met; together they went beyond themselves; presently they lay at peace with the universe. Outside, the wind hooted, rattled shutters, carried a noise of waves breaking mightily on the sea wall. Yesterday the King had barred the gate and locked it with the Key that he alone bore, lest the waters fling it open and rage into Ys. He did not expect to free those doors for a while; and few vessels would come thereafter. As winter neared, Ys drew into itself, even as he and his Queen did this day.

She chuckled. 'What's funny?' he asked.

'Oh, you,' she said. 'Dutiful you, hiding away from work like a boy from the schoolmaster. It's good to see you taking your ease, dear, merely enjoying yourself. You should do it oftener.'

Reminded, he sat up. 'I forgot my morning prayer!'

She arched her brows. 'For the very first time?'

'Uh, no.'

'I'm sure your Mithras will understand, and overlook it. Belisama does.' Bodilis's glance went to the figurine that occupied a niche in her otherwise plainly furnished bedroom. Carved of oak whose grain followed the folds of Her hooded cloak, it showed the Goddess as a woman of middle age, serene, an enigmatic smile on Her lips.

I could adore a deity like that, he thought, if this were Her only aspect.

Putting solemnity aside, 'We spoke of breakfast – ' he began.

A knock on the door interrupted. 'My lord, my lord!' called the voice of Bodilis's chief manservant. 'Forgive me, but a soldier of yours is here. He says he must see you this instant.'

'What?' Gratillonius swung feet to floor. His immediate feeling was of resentment. Could they never leave him alone? He took a robe off a peg and pulled it over himself. Bodilis rose too, with a rueful look for him.

His deputy Adminius waited in the atrium, wearing civil Ysan garb that he had donned with unmilitary hastiness. He saluted. 'Begging your pardon, sir.' The lean, snaggle-toothed countenance was full of distress. 'I'm afraid I got bad news. 'Ard news, anyway, though I'm sure the centurion can 'andle the matter.'

Gratillonius dismissed whatever happiness had still been aglow in him. 'Speak.'

'You got a challenger, sir. At the Wood. One o' the lodgekeepers came asking where you was, and I thought you should 'ear it from me.'

It was as if the wind came in off the street and wrapped around Gratillonius. 'Do you know more?'

'No, sir. Should I go look? I can tell 'em I couldn't find yer right away.'

Gratillonius shook his head. 'Never mind,' he said dully. 'Let me get shod.'

He turned back towards the bedroom. Having covered her own nakedness, Bodilis had followed him and heard. She stood at the inner doorway, the colour drained from her face. 'Oh, no,' she whispered. The hands that groped across his were cold. 'Not already.'

'The way of Ys,' Gratillonius rasped. He brushed past her.

Returning with sandals and cloak, he found she had not

stirred. Those widened eyes struck remorse into him. He stopped, clasped her by the shoulders, and said, 'I'm sorry. I forgot how terrible this must be to you. A total stranger, who may be another Colconor or, or anything. Don't be afraid.' It might be kindly of him to change from Latin to Ysan: 'Nay, fear not, heart of mine. I'll smite the wretch ere he can slice a hair off my knuckle. For your sake.'

'I dare not pray,' she whispered. 'This thing lies at the will of the Gods. But I'll hope, and – and weep for you, Grallon, who so loathes this need laid upon him.'

He kissed her, quickly and roughly, and went forth with Adminius. The wind shrilled, sent dead leaves scrittling along the street, roused little breakers on rain puddles. It drove clouds before it, making light and shadow sickle over roofs, half veiling the towertops. Rooks winged dark on the blast. The garments of such folk as were out flapped as if they too were about to fly away.

'You'll take 'im, sir, same as you did the last 'un,' Adminius avowed. ''E'll've 'ad a scant night's rest in the wet. 'E can't be very smart, or 'e'd've waited till later ter arrive.'

Gratillonius nodded absently. The rule that the King must respond at once to a challenge, unless absent from the city, was doubtless meant for more than the immediate gratification of Taranis; it gave him an advantage. Frequent changes were undesirable, even when the monarch was a political nullity.

'And if perchance you don't win, God forbid, w'y, 'e won't last out the day 'imself,' Adminius went on. 'Yer lads'll see to that.'

Shocked before he felt also touched, Gratillonius growled, 'No. No legionary will raise a finger against him. That's an order.'

'But, but yer the prefect o' Rome!'

184

'The more reason to maintain law. Including this damnable law of Ys. We *can't* have the city fall into disorder. Don't you see, it's the keystone of everything I've worked to build in Armorica.' Gratillonius considered. His mind had become as bleakly bright as the sunbeams. 'If I fall, report to Soren Cartagi. He'll be the effective governor for at least a while. Remind him of the need to continue my policies, for the good of Ys. Give him whatever help he requires. When he can spare you, bring the legionaries to the Duke and put them under his orders.'

Anguish asked: 'Wot about yerself, sir?'

'Let them burn me and scatter the bones and ashes at sea. That's what Ys does with her fallen Kings.' And I shall go home to Dahilis. 'My brothers in Mithras will hold their own rites for me.'

Gratillonius stiffened his neck. 'Enough,' he said. 'I do not plan on getting killed. Forward march! On the double, soldier.'

At Dragon House he donned his centurion's armour. All twenty-four of his men formed ranks and followed him out High Gate, battle-arrayed. By then word had spread and the streets were aswarm, ababble. Where Processional Way started north out of Aquilonian Way, a sqaud of marines formed a line to hold back the crowd. Through the wind, Gratillonius heard shouted wishes for his victory.

That warmed him a trifle. He had much to live for, and live he proposed to do. This challenger would scarcely be another pitiable Hornach, but rather some sturdy rogue prepared to take his chances. Quite possibly he was a barbarian. It would be almost a pleasure to kill a Frank, say. In any case, a fair fight which Gratillonius had not provoked was no butchery. As always, he did not dwell on the possibility that he might lose. To do so would merely weaken him.

185

The road bent east, under sere hills, and the Wood of the King loomed ahead. The gale had torn off nearly all the leaves that earlier turned it bronze. Now trunks and boughs were winter-grey, though shadows still made a cave of the depths beneath them. Twigs clawed at the sky. Timber creaked. Wind eddied about, wailed and mumbled.

Half a dozen more marines had reached the courtyard of the Shield and Hammer. They saluted the King. Tethered nearby stood their horses, and leashed hounds whined impatient. If either contestant fled, he would be hunted down and brought back for the death stroke.

Red-robed, Soren emerged from the blood-coloured house when an attendant called. He had been delayed by no need to equip himself; his was only to lead the ceremonies, before and after. 'In the holy name of Taranis, greeting, King of Ys,' he said.

For the sake of Dahut, Bodilis, Rome, Gratillonius bent his helmeted head to the God he abhorred. Mithras would understand.

'The challenger has chosen his weapons and is prepared,' Soren said. Nothing in his heavy visage bespoke how he wished the combat would go. He was the instrument of Taranis. Turning, he cried: 'Come forth, O you who would be King of Ys!'

A wiry, long-legged young man stepped from the gloom within, on to the porch and down the stairs. His movements were quick, suggestive of tension, but there was no hesitancy in them. A forked black beard, well trimmed, decorated clear features marred by poor teeth and a scar puckering the right cheek to pull that corner of his mouth into the hint of a sneer. From the outfits available he had chosen a nose-guarded helmet, knee-length chainmail coat, thick cross-garters over the breeches to protect calves, small round shield, long Gallic sword in a sheath, a javelin in his free hand. Plainly, he meant to make the best of agility against a larger opponent.

Plainly, too, he was not fatigued as Adminius had predicted. Springiness was in his gait and clarity in the green eyes. Browned skin gave a clue. This was an outdoorsman, skilful to contrive shelter and sleep soundly on the wildest of nights. He would be dangerous as a panther; and well he knew it.

He approached across the flagstones, peered, and halted. In Redonic-accented Latin he cried, 'Are you the King? But you're a centurion!'

And Gratillonius knew him. 'Rufinus!' Rufinus, leader of those Bacaudae whom the legionaries had driven from their prey on the road to Juliomagus –

The young man lifted spear and shield. Laughter whooped from him. 'Why, you rascal, you never told me! I'd not've bucked you elsewise. Better to've asked for a place in your command, hey?' He sobered, apart from a savage grin. 'Too late now, I suppose. Right? Pity.'

'What's this?' Soren demanded. 'Know you each other?'

'We've met,' said Gratillonius. A knot formed in his guts. 'He'll withdraw his challenge if I ask.'

'Impossible, as well you remember,' said the Speaker for Taranis. 'Let us pray.'

Rufinus glided close to Gratillonius. The smile kept flickering as he murmured, 'I'm sorry, centurion, truly I am. You're a decent sort, I think. But you should've told me, that night in your tent.'

They knelt at the royal oak. Soren signed them both with holy water and invoked the Father God. Wind boomed. A raven flew low overhead.

'We go off by ourselves,' Gratillonius said bluntly.

Rufinus nodded. 'They've explained.'

Side by side, the two men pushed through snickering

underbrush to the opening, out of sight from the house, where Gratillonius had killed Hornach and Colconor. Strange that underfoot were rain-sodden leaves and humus; this earth should be gory red.

His mood had not caused him to lose wariness. However, Rufinus attempted no sneak attack, simply leaned on his spear and sighed, 'This is too bad. It really is.'

'What made you come?' Gratillonius wondered.

Rufinus barked laughter. 'I wish I could say a mischievous God, but it was just chance – and myself – though it did seem, one midnight, moonlight hour, that stag-horned Cernunnos danced His madman's dance before me, to egg me on . . . Well,' he proceeded in a level tone, 'you roadpounders gave us brethren a nasty setback, you know. Not just our dead and wounded. You hit our spirits in the balls, and we skulked about for a long spell, living more off roots and voles than plunder and, hm, donations. My standing as duke was in danger, not that it meant much any more. Bit by bit, I rallied the boys, we got new recruits, till at last I had the makings of a fresh band. What it needed next – you'll know what I mean – what it needed was blooding, to prove itself to itself.

'Then the news ran this summer, civil war begun again and the Emperor marched off south with his army. I remembered Sicorus. Do you? My landmaster, who debased my sister till she died whelping his get.' Fury went like lightning over the face and through the voice, and vanished as swiftly. 'We all had things to avenge on Sicorus. The upshot was, one night we came and ringed Maedraeacum manor house in. We let women, children, harmless slaves go out, free; I told the boys that whoever touched them in anything but helpfulness would answer to my knife. Then we pushed Sicorus's overseers in to join him, and set fire to the building. That damaged the loot, of course, but next day we still picked a grand amount of gold and silver from the ashes.'

Rufinus sighed once more, shrugged, and finished: 'My mistake. I reckoned the Empire would be too busy with its own woes for doing much about this. That's how it was in past civil wars. But it turns out Emperor Maximus has driven his enemies before him right handily. The Roman – the Armorican Duke, is that what they call him? My fellow duke – I reckon he decided he could spare the troops to make an example of us. They scoured the woods for a month or more. Most of my Valiant are dead, the rest are fled. Me, I remembered a centurion who reminded me about wonderful Ys, and decided I'd scant to lose. So here we are, Gratillonius.'

Wind brawled, swirled under armour, made the Wood groan. Gratillonius said slowly: 'Too late, you thought of asking me for a berth in my service. How could I give you any, after what you did?'

'At Maedraeacum?' answered pride and reason. 'Had I no right to bring Ita's ghost peace? Every ghost that Sicorus squeezed out of life? Hasn't Rome made friends of her foes, like you Britons or us Gauls? I could serve you well, King. I'm a good man of my hands. And . . . My own Bacaudae may be gone, but I know many more, up and down the valleys and off in the hills. Outlaws; but they could be useful scouts, messengers, irregular fighters, for a King who showed them a little kindness.'

Gratillonius realized he must not listen. 'Try that if you overcome me,' he said. 'But remember that Rome is the Mother of us all. And be gentle to the Nine Queens and – and their children.'

For the first time, he saw complete calm on Rufinus. It was eerily like the peace he himself had felt this dawn after he and Bodilis made love. The wanderer traced a sign with his spear, in the wind. 'I promise,' he said low.

Thereupon he dropped into a feline crouch and asked, 'Shall we have at it, friend?'

'We must,' said Gratillonius.

They circled about the glade. Wind keened; the raven, settled on an unrestful bough, croaked hoarsely; fallen leaves squelped. Rufinus moved his buckler to and fro while his arm stayed cocked, ready to cast the javelin. Gratillonius kept his big Roman shield in place and squinted across its upper edge, the sword poised in his right hand.

Glances met and held fast. It was always a peculiar feeling to look into the eyes of a foeman, not unlike looking into those of a woman in bed, an ultimate intimacy.

They stalked, he and Rufinus, each in search of an opening. Now and then the Gaul made tentative movements of his spear. Gratillonius remained stolid. The wind blew.

Abruptly Rufinus cast. Immediately he snatched for the sword scabbarded across his back, and charged.

The Roman missile should have sunk its iron head into the Roman shield and hung there, its shaft dragging in the earth. Gratillonius was ready for it. His blade flipped it aside. It spent its malice in a rotten log. Rufinus was upon him. The Gallic sword crashed down. Gratillonius shifted his shield enough to catch the blow. His own weapon snaked forward. Rufinus sprang back. Blood from his left thigh darkened that trouser leg.

He's mine, Gratillonius knew. But let it be quick. Let it be merciful.

Rufinus gave him a wry grin and, again, circled, alert for a chance to pounce. Man for man, outlaw and centurion should be equal. It was not individual Romans but the Roman army that had broken the Gauls. Rufinus, though, had taken a wound not mortal but deep; and whatever carnivore skills he had picked up, he was untrained in the science of killing.

Gratillonius let him attack, over and over, wear himself down, retreat with more blood running out of him. Two or three times he got through the defence, but the injuries that the hare inflicted on the tortoise were minor slashes.

The end came all at once. Gratillonius manoeuvred Rufinus up against a thicket, which blocked retreat. Rufinus hewed. By that time the long sword was weakly held. Through the wind, Gratillonius heard how Rufinus panted, while blood soaked his breeches and footsteps. Gratillonius's shield stopped another blow. His short, thick blade knocked the weapon from his opponent's grasp.

A moment Rufinus stared, until his laughter cried out. 'Good work, soldier!' He spread his arms, while he swayed on his feet. 'Come, what're you waiting for? Here I am.'

Gratillonius found he could not move.

'Come, come,' Rufinus raved. 'I'm ready. I'd've done for you if I could.'

'Pick up your sword,' Gratillonius heard himself say.

Rufinus shook his head. 'Oh, no, you don't,' he crowed. 'I bear you no ill will, buddy. You won, fair and square. But be damned if I'll let you pretend – *Roman* – you're still in a fight. Make your offering.'

To Taranis, Who deigned to be Colconor. And Lir had slain Dahilis.

'Are you playing games with me?' Gratillonius brought forth.

'No,' said Rufinus, feebly now as the loss of blood swept him further along. He staggered. 'I only . . . want you . . . to stop playing games with yourself . . . and whatever Gods are yours, Roman.'

He lurched, sank to hands and knees, crouched gasping.

Mithras forbade human sacrifice.

It was as if Bodilis were suddenly there in the wind and the wet, Bodilis whom Gratillonius would seek back to as soon as he was able. Not losing time in cleaning it, he sheathed his sword. 'I cannot kill you, helpless,' he said, dimly amazed at his own steadiness. 'Nor can I let you lie there. Not if you surrender to me, altogether. Do you understand? I think I can save you if you'll declare yourself my slave, Rufinus.'

'I could have worse masters,' muttered back around the reborn grin.

Gratillonius knelt and set about staunching the wounds of his man.

5

Throughout the years, Soren Cartagi and Lanarvilis the Queen had held many a private meeting. None was as grim as this.

The gale had died away, but seas still crashed against the wall and gate of Ys, spume flying higher than the battlements. Their sound went undergroundishly through the whole city, as if earth responded to that anger. Starless dark engulfed heaven, save for what towertop windows glimmered alone. Lights and luxury in the room where Lanarvilis received her visitor could not really stave off night.

Motionless in a high-backed chair, she watched him pace to and fro before her. Flamelight sheened on her russet gown and silver fillet. It flickered within her eyes, making them demonlike, though on her face was only

192

compassion for him. He wore his red robe of office, the talisman of the Sun Wheel hung on his breast – so fateful did he think this occasion – but had removed his mitre on entering the house. In the uneasy illumination, his hair and beard seemed largely grey.

'Aye, thus it was,' he told her in his pain. 'He came back upholding the bandit. Said he'd bed him down in the Lodge. Ere I could shake off stupefaction and protest, Gratillonius declared himself winner in the combat and that that sufficed; no good would come of slaying a captive. Instead, he would give Taranis a hecatomb of beasts, bought out of his own purse.'

Lanarvilis nodded. 'The Gallicenae have heard that much, of course,' she said softly. 'He sent a written account among us – written by Bodilis, with whom he stays closeted in the palace, his Roman soldiers standing by. They've brought the Gaul there too. That is all I know thus far. His words to us were few and hard, no matter that Bodilis tried to milden them.'

'I'll give you the rest.' Soren's feet thudded on the carpet, a drumbeat above the sea-noise. 'I shouted my outrage. Ys lives by Her Gods, Who require Their ancient sacrifices. He replied that – he would fight future challengers, and those who did not yield must take their hazard of death; but he would not believe the honour of any God was served by – he called it murder!' Soren struggled for breath. '"Stand aside," he said, and began to help the scoundrel to the house.

'I called on the marines to kill the challenger, since this traitor King would not. "Be still," Gratillonius said – oh, how quietly. "It is not meet that anybody die here." His Romans trod closer, hands on hilts. Yet I – Elissa, Lanarvilis – I saw it was not they that stayed the marines. Our guards too were shaken, but 'twas the King they

193

would obey, this king who scorns the Gods That raised him up.'

Soren ground fist into palm. 'I swallowed vomit, though it burned my throat,' he related. 'After the injured man was at rest and a Roman – not our standby physician for a wounded victor, but a soldier with rough surgical skill – was tending him . . . Gratillonius returned and I sought to reason with him. Whatever his beliefs, I said, surely he could see that this – blasphemy, violation of the Pact – this would make him hated and undermine all he has done for his Rome. He answered that he thought not.'

'I fear he was right,' Lanarvilis said.

'Aye,' Soren groaned. 'Have you heard? Late in the day, when that Rufinus was somewhat recovered, Gratillonius brought him to the city. Beforehand, he had sent for heralds and told them to proclaim his intent. Folk were packed along Lir Way. He entered High Gate at the head of his marching men and, and a squadron of our marines, he riding, with Rufinus tethered at his saddlebow – Do you understand? He gave himself a Roman triumph; and the people cheered!'

'I heard,' Lanarvilis said. 'I was not surprised.'

'He has won them over. In spite of his alien God, in spite of his protecting that Christian priest, in spite of everything, he's their dear King Grallon, for whom they'll take arms against anybody. How long before the Gods take arms against them?'

'Have you thought, Soren,' she asked low, 'that we may in truth be at the end of the Age that Brennilis began? That mayhap Ys is once more offered the cup of youth, and if she will not taste of it must soon grow old and die?'

He halted. He stared. 'You too?' he breathed at last.

She shook her head. 'Nay, my darling. Never would I betray you. But my Sisters and I – other than Bodilis, though she laid certain words of wisdom in that letter –

we had Maldunilis brought back from Sena and spoke together. I knew you would seek me out.'

His bulk trembled. 'What did you decide?'

'It may be that Gratillonius will satisfy Taranis with his hecatomb.'

'I think not; for no sacrificial blood will flow in his heart.'

Lanarvilis shivered likewise. 'Wait and see. Taranis did not cast a thunderbolt this day. But if the Gods are indeed wrathful – Their revenge is often slow, but always cruel.'

Soren traced a sign, braced himself, and said, 'I'm concerned that all Ys not suffer because of a single man's wickedness. Might you Gallicenae curse him, as you did Colconor?'

Lanarvilis made a fending motion. 'Nay! How could we? He may be mistaken, but evil he is not. A curse without passion behind it can no more fly to its target than an arrow from a stringless bow.'

'And anyhow, several of you would refuse.'

'The whole Nine would, Soren.'

'So be it,' the man said. 'Well, Ys has been saddled in the past with Kings about whom something must be done. I mean not those who were . . . simply bestial, like Colconor, for to conspire against the Chosen of Taranis is an act of desperation – but some who posed a threat to the whole city. We'll send our agents out through Armorica, bearing gold and promises. Gratillonius will have challenger after challenger, month after month, till one of them cuts him down.'

Calm had descended on Lanarvilis. 'We guessed that idea would be broached, we Gallicenae,' she said, 'and we forbid it.'

'What?'

'Some of us love him. But put that aside. We too can lay our hearts on the altar when it must be done. Think, though. You and I are the politic persons, the worldliest among those who serve the Gods. Is it not really Ys we serve, Mother Ys?

'Think what Gratillonius has done and is doing. He has strengthened us, within and without our wall. He has quickened our stagnant trade. He has reconciled the high and the low. He has kept us free. Who else has the least hope of holding Emperor Maximus at arm's length? Who else have the Scoti and the Saxons learned to fear? Why, his very Mithras is a counterbalance to that Christ Who would take from us our Gods.

'Dare you imagine that some filthy barbarian or runaway slave can replace him? I say to you, Soren Cartagi, and if you are honest you will concede it – ill shall Ys fare if she loses King Grallon.'

Silence followed, apart from the subterranean thunder of Ocean.

Finally Soren dragged forth: 'I am . . . aware of this. I awaited that response of yours. I have even begun talks with my colleagues. Hannon is bewildered with horror, but I should be able to talk him over, along with the rest. We will not rebel, not conspire, but bide our time. Let the Gods work as They will.'

He stood quiet for a space before adding, 'Yet we, Their worshippers, cannot sit passive. They make us what we are, our unique selves, *Ys*. How shall we make our amends for this harm that has been done Them?'

'The Nine have thought upon that,' Lanarvilis replied gravely. 'We, his wives, know what stubbornness is in Gratillonius. But patience, endurance, that is woman's weapon.

'Therefore we will lay the foundations of the future, that ineluctable morrow when he has fallen and we are done with mourning him. We will take triple care that our daughters grow up in the awe of the Gods. First and foremost will we instil devoutness in Dahut, child of Dahilis, whose nurturing we share. Forsquilis senses fate within that girl. Its form is unknown, but its power waxes year after year. We Nine will set upon her brow the sigil of the Three.'

Again Soren signed himself.

'It is well,' he said, took up the wine cups that stood on the table, handed Lanarvilis one and took a long draught from its mate.

Thereafter, soothed a little, he sat down opposite her, ventured a smile, and said, 'You've lightened a huge burden for me. Thank you.'

She smiled back. 'Nay, you let it off yourself.'

'Well, mayhap, but first you loosened the bonds holding fast. Ever have you been kind to me.'

'How could I be aught else . . . to you?' she whispered.

They withdrew from the edge of that. 'Well,' he suggested, 'can we spend a while talking of small things? How have you fared since last I saw you? What will you share with me?'

'All I am permitted to,' she said.

IX

1

Winter's early night had fallen when three Romans entered an alehouse in the Fishtail district. The first was well known there: Adminius, deputy commander of the legionaries. The second had come occasionally, young Budic; he, who carried a lantern, now blew it out and put it down on a remnant of mosaic. The third was a tall, craggy-boned, middle-aged man, clad in ordinary tunic and breeches, but with his hair shaven off the front half of his scalp.

This taproom had been the atrium of a fine house – long ago, before sea level began to rise, driving the wealthy to higher ground and eventually forcing construction of the great wall. Bits of relief sculpture and hints of frescos peered out of soot and grease. Tables and benches on what was mostly a clay floor were rough wood, though themselves time-worn, haggled by generations of idle knives. Tallow candles guttered and dripped on the boards, enough light to see by after a fashion. Shadows curtained every corner, flickered across peeled plaster and thin-scraped membrane stretched over windows, parodied each movement. The stench of burning fat mingled with odours of cooking from the kitchen, of sour wine and worse beer.

Withal, it was a rather cheery place. About a dozen fishers, merchant sailors, wherry oarsmen occupied two of the tables. They drank heartily, jested roughly, laughed loudly. A woman sat with one group, teasing them while she sipped what they bought her. As the newcomers entered, another man came in from the hallway beyond. He grinned in lazy wise and secured his belt. The rest gave him a ribald cheer. 'Did your ram sink that hull for good this eventide?' shouted someone.

'Nay,' he replied, 'you know Keban better than that. She'll soon bob back to surface. Me, I'm thirsty. Mead, potboy, none of your horse piss but good, honest mead!' He was young, strong, ruddy of close-trimmed beard and queue-braided hair.

Adminius and Budic recognized him. 'That's Herun, of the navy,' said the younger soldier in his diffident way, and the deputy whooped, ''Oy, there, 'Erun, come drink it with us!'

Their companion shook his head. 'Poor, forlorn soul,' he murmured in Latin. 'Has he no wife, that he couples with a whore?'

Budic flushed. 'W-w-we warned you, sir, what kind of place this is. Should we g-go away?'

'No.' A smile. 'It's not as if I didn't recognize the surroundings.'

Herun trotted over. 'We got a guest 'ere,' Adminius said. 'Corentinus.'

The mariner halted, squinted through the murk, responded slowly: 'Aye, now I know him. Every sennight he preaches at the Forum, from the steps of the old Mars temple. What would a Christian priest among us?'

Corentinus smiled again. 'Naught to frighten anybody,' he said in Ysan that had become fluent though heavily accented. 'I hope to grow better acquainted with folk. These men kindly offered to show me where sailors hang out. After all, I'm a sailor myself.'

'Indeed?'

'Or was. 'Tis another kind of sea I ply nowadays. If I pledge not to evangelize, will you let me drink with you?'

A staring, listening stillness had fallen. ''E's a right sort,' Adminius declared. ''Oly man, but not sanctimonious, if you take my meaning. Nobody minds Budic or me or most of us soldiers being Christian, so why mind Corentinus?'

Herun recovered himself. 'Welcome,' he said, a bit grudgingly. 'Shall we sit?' He joined the three at a separate table. 'Only the mead here is fit for aught but swine and Saxons,' he warned, becoming more genial, 'but 'tis pretty fair stuff at the price.'

The potboy brought a round. Corentinus watered his. 'How like you our city?' Herun asked him.

'Oh, dazzling, a whirlpool of wonders,' the chorepiscopus replied. 'I've never seen aught to rival it, and I've been widely about in my time.'

Adminius laughed. He waved a hand around. 'This 'ere's 'ardly any palace,' he said.

'Nay,' Corentinus agreed. 'But see you, I've had my fill of elegance. Thanks to the King, I've seen the inside of most wealthy homes in Ys and its hinterland. Beautiful, as I said; but my flock numbers few, and they poor and lowly.'

'Get ye no Christians in summer?' growled a man at an adjacent table. 'I've met 'em aplenty whilst faring to Roman harbours.'

'Aye, aye. They attend services. But my true ministry is to Ys.' Corentinus chuckled and shrugged. 'Not that my sermons on the steps – my rantings, some call them – draw large audiences. So I thought I would go forth among ordinary folk and get to know them well enough that, God willing, I can find what words will appeal to them.'

Herun frowned. 'You'll find us a tough lot,' he said. 'For see you, 'tis by the favour and power of her Gods that Ys lives. Else would the sea overwhelm us.'

200

'God, the true God, He has power to save Ys,' blurted Budic.

Corentinus raised a hand. 'Belay that, lad. You mean well, but I did promise no preaching this night. Can we not just spin yarns? Or continue whatever else your pleasure is.'

'What is yours?' purred a female voice.

They glanced up. The harlot Keban had tidied herself after Herun and come back downstairs. She was pleasant to look upon, in her close-fitting gown over a buxom figure and her deliberately tousled hair. She dropped her eyelids and smiled. 'Care for a bit of fun, you?' she went on in Corentinus's direction.

He shook his head. 'Not for me, thank you.'

She looked about. 'Anybody? . . . Not yet, anyhow? . . . Well, who'll buy a girl a drink?'

'Allow me,' said Corentinus, and gestured her to sit beside him on the bench.

'Huh?' muttered from another table. 'Keban, don't you know that's the new Christian priest?'

'Mayhap I can seduce him,' she said impudently, and settled down.

Corentinus laughed. 'Or I you? We'll see. What'll you have?'

'Wine.' She stuck out her tongue at Herun. 'Despite what you say 'bout it.' To the pastor: 'I'm surprised. I truly am. I thought somebody like you would hate me.'

Again he shook his head. 'Nay,' he told her solemnly. 'I must hate what you do, but never you, poor child. Tell me, do you never weary of being a thing? Do you ever think what becomes of old whores?'

She defied him; forlornness lay underneath: 'What else have I got, unless to be a scullion in some household where the master and, and all of them'll hump me anyway?'

201

Budic was appalled. 'Why, Keban – ' he began, and stopped.

'You've been sweet,' she said to him. 'Few are.'

He withered under Corentinus's sardonic look. The pastor, though, merely declared to the woman: ''Tis never too late for God's grace, while life remains. Did you choose to accept His mercy, I would for my part undertake to find you a decent situation. In due course, my church may found a home for those who were lost aforetime.'

The outer door creaked. Boots thudded under the weight of a bear-solid man, roughly clad, who snuffed the link he had been carrying by scrubbing it against the clay and tossed it down. As he approached through the gloom, first Herun, then the soldiers and most of the mariners recognized his rocky visage. 'Maeloch!' cried one. 'What brings ye hither?'

The fisher captain spouted a laugh. 'What d'ye think? A bumper of mead, and – Ah, two girls on hand, I see. Hoy, Keban, Silis, which of ye'd fain be first?'

The former caught at the table edge before her and sat unwontedly silent, but the second, merry, asked, 'What, are you well-heeled tonight, Maeloch?'

'Aye, and horny as a narwhal,' he said, striding close to rumple her locks. 'Been outside o' town this past month, helping Kadrach the cooper.' No boats like his, and few ships, put far out to sea at this time of year. Maeloch sobered. 'And now I'm done, well, looks to me like a spell o' calm weather ahead, after the blows and high seas we've been getting. Belike there'll soon be a summons for the Ferriers. I'll enjoy myself here, for I'd better be home tomorrow night.'

Mirth had retreated as he spoke. Several men drew signs. 'Lackwits!' Maeloch said amiably. 'Why shrink ye when I bespeak yon duty? Would ye liefer the ghosts spooked about ashore, for aye?'

Since other benches were crowded, he sat down with Adminius and Herun. Opposite were Budic, Keban, and Corentinus. He peered past sputtering candles. 'But ye're the Christian priest!' he exclaimed.

'Not precisely my title,' the chorepiscopus replied. 'No matter. I've heard talk of you, if I mistake me not.' He offered his hand across the board, for a clasp in the manner of Ysans who were equals.

Maeloch ignored it, scowled, said harshly, 'Why d'ye pester honest men at their hard-won ease?'

'My son, I came not to pester, only to make acquaintance. And ever since I heard of your strange task, I've wished to talk with one among those who do it. Somehow the chance has not come.'

'Nor likely will.' Maeloch grabbed his mead from the servant and swilled deep. 'We're no puking preachers, we're plain working men, but this duty we have from our fathers, 'tis holy, and we'll not speak of it with any who share it not, let alone ye who'd mock it.'

'Oh, but I would never mock,' said Corentinus quietly. 'You have right, 'tis far too sacred a matter. I wish to understand what happens on those nights.'

'That ye may scuttle it?' fleered Maeloch. He drank more, snorted, grinned. 'Enough. I seek no fight. Keban, honey, are ye ready to frig?'

The woman looked downward. 'I don't – sudden-like, I don't feel so well,' she mumbled. 'I'm sorry, but could I just sit a while?'

Maeloch stiffened. 'Next to the priest? What's he been feeding ye?'

'Let her be,' Corentinus snapped. 'Yonder's a wanton for you.' His tone sharpened. 'Or is it unthinkable you seek the wife that I suppose you have?'

Rage flared. 'What business of yours, shavehead? I've heard ye deny the Gods of Ys, the Pact of Brennilis, in the Forum; and I've heard the sea growl in answer at the gate. No more! Get out!'

'Now, wait a bit,' Adminius urged.

Maeloch scrambled to his feet and around the table, to stand behind Corentinus and ask, 'D'ye leave on your own shanks, or do I frog march ye forth? Quick!'

Corentinus rose, stepped over the bench, looked down an inch or two into the malachite eyes. 'Are you that afraid of me?' he murmured.

Maeloch snarled and seized the right wrist of Corentinus. Instantly, the pastor jerked between thumb and forefinger and freed himself; and something happened with an ankle and a shove; and Maeloch sprawled on the floor.

Men swarmed up and around. 'No brawl, hoy, let's ha' no brawl!'

'God forbid,' said Corentinus mildly. As the fisher climbed back up: 'Maeloch, friend, I know you're awearied, overwrought, and belike I provoked you. 'Twas not my intent. I humbly beg your forgiveness. May I stand you a drink?'

What could a sailor do but accept?

A fresh beaker, drained, had him asking where a priest had learned such a trick for a tussle. 'Well, that's a bit of a story,' Corentinus said. 'Care to hear? Later I'll be happy to teach you the art, if you like.'

Men crowded around. Corentinus leaned back, laid ankle over knee, and began: ''Twas from a Sarmatian, on the south coast of the Suebian Sea, back when I was a deckhand. He was a wanderer himself, an outrunner of those Sclavonic and other tribes that're pushing in, now when the Goths and their kindred have pulled out. My ship was adventuring in hopes of getting amber at the source, 'stead of overland. First, you may know, we had to round the Cimbrian Chersonese and pass through the straits to the east. Those're wild and haughty folk there, Angli, Jutii, Dani, not really German although they claim the royal houses of the German tribes stem from them; and they have some mightily curious customs – '

Keban, too, listened. Silis sat apart; she had no interest in geography. One hand cradled her cheek, the fingernails of the other drummed the table.

2

Merowech the Frank and his grown sons had been in Condate Redonum buying slaves. They did this four times a year – a healthy young male shortly before equinox and solstice. Everybody in the city knew why; nobody dared speak about it. A few times the Roman authorities had, in private talks, offered to supply condemned criminals free. The Frankish headmen spurned it. They would give their Gods nothing but the best.

Merowech always obtained the victim, using money collected from the laeti, because the sacred grove stood on his land. It was he who speared the naked body that sprattled strangling from a rope flung over a bough. (The corpse was left for the carrion fowl. Eventually the bones were taken away and stacked on that hill where the midsummer bonfire burned.) To other leading men of the neighbourhood fell the honour of poleaxing and bleeding the animals that were also sacrificed, drinking some of the blood and sprinkling the worshippers with the rest. Afterwards the carcasses went to Merowech's cookhouse, and everybody feasted in his hall. Thus nourished, Wotan and His sky-riding war band ought to grant victory in battle.

For the vernal equinox an additional purchase was required, a young woman. While the slain kine roasted, the men took her to a newly ploughed field nearby. There Merowech swived her, followed by as many more as wished to call Fricca's blessing on their crops and their wives. She then went to work for the household whose turn it was, if she survived. Often she did not.

This day was glorious. Throughout the forest, buds had swelled and burst into leaf, blossom, a tumble of tender colours leading off towards reaches where sunlight speckled shadowiness, a whispering in breezes that were mild and laden with fragrances. The lesser birds jubilated. Overhead passed the great migrators, homeward bound.

Regardless, Merowech, Fredegond, Childeric, and Theuderich rode in helmets and ringmail, weapons at hand. Their dignity demanded it. They were not only the holders of acres broad and rich, they were garrison officers. It was on condition of the Franks providing the principal defence of the Redonian canton that the Romans had allowed them to settle there. Or so the official agreement read. Judging from what his father had told him, Merowech didn't think the Romans had had much choice, as weakened as the Empire was by its internal wars. Nowadays it seemed somewhat recovered, but the precedent had been set; and who could say how long till the next collapse?

A prudent man always went armed. If nothing else, the Franks had their own quarrels. Merowech, for instance, had a dispute over grazing rights under way with his neighbour Clothair, in which bickering half a dozen carls had got cut down. Clothair might take it into his head to waylay Merowech; success at that could be worth whatever weregild was negotiated afterwards.

Wariness did not forbid mirth, as the warriors rode along the track that twisted towards their farm. They swapped tales of what they had done in town, brags of what they would do elsewhere. When their japes turned to the woman and her expectations, they used their German-laced Latin so she would understand. She gave small response. It was as if she had shed all the tears that were in her. Numbly, hands bound, she trudged along at the end of a cord around her neck, secured to a horse. The man still grimaced to hear, but kept his mouth shut. At first he had cursed the Franks, and when they bade him be still, gibed that he had nothing to lose. A couple of judicious kicks taught him that that was mistaken.

Talk veered to politics. Merowech kept his ears open and his mind well-stocked. 'Yes,' he said, 'as nigh's I can guess, the latest news from Italy means Theodosius will indeed bring a host against Maximus. Which one'll outlive that day, the Gods will decide; but we'd best strengthen ourselves. At this coming feast, I mean to broach a thought – '

Abruptly men were on the road, ahead, behind. They numbered about ten, Gauls from the look of them, gaunt, ragged, unshorn, armed mostly with peasant's weapons, knife, wood axe, hook, sickle, sling, just a couple of spears and swords in grimy hands. The exception was a fork-bearded, scar-cheeked young fellow who must be their chief. He bore no marks of starvation or disease, but moved like a cat; though travel-worn, his garb of green had been cut from excellent stuff; a helmet covered his head, a metal-reinforced leather corselet his body; in his grasp were buckler and javelin, across his shoulders a scabbarded blade.

'Halt!' he cried cheerily. 'Get down off those horses. Pay your toll and you go unharmed.'

'What's this?' Merowech bawled. 'Who in Frost Hell are you?'

'The Bacaudae, the Valiant.'

207

'No, none of them infest these parts.'

'We do now. Dismount.'

'Donar's whang, he blunders in that!' Merowech growled to his sons in their native language. He had heard about modern cataphracts, but those were afar in the South and East; his kind were fighters afoot. 'Snatch your weapons while you jump down, and let fly. I get to cast at him. Then form a shield-burg with me, and we'll go reap them.'

In the same motion that brought him to the ground, he released the francisca hung at his saddlebow and hurled it. The dreaded throwing-axe, which flew ahead of every Frankish charge, should have cloven the young Gaul at the throat. But he was alert for it, dodged, launched his spear – and Merowech's round shield had a dragging shaft in it that he could not dislodge.

From boughs and from behind boles on either side, arrows whistled. Childeric howled and sank to his knees, a shaft through his left calf. 'Hold, hold!' shouted the Bacauda headman. 'No more shooting yet!' He glided nearer to Merowech, his own sword free to meet the Frank's iron. 'You're neatly ambushed, dad,' he laughed. 'Admit it, throw down your arms, and you needn't get hurt worse.'

Merowech bristled. 'Honour – '

'Oh, stop quacking. What use will you be anybody but the crows if you make us wipe you out? We can do it quite handily, you know. But we want you to carry a message for us.'

'I fear he's right, father,' Fredegond muttered. 'I'm learning his face. We'll get revenge later.'

Merowech nodded. 'You do have us trapped,' he forced from a throat that felt as if noosed. 'What do you want?'

'To start with, drop your weapons,' said the Gaul. 'Then listen to me, and pass on what I tell you.'

The Franks made themselves surrender. Horrible humiliations followed. The Bacaudae did them no injury. Rather, they removed the arrow from Childeric and bound up his wound. However, they took from them their arms, armour, horses, money, slaves, everything but undergarments – even shoes, because several of the brigands had only crude footgear.

The man and the woman who had been destined for sacrifice wept, she too, in the embraces of their rescuers. 'There, now, there, now,' said the leader, who called himself Rufinus, 'you're safe, you're free, you'll come along with us to a wonderful city and I'm sure its King will make good places for you.'

'What King is he?' asked Merowech.

'You've no need to hear that,' Rufinus answered. 'But listen to me. I went on a mission to such of my old comrades as I could find in our old haunts. They followed me back. I chose you to catch because of knowing what errand you'd be on. Your Gods gave you no help, though we were spoiling Their sacrifice. Think about that, Frank. Become a little more respectful of civilization.'

'You say that, you, a highwayman?'

'We're none like that,' Rufinus said sternly. 'We're honest folk who want nothing more than to come back under law, a law that is just.

'Listen well. There are going to be more like us in the woods and on the heaths roundabout. In time they'll find wives and beget children. By then they won't be hungry ragamuffins, but well outfitted and dangerous to run afoul of.

'Their first equipment they'll get from . . . my master. Food? The woods have plenty of game, as shrunk as the population is. Whatever else they need, they'll trade for, or pay for out of some very reasonable tolls they'll levy.

They'll harm nobody unless they're attacked, but if they are, they'll punish it hard. Do you hear me?'

'You mean outlaws intend to settle our lands?' Merowech choked on his indignation.

Rufinus laughed. 'Not quite outlaws. They'll earn their keep. They'll keep down the real robbers. In case of invasion, they'll be scouts, and they'll harass the barbarians while the cities raise troops, which they'll guide. In a while, I think, they'll be ready to make you Franks settle for just giving animals to your Gods. That'll cost you a great deal less!

'Tell your people at their gatherings. I don't suppose they'll be overjoyed. However, my word may start some of them thinking. We don't really want to teach you the lesson with fire and steel. We've got better things to do.'

Merowech stared a long while before he said, 'This is no Roman thing. Who's behind it?'

'I can't name him yet,' Rufinus replied. 'But I will say he's the grandest lord any man could dream of having.'

3

On the south side of Ys, between the city wall and the bluffs rising to Cape Rach, was a small crescent of beach. To the east the land mass butted against Aurochs Gate. Thus enclosed on three sides, the strand was often sunless and chilly. An incoming tide could make it dangerous, and the steeps were also a menace to the children whom they tempted to climb. Hence the place was not much used.

Occasionally, on sunny afternoons with ebbing water, Vindilis and Innilis took Dahut there. The girl loved it and was forever begging to go, no matter how raw the weather. She had discovered her chances were best when one of these two Mamas had her in charge. That woman would send for the other one, and the three would walk between those towers called the Brothers, and turn off Pharos Way on to the trail that went precariously down. Thereafter Dahut could do whatever she liked, within reason. Sometimes she wheedled her guardians into allowing what might seem unwise, but they had learned how sure-footed she was, and how strong a swimmer. Frequently, though, she would keep motionless for an hour or more, listening to a shell or the surf or the wind, staring out over the deeps where seals and dolphins played, gulls and cormorants winged, ships and great whales passed by.

On this day there was a slight haze, and enough breeze eddied past the headland to make the air nip. It smelled of salt, kelp, clean decay, things less readily knowable. Vindilis and Innilis settled themselves on a driftwood log. In front of them the sand reached coarse, tawny-dark, to a wet edge that was almost black. Beyond glimmered and surged the water, and the wall of Ys curved away, ruddy-hued, dizzyingly high up to the frieze of mythic figures and the battlements. On the other side the promontory bulked westward. Stones and boulders lay jumbled on its flanks, below scaurs where grass clustered silvery. Farther on, sight of land ended and the sea heaved grey-green, bursting white over the reefs. Birds skimmed about, creaking, or walked on the grit, to flap off when Dahut scampered their way.

The Queens had brought a large blanket as well as a basket of refreshments. No servant had carried these; they would not miss an opportunity to be by themselves. Vindilis's aquiline features softened as she brought the cover around them both. Once they sat wrapped in it, arms went about waists. Innilis sighed, almost happily, and laid her head against the taller woman's shoulder.

'How dear a moment this is,' she murmured after a while.

Vindilis nodded. 'All too uncommon.'

'When . . . we go back up . . . and you take the child to your house . . . shall I come along? Spend the night?'

Pain replied: 'Nay, that would be too risky.'

'Why? Grallon won't be there, in spite of her. 'Tis Guilvilis's night, if he beds with any of us.'

'I know. Yet – Dahut sleeps lightly at this stage of her life. Two days ago, with Forsquilis, she was wandering around thrice in the night. Maldunilis told me earlier, giggling, how when father and daughter were both with her, Dahut came in as they were making love.'

Innilis flushed. 'Really? What did G-Grallon do?'

'Oh, he scolded her mildly, shooed her out, and continued. She can do no wrong in his sight.' Vindilis scowled. 'You and I – She'd surely babble to him. Whether or not she saw, she has sharp ears and an uncannily quick little mind.'

Innilis drooped. 'I see. We must go back to stealing our times like chicken thieves.'

'The Gallicenae require their secrets kept from the King, now more than ever.' Vindilis glanced at the girl. She was piling sand together near the waves. Vindilis brushed lips across Innilis's cheek. Under the blanket, her free hand cupped a breast. 'We will have our times,' she promised, 'and do not think of them as stolen. They are our right. Blame not yonder child. Through her, we may win a happier morrow for ourselves.'

'What? How?'

'I know not. But clear it always was, Dahut has been born fateful; and the Gods have yet to claim Their due from Grallon.'

212

'Nay, no harm to him, please,' Innilis begged of the wind.

'I too hope 'twill be mere chastisement. We must wait and see. But, dearest, if They remain well pleased with us twain, and if Dahut is she who shall make a new Pact with the Gods – ' Vindilis held Innilis close.

A seal splashed and slithered on to a rock not far off the beach. Dahut saw, sprang to her feet, strained peering into sunlight and sea-blink. The gown fluttered about her taut slenderness. She called, a wordless quaver. The seal rested quiet. Dahut's head drooped. She turned about and walked towards the women.

Vindilis released Innilis, who reached out from under the blanket and inquired, 'Darling, what's wrong?'

'I thought 'twas *my* seal.' Dahut stopped, stared downward, dug a toe in the sand, clenched fists. ''Twasn't. Just an or'nary ol' bull.'

Innilis smiled and, seeking to humour her, asked, 'How can you be sure of that?'

Dahut looked up. Under the wild blond locks, her eyes were the hue of lapis lazuli, and as steady. 'I know. She taught me.'

'Indeed?' said Vindilis. 'I've heard you make mention, and heard from others – But what is this seal you call yours?'

'She loves me,' Dahut said. 'Better'n anybody, 'cep' maybe father.'

'Seals are sacred to both Lir and Belisama,' Vindilis said mutedly. 'I can well believe certain among them have . . . powers.'

Dahut's mood brightened. 'Can I get to be a seal? Like her?'

Innilis traced a sign against misfortune. Vindilis said, 'Nobody knows. There are stories that – that sometimes good people come back as seals after they die, because

213

the Goddess hears their plea at the Ferrying to Sena. That's so they can wait for those they loved and left behind. But nobody knows.'

'I wouldn' be 'fraid to,' Dahut declared.

'Peace,' counselled Innilis. 'Beware of overprideful-ness. There are stories that bad people come back too, when the Gods are very angry with them – but as sharks, or things still worse.'

Dahut suppressed a retort, flung her head high, and stood straight.

'I think,' said Vindilis, 'when we go home this evening, I should teach you a new prayer. "*Mother of Death, come softly, I beseech.*" You may, after all, not be too young for learning such things.' She unbent. 'Afterwards I'll tell you about a vestal long ago, who by the favour of Belisama had wonderful adventures.'

Likewise seeking to please the girl, Innilis said, 'That's a splendid fort you're making there.'

Dahut nodded. She was not shy about accepting praise. ''Tis Ys,' she answered. 'I'm making Ys.'

And she did, remarkably well, before she watched the tide come in and wash it away.

4

That year huge rainstorms arrived in succession, with lightning and hail. Harvests throughout western Armorica were meagre, or failed altogether. There were those who muttered that Taranis was avenging the wrong He had suffered in the Wood. They were not many, though. King Grallon had long since established royal granaries and filled them with the surplus of good seasons, bought from the Osismii. Now the folk for whom his agents provided

generally blessed his name. Rejoicing followed his procla-
mation that as soon as possible, he would commission
ships to go fetch more from Britannia and Aquitania. As
trade revived – in considerable part because of his measures against bandits and pirates – wealth had flowed into
Ys until now the city could readily afford whatever it
needed to see it through the next twelvemonth. Thus did
disaster not undermine Grallon's authority, but rather
strengthened it.

Corentinus therefore expressed surprise when Budic
came to his church with word that the King had urgent
want of his presence. He said nothing further, threw a
hooded cloak over his coarse dark robe, and followed the
soldier out. The midday was murky, rain driven thick and
chill before a shrieking wind. It scourged faces, forced
itself through garments, coursed down ribs and legs,
swirled in the streets higher than shoesoles. Often heaven
flared, and thunder followed like the wheels of a monstrous war chariot. The sea raged at the gate which the
King had locked.

At the palace, the majordomo took the newcomer's
cloak and offered him a towel and change of clothes. 'I
thank you, but nay,' Corentinus replied. 'Let my wet
tracks be a sign to you that here also is no hiding from
God. Lead me to your master.'

Gratillonius sat in the upstairs room he favoured for
private conferences. Cups, jugs of wine and water, a lamp
stood on the table before him. Next to them lay a papyrus
roll. Neither the flame nor the greenish-glassed windows
much relieved a dimness in which pastoral frescos became
an irony, nor did a brazier give much warmth. Beneath
his everyday outfit of tunic and trousers, Gratillonius
huddled in a cape; and that was strange, for cold did not
usually trouble him. He had left off any ornamentation.
When he looked up at Corentinus's entry, the chorepis-

copus saw the strong-boned countenance drawn into haggardness.

'Shut the door,' Gratillonius rasped in Latin. 'Be seated.'

Corentinus obeyed. Gratillonius leaned over the table between them, stabbed a forefinger on to the document, and said in the same tone, 'Magnus Maximus is dead.'

'What?' Briefly, Corentinus registered shock. He crossed himself, bowed his head, whispered a prayer. When he again met the other man's gaze, his own was firm. 'You've just had word?'

Gratillonius jerked a nod. 'From the Duke. It happened well over a month ago, but couriers to bear the news were few.'

'Theodosius overthrew Maximus, then? He died in battle?'

'No. Theodosius defeated him decisively near Aquileia. I think the Gothic cavalry made the difference. Maximus surrendered and renounced his claim to the throne. That should have been the end, hey? Exile somewhere, to an island, likeliest. Let the man who saved Britannia close his days in peace and honour. But no, soon afterwards Maximus and his young son Victor were killed. This letter to me isn't clear as to whether it was beheading at the express order of Theodosius, or murder by stealth.' A fist smote the table. The lampflame quivered. 'Whichever, we know by whose will they died!'

'God rest their souls,' Corentinus said. 'And yet He is just, is He not? Maximus's rival Gratianus perished miserably too – and Priscillianus, and how many more? – because of that man's ambition.'

'I'd grudges of my own against him. But he was my old commandant!' Gratillonius shouted. 'He held the Wall for Rome! He should not have died like that!'

He seized the wine jug and sloshed full a cup. Without

216

adding water, he swallowed. 'Pour for yourself, Corentinus,' he said. 'Drink with me to the memory of Magnus Maximus.'

'Is this why you sent for me?'

'N-no. Not really. Though I do want, need, to talk with you, and I expect I'll get drunk, and that's nothing a man should do alone.'

Corentinus took a small measure of wine, diluted it well, and sipped. 'May I offer a Mass for the repose of those souls?'

'Do. I meant to ask it of you. I thought of a funerary rite before Mithras, but – but Maximus wouldn't have liked that, would he? I'll pay what it costs to have you give my commandant a Christian farewell.'

Wind keened, rain runnelled down the glass.

'Am I the first you have told about this?' asked Corentinus.

Again Gratillonius nodded stiffly. 'I've got to convene the Suffetes and break the news. But first I'd better have a plan to lay before them. Else they'll debate and squabble and bargain, while matters drift. That kind of delay could prove fatal.'

'I am no politician or soldier, my son. I couldn't advise you.'

'Oh, you can. You've been around in the Empire more than I have. You've got the ear of Bishop Martinus, who's more powerful than he pretends, even to himself. Theodosius has re-installed Valentinianus, his brother-in-law, as Augustus of the West, but Theodosius is staying on for a while in Italy, and you know very well who's really going to rule. From what I hear, he's a zealous Catholic. You can better guess than I how he'll use the Church, and it him.'

Corentinus frowned. 'Watch your tongue.' He paused.

'What do you fear, exactly? Won't everyone benefit from peace and a strong Imperium?'

'Once I'd have supposed so,' Gratillonius answered starkly, 'but I've learned otherwise. And . . . I belong here now, I belong to Ys. Rome is still my Mother, but Ys is my Wife.'

Within the short beard, Corentinus's lips quirked the least bit. Sobering, he lingered over a fresh taste of his wine before he said: 'I see. Maximus appointed you prefect. There will doubtless be a pretty deep-going purge of his officials.'

Gratillonius drained his cup and refilled it. 'I'm not frightened for myself. I honestly think I'm not. But if I'm ordered back and – and obey, what then? Who'll succeed me? What'll he do?'

'Do you fear Roman occupation, the pagan temples destroyed and rites forbidden, Ys rising in revolt and Rome laying it waste as Rome long ago did to Jerusalem?'

Gratillonius shivered. 'You've said it.'

Corentinus regarded him closely. 'Then I'll also say that this strikes me as being a terrible evil. They're not simple rustics in Ys, the kind whose sanctuaries I helped Martinus overthrow. There it was enough to show how the old Gods were powerless to stop us. They'd never been very large in the lives of the people. A spring, a hill, any sacred site meant more; and it can as well be under the tutelage of a Christian saint. The Gods of Ys will not fade away like that. Before yielding up Their worshippers, They would bring Ys itself down in ruin.'

'You understand,' Gratillonius breathed.

'My holy duty is to win your people to the true Faith. My single hope of doing so without bringing on catastrophe is by persuasion, patience, year after slow year. Not to attack the Gods, but to sap Them. If only you would unlock your heart – But at least, under you, Ys

218

flourishes, open to newness as it has not been in centuries; and your protection is impartial. We need you as our King.'

'If you'd write to Martinus – '

'I'll do that, and more. He, in his turn, can convince the bishops throughout Lugdunensis that Ys should be spared. The Imperium ought to heed them. Besides, in worldly terms, better a loyal foederate, a keystone of defence and a cauldron of trade, than wreckage.'

Gratillonius eased somewhat, achieved a smile, said: 'Thank you. The Duke is on my side already. I don't think they'll dismiss him; he goes back to before Maximus. If you can make the Church our ally as well – ' Impulsively: 'Listen, Corentinus. You know the Ysan charities are mostly run by the Gallicenae. I know your mission hasn't much to spend. Help me, and I'll endow your good works, generously.'

'The thought does you credit,' replied the pastor with care, 'but the deed could endanger you. Your magnates would see it as yet another defiance of the Gods.'

'What I lay out of my privy purse is no concern of theirs, or of Theirs.'

'M-m, you realize that such of the poor and unfortunate as you enable us to aid – they will be grateful more to us than you, and this will incline them towards Christ.'

Gratillonius laughed and drank. 'Manly of you to warn me, but of course I knew it. No harm done. Why should I bar anybody from forsaking the Gods of Ys?'

Corentinus studied him. 'Wouldn't you want them to come to your Mithras?'

Gratillonius shrugged. On the heels of his merriment trod pain: 'Few ever would. His is no longer a conquering army. We hold the wall for Him while we can, but the foe has marched around it.'

He upended his cup and filled it anew. 'The Wall!' he shouted. 'We stood on the Wall under Maximus. My buddies – How many went south with him? What's going to become of them? Those are men of *mine*. I barracked with them, and pounded the roads and dug the trenches and fought the raiders and diced and caroused with them, and after I'd made centurion I led them, punished them when they needed it, heard out their troubles when they needed that – my Second Augusta and – and there were others with us on the Wall that year, Corentinus. Like Drusus of the Sixth; we saved each other's lives, d'you hear? So they fought for our old Duke, and lost, and what's that Emperor who killed Maximus and Victor out of hand, what's he going to do about them?'

'You are getting drunk in a hurry,' Corentinus observed in the sailor's lingo he used when he wanted to.

'I don't expect Theodosius can massacre them,' Gratillonius went on. 'Too many. But what, then? Think he'll send them back to their bases in Britannia, Gallia, wherever? I think not. He'll be afraid of them, and want to make an example, too. He'll discharge them, maybe. And what are they supposed to do then? They'll lose their veterans' benefits. Are they supposed to starve? Become serfs? Join the Bacaudae? What?'

'A knotty question, in truth,' Corentinus agreed. 'Christ bade us forgive our enemies, and I should hope Theodosius will, if only for his own soul's sake. But those men *were* mutineers, in a sense, and they'd too likely be an unsettling element in the army. You feel Maximus should simply have been exiled. But how can thousands be?'

Gratillonius straightened. Wine splashed from his cup as he crashed it to the table. 'Here!' he exclaimed. 'By the Bull, you've hit on it! Armorica's half empty. What we need most is more people, to make their homes and stand guard over them. And there we've got those fighting men, and here we've got a peninsula at the far end of the

Empire where they couldn't possibly be any threat to our overlord.'

Excitement seized Corentinus likewise. 'Write to the Duke and the governor at once,' he said. 'Urge them to propose it to the Emperors. Offer the influence, experience, help of Ys in getting settlement started. God willing, you'll have a glad acceptance.'

'I'll write tomorrow,' Gratillonius roared, 'and afterwards tell the Council. Now let's drink and sing songs and remember Maximus and all old comrades.'

Corentinus smiled – wistfully? 'I may not do that myself. But I'll keep you company if you like.'

They had been at it for a while, as the day darkened further, when a knock on the door brought Gratillonius there. He opened it and stood aside, still steady on his feet though the flush of wine was on his cheeks and the odour of it on his breath.

Bodilis entered. Her hair hung as wet as her garments. The hands with which she took his were cold.

'I thought you should hear this from me, beloved,' she said, oblivious to anybody else. 'Word reached me, I went to see, and, and I think Quinipilis is dying.'

X

1

The agony that speared through breast and left arm, the stranglehold that closed on a heart flying wild, gave way to quietness. She slept a great deal, though lightly, often rousing from dreams. Her pulse fluttered weak, like a wounded bird, and she had no strength. Nonetheless she whispered her commands that she be helped out of bed for bathing and necessities. Such times left her exhausted for hours, but her head remained always clear. Besides the wedded couple who were her only servants, the other Gallicenae insisted on abiding in her house, each a day and night in turn. They allowed no more than very brief visits by the many who came, nor did they themselves tax her with much talk. Often, though, they read aloud to her from books she loved.

Rainstorms gave way to fog. As summer waned, Ys lay in a chill dankness and a white blindness that seemed to go on without end. Quinipilis could not get warm, even when the hypocaust had made the floor too hot for bare feet. The Sisters kept her tucked in fleece blankets and rubbed her hands and feet – carefully, as deformed and tender as those had become. They brought soup and upheld her maned skull while spooning it into her.

Innilis had musicians on call, for such times as harp, flute, song might briefly cheer. Bodilis translated some lyrics of Sappho into Ysan, because Quinipilis had admired those she already knew. Whenever she rallied a little, however, the dowager was apt to ask for something more vigorous, renditions from the Greek, original in Latin or Ysan: the clangour of Homer and Vergilius, sternness of Aeschylus and Euripides, comedy of Philemon and Plautus, or (wickedly grinning) the bawdiest bits from Aristophanes and Catullus, as well as Utican the Wanderer and Witch-Hanai of this city. A couple of times she herself recited snatches of Gallic or Saxon.

That was near the beginning of her invalidity. Soon she slipped deeper down, and mostly lay with her thoughts and memories.

Then on the ninth morning she told Fennalis, who had the watch: 'Bring my Sisters hither.'

'Nay, you'd wear yourself out. I can scarce hear your voice, though you've had a night's rest. Take care so you can get well.'

Wrinkles formed a hideous frown. Somehow the words loudened enough. 'Stop that. I am not in my dotage, thank you. I *am* outworn, for which there is no healing.' The scowl turned into laughter lines. 'I've somewhat to convey to the lot of you – at once, ere the wheels altogether fall off the old oxcart. Prepare me your strongest strengthening draught.'

'That could easily kill you.'

'Another day or two would do that anyhow, with naught to show for it.' Quinipilis must halt a while to breathe. Her fingers plucked at the covers. 'Fennalis, I conjure you . . . I conjure all of you . . . by Our Lady of Passage.'

The short grey woman wrestled with herself a moment before she nodded, bit her lip to hold it still, and scuttled out.

Presently there were seven crowded at the bedside. Guilvilis was absent, having the Vigil on Sena. Forsquilis, who was this day's presiding high priestess, had come directly from the Temple of Belisama in her blue gown and white headdress. Innilis clutched the hand of Vindilis, like a child her mother's. Maldunilis wept, striving to hold it quiet and not blubber. Lanarvilis kept stoic. Bodilis kissed the withered lips and stood aside. Fennalis plumped pillows, got Quinipilis half sitting up amidst them, fetched the decoction of foxglove, willow bark, and herbs more curious, held the cup while it went its way, took a post hard by.

Quinipilis's breath quickened and grew noisy. That was almost the single sound. Fog made windowpanes featureless. Within, candles kept shadows at bay, though they filled every corner. A few things were clear to see – a vase of aster and fern from the woods, shelved toys that had been her daughters' when they were small, the hanging sword of King Wulfgar who was her first man, in a niche with a taper at its feet a statuette of Belisama as a young matron holding Her infant. Air lay overheated and sullen.

A hint of blood mounted through the waxiness on Quinipilis. Her glance brightened and steadied. When she spoke, it was clearly: 'Welcome. Thank you for coming.'

'How could we not come, mother, mother to us all?' replied Vindilis.

'This is our goodbye, of course.' Quinipilis's voice was matter-of-fact. She raised a palm against the protest she saw in some of their faces. 'Nay, we've scant time left. Let's spill none in foolishness. For myself, I'm more than ready to go to my rest. But first I've a thing to deal with – or, rather, leave to you.'

'Hush,' Forsquilis bade the Sisters. 'The Spirit is upon her.'

Quinipilis shook her head and coughed out a chuckle. 'I misbelieve that, my dear. 'Tis no more than the same vixen that ever made her den in me.' She grew serious. 'Yet lying here quietly, so quietly, feeling time slip away

224

– that gives one to think, in between the visits of the living and the dead.'

The high-crowned head nodded. 'You've wondered whom the Gods will choose to reign after you, and why.'

Quinipilis sighed. 'Aye. I told you I am content to go. But I would have been earlier. Or I could have stayed longer, equally content to watch the seasons pass and the children grow. Is it chance that I must depart just now? I fear very much the Gods are not done with our King.'

'Nay!' broke from Bodilis. She slammed control down on herself. 'If They are still angry because of – that unfulfilled sacrifice and – other matters – why have They not struck him already?'

Quinipilis closed her eyes. The power of the medication was flagging. 'You can guess?'

'Mayhap I can,' Lanarvilis said slowly. 'This year agone has been the most dangerous for Ys since the year he came. The Empire has been in upheaval while the barbarians snuffed blood and grew hungry. Then the Imperial peace returned, but the victors would fain destroy everything that Ys has ever been. Who could cope save Gratillonius? Even his man Rufinus who should have died in the Wood, Rufinus has proved an instrument for him to begin shoring up our bulwarks. Therefore the Gods have stayed Their hands.'

'Until now,' whispered Forsquilis.

Quinipilis reopened her eyes. 'So have I thought,' she told them. 'Also this have I thought, that They cannot yet spare him, but They will seek to humble him; and in that They will fail, but They can wound him terribly. He's a good man, under his iron – '

'He came to me yesterday, straight from having been with you,' said Bodilis, 'and that whole eventide he was swallowing tears.'

225

'Stand by him, Sisters,' Quinipilis pleaded. 'Whatever happens, never forsake him.'

'We can ill do that, like it or not,' said Vindilis.

'W-w-we did bring him!' blurted Maldunilis. 'We made him King. Could we have a better one? Nay!'

Fennalis began to reply but thought better of it.

'Help him,' Quinipilis bade them. 'Promise me. Give me your oaths.'

'By the Three I swear,' said Bodilis immediately.

Vindilis pinched lips together before she lifted her arms and exclaimed, 'Hold! Hard is this to say, but bethink you, we cannot foreknow – '

Quinipilis gasped. She slumped into the pillows. Her eyes rolled back. Her breath raced in and out like riptides between reefs, then died away to nearly nothing, then raced, then died. Froth bubbled around her lips.

'Goddess, nay!' screamed Fennalis. She flung herself down on the bed. Her fingers sought to clear the foam away, let air get through. 'Quinipilis, darling Quinipilis, are you there, can you hear me?' Only the rattling and whistling answered.

Soon they ended. Fennalis rose. Having signed herself, she beckoned to Vindilis, the blood daughter, who trod forward to fold the hands, bind up the jaw, close the eyes.

2

Lir's fog did not reach far inland. At the Nymphaeum, the end of the rains had brought a last upwelling of warmth and lightfulness. The forest that decked the heights glowed a molten green, a thousand hues which a breeze made ripple and weave. Likewise did the lawn in the hollow drink the sunshine that spilled on it from

226

among a few swan's-wing clouds, and give it back to heaven. Blooms had mostly died, but leaves in flowerbeds and hedgerows lived yet. Brooklets glittered and chimed on their way to the glimmery pond. In the shadow of the linden above the sacred spring, the image of the Mother smiled mysterious.

Forth at noontide from the colonnade of the building came certain vestals, as was appointed for this phase of the moon nearest autumnal equinox. Their garments were as white as the walls and pillars. Their hair flowed loose and their feet danced nimble, for they were young girls, less than three years into their service – descendants of Queens in Ys unto the third generation, whereafter the Goddess released a lineage. More fully clad, a virgin near the end of her term led them, as did an ageing woman who had returned to the Temple and become a minor priestess when she was widowed.

Blue sheened on peacocks; three spread their tails, like a salute of banners. The grown maiden put syrinx to lips and sounded the tune, while the girls joined hands and skipped the measure, on their way to do reverence before the eidolon. Their voices rose clear as the pipe-notes.

'Belisama, all-sustaining,
Lady of the golden year,
Now that summertime is waning,
Guard this world You hold so dear.
Soon the leaves must fall to cover
Earth grown weary of the sun.
Bring our lord, our King, our lover
Home to us when sleep is done!'

Suddenly one of them screamed.

The music stopped, the dance jarred to a halt. 'What is it?' cried the maiden. 'Come here, sweetling.' She held out her arms.

227

The girl touched her bosom, 'It, it burned,' she half sobbed. 'For a heartbeat, it burned.' Her eyes widened. Her face went chalky. 'I'm well again. I am.'

The old woman approached her through the silent stares. 'We must look at this.' She took the small hand. 'Fear naught. We love you.'

The maiden mustered courage. 'We have our rite to finish,' she told the rest. 'Follow me onward. Sing your song. Remember, we are children of the Goddess.'

The procession resumed, raggedly. Meanwhile the priestess hastened towards the Nymphaeum. Semuramat, daughter of Queen Bodilis by King Hoel, stumbled at her side.

3

The fog lifted. After sunset, a nearly full moon dazzled away from itself the stars that otherwise crowded heaven. So wild was Gratillonius that at length Bodilis suggested they leave her house. 'Space, air, a wholesome tiredness of the body, and then you may perhaps win to sleep for a while, my poor beloved.' They dressed warmly and went forth.

Silence enwrapped them, save for their footfalls on frosty paving and for the sounds of the sea, rising as they drew nearer. He had ended the ravings and curses and desperate schemes he brought her after the word reached him. Their breaths smoked wan, like the utterances of ghosts. Walls shadowed streets from the moon but not from starshine. Man and woman found their way readily down the lanes that twisted from Elven Gardens, and thence along broad Lir Way, over the deserted Forum, south on Taranis Way to Goose Fair plaza, across it and the pomoerium to a staircase and thus up on to the city wall. Guards at the Raven Tower challenged them; armour shimmered icy in the moonbeams from beyond eastern hills. Recognizing who came, the marines saluted and let them by. Under the high helmets, awe was on faces.

Gratillonius and his Queen walked onward along the battlements, past the war engines that slumbered in their housings, almost to the sea gate. There they stood looking outward.

The moon had cleared the towertops. Above the clustered roofs of Ys, they seemed spires of glass, ready to shatter at the least shaking from the sea, upraised out of a stonefield already sunken. Tonight there was no turbulence. The waters swelled and broke and swelled anew, fluid obsidian over which ran mercury. *Hush*, they murmured, *hush-hush-hush*. So clear was the air that Gratillonius saw a spark out yonder that must be light in the building on Sena, where Forsquilis of the Gallicenae held communion with the Gods.

Bodilis took his arm. 'Let us take comfort from such great beauty,' she said low.

'Beneath it lies terror,' he answered.

'Great beauty is always terrible. Life is.'

'Why? What have we done – no, not we, you and little Semuramat – that this has happened?' Gratillonius shook his head. 'Oh, I know. You, as close as you were to me, must be hit when They struck. What worse loss than you could I suffer?'

'Dahut,' she said.

He snapped after air.

'And you have not lost me,' she went on. 'Stop treading the same ground. You've pounded it barren. Let me tell you for the twentieth – or fiftieth or hundredth, but the last time – I remain your Queen Bodilis.'

'Whom I may never again touch in love.'

'That is your choice.'

'My choice?' His gaze sought the Raven Tower, black against the sky. Beyond hulked Cape Rach, and at its end guttered the pharos candle. 'My faith. Mother and daughter – Mithras forbids. If I denied Fennalis on that account, how can I do otherwise with you?'

'It would be . . . bad politics.'

'No politics tonight, no damned politics! This is of the spirit, as well you should know.'

She winced in the colourless light: she, both daughter and granddaughter of Wulfgar. It was not that her mother had sinned with her father. There could be no incest when the Gods decreed the wedding. It was that he, who could not help himself once Their will was upon him, had afterwards lost courage to live, and presently lay dead at the feet of Gaetulius.

Gratillonius saw the hurt he had given, caught Bodilis to his breast, and stammered, 'I'm sorry, I didn't mean that, shouldn't have spoken so to you – you, half-sister of Dahilis – ' through King Hoel: Dahilis, who perished in giving birth to Dahut.

Bodilis stroked his hair, stepped back, and smiled at him. 'I understand. These are roads that double back and back on themselves, aren't they? Well, of course I'll long for you, but we'll always stay friends, allies; no God commands our hearts.'

'Unless I refuse this marriage. The girl *is* too young. Oh, she's passed her Rite of Welcome; but so short a time ago, she so small yet and – and frightened.'

'You will be kind to her. You've been like the father she never really knew.'

Now he flinched. Casting weakness aside, he said, more calmly than he had said it before, 'Best for her, too, if I balk.'

'You would rip Ys apart. This is the holiest rite we were ever given, the renewal of the world.'

'I meant, well, carry out the service, but not c-c-consummate the marriage.'

Bodilis shook her head. 'No, you can't escape that either.'

'I did with Quinipilis and Fennalis.'

'They were past childbearing age.'

'Is Semuramat at it?'

'She will be. And . . . the bloodied sheet is given the Goddess next morning. No, Gratillonius, dear bewildered man. Unless you'd flee at once, abandon us forever, you must marry Tambilis tomorrow.'

He battered a fist against a merlon. That was the name Semuramat had chosen, to honour her grandmother who died in the horrible reign of Colconor. Such was traditional. Yet the older Tambilis had been the mother of both Bodilis and Dahilis.

'At least this time you've said rationally the things you shouted in fragments at the house,' added the Queen. She hesitated, glanced out across Ocean, added low, 'We do have tonight left us, you and I.'

A while he stood, hunched over. Moonlight caught a few tears. Finally he shook his head. 'No. Your advice is right, hard but right. Then I dare not – '

'You are doubtless wise,' she sighed.

He started back. 'Go home, Bodilis,' he said. 'Rest yourself as well as you can. Your daughter will need you very much tomorrow.'

She followed. 'What of you?' she asked at his back.

He looked straight ahead. 'I'll commandeer a lamp at the tower, and go down into the Mithraeum, and be with my own God.'

231

4

There was the ceremony in the Temple of Belisama, where vestals sang and the Eight stood veiled together with her who would be the Ninth, flanking the altar behind which lifted images of Maiden, Mother, and Hag. The bride came to the groom, they knelt under the prayers and hymns, rose again when bidden; he lifted her veil while the Sisters raised theirs. 'Gratillonius, King of Ys, in homage to the Goddess Who dwells in her, and in honour to the womanhood that is hers, receive your Queen Tambilis – ' Fennalis, the senior, brought the consecrated wine for them to share.

Public coronation and festivity waited until Quinipilis should have had her sea burial. This day the Gallicenae merely accompanied the King to his palace, where a simple meal was set forth. They talked sparingly, Tambilis not at all. What conversation did take place was mostly reminiscence of the departed.

Afterwards, one by one, each of the women kissed the girl and, in their differing ways and words, made her welcome, wished her well, promised her their help and love. By tacit agreement, Bodilis came last. The two clung together a short spell. Gratillonius stood aside, alone.

The guests and their attendants bade him goodnight and left. Dusk was blue beyond the doorway. The household staff were now free to come forth and, through the majordomo, request the benediction of the new Queen. 'Blessing on you, blessing on you.' Her voice was as thin as the hand with which she touched their heads where they knelt.

Thereafter they escorted the bridal pair to the royal

bedchamber. They had cleaned everything that was in it, arrayed green boughs and, in lieu of flowers at this season, clusters of berries. Candles burned in abundance. The broad bedstead carried a richness of furs and embroideries. A table inlaid with nacre held wine, water, fruits, confections. Incense sweetened the air. Frescos on walls, paintings on shutters, mosaic on floor, gave images of woodland, meadow, lake, sea, cloudscape; beasts real and mythic pranced, swam, flew; youths and maidens were joyful together. Outside, in silence, the stars were coming forth.

The door closed.

Gratillonius turned from it, towards his wife. She stood with arms straight down, fists clenched, staring before her. It came to him that in the chaos of his heart he had not yet really looked at her. And earlier she had been only Semuramat, daughter of Bodilis, stepdaughter to him, a bright and blithe child with whom he enjoyed passing time whenever he was able. She had, indeed, been like a true older sister to Dahut, more and more so as she blossomed towards womanhood.

At thirteen years of age, she reached not quite to his throat, and much of that height was leg. The rest of her seemed to be mainly eyes, underneath formally dressed hair which had changed from the gold of childhood to a light brown. They were the deep blue of her mother's, those eyes, or of Dahilis's or Dahut's. Her features were delicate, lips always slightly parted over teeth. Because she was often outdoors, summer had tinged her skin and dusted freckles across the tip-tilted nose. Bridal gown and jewelled pectoral hung heavy from her shoulders.

Remembering his first night with Guilvilis, he willed resolution upon himself. There was that which must be done, and shilly-shallying about it would be no kindness.

233

He went to her and smiled, and took her hands. They lay cold in his. 'Well, dear,' he said, 'here we are.'

She remained mute. Releasing her left hand, he brought his right under her chin and raised it until their gazes must meet. She blinked and breathed hard. 'Be at ease,' he said. 'You know your old friend. He hasn't changed. I wanted this not myself.' Louder than intended: 'O Mithras, nay!' Softly again: 'We've had a duty laid on us. We'll carry it out like good soldiers, you and I, eh?'

She nodded. It caused his hand, yielding, to slide down her neck. How frail it was, how silken the skin. A blue pulse throbbed.

'Come,' he said, 'let's be seated, let's drink to a happier morrow.' Let her become warmed, at rest, wine-dazed.

She ran tongue over lips. 'My lord is, is gracious,' she whispered.

He guided her to a settee before the table and, with a faint pressure, caused her to sit down, before he himself did. 'What nonsense,' he chided, attempting laughter. 'We'll have no "my lord" any longer. You're a Queen of Ys, Tambilis. You'll be a guiding star to the people, a healer, a strong voice in council; you'll command wind and wave; you'll be – with the Goddess. Better I call you "my lady".'

He filled two silver goblets, diluting in neither, and urged one into her clasp. 'Drink,' he said. She obeyed. He saw her grimace and realized that the wine by itself, dry as most Ysans preferred, was harsh on a palate that had usually known water. 'I'm sorry. Here, I'll pour some back and weaken the rest. I do think if you take a draught or so you'll feel calmer. And, uh, behold, wouldn't you like these raisins, these sweetmeats?'

Partaking did seem to help. After a few minutes Semuramat–Tambilis gave him a steady regard and said with childish seriousness: 'Mother told me you would be kind.'

'I promised her. I promise you. As far as lies in my power, I will.' *And may you never know how I miss her.*

'Then do what you shall, Grallon.'

His face heated. 'Wait, wait, no haste, let's talk a bit, let me tell you something about what to await – '

He avoided grave matters but bespoke feasts, games, foreign visitors with wonderful stories. She drank faster without noticing. A sparkle awoke. She leaned into the crook of his arm, snuggled against him, as she had done when she was a small girl and he yarning to her in the presence of her mother.

Desire flamed up.

No! he snarled to the Power. *You'll have Your way with us, that's fated, but not yet.*

'What's the matter?' she asked when his words stopped.

'Naught, naught.' He went on with the tale. His loins raged.

– 'That had better be all, darling,' he said around the dryness in his mouth. Thunders went through his breast. 'You need your sleep.'

Her nod wobbled, her voice was slurred: 'Aye. Thank you, kind Grallon. Now make me a woman.'

She caught her wits back to her. 'First I should pray to the Goddess, oughtn't I?'

He ordered his arm, that had been about to close tight, to let her go. He stood aside while she went to pray. He had long since had images of the Three removed from this room, but she found a nymph among the revellers who looked older and more modest than the rest. Her slight form took stance before the picture, she raised her hands, and Gratillonius stood fighting off the Bull. He heard:

> 'Belisama, to Your keeping
> I entrust my soul this night.
> Guard Your child while she is sleeping;
> Wake me to the morning light.'

Tambilis turned towards her husband, held out her arms. He went to her through the roaring. She did not know anything else than to let him undress her. Tortoise shell comb and ivory pins clinked to the floor. He had no skill in loosening hair, and she giggled a bit, while crying a bit, when he tugged a bit too hard. The pectoral and golden bracelets dropped with a clang. The girdle slithered aside like a snake. He shook as he undid the dress and pulled the undergarment off over her head.

Thereupon she stood with an uncertain smile on her lips. Hands flitted for a moment, seeking to conceal, but drew aside. As yet, he saw, her figure was almost a boy's. The crescent of the Sign burned red between tiny breasts. Hips and buttocks had, though, begun to fill out, and above her thighs was a shadowiness that caught glints of light.

Cast her down and have her!

Gratillonius stepped back. 'I'll first blow out the candles,' he said somehow.

Did the flush upon her cheeks pale? 'Nay, please, can we keep them?' she asked. Thus could she see what happened, and maintain bravery.

'If, if you wish.' As quickly as he could, he disrobed. When she saw him in his maleness, she gasped, quailed, rallied, stood fast. 'Be not afraid. I'll be gentle.'

He led her to the bed, drew blankets aside, guided her down, joined her, pulled the covers over them both. She shivered in his clasp. He stood on the wall against the Bull, while he murmured and stroked and kissed. Finally, of course, he must take her.

He *was* gentle. That much victory did he win over the Gods.

It hurt her nonetheless. She shed more blood than was common, and could not help sobbing afterwards. He held her close. 'There, there,' he crooned into her ear, ''tis done, you'll soon be well again, and we need do this no more until you are ready for it, years hence. I will not press you. Sleep, child.'

That also was territory he could defend.

XI

1

'Maybe here at last we'll find peace,' Drusus said low.

'I can't promise that,' Gratillonius told him. 'At best, you'll have to work for it, and most likely fight, too.'

Drusus sighed. 'It'd be worth it. If I could know my kids, anyhow, will have a chance to live their own lives.'

Gratillonius regarded his comrade of the Wall with compassion. The centurion of the Sixth Victrix seemed grotesquely out of place in this frescoed, mosaic-floored room. The tunic upon his stocky form was patched and faded. A deep inward weariness bowed the shoulders and looked out of the weatherbeaten, ill-barbered face. There was even a listlessness in his grip around the wine cup that rested on his knee where he sat.

Through doors open to the summer's warmth drifted the sounds of Aquilo, voices, footfalls, hoofbeats, wheel-creak, hammer-clash, together with odours of smoke and of green growth beyond the town. Those too seemed remote from the visitor.

It was Apuleius Vero who found words: 'Your life has been one endless march from battle to battle, homeless as the wind, over hill and heath and fields laid desolate, has it not?'

Publius Flavius Drusus cast a glance of startlement at the senator, the antiquated but immaculate toga that wrapped his slenderness and the handsome, still fairly youthful countenance above. 'Feels that way, sir,' he agreed.

Gratillonius harked back across the years. He had not been much together with this man, but those times were burned into him: combat against the barbarians, fellowship of miles and campfires and barracks, later a chance meeting in Augusta Treverorum and a drunken evening when hearts were unlocked. But Drusus had earlier fought the Saxons as they came reaving out of the eastern sea; he had crossed to Gallia to fight under his Duke Maximus and win for him the Imperium; he had stood guard on the German frontier and campaigned beyond it; he had tramped south over the mountains into Italy and had done battle again with legionaries like himself; he had followed his Emperor eastward, and seen their cause go down before Theodosius's Gothic lancers; half a prisoner, he had done hard labour on lean rations through month upon month of autumn, winter, spring; then he had made the trek across Europe to Armorica and a fate still unknown. Gratillonius did not wonder at seeing him slumped.

I hope I can straighten that back of his, the King of Ys thought.

'You may indeed have come to haven,' said Apuleius.

'Sirs, excuse me, but I don't understand,' the centurion faltered. 'I mean, well, all right, we veterans of Maximus have been sent north. We'll get our discharges, and places to stay, and – it's better than we hoped for, back there with the cataphracts on their tall horses herding us along – but what do you want of *me*? Why am I here?'

Gratillonius smiled. 'That's a long story, old buddy,' he replied. 'Let me just give the gist of it now, because I think dinner time's close and we'd like to relax then.

'This resettlement was my idea, when I heard about the

239

fall of Maximus last year. A priest – chorepiscopus, I mean, name of Corentinus, gave me a lot of help, and we got Bishop Martinus in Turonum and other big men interested, and – Never mind. The upshot is that here we have Armorica, half depopulated, screwed over by pirates and bandits and barbarians who've actually taken up residence. And yonder we had you soldiers, good men, but men that the Emperors could neither trust nor massacre. Let's bring them together.

'I thought of establishing a colony. If it was near Condate Redonum, it'd keep the Franks there in line. But that was refused. Not unreasonable, from Theodosius's viewpoint. He wants you dispersed as well as discharged, so you can't ever get up another revolt. So be it.'

As he paused, Apuleius interposed gently: 'None of you shall be left destitute. Each man shall receive his plot of land and the basic tools he requires. The tribesmen will surely help him, for they ought to welcome such a strong new neighbour. From among their daughters he can soon find a wife. Praise God for His mercies.'

'We'd not every one of us make a farmer,' Drusus objected. 'Many of us wouldn't know one end of a cow from the other.'

Gratillonius laughed. 'True. Well, any legionary has skills that're in demand, what with trade reviving hereabouts. There'll be work for all. I can use a few engineers in Ys, as a matter of fact. And if nothing else, the granaries of Ys will keep you from starving before you can support yourselves.'

Drusus shook his head dazedly. 'My partner in the mud, a king,' he marvelled.

'Let's get to the point about why we've sent for you,' Gratillonius went on. 'You owe a heap – I think you'll

240

agree – to my friend Apuleius. He kept up the correspondence and the political pressure and everything else I didn't have the time or the connections for. You see, I knew you'd be with your outfit if you were still alive, Drusus, and knew you could be depended on. So we managed to get a fair-sized number of men in your century assigned to this area.'

'No gratitude is due me,' said Apuleius. 'I only wish to see the district well served, and therefore accepted Gratillonius's recommendation. Aquilo and its environs are poorly defended. We have nothing but a handful of native troops, ill-trained, and reservists with no training to speak of. Despite my repeated pleas, the Duke has never stationed any legionary regulars here.

'Well, of course you and your, ah, vexillation are going to be civilians. As such, you cannot, under Imperial law, form yourselves back into a military unit. You will be farmers, artisans, and so on. However, you will not have forgotten your martial trade, and equipment can be gradually obtained. I expect you to hold periodic drills and exercises which will include Osismiic men. Thus you will eventually provide us with a reserve force that is effective.'

'Almighty God!' Drusus exclaimed. 'You *mean* that?'

'I was never more serious,' assured Gratillonius. 'I'm hoping you'll take the lead, under Apuleius the tribune, in getting all this organized. Think you can handle it?'

Drusus put down his cup, sprang to his feet, squared his shoulders, and gave the Roman salute. 'Sir, I do.'

Gratillonius stood up too, refrained from hugging him, but said, 'Splendid. We'll discuss details in the next couple of days. First let's enjoy ourselves. Isn't food about ready, Apuleius? My stomach believes it's been sent to hell for the sin of gluttony.'

A trifle shocked by the irreverence, the senator none-theless answered graciously, 'Soon, I pray your patience. Would you two like to go to another room and talk? You see, we've developed a custom in my family. Before the main meal, I spend half an hour with my daughter.'

'Verania?' asked Gratillonius.

Apuleius nodded. 'I'm surprised you remember.'

'Why shouldn't I? Charming child.' Abruptly it came to Gratillonius: Rovinda, the wife in this house, was again pregnant; but there had been no sign or mention of another infant. Whichever she had borne since Verania must have died, as infants so often did, unless their mothers were Gallicenae who had medical arts and magics and the blessing of Belisama.

Impulsively, Gratillonius proposed, 'We'll stay, if you don't mind. She might like meeting newcomers.'

'Oh, that would be wonderful,' Apuleius said. 'You are too kind.'

Gratillonius shrugged and laughed. 'I'm a father myself, several times over.' He regretted it when he saw the flicker of pain across Apuleius's lips, but dismissed remorse; he knew himself for a man not especially tactful nor the least bit subtle.

Drusus sat back down and reached for his cup, looking resigned.

Apuleius went to the inner door and called. A female slave led Verania in. She moved shyly towards him, her gaze big and hazel in the direction of the strangers. Gratillonius's heart lost a beat. O Mithras! Just about four years old, she was a trifle younger than Una, and her colouring was different, lighter; but how those delicate features and that graceful gait recalled the daughter that Bodilis had given him.

Daughter of Bodilis – A year had passed without much

blunting his longing for Bodilis as more than a soft-spoken counsellor, a carefully correct friend.

Gratillonius mastered himself. From Dahut he had learned how to court little girls. You didn't stare or beam or gush or grab. You were cheerful, casual, always respectful of the child's dignity; and before long she would listen to you, then come to you, with the dawn of adoration in her eyes.

2

'The centurion will be away,' Adminius lamented. 'Not the King, 'e don't matter now, but my officer Gratillonius, centurion o' the Second. Slice and gut me, wot a shame! The single thing wrong, that 'e can't be there ter stand me by and lead the celebration afterwards. 'E would, you know. I've 'alf a mind ter put it all off till 'e gets back.'

He knew that was impossible. The family into which he was marrying would have taken grievous offence. The Powers might too, since the astrological signs were propitious for the date set and for none other in the near future. Besides, nobody could say when Gratillonius would return from this latest journey of his.

Adminius found consolation in knowing that his whole Roman squadron would be on hand. This time the prefect had left them behind and travelled with an escort of Ysan marines. In part, he had explained, that was to allay a certain jealousy he had seen growing. To take them beyond the frontier not only gave them a pleasurable outing but acknowledged that he was *their* King. And in part, when he was to deal with former rebels, he had better avoid anything that might look suspicious to the Imperial authorities.

The wedding would be an event of some importance, joining the deputy commander of the legionary cadre to Avonis, sister of the naval officer Herun, who with her belonged to the Taniti clan of Suffetes. It would take place at the Nymphaeum, and a Queen would preside. Adminius proposed that his soldiers form an honour guard. They cheered, except for Budic. 'What's the matter with you?' demanded Cynan.

The young Coritanean reddened like a maiden. He must gulp before he could mumble, 'A pagan rite. The chorepiscopus was warning again, in his last sermon, about d-d-danger to the soul.'

'Ha!' Cynan sneered. 'Some faith, that won't let a fellow show friendship! When are you due to be gelded?'

'Lay off that,' Adminius ordered. 'Honesty's too flinking rare as is . . . Budic, lad, I won't force yer. But well you know, I'm not the first among us ter settle down with an Ysan wife, and me a Christian too. It's an honourable estate, better than 'oremongering, 'specially when we'll likeliest leave our bones 'ere. You needn't bow down to 'eathen idols – I won't meself – just because you join our party.'

Budic caught lip between teeth, shivered, and said, 'I'm sorry. I'll come, and, and hope Corentinus will understand.'

'Good.' Mollified, Cynan slapped him on the back. 'The centurion would be disappointed to learn you hadn't.'

'I thought of that,' Budic whispered.

– On the day, the legionaries departed in full and polished armour, up the valley to the hills. The groom rode ahead of them, finely clad, on a white horse, next to his intended father-in-law. Behind followed other kin and well-wishers, together with pack beasts carrying supplies for a feast. The weather was superb. Merriment carolled along the whole way. The bride had fared a day in advance, accompanied by attendants and Queen Forsquilis, that she might be purified and then well rested.

At noon the group reached the sacred site. A vestal guided them by a short woodland path to the barrack. They would sleep there – floor space and pallets were sufficient – before returning home in the morning. While they refreshed themselves and took their ease, the small garrison hospitably carried back the food and wine they had brought, for the women of the sanctuary to set forth on tables which had been placed on the lawn.

At mid-afternoon a procession of girls arrived, led by a full-grown virgin who was near the end of her term of service. Hair garlanded and flowing loose over white gowns, they sang and fluted hymeneals while they conducted the groom and his friends to the Nymphaeum. Beautiful among them danced Princess Dahut. Already she was often here, as well as in other places hallowed to Belisama. It was unusual for one so young, but she was being raised in piety.

Around the greenswarded hollow brooded forest, above it cloud mountains and blue depths, heavy with summer. The air was as sweet as the music. Peacocks walked on closely-trimmed grass, swans floated on the pond. That water came from several brooklets out of the hills and the spring at its edge; thence ran a stream which fed the slender canal that joined with rains to quench the thirst of Ys. The spring bubbled from a pile of boulders, atop which smiled a statue of the Mother, shaded by a huge old linden. Flowerbeds blazed with colour, hedgerows and bowers drew the eye onward to the building. It was wooden and of no great size, but its white, colon-naded, large-windowed form was as of a jewel.

Adminius uttered a command. The soldiers formed a double rank below the stairs. Forth on to the portico came the aged chief priestess and her coadjutresses, in blue gowns and high headdresses. Gravely, they summoned the groom. He mounted the steps and followed them inside. After him went the rest of the wedding party, and then the choir. The legionaries stayed behind.

Through open doors came sounds of hymn, chant, prayer. Budic strove not to listen. He failed. Those words, those melodies were at once too joyous and too solemn.

They ended in a benediction uttered by a woman's purring voice. The bridal couple appeared, plump blond maiden on the arm of lean sandy man. They descended. As they passed between the soldiers, swords flew from sheaths and '*Ave!*' roared aloud.

The guests followed, the girls, the votaresses. Last was the Queen. Tall and stately walked Forsquilis, her face almost inhuman in its classic lineaments and pallor, save for the faint smile.

Dahut had been named to cry, 'Rejoice! The blessing of the Goddess is ours! Rejoice!' Thereupon everything broke up in shouts and laughter. Folk mingled, embraced, made for the laden boards. Forsquilis went back inside. When she returned, her golden-brown hair was coiled around a silver coronet and cloth of gold clung to her litheness. She herself called for drinking to the health and happiness of the newly wed, and in the hours afterwards chatted freely with any and all.

The gaiety, and perhaps the wine, soon overwhelmed Budic. Every nuptial feast in Ys, other than the King's, was mirthful, and apt to become erotically charged. Here there could be no stealing off with a newly met woman.

However, nothing forbade the vestals to smile, joke, dance, exchange glances, murmur hints. When they attained their majority, most would want husbands, some would want lovers, and surely Belisama breathed higher the fire that She had kindled in young hearts. Budic blundered bewildered through a whirl of loveliness.

The sun went under western hills. Clouds burned golden. Forsquilis signalled to the virgins. They formed a line, their feet skipped, their epithalamium lifted, as they brought Adminius and Avonis back to the Nymphaeum. Dahut bore a candle before the two, lighting their way to the flowerful chamber that was theirs for the night.

Festivity outside continued a while. Twilight deepened, stars blinked into view, moon-glow silvered heaven above high eastern darknesses. First the oldest and the youngest yawned goodnight, then presently all revellers departed to their rest.

– Budic awoke. He could not have been long asleep. The barrack was pitchy black and steamy hot. He felt bodies pressed close to his, and for a moment a surging took him; but they were merely two roadpounders like himself, and snored. He rolled over, hoping to regain oblivion. The straw of his pallet rustled. He remembered youths in Britannia, when he was a boy, boasting of what they had done with girls in the hay. He remembered that he had not really been down in peaceful nothingness. Slim forms with voices like the chiming of brooks had undulated through his dreams.

Sweat prickled and reeked in his armpits. His member swelled and strained. Almost, he groaned. *Christ guard me from the demons in this haunt of heathendom!* Useless to lie here. He would only toss about till he roused his mates, who'd swear at him. Maybe some fresh air would soothe. He groped his way to the door, and out.

How solid, how soft the earth was beneath his feet. The night laved his nakedness; he felt every smallest cool ripple in it. The forest smelled of damp and musk. He heard rustlings, chirrings, a hoot, a wing-beat. They seemed to call him. Moonlight dappled leaves and ground. As his night vision strengthened, he saw the path winding off to the holy grounds. Yonder was water. Thirst smouldered in the thuttery thickness that held him by the gullet. He thought confusedly that he would not drink from the pond, for it was given over to the lustful she-devil; but the stream that ran from it, off to the canal and thus the city, ah, he could fling himself belly down, grip the moss in both hands, and bury his mouth in that chilly kiss.

He moved ahead. Twigs fingered him. A moonbeam touched a great fungus growing on a log. It stood forth like a phallus or the flame of a lamp in a bridal chamber. Was it a nightingale that trilled, or a girl's laugh?

The woods opened on the lawn. Budic slammed to a halt.

The full moon hid most stars behind a veil of brilliance. Trees, hedges, grass reached asheen. Above the spring, below the linden, the idol stood livid against shadow. Darknesses limned the rich curves of breasts and hips. Argency glimmered and sparkled over the pond. Around it, upon it, out from within it, the nymphs were dancing.

They were not vestals, innocently asleep, they were mist and moonlight made female, shapes that flitted, wove, flickered, soared, twined, caressed, parted to tremble on the edge of flight, came back together to embrace, one with one another and the night and the burgeoning summer. Not with his ears but with his soul, he heard them sing and cry and yowl desire. He knew not whether they were aware of him or cared; but he was about to plunge forth and lose himself in them.

248

Out of the gloom that bulked against the northern sky trod a man. He was huge, naked, stallion-erected. Each fist held a writhing snake. It was as if stars glittered trapped in his unbound hair. From his temples sprang a mighty rack of antlers. Slowly he paced from the wood towards the nymphs, and their movements turned in his direction.

Budic huddled behind a tree. He could not help himself, he must peer around its trunk.

Moonlight flooded her who came down off the portico and across the lawn. White, white, blue-white was her skin, also nude except for the tresses streaming loose. She held out her arms to the man-shape. Distant though she was in this dimness, Budic knew that Athene countenance.

The male wheeled and strode to meet her. She ran. When she reached them, they halted and he took both her hands in his. The serpents wrapped around their wrists, moonlight icy along scales. For an endless while, male and woman stood unmoving. Then at last they went side by side into the forest. The nymphs took up their frolic anew.

Lightning through the thunder that filled Budic's skull: Everybody knew Forsquilis was deepest versed in sorcery of the Nine witches, and gossip muttered how she bore the air of a passionate woman and how hard it must be for her to share a single man. None, even Christians, ever dared hint that any among the Gallicenae might betray the King. But what about a God – a demon?

A nymph-shape left the dance and swayed across the dew towards Budic.

He shrieked and fled. Yet he did not re-enter the guards' house when he got there, but spent the rest of the night outside, shuddering, grovelling, weeping, and praying.

3

'Have you told anyone else?' asked Corentinus.

Astounded, Budic gaped at him. Dusk gathered around the minister of Christ where he sat on his stool, in the room of his church that he had designated private, like a black-feathered bird of prey on its perch.

'N-no, Father,' the Coritanean stammered after a moment. 'I p-pretended I'd had nightmares, that was why I was so numb and weak this morning.'

'Good.' The knaggy head nodded. 'No sense in letting rumours get started. They'll force people to take firm stances, which is the last thing we want the pagans to do. Of course, you realize what you saw may well have been just a dream.'

'What? No, Father, that can't be. I mean, I beg your pardon, but I do know the difference – '

Corentinus raised a palm to cut off the words. 'Peace. Don't fret yourself. It matters little. The forces of Satan prowl always around us. Whether they work as mirage or material, their purpose is the same, to lure us from our salvation. If what you saw really happened, I'll feel sad for that poor benighted woman. But you, my son, you may thank God that He strengthened you to resist.'

Budic wailed and covered his face. 'No, Father. Th-th-that's why I came – not even to warn you, but, but the vision won't leave me, the lust is fiercer than fire, what shall I do, Father?'

'Ah. Hm.' Corentinus rose, bent over the hunched

figure, briefly hugged the bright head to his bosom. 'Don't be afraid. You have wisdom beyond your years, that you seek help here instead of in a brothel.'

'I have sinned that way before. But this, this *called* me.'

'I know. I too have heard.' Corentinus began pacing back and forth. He made his voice dry:

'Listen, Budic. You've been a pretty good catechumen, and this isn't the first time I've given you some thought. Now, I can't compel your spirit. Only God can do that. But I can, in my left-handed mortal fashion, advise you. So listen, and think.

'Your trouble is that you're devout, but you haven't got the makings of a monk. No disgrace in that. The Lord bade Adam and Eve be fruitful and multiply. What're you waiting for?'

Budic gave him a dazed look. 'Where'll I find a Christian wife? I knew I did wrong, going to that pagan wedding. Isn't this my punishment?'

Corentinus smiled. 'I'm not sure you did do wrong. I've never reproached any of my flock who married unbelievers. It can't be helped, and grace may come on the spouses. I only require that they allow their children to hear the truth. You, though – you're not the sort who could live with an infidel woman. But you need a woman, in the worst way.'

He took stance before he went on, almost sternly: 'I have one, if you're Christian enough, man enough, to take her for your wife.'

Budic stared up at him. The chorepiscopus seemed to tower as if he spoke from the peak of Sinai. 'Who?' Budic whispered.

'You know her well. Keban, the harlot from the Fishtail.'

Budic sat dumb-stricken.

251

'She has repented,' Corentinus went on relentlessly, 'she has washed herself clean with her tears, she acknowledges Christ her Lord and Saviour. But who among the haughty goodfolk of Ys will have her, even as a scullion? I give her shelter and employment here, but it's made work, as well we both know, and her days are empty, and Satan understands very well how to fill that emptiness with old carnal cravings. I've dreaded that she may fall by the wayside. But if not – what an example to shine before every wretch forsaken in this city of sin!

'Budic, she's still fairly young, healthy, a fit mother of sturdy sons, and reborn in Christ. What she was before is nothing in the sight of God. But is everything in the sight of man.

'Who will have courage to take her under his protection, for the salvation of both, and shield her, and turn his back on the sly, unspoken mockery, till at last it is outlived, forgotten, and an honourable old pair go hand in hand towards Heaven? Might you be, Budic?'

Silence lengthened, underneath harsh breath.

Corentinus eased. 'Ah, well, I know better than to force things,' he said. 'Come, lad, let's share a stoup and talk a bit. I can always use barrack-room gossip. As for any sins of yours, consider them forgiven.'

– But later that evening, summoned, Keban entered. In wimple and full, coarse gown, timidly smiling, by lamplight she seemed twice comely. All she did was prepare and set forth a frugal meal, and answer a few inconsequential questions. Yet the glance of Budic followed her everywhere she went.

Often around the autumnal equinox, storms caused Ys to lock its sea gate, lest waves force an opening and rush through the harbour into the city. When calm was restored, the King freed the portal. It was his sacral duty. Only if he was absent or disabled did Lir Captain take it in his stead.

As usual, he performed the task at high tide, which this day happened to come in the afternoon. 'You see,' he explained to Dahut, 'the doors are hung in such a way that they always want to be shut. As the water falls, the floats that hang from them do too, and draw the doors open. At low water, they would pull so hard that I couldn't get the bar out of its holder.'

'But what if you *had* to close the gate then?' she asked.

Gratillonius smiled. 'Sharp question!' There was quite a mind below those golden curls, behind those big eyes. 'Well, we have machinery, so gangs of men can haul the doors shut against the weight of the balls. Just the same, it's hard work.'

Lanarvilis had told him he should let Dahut witness the rite. All the Queens were touchingly concerned about the upbringing of Dahilis's daughter. Delighted, he had sent a messenger to temple school. She came from there in company with Guilvilis, whose turn it was to foster her. He was twice happy that that turn coincided with his night at Guilvilis's house.

Woman and child followed him from the palace. Guilvilis had donned finery, a silken gown that showed to disadvantage her tall, awkward, heavy-haunched figure.

The thin dull-brown hair would not stay properly in its elaborate coiffure, but did call attention to small eyes, long nose, undershot chin. In a schoolgirl's brief white dress, Dahut went like wind and waterfall. Gratillonius wore a ceremonial robe of blue-grey wool embroidered in gold and silver thread with sea beasts. In full view on his breast hung the iron Key.

A squad of marines waited in their conical helmets and shoulder-flared loricae. Pike butts crashed a salute on the stones. They took formation behind the King. Traffic on Lir Way was thick and bustle was loud, but a path opened immediately before the procession. Many folk cheered, some signed themselves, a number of youngsters trailed after to watch from the wharf.

The Temple of Lir stood under the Gull Tower, just before the pomoerium. Ancient, it lacked the Grecian exquisiteness of Belisama's, the Roman stateliness of Taranis's. Despite small size, here was brutal strength, menhir-like pillars and rough stone walls upholding a roof of slate slabs. The interior was dark, revealing little more than an altar block within an arch formed of the jawbones of a whale.

Gratillonius entered. The man on watch today greeted him. Every ship's captain in Ys was ordained a priest of Lir; Hannon Baltisi simply presided over meetings of the guild and spoke for it and its cult in Council. Gratillonius knelt to receive on his tongue the ritual pinch of salt and voice the ritual plea that the God withhold His wrath. Emergence was like release from captivity.

It was a bright, bracing day. When he had climbed the stairs to the rampart heights, he looked out across utter openness. Waters shone blue, green, purple, white-capped, save where they burst on rocks and reefs, brawled against wall and cliffs; there fountains leapt. In this clarity he could see the house on Sena, miles away. Only wings beclouded the sky, hundreds of them soaring and circling on the breeze whose tang washed his face.

He looked inland, across the broad arc of the basin. How still it lay, nine or ten feet beneath the tide, lower yet whenever the combers climbed and broke. Ships and boats crowded the piers. Men were busy with cargo. Mariners of Ys would venture another voyage or two before winter closed in. The knowledge that he had put life back into that trade made a glow in Gratillonius.

And the city behind shone in roofs, towers, on its higher eastern half gardens, temples, mansions. Hinterland stretched beyond, valley and hills where homes nestled, the gaudiness of leaves muted by distance to a tapestry laid over the earth, a sign of ingathered bounty. God Mithras, said Gratillonius, watch over all this, stand guard upon its peace.

Dahut tugged at his hand. 'Won't you start?' she piped.

Hauled from his reverie, he laughed and tousled her hair. 'Ever are you the impatient one, eh, sweetling? Aye, let's . . . Have a care! Lean not so far over the parapet. I know you love the sea, but remember, 'tis forever hungry.'

He led her past the Gull Tower and the sheltered war engines to that fifty-foot gap in the wall which was the portal. Dahut, who had been here before, cried greeting to the block that jutted from the wall below the battlements. It had the time-blurred form of a cat's head. A chain ran from the inner top corner of the adjacent door, into the block, over the sheave within, and down out of its mouth. Most of the chain hung submerged, for the leather-clad bronze ball at its end floated not far beneath, idly swinging in the waves. Gratillonius heard the thuds when that great weight rolled against the wall. Those dry-

255

laid blocks were well fitted indeed, to have withstood centuries of such battering. And even the doors, oaken though copper-sheathed and iron-bound, had only required replacement twice.

He let go of Dahut's hand. 'Now 'tis single file,' he said.

A flight of stone steps angled down the inside of the wall to a ledge beside the gate, halfway up. There stood a capstan, from which a chain ran through another cat's head to the inner top corner of the door. Opposite, fifty feet away, was a similar arrangement. 'This is the machinery for closing at low tide,' Gratillonius explained. 'The doors are made so they never swing too widely for that. Follow me onward.'

From the ledges, narrow, railed walkways ran across both doors, meeting in two platforms at the juncture. Dahut touched the riveted green plates and black iron reinforcing strips that she passed. 'Why must you ever lock the gate?' she asked. 'Less'n you want it shut up at low tide.'

What a quick person she is! marvelled Gratillonius. 'Well, think of a big storm with huge waves. They don't only have high crests, they have deep troughs. The floats drop down as well as bob up. Were it not for the bar, they'd jerk the doors wide. The sea would pour through and do terrible things to poor Ys.'

'Thank the Gods that They don't let that happen,' admonished Guilvilis. Gratillonius thought, irritated, that man had somewhat more to do with it.

He reached the platform. There a titanic beam, pivoted on the southern door, fitted into an iron U on this northern one. A cable ran from its free end to a block and tackle above. The bar was secured by a chain through it and through a staple, closed by a ponderous lock whose hasp went between two links.

Looking down into the girl's eyes, Gratillonius wondered how he appeared in them. 'This is my work,' he said.

The marines had deployed along the walkway. Gratillonius unslung the Key from his neck and raised it aloft. 'In the name of Ys,' he called, 'under the Pact of Brennilis that the Gods did grant unto us, I open the city to the sea.'

He fitted Key into lock. It turned stiffly, with a clicking as of footsteps. He withdrew the Key and laid it back in his bosom. With both hands he removed the lock and hung it on a single link. Drawing the chain out, he fastened it in a loop by locking the loose end to the staple.

Crossing over to the opposite platform, he uncleated the cable and hauled on it. Cunningly counterweighted, the bar rose easily for all its massiveness. When it was almost vertical, he refastened the cable. Returning, he clasped his hands and bowed before the lock.

It was done. The party went back to the top of the wall. Soon, as tide ebbed, the doors would begin to draw apart. The sea would come hissing through, but gently, by that time not raising the level of the basin too much. Ys would again have the freedom of Ocean.

'I've other matters to attend to,' Gratillonius said regretfully. 'Guilvilis, there's scant sense in taking the child back to class today. Why not show her about this quarter? The Cornmarket, Epona Square, the Ishtar Shrine, whatever she'd like to see. She's grown enough for it. I'll seek your house this evening.'

Dahut skipped for joy.

That ended an hour later.

Passing through the narrow, twisted streets near the waterfront, on the edge of the Fishtail slum, the girl halted. 'What's in there?' she asked.

Guilvilis looked around. The cobblestones of Crescent Way lay nearly deserted, for dwellers in the tenements that hemmed it in were still off at work. On the right a building lifted four storeys high, balconies cantilevered from the upper floor, the lower wall stuccoed and inset with shells which centuries had chipped and discoloured. A couple of children had stopped their play to stare at the finely clad lady. A porter with a laden frame on his back had just come around a corner; Ys restricted draught and burden-bearing animals to a few principal thoroughfares. 'Where?' the Queen replied vaguely.

'*There*,' said Dahut with exasperation, and pointed.

Opposite stood a building unique to Lowtown. It was of black marble, broad and deep though not high. Pilasters flanked bronze doors on which were life-sized reliefs of a veiled woman and a man with bowed head. The entablature was granite, sculptured into a frieze: a row of skulls and at the centre, floating above, an unborn babe.

'Oh,' said Guilvilis. 'Why, that, that's Wayfaring House.'

'What's it?'

'You haven't heard? Well, 'tis, um, 'tis thus. You know dead people get taken out on the funeral barge and put in the sea.'

Dahut nodded solemnly. 'Father's told me. He says that's where my mother went.'

'Well, the barge is supposed to go out each third day, but often the weather makes that too dangerous. Sometimes they have to wait a long while. They did this month, with those awful storms we got. Here, Wayfaring House, here is where they wait.'

'Oh.' Dahut's eyes widened.

''Tis all good and quiet for them,' Guilvilis said hastily.

'Can we go see?'

'What? Nay, I think better not. Later, when you're older.'

Dahut's face drew into an expression the Gallicenae well knew. 'Why? You say 'tis good and quiet.'

'Well, it is – '

Dahut stamped her foot. 'Father said show me everything I wanted!'

Guilvilis searched her memory while the child fumed. 'Aye, he . . . he did that, I think. But – '

Dahut darted from her, up the few broad stairs. The doors were unsecured. She pulled them apart and was inside before Guilvilis got there.

'What's this?' called the old man on duty. His voice made echoes in the twilight of a huge chamber. He shuffled forward. 'My lady, you shouldn't bring a wee one here. Leave her with me. Which beloved would you bid goodbye to? – O-ah.' He recognized the woman. 'My *lady!*' Touching his brow in reverence: 'How may I serve you?'

'I, well, 'tis thus – ' faltered Guilvilis.

Dahut dashed past them.

Stone tubs, a few feet apart, covered the floor. She came to the first and looked over its edge.

Brine filled it. Within, full length, lay a dead woman.

259

While a sheet wrapped her body, its soddenness revealed the bony contours. Cords bound wrists and ankles and held her to eyebolts. Hair floated loose. It had been an old woman, withered and toothless. The jaw had been tied up and the eyes closed, but lips and lids were shrivelled back, while the waterlogged face bloated around the beak of a nose.

'You shouldn't'a done that, little girl,' wailed the attendant.

Dahut made a mewing sound. Like a sleepwalker, she stumbled to the next vat. There was a man more newly dead. He had been young and healthy, though now his skin was ashen. Some mishap had shattered the right side of his head.

'Get her away from that, my lady,' the attendant implored. 'She's too young for the sight, she is.'

'Aye, come, let us go, Dahut, dear, let's go see Corn-market and I'll buy you a honeycake.' Guilvilis lurched towards the princess. 'Cry not, be not afraid.'

'Nay,' said the man, 'these are but the harmless dead. We'll take them to their rest on the morrow, and the Ferriers will bring their souls to Sena and the Gods will make happy those who were good.'

Stiff-legged, Dahut walked to the door. She stared before her, never a tear, never a blink. As daylight touched her, it showed a visage with no more colour or movement than any in the brine.

Nor did she speak the whole way back to the house, and scarcely at all when Gratillonius arrived there. But when she had gone to bed, and man and wife were about to, they heard her scream.

– He stood holding her in his arms. She had hidden her face against his breast but did not give him back his

260

embrace, only shivered and mewed. By the light of a single candle, he glared at Guilvilis.

'You dolt,' he snarled. 'You unspeakable clod, lackwit, bungler. What have you done to her? How could you do it, even you?'

She opened and shut her mouth several times, and he thought how very like a fish she looked, before she could stammer. 'Y-y-you said take her where she wanted, and, and she got away from me. Oh, I'm sorry!' Tears coursed from her eyes. Her nosed dribbled.

'A squid would have had better judgement, more command. And 'tis you who dwell in the home of Dahilis! Take you hence. Leave us ere you do worse harm.'

She stared, and now he thought of a poleaxed cow.

'Get you to the nursery.' To the Sasai, Antonia, Camilla she had borne him in such quick and glad succession. 'Dahut and I will be together this night . . . Not so, darling?' he murmured into the child-fragrance under her hair.

Guilvilis lifted her hands. 'I love you, Grallon. I wanted to do what you said. I wanted to please you.'

He brushed her aside as he carried his daughter out of the room.

They must cross the atrium to reach the main bedchamber. Every trace of Dahilis was gone. That had been at his insistence. Guilvilis would passively have left the dear things in place. He had ordered them brought to the palace. Guilvilis had acquired a few objects of her own. They were mostly garish. He didn't care.

He heard her weep on her way to the nursery. His anger sank a trifle. Thanks to her, Dahut had seen an unpleasant thing before she was ready for it, and it had given her a nightmare, but surely she could overcome any

261

fears, as lively and self-willed as she was. Sometime soon he'd toss Guilvilis a friendly word or two.

He laid the ivory shape down on the bed. Though there was hardly any light here, she burrowed into a pillow. It was as well, since he must now undress and – better find himself a nightgown, which he generally did only in the coldest weather. Dahut was naked, but, Mithras, she was five years old. Yet, holding her, he had felt the first slight filling out of her slenderness.

'Be not afraid, sweetling,' he said. 'You saw no people yonder. You saw the husks they've no more use for. 'Tis like a – a dandelion, when the seeds blow away on the wind to become new dandelions.'

Still she was mute. He got into bed and held her close. How moveless she lay, except for the faint trembling and catches of breath. Couldn't she cry, talk to him, have it out? Well, she'd always borne a strangeness about her. 'I love you, Dahut,' he whispered. His lips brushed her cheek. 'I love you so much.'

She did not answer. He got scant sleep that night.

6

Morning was bright and bleak. The funeral barge departed on the tide.

Dahut saw it from the heights. She had said at breakfast that she wanted simply a crust of bread and a cup of milk – which was true; she must force them down – and that she would make her own way to school – which of late she had been proudly doing. Father had left, and Mama Guilvilis was too crushed to respond. Freshly clad, Dahut

262

set forth. Then she followed side streets to Northbridge Gate and went out on Point Vanis.

Few whom she passed paid her any heed. To them she was merely another lass bound somewhere, uncommonly pretty and curiously intent, but nobody to question. Women and girls walked about Ys as freely, safely as men. However, once on the headland, she left Redonian Way and went along the cliffs. A shepherd, carter, merchant, courier would have been too surprised by the sight of a child alone beyond the city wall. When she glimpsed anybody, she hid behind a bush or a boulder. Sometimes she stayed a while, staring out to sea or downward at earth and insects, before she wandered onward.

The promontory reared stark out of the water and stretched inland nearly bare save for grass turned sallow, gorse, thistle, scattered trees that the wind had dwarfed and gnarled, lichenous rocks. In a few places stood beehive-shaped stone shelters or menhirs raised by the Old Folk to Gods unknown. Wind boomed from the west, a torrent of chill. Clouds scudded before it, gulls, cormorants, a hawk on high. Shadows harried each other across the miles. In between them, sunlight made the waters flame.

Finally Dahut reached a low mound and a headstone, out near the northern end of the point. She sat down to rest. At school she was learning the Latin alphabet. She had not been here since that began. Now, slowly, with a tracing finger, she followed the letters chiselled into the stone.

> Q IVN EPPILLO
> OPT LEG II AVG
> COMMIL FEC

Father had told her that a brave man lay beneath, who died fighting for Ys and Rome before she was born. He put off saying more, and when she asked two or three of the Mamas they put her off too. They seemed uneasy about it.

Abruptly Dahut sprang up. Her glance flung itself around. Against the dazzle on the sea she spied and knew the funeral barge, crawling out upon its oars. She choked down a scream and fled.

Nearby, where the cliffs turned east, a footpath led to them from the bend in the highway. Dahut sought it. Downward bound, it became a mere trail, steep and slippery. Father had held her in the past when they visited. Dahut picked her way alone, breathing raggedly but never losing balance.

A few blocks, canted and overgrown, showed that once a stair had led up. At the bottom were crumbling walls and the remnants of a jetty. Father had said this was a Roman marine station, smashed to pieces and fired long, long ago by the nasty Saxons. Dahut scrambled past the wreckage. Charred baulks and newer driftwood had jammed around the stump of the jetty to form a rough little ness. On this face of the headland the surf did not, today, assault it, though whitecaps smote and whooshed and sent spindrift flying.

Dahut stooped and took off her sandals. Barefoot, she could go out on the logs. Wind ripped at her. She cupped hands about mouth. 'O-ho, o-hoo,' she called. 'Come to me, come to me!'

The wind flung her cry down into the waves.

'O-ho, o-hoo! Please come. I need you.'

A shape appeared and swam rapidly towards her. It was golden-brown and huge-eyed. 'Welcome, thank you,

264

welcome,' Dahut shouted; and tears started to run. She hunkered down into what shelter an uptilted slab offered. It was of planks, bleached and warped, still held by corroded nails to a pair of snapped-off crossbeams: a piece from the deck of a lost ship.

The seal came aground and slithered over the jumble. Dahut flung arms around her neck. The fish-breath was not foul, it was strong, like a soldier's trumpet. The wetness didn't matter, when such warmth and sleekness were there to lie against. A flipper enfolded Dahut. The seal nuzzled her. Whiskers prickled, then a tongue kissed, a voice hummed deep in the throat behind.

'O-o-oh, I saw the dead floating. They were all ugly an-an-and eels will eat them, *me too*, like my mother that father says was so beautiful, o-o-oh, they come after me in my dreams. I thought one of them was mother.'

The seal held her close.

'Nay?' Dahut whispered after a while. 'Not really? Never?'

Somehow the seal got her looking outwards and opened her to what she saw.

'Papa told me 'bout dandelions – '

Radiance lit the wings of a hovering gull. Its voice was like laughter

'Aye, shells on the beach, kelp, starfish, but they all go back, they all go back.'

The waters no longer roared, they sang.

Dahut snuggled. Here, shielded from the weather, held in this comfort, she could let her weariness overwhelm her, she could sleep and be healed. 'They all return. Ever'thing returns . . .' The voice of the seal went lulling. ''Tis mine.'

> Oh, darling, lie peaceful. The sea is before us,
> The mothering, cleansing, all-powerful sea,

And borne on the wind and the foam is a chorus
Of surges and surf to your nest in the lee.
From depths that are darkling the billows lift sparkling,
As eager and salt as the beat of your blood.
No horror shall snare you, but life shall upbear you.
Dear sea-child, the tide of your hope is in flood.

XII

1

There was a man called Flavius Stilicho. His father had been a Vandal who entered the Imperial army and became an officer. Stilicho did likewise, rising high and fast until he was the mightiest general Rome had known for generations. This made him a power in the state. After military and diplomatic exploits in Persia and Thracia, he moved against the barbarians of the North. In Britannia his campaigns piled the bodies of Saxons, Picti, and Scoti in windrows and sent the survivors reeling back.

That spring, Uail maqq Carbri had led a seaborne raid up the channel to the mouth of the Sabrina and along the Silurian shore. Newly reinforced, the Romans fast marched from Isca Silurum, surprised the Scoti, and harvested a goodly number of them before the rest could escape. Uail's outsize currach did keep its load of booty from a town his reavers had sacked, including some captives. Among those was a lad of sixteen, a son of the curial, named Sucat.

Gallia had become an even worse hunting ground. Armorica guarded the approach, strengthened by the newly enlarged navy of Ys. No man of Ériu in his right mind would go there, unless it be as a peaceful trader.

Uail sought Niall maqq Echach, King at Temir, and gave his ill tidings. Unlike most of the chieftains who were on hand, Niall did not rage. Time had taught him patience. If the sun-brightness of his locks had begun, ever so faintly, to dim, the wits beneath were whetted as keen as his sword had always been. He accepted Uail's gifts out of the plunder, and made generous return. 'It's kindly your mood is, lord,' said the skipper.

Niall laughed. 'It is not,' he replied. 'The Romans must simply wait their turn. I have built up my strength over the years. Now we will build it further still, beginning with an undertaking that men shall remember forever.'

Towards that end, he had been seeking the goodwill of his Condachtach kinfolk. One of these, a tuathal king from the western shores, happened to be guesting him just then, a man named Mílchu. When this man went home, among the gifts he took along was the slave Sucat, whom Uail had presented to Niall.

Alliance was natural. Warfare between the Ulati of the north and the Firi Condachtae south and west of them was as ancient as when Cú Culanni stood off the cattle raiders of Queen Medb, if indeed the strife had not begun between the sons of Ír and Éber just after they conquered the Children of Danu. Being of Condachtach origin, the royal house that lorded it over the tuaths of Mide had inherited those feuds.

Equally haughty were the Ulatach kings who foregathered at Emain Macha. The chief among them claimed descent from Conchobar maqq Nessa, the lesser ones from the warriors of the Red Branch, as did the landowning nobles.

Tributary to them, between Qóiqet n Ulat and Mide, were humbler folk. Ulati had established themselves in those parts as chieftains, but scorned the dwellers, calling them mere Cruthini or outright Firi Bolg, exacting heavy rents, being careless about rights. Often a poor man could only get justice by starving at the door of the rich.

268

Sometimes this, too, failed to shame the defendant, whose well-nourished flesh could endure hunger far beyond the day when scrawniness must either give up or die.

Thus, when the chariots of Niall and his sons rumbled north at the head of a host, victory winged above them. They found few earthworks and strongpoints to overrun. The enemy leaders fought valiantly, but many of their followers, especially bond tenants, were half-hearted and quick to flee. Reinforcements from the King at Emain Macha arrived too late, too little. At the end of the second summer's warfare, Niall had prevailed as far as the headwaters of the River Sinand, almost to the Ulatach lands proper. The petty kings whom he had beaten plighted faith to him. He took hostages from them and went home.

There he would bide a while, waiting to see what happened in Ériu and overseas, before moving onward. Anything else would have been foolhardy. What he had won promised wealth, power, glory, but also unforeseeable trouble. It was more than ploughlands, herds, salmon streams, forests for game and timber, gold, weapons, men. His now was mastery over Mag Slecht, the holiest place in all Ériu. He must be careful not to rouse the anger of its Gods or too many of Their worshippers.

2

The months wheeled onward, through winter and spring and again to summer.

Esmunin Sironai, chief astrologer in Ys, predicted a lunar eclipse some three sennights after solstice. His tables and formulae went back to the Chaldeans, with much added by the Greeks and no little by his own people over the centuries, hampered though they were by their climate. The Queen who would be in charge of the Temple of Belisama at the time prepared for a special service, and she who would have the Vigil on Sena rehearsed special prayers, for the moon was the Lady's. Forsquilis arranged to have neither duty; she would be casting spells and taking omens by herself. Bodilis planned to be at Star House.

The weather proved clear. The Symposium met early for dinner and discourse. King Gratillonius had attended such meetings when he was able, but excused himself from this. The word went, very softly, that he intended a rite in his Mithraeum.

At sunset the company entered the Water Tower and climbed a helical staircase to the observatory on top. Esmunin's students busied themselves with armillary spheres, goniometers, and other instruments. The old man sat in a corner wrapped in his cloak. He was nearly blind. 'But we will tell you all as it happens, master,' they said lovingly. 'We will write it down with exactness, that you may draw forth meanings we would never find.'

Bodilis went to the parapet. Ys made a basin of darkness, save where fire glowed from windows, but towers still caught light on their uppermost metal and glass. In the opposite direction, the canal drew a thread of silver through the dusk in the valley. Air was as yet warm, moist, full of scents and whispers. And yonder above the hills rose the full moon. Already a gap was out of its limb.

'A-a-ah,' murmured voices, and 'Goddess, be gentle us-ward,' and 'Quick, now, set the clock.' Nearsighted, Bodilis squeezed forefinger against thumb to make a peephole through which she could more clearly see the marvel.

Blackness advanced until it became red. That veil gave way in turn to blackness again as it withdrew from ashen white. It had been an eclipse longer than some, shorter than some. It would go into Esmunin's book, another grain of truth laid down for a harvest he would never see. Bodilis wondered how many learned men in the Empire had troubled themselves to observe this, or watch at all.

A little talk followed, comparison, speculation; but most of the philosophers were ready for bed. Bodilis remained wide awake. As folk descended and said goodnight, she started home, thinking that she would read for a while, or perhaps attempt a little further translation of the *Oedipus*, or perhaps do a sketch for a painting she had in mind. Her place had grown lonesome since Gratillonius ceased sleeping there. Semuramat – Tambilis – was lonely too, but it behoved a Queen to maintain a household; and, to be sure, Tambilis was still studying those things a cultivated woman should know. Kerna and Talavair were good daughters who tried to see their mother often, but they had their families to attend first.

Bodilis had no need of a lantern, so brightly did the moon shine. The streets she took were empty, which made the glimpses she got through the windows of lighted homes seem doubly snug. Her rangy stride sent echoes rattling along the up-and-down twistiness.

It happened that her way led her by a house lately firegutted. That was rare in Ys, where only the upper storeys of the tallest buildings were wooden. When conflagration did occur, the marines at Warriors' House were as quick to come put it out as they were to come stamp down violent crime. In this case, a high wind and a broken amphora of oil defeated them. The family moved elsewhere, pending repairs.

A man had climbed up to sit on the blackened front wall, whose roof had collapsed. Swinging long legs, he was dressed in forester's wise, coarse shirt, leather doublet, cross-gartered trews. The moonlight showed a silver headband, gold earrings, forked black beard. A scar puckered the face that he kept turned aloft.

The sound she made caught his attention. He came down in a rush via a windowsill and made a sweeping salute of deference. 'My lady, Queen Bodilis!' His rather high voice spoke easy Ysan, though with a Redonic accent. 'What a grand surprise. How may I serve you?'

She recognized Rufinus. They had met seldom and fleetingly, as much as he was off on errands of the King's about which neither man said much. 'What were you doing?' she inquired.

'Watching the eclipse, of course,' he laughed. 'Such marvels are all too few, and then this wretched weather of ours most likely hides them.' Immediately he grew serious. 'Afterwards I sat trying to think what makes such a thing happen. Surely the Queen knows, but I'm only a runaway serf.'

'You've no ideas?' she found herself asking.

'Naught but folk tales. Not erenow have I had leisure to wonder about the world, thanks to King Grallon, best of lords.'

Bodilis winced and replied in haste: 'Well, 'tis simple enough. The sun and the moon move opposite each other when the angles are just right, and so the shadow of the earth falls on the moon. Have you not noticed how that shadow is curved?'

Rufinus stared. 'Why – yea, my lady – but, but do I understand you to say the world, this earth, is *round*?'

'Indeed. That's well known. Think how a ship goes below the horizon on a clear day. First the hull disappears, then the mast. How could that be, save on a globe?'

Rufinus drew a long breath. His voice pulsed: 'True, true! I said I'd never had a chance to think beyond the needs of staying alive, till lately, but – Yea, clear 'tis to see. But more riddles boil forth – ' He fell to one knee in his extravagant fashion. 'My lady Bodilis, wisest of the Gallicenae, may I beg a favour? May I accompany you to your doorstep, listening to whatever you care to share of your knowledge? If ever you'd make for yourself an adoring servant, here is how!'

Bodilis smiled. 'Why, certainly, if you like.' As devoted as he was to Gratillonius, this young man would be no menace to her; and he was charming and his appeal was touching. Besides, she recalled vaguely, gossip was that when in Ys Rufinus did not take advantage of the novelty that could attract many a well-born woman to him.

He capered for joy.

The questions he put as they went along showed ignorance, but also a mind amazingly quick to comprehend the truth. At her house she was tempted to invite him in. Few pleasures matched teaching a bright pupil. She thought better of it; but they agreed to meet again when opportunity allowed.

3

That had been a quiet year in Ys. Yet folk came to believe that mighty things were astir in the womb of time. One month the moon had darkened; then in the very month that followed, a comet appeared. For seven-and-twenty nights it followed the sun, drawing ever nearer as a wolf overtakes a stag. Even when clouds hid it, all knew that it prowled above, a maned star trailing tails of ghostly flame.

The Gallicenae met shortly after the apparition. 'This fear is nonsense,' Bodilis declared. 'Whatever comets are – Aristoteles thought them mere vapours in the upper air – the chronicles tell us they've come and gone with less serious consequences than so many thunderstorms.'

'The fear may be groundless,' replied Lanarvilis, 'but 'tis real just the same. 'Twould help were the King on hand, but – ' She shrugged. Gratillonius was off to the Romans again, helping Maximus's veterans organize the training of reservists. 'Unrest grows. Some mariners are afraid to put to sea. Nagon Demari stirs up the workers.'

'And Christian Corentinus makes converts,' Vindilis sneered.

'The trouble will die out, won't it?' ventured Innilis.

'One hopes so,' Fennalis answered. 'Still, 'twould be wise as well as kindly to quell these dreads now if we can.'

'That's why I called you hither,' Lanarvilis told them, and went on to explain her idea. After some discussion, the Queens reached consensus. Let heralds go forth, promising that at new moon, some nights hence, the whole Nine would be on Sena, there to divine the will of the Gods and set right any wrongs.

Towards the end of the talk, Forsquilis proposed: 'We should take Dahut with us.'

'What?' exclaimed Maldunilis. 'But we can't. She's no Queen. She may well never be.'

'True, she may not go ashore with us,' Forsquilis said. 'But she can abide on the barge, which will wait overnight to take eight of us back.' Her seeress's eyes searched them. 'It should strengthen that awe of the Gods we want her to feel.'

– Dahut was enraptured. The barge of state had always been so splendid, and here she got to ride on it, and to holy Sena! Tambilis, who was familiar with it because of the Vigils she took, led her about and showed her everything, from the swan's head at the prow, through the flagstaff and temple-like deckhouse at the waist, to the gilt fishtail at the stern. The sailors made much of the little princess; even those at the oars had a grin and a jest for her. It was a brisk day, wind whittering, the sea all grey-green and whitecapped.

The mainland cliffs sank into horizon haze. Low and flat, the island grew in view. Tambilis's pleasure dwindled. She had not told Dahut that she was often terrified yonder, alone after dark with the wind and the sea and Lir.

The barge docked. Guilvilis, who had been on duty, came down from the House of the Goddess to meet her Sisters. Its stonework bulked murky, foursquare, crowned by a turret of equally grim aspect. Beyond reached scrub, harsh grass, naked rock. Dahut tried and tried to see the two menhirs she had heard about, but they were at the heart of the island and she couldn't.

Tambilis bent down to hug her. 'You shall stay with the men, dear,' said the youngest of the Nine. 'They'll want to amuse you, and that's fine, but remember we brought you along so you could think hard about the sacred mysteries.'

Bodilis smiled a bit sadly down on the two. 'You were ever a good girl, Semuramat who was,' she murmured.

– While the high priestesses did not believe eclipse and comet were evil portents, neither had they come here as a political gesture. That would have been mockery of the Three. Their sundown rites were solemn. Thereafter they filed inland to the Stones. Wind hooted and bit, waves crashed. Low in the west, the invader star seemed to fly through ragged clouds.

Eight of the women formed a ring around the pillars. Fennalis, the senior, stood in front and called in the ancestral language, 'Ishtar-Isis-Belisama, have mercy on us. Taranis, embolden us. Lir, harden us. All Gods else, we invoke You in the name of the Three, and cry unto You for the deliverance of Ys.'

Tambilis had carried a firepot. She set alight the wood which a keeper of the Vigil always made sure was ready. The tasting of salt followed, and then the knife, to nick forth a drop of blood that each flung into the flames. Together the Gallicenae sang the prayer for guidance.

Meanwhile the clouds came in hordes out of Ocean, until blackness overwhelmed Sena. The wind loudened, the waves raged.

– By morning a full gale was under way. Noise, chill, and spindrift filled the air. Fury ran free on the waters. There could be no question of return.

The Queens were safe enough. Ascetical though it was, the House gave shelter and held supplies. In the unlikely event that combers washed over the island, the tower offered refuge. Yet this looked like keeping them weatherbound for days. Tasks ashore would go neglected while anxiety tightened its grip on the people, who would see this as another bad omen. Said Forsquilis bleakly: 'Once the weather was at the command of the Gallicenae. We ourselves have summoned it. But more and more does the power slip from us. The world blunders blind into a new Age which holds terrors unknowable.'

Tambilis and Bodilis went to the barge to reassure the crew and, especially, Dahut. They found the child wholly fearless, out on deck as much as the men dared allow, peering into the wind and chanting some wordless song of her own.

– Next morning the gale had dropped to a stiff breeze, while sunlight straggled down between rain-squalls. The seas remained heavy, and the captain of the barge told the Nine that he could not yet start forth. The reefs were too many, too treacherous. He guessed departure would be possible in another two or three days.

Dahut trilled laughter.

Towards noon, those on the island were astounded to see a vessel bearing in. On eight oars, it was a fishing smack, tarry, battered, but stout. '*Osprey*!' Dahut shouted, dancing in glee. '*Osprey*! Maeloch's come!'

Standing on the dock, Fennalis clutched her cloak to her. 'What's this?' she asked. 'Whom do you speak of?'

Dahut grew grave. 'Maeloch's my friend,' she said. 'I called to the seal and got her to bring him for us.'

'I don't understand,' Maldunilis whimpered.

Innilis explained: 'Maeloch, a fisher captain, also a Ferrier who knows this passage well. Sometimes he's been the boatman when Dahut's gone out on the water. I've taken her myself down to his home at Scot's Landing, where he fills her with goat's milk and stories.'

'She's had me do the same,' said Bodilis. 'Child, what's this about a seal?'

Dahut paid no heed, and then the boat was close in, its crew looking lively under profane orders. They made fast. Maeloch sprang on to the dock. He drew the cowl of his leather jacket back from his shaggy-maned head, made a reverence like a bear's, and boomed: 'Ladies, we'll take ye back. Fear nay. She's a cramped and smelly craft, but the crossing will be quick and safe.'

The captain of the barge huffed. 'Are you mad?'

Maeloch spread his huge hands. ''Twasn't my thought,

277

mate,' he admitted. 'A dream came to me last night, and when I stepped out at dawn I saw a seal that swam in a beckoning way. She led us. We might have been skerry-prey without her for a guide; but 'tisn't the first time we did well to follow a seal. She'll bring us to harbour again.'

'She *will*!' Dahut cried.

Forsquilis came forward. 'This is true,' she said into the wind. 'I too had dreams. I cannot read them, not quite, but – Come, Sisters, let us embark.'

Tambilis sighed almost happily. She must stay behind, today's Vigil being hers, but she would not be entirely by herself. The barge would convey her when the sea had calmed enough for that awkward vessel.

Maeloch beamed. 'Aye, welcome aboard, ladies. We'll do our poor best to make the trip easy for ye. I did need to whack a couple of the crew ere they'd go, but they've come to see this is a right thing to do. We ask no reward but your blessing.' His hand dropped over the head of Dahut. 'For how could we leave the princess waiting here, the daughter of Queen Dahilis what everybody loved?'

4

The tower named Polaris was the westernmost of its kind, in Lowtown although on the mildly prosperous south side of Lir Way. Equidistant from the Forum and Skippers' Market, it contained something of both. Respectable folk occupied the lower storeys, the poor and raffish dwelt higher up. When he was in Ys, Rufinus had an apartment on the topmost thirteenth floor.

Thither came Vindilis one winter afternoon. Fog had taken over the city, making its traffic a migration of

278

phantoms, but a breeze from the south had now begun to rend and scatter the blindness. Clumps of it still greyed vision, and air remained raw. In plain black cloak and cowl, Vindilis strode unrecognized.

Approaching Polaris, she got a full view of it save where shreds of mist blurred vision. Less lavishly built and ornamented than some, it nonetheless lifted arrogantly. Marble lions with fish tails for hindquarters flanked the main entrance, whose entablature depicted a ship at sea and its lodestar. The first five storeys were of the dry-laid stone the Gods had required, beneath tawny stucco inset with images of Ocean's creatures and plants. Construction above was timber, its paint shading from the same yellow to pearly white. Grotesques were carved into the vertical beams. The tower narrowed as it mounted to its roof. From that bronze cupola, green as the sea gate, curved four serpent heads. Each wall was agleam with window glass.

Vindilis mounted the low staircase, whose granite lay in concavities worn by centuries of feet. Entering, she found herself in a corridor on to which opened a number of shops and workplaces – a wineseller's, a spicer's, a draper's, a jeweller's, and more, including a small establishment selling food. Lamps lightened their dimness. Trade and craftsmanship happened softly. At the middle of the corridor was an alcove where a strong man sat by a wheel and crank. A rope went upward. By raising water and other needs, and bringing wastes and rubbish down for disposal, this hoist took some of the curse off living on the higher storeys. Adjacent stairs went steeply aloft. Vindilis began the climb.

Doors on the first several residential floors stood mostly shut. Many bore the insignia of families that had lived for generations in the suites behind. Higher on, occupants were more transient. There was a measure of shabbiness, odours of cooking cabbage, loud voices, raucous laughter, children milling in and out of doors left ajar. Everybody goggled at the stranger lady.

Yet no one menaced her, nor did she see outright filth or poverty. Tower folk on the various levels formed their own self-policing communities, often with their own argots and customs. They were apt to scoff at groundlings. It added much to the intricate, many-coloured tapestry that was life in Ys.

The thirteenth floor had space for just one apartment. The landing was a narrow strip lighted by a small window. Vindilis scowled at the door. Rufinus had replaced its former knocker with the penile bone of a walrus. Distastefully, she struck it against the wood.

He opened for her at once. Her messenger having told him she wanted to visit, he was neatly attired in a Roman-style tunic. 'My lady!' he greeted. 'Thrice welcome! Pray enter, let me take your cloak, rest yourself while I bring refreshment.'

'Did you think I'd be winded?' she answered. 'Nay, I keep myself fit, and forty years leave me somewhat short of senectitude.'

Her coldness failed to dismay him. Smiling, he bowed her through, closed the door, relieved her of her outer garment. For a moment they regarded each other, his green eyes even with her black. She had drawn her hair straight back. The white streak through the middle of it seemed to recall the comet of summer. Whiteness had begun to fleck the raven locks throughout.

'Do be seated, my lady,' Rufinus urged. 'Would you care for wine or mead? I've laid in cheeses, nuts, dried fruits as well.'

Vindilis shook her head. 'Not now. I've business on hand that cannot wait.'

'Aye, daylight wanes. Yonder door gives on to a balcony. Or would you liefer look through a window in this dank weather? The glass is fairly clear.'

'Why do you live in an eyrie?' she asked. 'I know you could have quarters in the royal palace if you wished.'

Startled, he said, 'Why, well, I like my privacy. And the view is magnificent. The very fogs – I stand on that balcony under the moon and look down on a city become a lake of flowing alabaster. By day I am kin to the rooks and hawks around me.'

'You certainly have changed your ways. Like your language.'

'My lady?'

'You neither live like a Bacauda any longer nor talk like one. I'll step outside. What I see should tell me more about you.'

Crossing the main chamber, she glanced everywhere around. The bedroom door stood shut. The kitchen was open, and ordinary: a cubicle minimally equipped, plastered and tiled against fire hazard. He kept the place clean. Rather, a hireling doubtless came in and did, for Rufinus had money these days. The atrium doubled as triclinium, with a table and chairs next to a sideboard. The ware on its shelves ran to the fanciful, sometimes the obscene, such as a ewer in the form of Priapus. Another table was of finely carved walnut inset with nacre. Likewise good were a pair of couches. A corner was taken up by his travelling gear, the weapons and tools and forester's outfit with which he fared on the King's missions. Two portrait busts on pedestals flanked it, one the beautiful ancient head of a boy, the second a modern likeness of Gratillonius. Elsewhere sprawled a jackdaw collection of objects, everything from a golden arm ring of Frankish workmanship to an earthen jug which must hold certain memories, whatever they might be.

Passing the central table, Vindilis spied a flute, a couple of books, writing materials, a shingle on which words had awkwardly been penned. 'I see you practise your literacy,' she remarked.

'I do, my lady, with more patience than is usually mine,' he said. 'You doubtless know Queen Bodilis was gracious enough to arrange instruction for me. She's promised me fascinating things to read when I'm able.'

He hurried to fling wide the balcony door. Vindilis trod forth into a chill that braziers kept from the apartment. She breathed deep. 'Fresh air cleanses,' she said.

Rufinus smiled. 'I pray pardon if my lodgings are stuffy. I get more fresh air than I care for, outside Ys.'

The view embraced a semicircle, from the sea portal to High Gate and beyond. Rampart, turrets, triumphal arch, streets, plazas were hers, an interweaving made mysterious by the vapours that drifted through it. Towers like this lanced above, to catch long sunbeams and bedazzle heaven. Afar she saw Elven Gardens and the purity of Belisama's Temple like an island rising out of the mist-lake. The sounds were of wind, wings, bird calls, and, faintly, the pulsebeat of the city.

'Aye,' Vindilis mused at length, 'you've deeper reasons than you perchance know for roosting here. All this calls to you.'

Rufinus blinked. 'What?' He cleared his throat. 'Hm, can I supply aught that my lady needs for her aeromancy? Shall I absent myself?'

Vindilis re-entered the room, closed the door, confronted him. 'Not for that have I come,' she said.

'But your message was – '

She smiled sardonically. 'My message was to head off rumours. I have no gift for reading the future in patterns of cloud and breeze. If I did, I'd mount the pharos for it. Nay, my aim is to talk with you in private.'

Unease passed through him. 'Indeed? A surprise. I'm nobody.'

'You are he whom the King defied the Gods to spare. That alone makes you fateful. Now you have also become his confidential agent, going to and fro on the earth. Surely you offer counsel as well. Sit down, Rufinus.'

'As my lady commands. But first let me pour wine and –'

Vindilis pointed to a chair. 'Sit down, I told you.'

He folded his long legs and stared up at her. 'Does my lady speak for the Nine?'

'Not altogether. Words concerning you have passed among us, but 'twas my decision to seek you out. What I tell anyone else will depend very much on what happens here.'

He wet his lips. 'I'll not betray my master's secrets.'

Vindilis folded her arms and looked above him into the shadows that were gathering as daylight ended. 'I need it not. I can guess, broadly, what goes on. The organizing of former Bacaudae into the King's forest rangers. Tasks they carry out at his behest. Linkage with the smallholders, the serfs, belike certain townspeople, the resettled veterans. He's gathering together a native Armorican strength, to protect the country better than Rome does. Yet the Imperial authorities would dislike learning that they are under surveillance and that so much they've mismanaged is quietly being done. *I* will bear no tales to them.'

Rufinus had regained balance. 'The Queen is shrewd. I beg leave to say no more.'

Her gaze smouldered at him. 'You may be required to. I think that from time to time you shall be recommending certain courses of action to Gratillonius, proposals that would not have occurred to him of their own accord.'

Forgetting her orders, he jumped to his feet. Pallor made the scar on his cheek stand lurid. 'Nay!' he cried. 'Grallon's my lord!'

'Calm down,' she snapped. 'Think you his wives would wish him steered towards harm? I've his best interests at heart. And yours, Rufinus.'

'Mine? My lady, I'll take no bribe – forgive me – no recompense.'

Her smile was hard. 'Not even silence?'

He stared. 'What mean you?'

'Unwise you were, Rufinus, to take your pleasures freely in Ys.'

He stiffened his back. 'Why should I not carouse?'

'Wine, song, shows, gambling, aye. But you're never seen in Tomcat Alley, nor do you avail yourself of the girls so readily available in taverns near the waterfront. For that matter, given your status and, yea, your personal charm, I'm sure a number of elegant women would be glad of a little sport with you.'

His hands lifted as if to fend her off. 'I'm not impotent – '

'I never believed that.'

'I've been with women – '

'Doubtless. After all, you came here intending to make yourself King.'

'If I choose now to be chaste – '

'Curse me if you must,' said Vindilis crisply, 'but insult not my intelligence. I suspected early on what you are. The Nine have their means of finding things out when they care to. Shall I name the foreign sailors? Some you brought hither, the young and handsome. That was most foolish. 'Tis sheer luck that your fellow tenants have not paid much heed . . . thus far. They soon will, unless you grow careful.'

The breath rasped in Rufinus's throat. 'What concern is this of theirs? Of yours?'

The sharp features softened, and the voice. 'It should be none. In olden Greece, I've heard, 'twould not have been, nor for a long time in Rome itself. But Ys is neither. Underneath all the sensuality, its heritage remains, of austere mariners from the South, ruthless charioteers from the East, and – who knows what of the Old Folk?' She laid a hand on his. 'Would it were otherwise. But this must needs concern me, because the revelation would destroy your usefulness to the King. It would cast suspicions on him that would wound him in his soul and undermine him in his power. You'd not do that to Grallon, would you, Rufinus?'

He shuddered. Anguish answered: 'O Gods, netherworld Gods, nay.'

'Then, first, be more discreet,' she said. 'You can do as you like beyond our borders, though best would be if you use a false name. While in Ys, amuse yourself as you wish, save for this.' Her tone thinned. 'Engage whores, if your fingers will not suffice you.'

He reddened. 'I can. I have. 'Tis only – I think my nature is, is because I was a boy when I joined the Bacaudae, who seldom see women, and – Nay, I pledge caution in Ys, for Grallon's sake.'

Warmth responded: 'Then I will accept your wine. Come, light wicks ere dusk overtakes us. Set forth food also, though I eat sparingly. Let us sit down and become acquainted. For I do not abhor you. I understand you better than you imagine.'

Heartened, he warned, 'Gladly will I plan with you how we may both serve Grallon, my lady. But remember always, he is my lord, to whom my faith is plighted.'

'Whom you love,' she said softly.

Rufinus flinched. 'He does not know.'

'Nor shall he ever,' Vindilis promised, 'if you bear yourself towards me as I hope you will.'

5

The Queens were all kind to Dahut, in their different ways, but she came to like Tambilis best and looked forward to her turns at staying in the house of the youngest. This was in spite of the fact that Papa never came there, with his romps and stories and tuneless but bouncing songs, as he did to the other Mamas whenever he was able (though he never spent the night with Fennalis or Bodilis). Dahut tried to find out why that was, but couldn't get any real answer from either one. They certainly smiled and spoke gently enough when they met.

No matter that eight years lay between their births, Tambilis and Dahut shared secrets, played little games together, went on trips, moaned about lessons, giggled at funny things. Tambilis had more learning, of course, which she could not readily explain to Dahut, only saying, 'Wait till you get that far.' However, she knew there was something mysterious and special about Dahut which could still less be put into words. 'I'm not afraid of you,' she said. 'You're my own dear cousin.'

The Council of Suffetes met around the quarter days. Tambilis confessed to Dahut that she merely listened, sometimes interested, sometimes frightened, sometimes well-nigh falling asleep. On the days themselves, the meetings adjourned for various ceremonies. Tambilis looked on the vernal equinox that year as a liberation.

After services at the Temple of Belisama, she sought Dahut out from among the departing choir girls. She herself had been one of the high priestesses. 'Would you like to come with me?' she asked, flushed and proud. 'I have the Shrine of Ishtar this time. 'Tis just open two days a year, you know, at spring and autumn.'

Dahut joyously agreed and got permission. She had heard that Ishtar was an ancient name of the Goddess and that the Founders had built Her a house when Ys was a new Phoenician colony. Nowadays Her first, simple dwelling stood unused, except when the wheel of the year bore back remembrance.

Hand in hand, the two made their way through crowds that respectfully parted, down into Lowtown. The blue gown and high white headdress of Tambilis only made her look as young as Dahut, who wore a flowing dress of silk, gilt sandals, and above her unbound blond hair a garland of primroses. The day was mild and sunny. Birds winged around flashing towers.

The Shrine was small, rammed earth and slate roof on a plot scarcely larger, which was marked off by four boundary stones. When Tambilis had unlocked the door, the interior proved equally plain, clay floor and rough altar block, though the Mirror was polished and the murals of Stars and Moon had lately been retouched.

After prayer, Tambilis seated herself on a bench together with Dahut and waited. In the hours that followed, a number of people came one by one or two by two through the open entrance. Mostly they were humble folk. Some simply wanted to make their devotions. Some approached the Queen and asked for blessing or help – a woman with child, a man who had lost his only son, a woman in search of her husband's forgiveness for adultery, a man soon to sail forth to distant lands, a girl who was deformed and lonely, a boy with soaring dreams . . . Tambilis could give the benison. Aid and counsel she was seldom prepared to render, but she knew where they might be found. In this wise Dahut saw what power was the Goddess's.

At sunset, after a final orison, Tambilis closed the shrine. The weight of solemnity fell off her. 'Now we are free,' she carolled. 'Come, let's go to the Forum. They'll be celebrating, you know, and the performers and musicians and, and everybody. There'll be stalls with food and drink and sweetmeats and, oh, all sorts of fine things. Innilis said I can bring you home as late as we want.'

'Till dawn!' Dahut cried.

They danced off, Tambilis forgetting that in public a Queen should be stately.

Between the Roman-like buildings that surrounded the central plaza, a throng milled. Their feet hid the mosaics of dolphins and sea horses. Dusk had gone flickery-bright, for the Fire Fountain was playing, oil ablaze, pumped high to cascade in red, yellow, green, blue flames down its three basins. Voices surfed, laughter rang, melodies whistled, throbbed, twanged, drummed. Raiment made a rainbow, and few were the brows without a wreath.

Wandering about, little noticed in spite of Tambilis's garb, the girl passed near what had been the Roman temple of Mars and was now the Christian church. Words slashed through the merriment: 'O people of Ys, hear the warning. Terrible is your danger.'

Tambilis paid no heed, but Dahut stopped and stared. A tall, rawboned man stood on the top step of the temple portico. His beard was black but grizzling, his hair abristle

288

behind a shaven slice of scalp that went from ear to ear. His robe was of cloth cheap and rough. At his back, drably clad, clustered a few men and slightly more women. 'Amen,' they chanted whenever he paused. His speech was quiet, but it carried.

' – yon cheerful ingle is in truth a will-o'-the-wisp leading you on to the burning that waits down in hell – '

The Ysans ignored him, talked, quaffed, japed, kissed.

'I beg you, listen. Ah, well do I understand, my plea tonight will win nobody over. But if you will hear it and think about it – '

Dahut's face paled so that the restless colours took possession of it. 'Come,' Tambilis said. 'No matter that old mouldy. Let's go on.' Dahut seemed to hear only the preacher.

'I do not scoff at your faith. Your Gods have brought you to much that is wonderful. But Their time is past. Like those unfortunates whom senility has turned mad, They do naught but mislead; and the road They have you upon goes into the Abyss. I love you too much, God loves you too much, to wish that for you. Forswear those demons you call Gods. Christ waits and longs to save you.'

'Nay!' Dahut yelled. She broke from Tambilis's clasp, dashed off and up the stairs.

An uneven sigh went over the revelry and damped it down. Many recognized the slim form with the beautiful face that ran to stand before Corentinus. They breathed her name to the rest. Eyes and eyes and eyes turned thither.

'Child,' called the chorepiscopus shakenly, 'beloved Princess Dahut, do *you* see the truth?'

She stamped her foot, clenched her fists, and shouted

up his height: 'You lie, old man, you're a liar! The Goddess is good, the Gods're strong!'

'Oh, poor darling,' Corentinus said.

'You're horrible!' she screamed. Turning to the Forum, she raised her arms. The light from the Fountain picked out her bright garment and hair, while casting Corentinus into murk. 'Don't you listen to him! The Goddess is good, the Gods're strong!'

'Child,' Corentinus groaned, 'you have but seven years in this world. How can you know?'

'I do know!' she flung at him. 'The sea tells me, the seal comes to me, an' an' today – everywhere – ' Again she faced the people. 'Listen to me. We *belong* to the Gods. If we forsake Them, They will forsake us, and Ys will die. Please be true to the Gods!'

Weeping, she stumbled back down the stairs. Tambilis hurried to embrace her. The crowd swarmed around them. It roared. Corentinus and his Christians stood alone beneath the pagan frieze on their church.

XIII

1

At Lúgnassat, King Niall must by law preside over the great fair at Tallten, its rites and sacrifices as well as its games and worldly dealings. His older sons had fallen into the way of representing him at such other gatherings of the kind as were important. They would be unwise to break that practice, when no warfare had call upon them this year. Besides keeping the glory of their house in view, it gave them a chance to gather news and strike useful bargains. With their north-faring dreams, the lords of Mide wanted no enemies at their backs. About the hostility of the Lagini they could do little; however it seemed that Niall's punitive expedition, and the wealth he took back with him, had sapped the eastern Fifth for a while.

Yet he was now master of Mag Slecht, where stood Cromb Cróche, Who had power over earth and blood. If he wanted the help, the goodwill, of that God, he for his part must not fail to pay honour and make offering. Having given the matter thought, he sent his son Domnuald on his behalf, with a goodly train of warriors and servants, a druid for counsel and magic, a poet for solemnity and power, several bards for entertainment when the company had made camp at eventide. Though still rather young, Domnuald had proved himself in battle against the Lagini and afterwards the Ulati. Among his own folk, his cheerfulness and common sense boded well for the future.

As he approached his destination, he departed from the main road and travelled about, collecting the tribute and rents due his father. These he took in the form of kine. To landowners in whose houses he overnighted when that was convenient, he explained his intention of giving the animals, in a huge slaughter, to the Bent One of the Mound. Thus should there come no evil creatures upon Niall or the sons of Niall.

Certain men cast dark looks. After their guest was gone, they rode off with word. Having become a cattle drive, Domnuald's progress grew slow. Nevertheless he ended his journey ahead of time.

The past few days had been hot. Air stewed in the nostrils, clothes clung to skin, breath was heavy and sleep unrestful. Clouds brooded enormous, blue-black, with mutterings in their depths and sometimes a wan flicker of lightning; but the blessed rain did not fall and did not fall. The herd became skittish, hard to control. Men's patience wore thin, until tempers often flared into quarrels.

Mag Slecht was a plain out of which rose small hills. Here the menhirs, dolmens, and cromlechs were many. Such folk as lived thereabouts tended the cult sites and, in return, shared in the sacrificial feasts that outsiders held. Otherwise poor and lowly, they were still regarded as having something eldritch about them. Domnuald went by their homes without stopping, more hasty than haughty, until his band spied the halidom of Cromb Cróche from afar. Then he galloped his horse ahead of everybody else, up the track through the woods that decked the hillsides, reached the clearing, and reined in.

Awe smote him. He saw a huge circle of grass surrounded by forest. In this windlessness, leaves were utterly silent, as if cut out of green stone, and shadows made caves beneath the boughs. At the centre blazed brightness almost too fierce to look at. It was the gold and silver that sheathed a giant standing stone which had somewhat the look of a hunchbacked man. Not much smaller were the menhirs that formed a ring around it, twelve altogether, themselves covered with brass kept bright by the rubbing of worshipful hands.

Domnuald's troop had remained below to set up camp, save for a couple of warriors who followed him more slowly. The trees hid them. Shouts, lowing and neighing of beasts, creak of cartwheels reached him faintly, as if the simmering stillness crushed every noise under its weight. He was alone beneath the thunderheads.

Of a sudden that ended. Three more roads led to this crest. Out from the eastern one trod armed men Their spearheads flamed in the ruthless sunlight. Domnuald dropped hand to sword hilt where he sat. The leader strode towards him, a man as heavy as Domnuald was slender, dark as Domnuald was fair. 'And who might you be?' called the Mide prince.

'I am Fland Dub maqq Ninnedo,' growled the stranger, 'king of the Tuath Ben Síde, who hold this land from of old. And you would be the upstart from Temir, would you not?'

'I am son to the Mide King, your high lord,' Domnuald answered as steadily as might be. 'What do you want? The rites are not till day after tomorrow.'

'Hear me,' Fland said. 'You would take over our sacrifices, ours by right since the Children of Danu reigned here. You would glut yourselves on offerings we should have made – '

'The holy meat we will share with all who come!'

Domnuald cried indignantly. 'Do you think the sons of Niall are niggards?'

'Do you seek to buy the favour of our tenants away from us?' Fland retorted. 'It shall not be. We, the landholders of three tuaths, say that.' He tried to fight down his fury. The breath grated in his throat. 'See here, boy. Let us be reasonable. We, my friends and I, we came early so we could catch you, talk with you, beforehand. Surely you and we between us can make a fair division of honour.'

Domnuald reddened. 'How can I parcel away my father's honour? If you bring livestock of your own to offer, I'll not be standing in your way.'

'You have taken as much as the land can spare.'

Youth and summer heat broke free like a lightning flash. 'And so shall it always be, Fer Bolg!'

As if of itself, Fland's spear stabbed upward. Domnuald's escort, arriving just then, saw their leader topple off his horse, to thresh about with blood spouting and flowing.

Fland stared. 'I did not mean – ' he mumbled. Wit came back. As soon as the Mide men knew, they would attack. And they outnumbered his. Did he surrender, Niall would not likely take éricc payment for this young life, not though the honour price that a man of Fland's standing must add was high. Best flee north. The King at Emain Macha would have need of warriors before long.

Fland waved and whistled. His companions loped after him into the woods that they knew and the Mide men did not. Behind them, Domnuald maqq Néill's blood ebbed out, slower and slower, like the blood of an animal slain before Cromb Cróche.

Landing at Clón Tarui, Conual Corcc left a guard with his ships, his wife, and certain others. The rest of his followers, a large and well-armed band, hurried through Mide to Tallten. They had hoped to attend the fair, but a storm held them past Lúgnassat. Thus they arrived only on its last day, as it was breaking up.

Even so, what they saw was a mighty thing. Here Lúg of the Long Arm had buried His fostermother Talltiu and founded sacred games in Her honour, ages past. Here the Kings at Temir were buried, their grave mounds surrounding Hers like warriors asleep outside the house of a queen. Here the contests still took place, races of every kind, wrestling, hurling, games of skill. Here were music, poetry, dance, both solemn and light-hearted. Here was a market to which traders came from all over Ériu and no few countries overseas. Here too was another kind of dickering, for the fair was reckoned a lucky place to make marriages, so that families sought it to discuss arrangements and couples were united in the Glen of the Weddings. Laughter and song resounded through the river valley. Its grass disappeared under tents and booths, and must afterwards grow back out of trampled mud. As they arrived and as they left, the lines of chariots and horsemen stretched for miles, not to speak of people afoot.

Above all, the fair was holy. The King himself conducted the great sacrifices; many lesser ones occurred as well. The laws were spoken aloud before the assembled chieftains and ollams. Serious matters were dealt with; an oath sworn or an agreement made here was doubly binding. For a crime committed at the fair, there could be no compounding by payment. Earth-walled fortresses frowned around Tallten, for it was among the royal seats of the realm, but at Lúgnassat season they stood empty; none dared break the peace, enmities were set aside, anyone could come from anywhere and his person be inviolate.

Conual Corcc made his way among the crowds, towards the hall of the King. It loomed on a rise of ground amidst its outbuildings, long and high, peeled studpoles gleaming from whitewashed cob walls, thatch woven in cunning patterns. Life brawled around it, warriors, attendants, artisans, visitors, men, women, children, horses, hounds, fowl – no swine, which it was gess for a King to possess though he could eat them; but prize cattle were there, sleek of red-white-black-brown coats, prideful of horns. Bright was the garb that swirled from shoulders and waists. Steel shone on weapons, bronze over shields, silver off brooches, gold about necks and arms. Talk surged like surf, along with clamour of children, beasts, smithwork, carting, footfalls, hoofbeats. Smoke from the cookhouse told noses that an ox was roasting.

This morning was brilliant. Conual stood taller than most. His hair burned above the hubbub. Folk stared, made way for him and his troop, but did not venture to address a lord unknown to them – until abruptly a voice cried his name. He stopped, looked, and knew Nemain maqq Aedo.

The druid had aged in the years since Conual went abroad. Stooped and skeletal, he leaned heavily on his staff and walked with the care of those who do not see well. Yet he made haste – a path opened immediately in the throng, and a hush fell – until he and Conual embraced.

'Welcome, welcome, a thousand welcomes, dear heart!' he cried. 'How I have waited for this glad day!'

Conual stepped back. An eeriness cooled his spirit. 'Did you, then, foreknow my coming?' he asked.

'Ah, there have been signs, not all of them good, but you strode into my dreams and . . . waking, I looked into the Well of the Dagdae.' Nemain plucked at Conual's sleeve. 'Come, let us go aside where we can talk.'

'Forgive me, but I should not hang back from greeting the King. That would be an insult.'

'It will not, if I enter with you, for I whispered in his ear that I must be off on mystic business. Himself is bidding farewell to his high-born guests who stayed here during the fair. It will take a while.'

The sense of trouble grew colder within Conual Corcc. He gave the druid his arm and beckoned his men to keep their distance. A way downslope was a grove of rowan, with a bench for those who might wish to linger among the sacred trees and breathe of their magic. Overlooking the turmoil of leavetaking along the river, it was a haven of peace.

The two sat down. 'Know that you have come at a time when grief is upon Niall maqq Echach,' Nemain began. 'The news has reached him that a son of his was slain at Mag Slecht by tuaths restive after he wrung their allegiance from them. Niall could barely keep showing the world a good face and carry on his duties. Now that the fair is ending, he is free to kill. Already he has sent for his hostages from those three tuaths. Tomorrow he will hang them. His vengeance will not stop at that.'

'It's sorry I am to hear this,' Conual said. 'Who is he that fell?'

'Domnuald – Domnuald the Fair, we called him, child of Queen Aethbe.'

Conual sighed. 'Domnuald, indeed? Ochón! I remember him well. He was only a little lad then, but always bright and merry. May he reach Mag Mell and abide in joy.'

'That is too strong a wish to utter at once,' Nemain cautioned. 'Well, Niall mourns the sorer because Domnuald, of all his sons, reminded him most of Breccan, his first-born, who died at Ys. You have heard about that?'

'Somewhat. I have been busy, you know, faring, warring, and . . . dealing . . . in Britannia.'

'You return to claim a dream you have cherished, do you not?'

'I do. It is nothing that threatens Niall. Else why would I seek him first? Rather, he should help me, speed me on my way, for the sake of our common fosterage and the shield I can raise at his back.' Conual frowned. 'This redoubles the misfortune that has befallen him. As for myself – ' He drew breath. 'Nemain, dear, could I meet with those hostages?'

'I knew you would ask that,' said the druid. 'Come.'

The prisoners were confined in a shed, tightly bound. Their guards durst not refuse admittance to Nemain, who led Conual in. The three men met his gaze proudly and spoke curtly. 'You are ready to die, then?' Conual inquired.

'We are that,' replied one, 'thinking on what our deaths must cost Niall later.'

'Hm, now,' said Conual, 'your three tuaths can scarcely stand against his might, nor can they look for much aid out of Ulati country. Would it not be better that he seek revenge on the killers instead of laying waste your homeland?'

He spoke with them a bit more. Thereupon he and Nemain went back out and talked at length.

The sun stood past noon when Niall's last guest had left. He slumped on his high seat, drinking horn after horn of ale. Uneasy stillness filled the hall. The rustle of movement and low voices seemed only to deepen it. Abruptly a shout broke through. The chief of the guard announced Conual maqq Lugthaci, who came in, resplendently clad, at the head of his warriors, at his right hand the druid Nemain maqq Aedo.

Niall roared. He bounded from his seat and plunged down the length of the hall to seize his fosterbrother to him. His folk howled, stamped the floor, beat fists against benches and shields, in their joy at seeing darkness lifted off the King.

Conual's followers carried gifts worthy of him, weapons, fine garments, Roman glassware of lovely shape and swirled colours, Roman silver which included a tray whereon were reliefs of heroes, maidens, and curious creatures. Niall made lavish return. Chief among the treasures he ordered fetched from his hoard and gave to Conual were a golden torc and a bronze trumpet whose workmanship drew cries of admiration from everybody who beheld.

Though the feast that day was hastily prepared, it was grand. After Laidchenn had hailed the newcomer in a poem and received a fibula in the form of a charging boar, he said, 'Fine this is, but before I know what the deeds of our guest have been, I can not properly praise them.'

The building became still as heed turned towards Conual. He smiled. 'That story will take long,' he answered. Scowling: 'Much of it is sorrowful.' Loftily: 'But I shall go to wrest out a new fate for myself.'

As he related or stopped to answer questions, he never conceded defeat. Yet clear it was that woe had betided the Scoti in Britannia. Under Stilicho's leadership,

Romans and Cunedag's Britons had pressed in ever harder. This year, the last Scotic settlers in Ordovician and Silurian lands had perforce abandoned their homes and gone back across the water.

'But mine was not a sad leavetaking,' Conual avowed. 'I had gathered picked fighing men from among them. Others have I brought with me too. They wait in my ships, for they would be strangers and awkward in this company; but they shall soon be working wonders.'

'What is your intent?' Niall demanded bluntly.

Conual laughed. 'Why, what else but to claim my heritage in Mumu? I am of the Eóganachta; I will be as great a King as any of them, and afterwards greater!'

Niall stroked his beard. 'That would please me well, darling,' he said. 'I fear I cannot offer you help. There is too much on my hands. However, abide here until Nath Í returns from the fair he was attending. Do you remember him? He is my nephew, and now my tanist. He has travelled widely in those parts and should be able to give you sage counsel.'

'You are very kind, darling,' Conual replied. 'So sweet are you that I make bold to ask a further boon.'

'You need but ask.'

Conual sat straight, looked the King in the eyes, and spoke weightily: 'You will recall the command laid upon me, that I am to redeem any captives I meet whenever I can. This day I have met with those hostages whom you have condemned to die tomorrow. What I ask is that you let me ransom them.'

A gasp went around the hall. Fists clenched, glances flickered between the two men and the hanging shields and the doorway.

Niall stiffened. The blood came and went in his face. At last he said, word by slow word: 'Do I hear aright? My guest and fosterbrother would not mock me, I am sure. Perhaps you have misunderstood. Know, the tuaths for which they stand surety have murdered my son Domnuald. Shall his blood cry in vain for revenge?'

Nemain lifted a thin hand. 'Not so,' he agreed. 'But they who slew Domnuald, Fland Dub and his fellows, have fled beyond the Walls of the Ulati. What honour lies in burning poor little shielings, driving off poor little herds, butchering innocent tenants? The Gods will raise the just man up, and They will cast the unjust down.'

'I will pay, in gold, the éricc, and add thereto my own honour price,' Conual declared. 'Deny me not, if you love me. I may no more refuse to seek the freedom of men in bonds than you may traverse Mag Callani after sunset or let sunrise find you abed at Temir.'

Niall hunched his shoulders. 'Shall those men go home free, to boast that I dared not avenge my son?' he growled like a wolf at bay.

'They shall not,' Conual answered quickly. 'I will take them south to Mumu. I think they will serve me well. And we are allies, you and I.'

'As for vengeance,' Laidchenn reminded, 'it awaits you at Emain Macha.'

Said the druid: 'The ransom that Conual pays will provide Domnuald a burial such as few kings have had, and endow honours for him for as long as Temir abides.'

Niall gusted a sigh. 'I yield you this, Conual. But it was not well done of you to trick me into making the promise.'

With his pride thus bulwarked, he was presently at his ease, still sombre but readier to talk than he had been of late. In the course of the time that followed, Conual remarked, 'I was surprised to hear your nephew Nath Í is your tanist. Would you not liefer have a son of yours succeed you?'

301

'Nath Í is worthy of his father, my brother Féchra, whose ghost ought to be pleased,' Niall explained. 'Of course, I would have preferred a son of mine. But they all hope to win sword-land, kingdoms of their own.' His gaze pierced the darkness gathering around firelight as the sun went down outside. It came to rest on one of the skulls fastened to the wall, a head he had taken in war upon the Ulati. 'They shall have that,' he said low.

3

Again the year swung towards equinox. Summer died in a last passionate outpouring of warmth, light, green, quick thunderstorms, high stars at night. Life pulsed strong in Ys, trade, shipping, foreigners from inland and overseas, readymaking for festival.

On such a day Dahut went from temple school to the home of Bodilis, whose turn it was to care for her. The time had been long, because first the Queen had had an illness that did not readily yield to medicine or even the Touch, then the princess had been a while at the Nymphaeum. That was customary with royal children, to get them used to the sacred site and its environs before they reached the age of full vestalhood. None had started these visits as young as Dahut, but the Nine had their reasons. Today the King had come back from business in Darioritum. He would not spend the night with Bodilis, he never did any more, but he would call on her.

Thus Dahut burst into the atrium crying jubilantly, 'Mother Bodilis, Mother Bodilis, is father here yet? He is coming, isn't he? He always wants to see me very soon.'

She stopped, looked, and breathed, 'Why are you sad?'

The woman smiled. It made crinkles around her lips and eyes, radiating into the cheeks as they had never done in Dahut's first memories of her. 'Oh, I am not, dear,' she answered softly. 'I am happy, in a solemn way. Something wonderful is to bless us.'

Dahut's eyes, the same blue as hers, widened. 'What? I know father will bring me a present. What is it going to be?'

'I fear you must wait. You should have been told erenow, but – '

Footfalls sounded at Dahut's back. Turning, she saw Tambilis enter from the street. The daughter of Bodilis was finely dressed in a gown of white silk embroidered with doves, on her feet gold-inlaid shoes, on her head a garland of roses from which her light-brown hair flowed free past the delicate features. She looked quite different all at once. It was as if overnight she had grown taller, her body had filled out and her bosom swelled. Another strangeness was in her as well: she seemed frightened and resolute and lost in a dream.

Bodilis hastened to her. They embraced. 'Darling, darling,' the mother said. 'Are you truly ready and willing?'

Tambilis nodded. 'Aye.'

'Be not afraid. You are now big enough, and this is Belisama's will, and, and be sure he will deal kindly with you. Be sure of that.'

'I know.'

Bodilis sobbed forth a laugh. 'Come, then. Let me show you what I've had prepared, and tell you what I think will be best, and – ' Hand in hand, they left the room and Dahut.

The girl stood where she was. Her face clouded, less with hurt than anger. A servant woman appeared from

303

the inner part of the house. Bodilis must have told her to absent herself. She was an Osismian, blond, plump, one of many who sought to Ys and worked a few years to earn a dowry, unless they could catch a husband here. 'Breifa,' Dahut snapped, 'what is happening?'

The maid was taken aback. 'You know not, Princess? Why, tonight the King makes Tambilis really his Queen.' She blushed, giggled, squirmed. 'Well, he knows not either, I hear. 'Tis to be an unawaited welcome-home gift for him. She is beautiful, the lady Tambilis, nay?'

'Oh,' said Dahut tonelessly.

'I could not but overhear,' chattered Breifa. ''Twas Queen Bodilis who thought it should be done thus. Messages and such, arrangements, those would be too slow and stiff, they'd take the joy out of this. And Tambilis would be – passive, only a thing, is that what Queen Bodilis said? I remember not. Anyway, better Tambilis sweep him off his feet when he arrives, thinking he has just been invited for a cup of wine and a chat. Then he'll sweep her off hers soon enough, ha, ha!'

Dahut said nothing.

Breifa covered her mouth. 'I talk too much, I do. What a bustle 'tis been, making everything right. Rejoice, lady Dahut. Someday you may be a Queen too.'

'The Queen . . . of the man . . . who kills my father?'

'Oh, dear, I'm sorry. Well, such is the law of the Gods.'

Dahut stalked off. She went into the street and stood arms folded, staring from this height out across the city to the sea.

Bodilis emerged, leading Una, her child by Gratillonius, a few months younger than Dahut but smaller and much more quiet. 'There you are,' the woman said. 'I looked and looked for you.' She paused. 'What is wrong?'

'Naught,' said Dahut, gaze held afar.

Bodilis laid a hand on her shoulder. ''Tis disappointment for you, I know, not to see your father this eventide. Be brave. You will soon meet him, I pledge to you. You and Una and I shall stay in Tambilis's house tonight. Won't you like that? And I will tell you why, and you will be happy for him and your friend, I'm sure.'

Dahut shrugged and trudged along.

4

At sixteen years of age, Tambilis had completed the education required of her. Each Queen served the Gods and Ys not only in set duties, but according to whatever special abilities she possessed. Tambilis had begun teaching elementary Latin in the temple school of Belisama, where Bodilis instructed advanced students of that language.

The young Queen was strolling about the flowerful intricacy of Elven Gardens during the noontide rest period. She smiled drowsily and crooned to herself. Rounding a hedge, she came upon Dahut. The child sat tracing pictures in the gravelled path. What they were was hard to guess, because the stones rattled back together behind her finger.

'Why, why, good day,' Tambilis said, astonished.

Dahut looked up like a blind person.

'But you're miserable!' Tambilis exclaimed. She hunkered down to hug her playmate. 'What's wrong?'

'Naught,' said the dry little voice.

'That's untrue,' Tambilis chided. 'Hark, you can tell me.'

Dahut shook her head.

Tambilis considered. ''Tis the King, nay?' she asked after a moment. 'You feel your father slighted you. Well, he did not. 'Twas but that he – he and I – well, the will of the Goddess was upon us. Is. Have no fear. Soon he'll greet you, and he does have the prettiest cloak for you, that he found among the Veneti, and, oh, all sorts of adventures to tell about.'

Still there was no response. 'Indeed,' Tambilis persisted, 'you must visit us. We're staying at the palace now while we . . . get to know each other better. We shall for several days yet.' Resignation laid a sudden burden on her voice. 'After that, all will be much as it was before.'

'I will see him somewhere else,' Dahut said.

'But why? My dear, I've not turned my back on you. I love you always.' Tambilis searched for words. ''Tis only that time goes, things change. Later you'll understand.' Impulsively: 'This was not my wish at first. 'Twas Guilvilis who caused it, stupid, clumsy, loving Guilvilis. She mustered courage at last to tell me I did wrong, withholding myself when I could gladden him, lighten his cares, and – And, Dahut,' glowed from her, 'the Goddess gives me joy too, as She will you someday.'

Dahut screamed. She scrambled to her feet and fled.

When she was not at her next class, the teacher sent an acolyte to inquire at the dwellings of the Gallicenae. Had she perchance been taken sick? It took hours to establish that she had disappeared, and then to organize search parties. They did not find her until sundown, after she had re-entered the city at Aurochs Gate and was stubbornly walking up Amber Street towards the home of Fennalis. Her clothes were wet, with smells of kelp and fish.

306

XIV

1

As autumn yellowed leaves, Conual Corcc bade Niall maqq Echach farewell. Since this must at first be a reconnoitring expedition, he left behind most of his men. Just thirty followed him south, among them the three hostages he had saved. His Cruthinach wife came too, for there is magic as well as comfort in women.

Shut off as Mumu was from the rest of Ériu, Niall heard nothing more until spring. When finally a messenger arrived to bid the remaining warriors now seek their lord, it was a strange story that he brought.

A day's travel northwest from the Mountain of Fair Women was the Plain of Femen, where Fedelmm the witch had troubled King Lugthach. It was fertile and well settled, save at one place where forest stood ancient. Few ventured in, for at the middle of the woods reared the Síd Drommen. This limestone outcrop, whose three hundred feet overtopped the trees around, was believed to be the haunt of elves, ghosts, every creature of the Other World. However, swineherds took their animals there in season for the rich mast. Though their trade be humble, it gave them ties to Those Beyond.

Once two of them were in that wood together. Each kept pigs for the king of a neighbouring tuath: Dardriu for the king of Éle, Coriran for the king of Múscraige. To his master King Aed came Coriran and said: 'We fell into a deep sleep, Dardriu and I. Adream, we beheld the

Ridge of the Beings. Before it were a yew tree and a flagstone. Somehow we knew that that was the tree of the Eóganachta, and that he who stands upon the stone shall wax great.'

The druid of Aed thought deeply, sought visions, and declared: 'The Síd Drommen shall become the seat of the kings over all Mumu. From him who first lights a fire under that yew shall they descend.'

'Let us go to light it!' cried Aed.

'Let us await the morning,' counselled the druid: for it was late, and the sun hidden behind lowering clouds. Soon a snowstorm began, this early in the year.

It caused Conual, his wife, and their men to lose their way as they fared down from the north. They blundered into the wood and took shelter below the rock. A yew tree growing there, its leaves withered but as yet unfallen, gave a roof of sorts, letting them kindle a fire. A flat stone at its foot made a place to stand while shoes dried out.

So did Aed find them. Although downcast, the king did not venture to quarrel with the Gods. Conual had, indeed, a birthright claim. Moreover, he was a friend of the mighty Niall, of whom they had report. The upshot was that Aed acknowledged Conual king of the surrounding territory and gave him his own son as hostage.

Thus the story that Niall heard in spring. He smiled and let the men go whom Conual had brought from Britannia. Among them were several ollam craftsmen – engineers, stonemasons – who understood the Roman arts of fortification. With them Niall sent rich gifts.

A year passed.

For Niall it, like the twelvemonth before, was less warlike than many had been. Both years were nonetheless busy. His sons champed to be off conquering, but their father held them back. 'Lay the keel, fasten the ribs, bind the strakes,' he said. 'When the ship is ready, we will sail.' They did not fully understand, not being seamen like him.

Niall did complete the taking over of those nine tuaths which had been tributary to the Ulati. He raised new kings among them to replace those he had felled in battle, and a high King above these: all obedient to him. They were well content, because he returned to them that governance over the sacrifices at Mag Slecht which had been theirs from of old. Despite yielding this, which cost him little and won him much in the way of goodwill, he never let wane his resolve to have vengeance for Domnuald – and someday, somehow, for Breccan.

The hostages that the tuaths gave him he treated so generously that they vowed to fight at his side when he became ready for his onslaught against the Ulati. Likewise would their kinfolk. The kingdom he had founded for these became known as the Aregésla, They Who Give Hostages, a name borne proudly. People began calling him Niall of the Nine Hostages.

– King Fergus Fogae in Emain Macha was fully aware of the storm that brewed in the south. He thought of launching an attack himself, decided that that would be ruinous, and set about strengthening defences throughout his realm. His poets reminded him of how Cú Culanni had brought Medb and her Condachtae low. Those songs echoed spookily in the hall.

– Next Imbolc came messengers from Conual to Temir. They bore gifts no less than those Niall had sent south, and fateful tidings.

Conual's power had grown like the antlers on a stag. While small, his force of exiles was schooled in ways of war unknown to Mumu. Each battle they won brought new allegiances, thus a larger host to call upon. Without fighting, even more chieftains swore faith to this new-comer whom the Gods had clearly blessed. Lately he had got for a second wife Ámend, daughter of Oengus Bolg, king of the powerful Corco Loígde. They holding land on the south coast, Conual thereby gained an opening to the outer world.

The magic that flamed around his name came not least from the seat he had chosen. It was the very Síd Drommen: an audacity that brought not disaster on him, but victory after victory. There he was building a stone stronghold of the Roman kind, impregnable to anything that Gaelic men could bring against it: Liss inna Lochraide, the Fort of the Heroes. Already, in the mouths of the folk, the name of the rock itself was changing to Latin Castellum, which soon got softened to Cassel.

The poet who related these things to Niall knew better than to say so, but unmistakably underlying his staves was glee, that his lord's rise was so swift that the deeds of the Temir King could not compare.

Niall sat silent a long time, staring into firelight darkness. Finally those who sat close saw his lips move. 'The Síd Drommen,' whispered forth. 'He dared. He *dared*.'

2

Forty days after solstice, the diminishing gloom of winter was made bright in Ys. Queen Tambilis bore her first child. Mother and daughter were in the best of health. As he was wont on such occasions, the King decreed festival immediately after the hallowing of the new little Semura-mat. Legionaries formed an honour guard when he led Tambilis from the Temple of Belisama to the palace. With

310

them came the rest of the Nine – on as high a holiday as this, the Gods required none to stay alone on Sena – and the magnates of the city with their wives. Wine, mead, and rich food from the royal stores were distributed among the poor, that they too might celebrate. Entertainers of every kind, having anticipated the event, swarmed merrily about. After dark the Fire Fountain blossomed, though weather kept the Forum almost deserted.

In a house near Menhir Place there was no mirth. It was a small but decent house, such as a married soldier could afford to rent. The matron was having her own first childbirth. Her labour started about when the Queen's did. Still it went on. She was Keban, wedded to Budic.

Adminius had excused him from duty, never expecting he would be gone this long. He sat on a bench in the main room, elbows on knees, head bowed between shoulders. A lamp picked furnishings out of the shadows that filled every corner. His breath smoked in the chill. Outside, the night wind hooted, shook the door, flung handfuls of hail against shutters.

The midwife came in from the bedroom holding a candle. She shambled in her exhaustion. Budic raised his face. The youthfulness it had kept through the years was hollowed out. He had not shaved all this while; the whiskers made a thin fuzz over jaws and cheeks. 'How goes it?' he croaked.

'Best you look in,' the woman said, flat-voiced. 'You might not see her alive again. I'll keep doing what I can, sir, but my arts are spent.'

Budic rose and stumbled into the other chamber. A brazier gave warmth that sharpened the reek of sweat, urine, vomit, burnt tallow. Enough light seeped through the doorway to show him the swollen form and sunken wet countenance. Her eyes were shut, except for a

311

glimmer of white. Her mouth was half open, her breath shallow. Now and then a feeble convulsion shook her. Helplessly, he laid his palm on her forehead. 'Can you hear me, beloved?' he asked. He got no answer.

A sound drew his attention – crash of wood against wall, suddenly loudened storm noises, the midwife's cry of amazement. He went back into the main room. A tall, grizzle-bearded man in a coarse robe and paenula had entered. One knotty hand gripped a staff. Beneath a half-shaven scalp his features jutted like the headlands.

'Corentinus!' Budic exclaimed in Latin. 'What brings you, Father?'

'A sense within me that you have need, my son,' replied the chorepiscopus.

The midwife traced a warding crescent. Tales had long gone about that this man of Christ sometimes had foreknowledge.

'Need of your prayers,' Budic said. 'Oh, Father, she's dying.'

'I feared that. Let me see.' Corentinus brushed past him. Budic sank down on the bench and wept.

Corentinus returned. 'She is far gone, poor soul,' he said. 'This was just a little late in life, maybe, for her to start bearing. I thought she was barren, and beseeched God to gladden the two of you with a child, but – '

Budic lifted his gaze. 'Can you pray her back to me?'

'I can only ask God's mercy. His will be done.' Corentinus pondered. 'Although – ' Decision: 'He helps us mortals, even unto an angelic summons, but we must do our share. My rough medical skills are of no use here. The Gallicenae command healing powers beyond any I've ever heard of elsewhere. I'll go fetch one.'

Budic gaped. 'What? But they're feasting at the palace.

312

I know because Cynan looked in on us on his way to parade.'

Corentinus rapped out a laugh. 'The more merit in the charity, then. Who can tell but what this may start the pagan on a path to salvation? Hold fast, son. I'll be back as soon as may be.' He went out into the night.

The midwife shuddered. 'What did he want, sir?' she asked. Her Latin was rudimentary.

Budic shook his head, numbed beyond his numbness at the thought of such a raven breaking into the King's banquet and demanding the aid of the Nine.

Whoo-oo called the wind, and more hail rattled over the cobbles.

Budic returned to the bedside. Time crept.

The door thumped open. Corentinus loomed above a slight form in a cowled cloak hastily thrown over splendour. Emerging, Budic recognized Innilis. He pulled himself erect and saluted. Behind the two came a servant woman with a box in her arms, and then Adminius in armour that sheened wet.

'Stand aside,' ordered the Queen. Budic had never before heard her anything but soft-spoken. She stepped into the bedroom. 'Light.' The midwife got the candle. 'We'll want more than this. I've brought tapers.' The servant, who had followed, began unpacking physician's things from the box. Innilis closed the door.

Adminius looked around. 'Filthy weather,' he said. 'You got something ter warm a fellow's belly? The centurion 'ad us inside, of course. We'd get our share when the fancy part of the evening was done and 'e relieved us guards.'

Mechanically, Budic set out wine and water jugs, cups, a loaf of bread and sections of sausage. 'He let you go just like that?' he asked.

313

"E's our centurion, ain't 'e? Told me ter convey 'is sympathy and best wishes. 'E can't leave the feast, that'd insult some of their 'igh and mightinesses there, but 'e'll stop by in the morning. I came along on be'alf of the boys.'

'The priestess Innilis – '

'She honours her calling,' said Corentinus.

Towards dawn she trod forth. Her face was pallid, eyes dark-rimmed, hands atremble. 'Keban should live,' she told the men. 'The child – it was a boy – I had to sacrifice the child for the mother, but I think he was doomed in any case. Nay, do not go in yet, not ere Mella has . . . wrapped him. Besides, Keban has swooned. But I think, by Belisama's grace, she will live. She may be in frail health hereafter, and I doubt she will conceive again. But your wife should live, Budic.'

He went to his knees. 'Christ b-b-be thanked,' he stammered in Latin. And in Ysan, lifting eyes burnt-out but adoring: 'How can I thank *you*, my lady? How can I repay you?'

Innilis smiled the least bit, laid a hand on his blond head, and murmured, 'The Nine take no pay, unless it be in the coin of love.'

'Ever shall I love the Gallicenae and, and stand ready to serve them, whatever their wish may be. By the body of Christ I swear it.'

She declined his offer of refreshment and departed with her attendant, promising to visit later in the day. Adminius escorted them. Corentinus stayed behind. 'Let us thank the Lord, my son,' he said. His tone was harsh.

3

At Imbolc Niall Náegéslach gave out that after Beltene he would fare overseas. Unspoken was: 'Let Conual Corcc down in Mumu have his fortress. The Romans threw him out of Britannia. I will carry my sword there.'

Remembering what had happened under the wall of Ys, some men were daunted. Most, though, felt no forebodings. In the ten years since, the King at Temir had won back everything he lost, and far more. This foray could well begin laying the groundwork of his vengeance on the city of the hundred towers. Well-informed chieftains knew that the terrible Stilicho had not only himself quitted Britannia, he had taken with him many troops to use against the Germani who threatened Gallia. Complacent and thinly defended, the island east of Ériu offered wealth for the taking.

So it proved. Those who met with the King and followed him in galleys and currachs found easy pickings. From Alba to Dumnonia they ravaged. Men they killed, women they raped, slaves and booty they took. What legionaries there remained never got to a place the raiders struck before they were gone, leaving smouldering ruins, beheaded corpses, weeping survivors who had fled and then crept back home. The Britons themselves were ill prepared and fought poorly – save for Cunedag's tough hillmen, whose territories Niall steered clear of. Elsewhere he opened a way for Scoti to return, resettling along the western shores.

In blood he washed away his bitterness. As hay harvest

and Lúgnassat neared he went home full of hope, he went home in glory.

He came back to wrath. In his absence, the Lagini had entered Mide and made havoc.

Eochaid, son of King Éndae Qennsalach, led that great inroad: Eochaid, whose first taste of battle seven years ago had become rank with defeat at the hands of Niall; Eochaid, whose handsomeness was forever marred by the scars of the blistering satire which Tigernach, son of Laidchenn, laid on him that same day. Since then he had known victory. He joined the Loígis clans when trouble broke loose with men of Condacht or Mumu, to repel the invaders and harry them past their own borders. He helped bring the allied kingdom of Ossraige to obedience, and collected tribute that subordinate tuaths in the mountains would have denied. Yet always the memory of the humbling festered.

They were, after all, as honour-proud in Qóiqet Lagini as men were anywhere. In Gallia their distant ancestors had been the Gáileóin, the Men of the Spears, which the Lagini claimed was also the meaning of their present name. Having entered Ériu, they formed their own confederation at the same time as the Goddess Macha of the Red Locks built Emain Macha to the north. Their seat of high Kings, Dún Alinni, was the work of Mess Delmon, who cast out the dark Fomóri, and pursued them into the very realms of the dead. The Lagini held Temir itself until the Condachtae who founded Mide drove them from it.

Long had Eochaid brooded upon this. When the news came that Niall was bound abroad with as large a following as could put to sea, he shouted that this was a chance given by the Gods Themselves. Éndae, his father, urged caution; but Éndae was weakened by age, while the

316

country throbbed with fierce young men eager to hear the son.

Thus Eochaid gathered a host on the west bank of the Ruirthech, which near Dún Alinni flowed north before bending eastward to the sea. His charioteers led the warriors on into Mide, straight towards Temir.

They failed to take it. Those sons of Niall who had stayed behind held it too strongly. Yet bloody was the fighting ere the Lagini recoiled. Thereupon they went widely about, killing, plundering, burning. Countless were the treasures, cattle, slaves, and heads they took home.

Niall came back. When he saw the ruin that had been wrought, he did not rage aloud as once he would have done. Men shivered to behold an anger as bleak as the winter during which he made his preparations.

It may be that at first King Fergus of the Ulati breathed easier, knowing that for another year he need not await attack out of Mide. If so, his happiness soon blew away, on the wind that bore the smoke out of Qóiqet Lagini. From end to end of that Fifth Niall and his sons went. They pierced and scattered the levies that sought to stay them, as a prow cleaves waves, flinging foam to starboard and larboard. His ship, though, ploughed red waters, and the spray was flames and the whine in the rigging was from women who keened over their dead.

Éndae yielded before his land should be utterly waste. Now Niall exacted the Bóruma; and when he brought it back, chief among the hostages who stumbled bound at his chariot wheels was Eochaid.

Never did Niall show honour to this prince, as he did to those he had from the Aregésla and elsewhere. The Laginach hostages lived crowded into a wretched hut, miserably fed and clad. They were only allowed out once a day to exercise, and that only because otherwise they would have taken sick and died – which some did anyhow. When Niall fared in procession, most of the hostages in his train wore golden chains, the merest token of a captivity which was actually a life full and free in the royal household. The Lagini went in shackles of iron.

On his deathbed a few months later, the druid Nemain reproached the King for this. 'You are ungenerous, darling, the which is not like you. Was it not enough to reclaim, in the Bóruma, threefold what that young man reaved us of?'

'I have my revenge to finish,' Niall answered. 'Let Eochaid meanwhile be my sign to the Gods that I do not forget wrongs done my kindred.'

The old man struggled for breath. 'What . . . do you mean . . . by that – you whom I love?'

'Eochaid shall go free,' Niall promised, 'when the head of Fland Dub is in my hand, and Emain Macha mine, and Ys under the sea.'

XV

1

It had become clear to the Nine and many others that Dahut would embark upon womanhood in her twelfth year. Suddenly she was gaining height and shapeliness. There was never any misproportion, outbreak in the clear skin, or loss of self-possession. While always slender, she would be more tall and robust than her mother, though equally graceful and lightfooted. The buds of her breasts were swelling towards ripeness, the curves beneath becoming rich. Golden down appeared below her arms, and under her belly formed a triangle, the figure sacred to the Goddess as the wheel was to Taranis and the spiral to Lir. She strode more than she skipped. Her voice took on a huskiness.

Above, she eerily resembled Dahilis. Great lapis lazuli eyes looked from tawny arches of brow, out of a face where the high Suffete cheekbones joined a chin small but firm. Her nose was short, a little flared at the nostrils, her mouth full and a little wide. Her hair billowed halfway down her back when she loosened it, thick, amber-hued with a tinge of copper therein.

What she lacked was the sunny temper that had been Dahilis's. Despite her beauty and quick-wittedness, Dahut was a solitary child. The Gallicenae and their maidservants had tried to find her companions of her own age, but those grew inclined to avoid her. At home the boys complained that she was too imperious, the girls shivered and called her 'odd'. Dahut did not seem to care. She preferred adult company when she was not off by herself, which came to be more and more in her free time.

She learned fast, read widely, was earnest in her devotions. Athletic, she walked or ran across long stretches, ranged the woods when at the Nymphaeum, rode the horses her father gave her or drove a chariot he had lately added, was a crack target splitter with bow or light javelin, spent as many hours as she could arrange on the sea, sometimes even demanded privacy to strip and swim in its chill turbulence. Female skills she acquired, but without much interest. Occasionally she made use of Gratillonius's workshop behind the palace, and he laughed that an excellent artisan was lost in her as well as in him. She appreciated good food, drink, garb, together with art, music, theatre; but it was as if she found her real pleasure in board games and other mental contests, or simply in listening to the King's conversations with visitors from afar.

His Roman soldiers doted on her. They called her their Luck, and practised special drills when she was there to see. Likewise, the fisher captain Maeloch was her slave.

The Queens held her precious too, though in various ways and for various reasons. They agreed she must not be spoiled – if anything, more was required of her than of the rest of the princesses – nor should weight be laid on the fact that they perceived a destiny in her, without being able to see what it was. Nevertheless, inevitably, Dahut got intimations of this.

And so in her twelfth springtime she embarked upon womanhood.

It happened when she was staying with Tambilis. Gratillonius did not these days, because Tambilis was near term with her second child, whom she meant to name Estar. Dahut came into her room by dawnlight, shook her awake, and said sombrely, 'I have bled.'

'What?' Tambilis sat up, rubbed her eyes, looked around. 'Oh, my dear!' She surged from her bed and hugged the girl close to her. 'Welcome! Be not afraid. Rejoice. Come, let me see.'

In the guest chamber she examined the cloth that had been for some time laid atop Dahut's nether sheet. A spot marked it, brilliantly red against white, however dim the chamber still was. 'Aye, this is your first coursing ever,' Tambilis said. 'May they be many and all easy. How feel you?'

'I am well.' Grudgingly, Dahut pulled off her nightgown at Tambilis's behest and let the woman show her how to wash herself and attach a pad.

'Now you remember what you must do,' Tambilis chattered. 'And me, oh, the glad load of duties on me! What do you wish for breakfast, darling?'

Dahut shrugged. Well, girls were often upset on this day of their lives. Yet Dahut was calm enough, withdrawn into herself.

'We shall have *such* a festival! We begin with our prayers, of course. I'll help you dress.'

Tambilis kept her image of Belisama in a room at the rear of the house. It was a miniature of the Goddess as Maiden, carved out of narwhal ivory and set in a niche painted deep blue with stars. Little of Quinipilis remained in this house; Tambilis favoured things bright and dainty. She held up the spotted cloth as she and Dahut gave thanks.

Now the girl did not change lodgings but stayed where she was, avoiding company, saying her orisons and meditating upon the mysteries. When the flow had stopped, she bathed in water not from a cistern-well but piped from the Tower, to which it had flowed down the canal from the Nymphaeum. Then it was time for celebration.

Sumptuously arrayed, Dahut went forth from the house into a glorious morning full of songbirds. Ocean sparkled beyond spires washed by last night's rain. Flowers and blossoms dappled the valley and its guardian hills. Airs blew gentle. King Gratillonius waited outside in full regalia, love and pride radiating from him, together with all the Gallicenae in their blue-and-white attire of priestesses. The magnates of the city were there too, surrounded by their families. Light blazed off metal as legionaries drew swords and shouted, '*Ave!*' while Ysan marines crashed pike butts down on paving stones.

Musicians played fore and aft of the procession that went to the Temple of Belisama. Ordinary folk flocked to join it and follow it into the halidom. In that twilit chamber they stood quiet. From the aisles, vestals sang praise.

The Nine stationed themselves behind the altar, before the tall images of Maiden, Mother, and Hag. Dahut knelt and asked their blessing. She received wine, a drop of ox blood, and salt. When she had laid her garland on the block, Fennalis, senior priestess, placed on her brows a coronet of silver studded with emeralds and rubies. In lieu of her mother, her father bowed to the Triune and put a toy into her hands. It was one among many he had made, chosen by her because she was particularly fond of it, a gaily painted wooden horse with jointed legs. This too she laid on the altar and dedicated to the Goddess. That took but a single word: 'Farewell'.

Again outside after the service, she received the embraces and congratulations of her kin, the cheers of the crowd. She responded sparingly, though she did dimple up repeated smiles. Thereafter Gratillonius brought the party to the palace for a feast. At this she had a final tradition to observe, albeit an event regarded as merry rather than solemn. She gave away the rest of her playthings to her younger half-sisters.

Who should receive what had taken forethought. Bodilis's Una, Guilvilis's Sasai, Lanarvilis's Julia, Maldunilis's Zisa, Forsquilis's Nemeta, Vindilis's Augustina were close to Dahut in years. Guilvilis's Antonia and Camilla were not far behind either; but her Valeria was only five, while Tambilis's Semuramat was two – and that last mother claimed a rattle also, because it was lucky for an unborn child to receive a gift.

Thus went the Welcoming of Dahut. Commoners did likewise for their girls, though usually the blessing was by a minor priestess at a small sanctuary and the meal afterwards modest. It was all the same in the sight of the Goddess.

For royal children, though, unto the third generation, more waited.

It happened quietly. In the morning Dahut rode to the Nymphaeum with an escort and a Queen. This one's task would be to stay there for a few days, consecrate the maiden a full vestal, and teach her certain secrets. Dahut would remain longer and receive training in her new duties. Thenceforward she would be at the Nymphaeum a sennight each lunar month, otherwise at the Temple in Ys, as housekeeper, gardener, participant in rites, and student. She would have ample leisure and a stipend which would enable her to live where and how she chose in the city, provided she remain pure. Her service was to end on her eighteenth birthday. Then she would be at liberty to marry, enrol as a subordinate priestess, pursue an independent career, do whatever she wished. Any daughters she might bear, and any daughters of these, must in their turn become vestals like her, enjoying the same advantages – unless, before the term of the vow closed, the Sign should come.

Bodilis had volunteered to be her sponsor at the hallowing. She had been half-sister to Dahut's mother.

The day of arrival went to settling in. Each virgin had a tiny room to herself. A newcomer was subject to japery and giggles in dining commons, but not too many questions. After all, she had been here before. Dahut bore it – neither cheerily nor ungraciously; aloofly – and retired early.

Her religious induction came the next morning, a brief ceremony. Later various instructresses interviewed her. They had already met the new votary, but hoped for closer acquaintance and some idea as to what kinds of education promised most for her. In the afternoon was a dinner more elegant than usual here, where everyday fare was simple. Later, until dark, pipe, drum, sistrum, and voice gave melody for dances on the greensward.

The morning after that, Bodilis drew Dahut aside. 'Before I go home, I am to explain to you the secrets,' she said. 'They're not really close-veiled. That would be impossible.' She smiled. 'But tradition insists that certain knowledge may pass only between Queen and vestal, and otherwise not be spoken aloud. Let's avail ourselves of this beautiful weather while it holds. Go dress yourself for a ramble and meet me.'

Dahut obeyed happily. When she and Bodilis had left the building, she could not forbear to prance about and bay the Wolf Chant. 'Ah, you are young still, sweetling,' the woman murmured. 'Come along.'

They took a trail uphill into the woods. A rivulet gurgled beside it. Birds trilled. Squirrels raced ruddy.

Sunlight filled leaves with green fire and spattered on the shade beneath. Warmth and savour steamed from the earth.

'There is naught arcane about most of what I shall tell you,' Bodilis said. 'Special prayers. Cantrips to ward off certain misfortunes and certain creatures. Minor medical skills; we *are* healers, we royal women, though lay physicians practise too. At the least, dignity requires we be able to treat our own lesser ailments. It begins with knowing how to brew a tisane of willow against cramps, albeit many a goodwife can do the same. But let us commence with the greatest and holiest of all, the gift that the Goddess bestowed upon Brennilis and those who should come after.'

They emerged where the hillside shouldered out to form a hollow. The spring that fed the stream was not much farther up, and here the water spread some three feet wide, ankle-deep, glittery beneath the sun. That light laid gold over the crowns of the beeches, hazels, and thorns walling in the grassy space. Masses of convolvulus clung to their innermost boles. Within their circle, blue stars sprang from plants with hairy stems and leaves, a cubit tall.

Bodilis signed herself. She knelt before a patch of them. 'Here,' she said, her tone now grave. 'Look closely.'

Dahut did perfunctory reverence and hunkered impatient. 'Why, that's just borage,' she said. 'They use it for flavour and colour in food. It helps against fever. What else?'

'It is the Herb,' Bodilis told her.

Dahut reared back. 'What? This?'

Bodilis nodded. 'Aye. Our name for it is "ladygift". If a Queen of Ys eats a spoonful of these flowers, fresh or dried, a small spoonful, she does not conceive that day. When she wishes a child, she need simply leave off the use – ' a fleeting, wistful smile – 'and open herself to the King, if she be not too old. It is the bestowal of Belisama, so that the Nine may have sovereignty over their wombs and thus freedom to uphold the law of Ys against any of our random Kings who proves to be bad.'

Dahut's fingers stole forward to touch the plant. 'But this,' she said, 'only this? I thought belike 'twas magical vervain.'

Bodilis chuckled. 'Not that, of all plants! It works to cure barrenness.'

'But the Herb should grow in a sacred place – the Wood of the King?'

Both now kneeling, Bodilis took the hands of Dahut in hers, caught and held the maiden's gaze, said slowly: 'All the world is sacred, and perhaps the commonplace most.

'The knowledge of what ladygift actually is has gone about underground – that could never be stopped – but 'tis a thing folk do not bespeak. For the Herb, not mere borage but the Herb, is for the Nine alone. To every woman else, this plant is what you said, a simple, a seasoning, a decoration, naught else.

'Remember, Dahut, you must remain chaste until the end of your service. Else the wrath of the Gods would be upon you, and as for the law of man, you could be thrown off the sea cliffs or whipped from Ys into the wilderness. It has happened in the past.

'The ladygift will cease to ward you if you pass your vestalhood unchosen. After that, you must care for yourself, or endure, as has ever been the lot of women.

'But if ere then the Sign appears between your breasts and you become a Queen: then before each time the King comes to you, or you think he may, until you desire to bear his child – take a few of these little flowers, and kiss them, and swallow them. For the kisses of the Gallicenae raise the Power.'

2

Very early in the shipping season, a large and well-laden merchant vessel stood out from Ys for Hivernia. The crew did not expect to have need for their fighting skills. Strengthened and vigorously used by King Grallon, the navy had scoured these waters clean. Beyond the Dumnonian end of Britannia there was a chance of pirates. However, Tommaltach had assured the captain it was most unlikely that they could bring anything more to bear than a few currachs; and such would not attack a ship with high freeboard, war engines, armoured men. The peace of King Conual was spreading fast across Mumu, where folk preferred trade to war anyway. Two years ago, Niall, the King in Mide, had wasted Roman territories. Since then, though, his attention was aimed north; the question was not whether he would fall on the Ulati, but when.

No prudent man would have fared just on the word of a young barbarian. It was borne out by other reports that had come to Ys as traffic between his people and the city grew in erratic fashion. Besides, Tommaltach maqq Donngalii was no ordinary adventurer. His father was king of a tuath and a friend of Conual Corcc. Tommaltach, age about sixteen, was a blooded warrior when he joined a venture to Ys, less in hopes of profiting from gold, sheepskins, and salt pork than to see the marvels. He had taken the trouble beforehand to acquire some of the language, as well as basic Latin. Meeting him, Rufinus readily persuaded him to stay through the winter. During those months, the Gael living in Rufinus's eyrie, the two of them had grown close, and Rufinus had got a working knowledge of Scotic speech.

After the stark headlands at Armorica, his goal seemed gentle, lushly fruitful, incredibly green. The Ysans anchored in a small bay, made camp ashore, gave presents to natives who approached. Tommaltach dickered for horses. The crew loaded three of these and put Roman saddles on the rest. It took a little while to get the animals used to that. Leaving most of their shipmates on guard, Rufinus and Tommaltach rode off at the head of ten. The journey to Castellum took a pair of easy days, broken at one of the free hostels which kings here endowed.

Rufinus observed carefully as he fared, and beswarmed his guide with questions. This was pastureland where it was not forest, sheep and cattle at graze, only a few small and scattered fields sown in rye, barley, oats. Some wattle-and-daub dwellings stood isolated, but most seemed to cluster inside earthen ringwalls with palisades on top. Towns did not exist. Armies were wild rabble, virtually without body protection, led by noblemen in chariots such as were four hundred years obsolete in Britannia and Gallia.

Withal, throughout Hivernia – Ériu, its people called it – arts and crafts excelled, while respect for learning was so high that the person of a druid or poet was inviolate. Women were almost as free as in Ys, infinitely better off than anywhere in the Roman world. Aside from slaves, who were mainly captives taken in raids, the relationship between master and follower, landholder and tenant, was contractual, either party able to abrogate it at will. Folkmoot and *brithem* – judge – gave out a rough justice;

wrongdoing was generally compounded by payment, and a rich man must give more in redress than a poor man. When this failed, frequently the aggrieved person sat down at the door of the other and fasted until the latter, who was supposed to starve himself also, yielded. 'Unless, I imagine, he outlasts the plaintiff,' Rufinus drawled. 'Still, you Scoti are not quite the two-legged wolves the Romans think you.'

'Ah, it's grand to be home, that it is,' Tommaltach exulted. 'Not but what I don't mean to be often again in Ys, for the exploring of its wonders and to carouse with you, darling.'

Rufinus sighed to himself. This race habitually talked in extravagances. The youth had no idea what they implied to his listener. Tommaltach was beautiful: medium tall, wide-shouldered but supple, the snubnosed, blue-eyed countenance as fair-skinned as a girl's except for a breath of beard, under a tumble of black hair.

No doubt it was just as well. Vindilis had counselled wisely. Less for hospitality than for appearances' sake, Rufinus had from time to time brought a pretty harlot to the tower. He performed competently, thinking it could not be denied that women were better constructed for the purpose, then let Tommaltach have the rest of the sport.

The Scotian left the road, which was dirt, but not badly laid out, to swing wide of a dolmen. In Ériu as in Armorica, works of the Old Folk brooded. 'Christians chiselled a cross on that,' he explained. 'Ever since, the dwellers inside have been angry and spiteful.' The religion had made considerable headway in Mumu.

Stepping from the hostel at sunrise, Rufinus peered aloft and conferred with Tommaltach and the innkeeper. He did not want to reach Castellum drenched. Opinion was that rain would hold off long enough. Rufinus ordered his men into full battle gear: peaked helmets, cuirasses with flaring shoulderpieces and spiral-ornamented loricae, greaves above leather breeks, studded shoes, leaf-shaped swords, long oval shields. He himself donned a silken shirt with flowing sleeves, jerkin of chased leather, woad-dyed linen trousers, calf-length gilt boots, belt and baldric set with carnelians, over his shoulder a red cloak trimmed in ermine and secured by a cameo brooch. A show counted for well-nigh everything when you dealt with Celts. Besides, Rufinus enjoyed it.

The troop rode briskly on, beneath mountainous clouds through which the sun cast lances. The air was cool and damp. Soon the countryside turned into stands of wood-land, meadows between them. Stumps showed that not long ago this had all been forest. 'The King is having it logged off,' Tommaltach said. 'Settlers come, making strength and wealth around his seat.' He pointed. 'Look, my heart. On the horizon, the Rock!'

Nearing, the travellers saw the limestone mass lift ruggedly, an island in a green sea, its clifftops three hundred feet above. Buildings clustered at its base and strewed themselves out across the plain. Many were larger and better made than Rufinus had seen until now on his expedition. On the heights frowned a fortress. It was the Roman kind, foursquare, turreted, built of mortared stone, a thing that had never before been in Ériu.

Therefore it was twice important to impress the King. 'Hoy-ah!' Rufinus cried. 'Smartly, on the double!' The horses trotted forward.

Warriors hastened from the dwellings and along the trail up the Rock. They were outfitted like other Scoti. Tommaltach galloped ahead to meet them. They cheered and formed a primitive honour guard.

– Inside the castle, barbarian ways remained strong.

330

The feasting hall was long and lofty. Smoke from a pair of firepits did not escape out the high-set small windows as readily as through thatch. Benches lined the walls. Above them hung painted shields, while skulls grinned from the many niches. Yet there were also finely woven hangings, intricately carved panels on the seats, imaginatively wrought tableware of wood, bronze, silver, gold, a general rude magnificence in which Rufinus found more subtleties the more he looked.

Conual Corcc, a tall man with flame-red hair, was gracious rather than boisterous as he received the Ysans. They distributed gifts from off their pack beasts, things as good as Ys could offer, and got thanks from the King's poet in intricate stanzas. Eventually, at their departure, he made them presents of value exceeding theirs. First they were his guests for over a month, and nothing was refused them.

During that time, Conual and his councillors made numerous occasions for private talk; and their queries were shrewd. 'I am an envoy of my lord, the King of Ys,' Rufinus said early on. 'He has heard of your rise to mightiness. He hopes for friendship, oaths exchanged, benefits shared.'

'He is afar,' answered Conual. 'True, I've no wish to make war on him or on the Romans like Niall of Temir. But what is to bind our two lands together?'

'Trade.'

'You've come too soon for that, my dear. The great fairs do not open before Lúgnassat.'

'I know. Granted your leave, we would like to take our ship's cargo round about and see what bargains folk wish to strike. But that is not why I am here, the voice of King Grallon. He in his wisdom looks beyond the gains that some Ysan merchants have made at your fairs. He hopes to arrange that many more will want to go, and many of your traders seek to us. We have much to give each other. Ys offers the harvest of the sea; amber from the Northeast, Roman wares transshipped from the South; the products of her own weaveries and workshops. Ériu has the yields of her fertile land, pearls, and also gold, which has long been draining out of the Empire. Surely, as traffic quickens, men will think of more than this.'

'Hm. What might hinder?'

'War, pirates, the rapacity of overlords, ignorance and distrust. You, who I hear have spent years in Britannia, you will understand. Consider, King. Think of an alliance between yourself and King Grallon. Imagine missions going to and fro, men becoming well acquainted, making agreements and planning joint ventures. Meanwhile, with help from Ys, your people build stout ships like ours, to trade farther than ever erstwhile and to patrol your home seas.'

'It's like a Roman that you are speaking. I follow you, but there are not many in Mumu who could. Just the same – Do let me think. Let us talk more in days to come. Already I know that the message I will be sending back with you will be a kindly one. May you come here again, Rufinus.'

3

Apuleius Vero and his wife Rovinda stared enraptured at the presents Gratillonius had brought them. For her there was a woollen cloak from the foremost webster in Ys, warm but light and soft as thistledown, its dusk-blue worked with silvery figures of dolphins and terns. For him

332

there were the poems of Ausonius, done on to parchment by a calligrapher who had access to Bodilis's collection, bound into a codex whose cover was tooled leather with gilt trim.

'Oh,' the woman breathed. 'It's gorgeous. How can I thank you?'

Apuleius gave his friend a long look. 'You *thought* about this, did you not?' he said quietly. 'You're less blunt than you let on.'

Gratillonius smiled. 'I've things for the children too, of course,' he told them. 'How are they?'

'Very well.' A cloud passed over Rovinda's face. She and her husband had lost all but two. She dismissed memories in favour of pleasure. 'They'll be overjoyed to know their honorary uncle is back. Their tutor is sick abed, so we've allowed them to stay on the farm. They love the countryside so.'

'And they deserve a reward,' the father added. 'You know Verania is quite the little scholar, when she isn't outdoors. Well, now, Salomon has begun taking a real interest in his own studies. That doesn't come easily to a headlong boy like him. Rovinda, dear, dispatch a slave to fetch them before you turn the kitchen inside out preparing the feast I'm sure you want to welcome our guest with.'

'Hold on,' Gratillonius suggested. 'Why don't you and I walk there? We can easily return with them before dinnertime.'

'Aren't you tired after your journey?'

'No, it went smoothly. And from my arriving this early in the day, you know darkness caught us quite nearby. We camped on Drusus's property. He took me into the house and poured with a free hand. A walk will clear my head, if you care to come along.'

333

Apuleius grew pensive. 'Hm-m . . . Very well. I'll let that replace my regular exercises for today. It will be much less tedious.' His smile was a trifle forced. 'Besides, I planned to take you there when we got an opportunity. I have something for you.'

Gratillonius took the package he had not unwrapped. Donning outer garments, the men went forth. Aquilo was abustle. The approximately annual visits from Ys were always occasions in such a small city. The escort were already mingling with the people. He recognized a few former legionaries. Drusus had told him that after six years the resettlement was still working well. The veterans were gradually making the civilian reservists militarily effective – more than Imperial law envisioned. Most of them had married Osismiic women and become farmers, artisans, tradesmen. They had a stake in Armorica. No hostile barbarians would get close to Aquilo, unless as prisoners bound for the slave markets.

Apuleius conducted Gratillonius out the east gate and north on the river road. The day was clear, chill, a wan-bright sun above the heights whose steepness hemmed in this bank. Across the stream, the land rolled away, its northern horizon forested. Scattered farmsteads stood among dun ploughfields, sallow meadows, orchards gone yellow and brown. Wind boomed from that direction. A buzzard rode watchful upon its torrent.

Apuleius must raise his voice against the noise. Indoors he would have spoken softly: 'You've more than a walk in mind.'

Gratillonius nodded. 'Privacy.'

'Nobody eavesdrops at the house.'

'I know. But – your letter urging me to come said only that you've news for me. Now, I've learned your style. You have to be thinking of something unwelcome. I'd have trouble sitting still while we discussed it. This wind ought to flush the fret and anger out of me, so we can have a pleasant evening together.'

'I see.' Apuleius's Hellenic-like features showed the distress he had been holding back. 'The truth is, I have little in the way of news. Mainly it's an accumulation of hints, overtones, mentions, incidents, the sort of word that the tribune at Aquilo, who sees higher authorities now and then and who maintains a rather extensive correspondence – the sort of word he gets, while the prefect in Ys, who is also the King of that nest of pagans, does not.'

The wind slipped fingers under Gratillonius's cloak. 'I have been notified that Lugdunensis Tertia has a new governor.'

'You've probably not heard yet that the Duke of the Armorican Tract is also being replaced.'

Gratillonius half stumbled. 'What? But he's done well. He and I have kept the peninsula at peace.'

'Precisely. He and you. Oh, I'm sure it will be an honourable retirement. No sense in provoking the many who feel grateful. But Honorius – Stilicho, rather – intends that his will, and none other, shall prevail everywhere in the West.'

Gratillonius's gullet tightened. 'If he means to recall me – Can you make them realize what insanity that would be?'

'My direct influence is slight. I do have communication with some men who are powerful. I will try. Just what I should write in my letters is one of the things we must discuss.

'Your policies were too successful, my friend. The Imperium has had unhappy experiences with such officers. Think back over the course of events since Maximus fell.'

Apuleius chuckled drily. 'If nothing else, those seven years were seldom dull.'

Gratillonius grunted response and fell silent, trying to recall and order them for himself.

– Following his victory, Theodosius reinstated Valentinianus as Emperor of the West, but remained two years more in Italy, organizing its shaken government, destroying every relic of the usurper he could find, before he returned to Constantinople. As chief minister to Valentinianus, he left his general Arbogast.

This man had been the real director of the battle. A Frank and an avowed heathen, he favoured barbarians over Romans for high office, pagans over Christians. On both counts, he was soon at odds with Valentinianus, and after a while he got the ineffectual Augustus murdered. Thereupon he proclaimed as Emperor a rhetorician named Eugenius. The real power was his. When Bishop Ambrosius appealed to him to desist from encouraging the cults of the old Gods, he threatened to stable his horses in the cathedral of Mediolanum and draft monks into his army.

After two years that army met the host of Theodosius, bound from the East to regain the West. For two days they fought, until Eugenius was killed and his cause lost. Arbogast fled, but committed suicide soon afterwards.

Theodosius marched on to Rome. He was smitten with dropsy and knew he had not much time left on earth. The Empire he redivided, the East going to his son Arcadius, the West to his son Honorius. Thereupon he retired to Mediolanum, made his peace with God as best he could, and expired in the winter that was past, some nine months ago.

Arcadius was an indolent youth of seventeen, under the thumb of his praetorian prefect Rufinus. (Recalling that name, Gratillonius smiled wryly.) Honorius was a boy of eleven, said to be a weakling also. His father had made Flavius Stilicho and Stilicho's wife Serena joint guardians of him. They betrothed him to their daughter Maria.

Further strife was ineluctable. Stilicho had begun this season's warring on the Rhenus, where German tribes had got troublesome. But after quelling them, he marched to Thracia. There he still was.

– 'It's given out that he aims to expel the Goths and Huns from that province,' Apuleius said when Gratillonius inquired. 'And no doubt he is working towards it. However, I've excellent reason to believe that his real objective is the destruction of the praetorian prefect Rufinus. If he can accomplish that, he will be the master of the whole Empire, both East and West.'

'And then – ?'

'The event is in the hands of God. But men can take measures.'

Beyond the inflow of the Stegir they crossed a bridge over the Odita and followed a road that went north along the tributary stream. An oxcart lumbered far ahead, distance-dwindled; a tenant forked hay into a wooden trough for the cattle in a paddock; at the house behind, his wife strewed grain for free-running chickens: a peacefulness at which the wind gibed.

'I wouldn't look for immediate woe,' Apuleius said after a time. 'Stilicho will be busy. Even here in the Northwest, surely his first concern must be the Scoti. You know how they took advantage of his departure from Britannia to ravage it, two years ago, and have since been re-establishing their enclaves there.'

Gratillonius scowled. His father's home had been spared, but barely. 'That was the work of Niall. I hear he's now preoccupied inside Hivernia. Some good luck does drift our way sometimes.'

'Who? . . . No matter. You're in touch with the Scoti as I am not, as I suppose no Roman – no other Roman is. That's one thing against you.'

Gratillonius bridled. 'See here, *I* broke the fleet that would have raided up the Liger a dozen years back. True, I'm cultivating relationships with Scoti, but friendly Scoti.'

Apuleius sighed. 'I don't doubt you. But they see it otherwise in Turonum, Treverorum, Lugdunum, Mediolanum – wherever it comes to mind that the man sent to be Rome's prefect in Ys has become its independent sovereign. For that you are, no matter if you continue piously calling yourself a centurion on special duty.'

'How have I subverted any interest of Rome? By the Bull, I've strengthened us!'

'And strengthened Ys. The city that once lay veiled is today chiefest in Armorica, its brilliance and prosperity outshining any of the Western Empire. Nonetheless it remains as alien, as un-Christian, as the seat of the Sassanian King.'

'Rome's made peace with the Persians.'

'How long can that last? How long will Ys choose to be our ally? You will not reign forever, Gratillonius. You will not reach old age, unless you can end that barbarous law of succession. Ys would be a most dangerous enemy. Already the grievances are building up.'

Gratillonius shook his head. 'You're wrong. I know.'

'You know what they think in Ys. I know what they think who govern Rome. When those men clamp down on the trade you have caused to flourish, how then will Ys feel?'

'Ha? But that's ridiculous! Why in the name of moon-

338

struck Cernunnos should they do any such thing? We gave Armorica peace; we're drawing it out of poverty.'

'By means that are . . . unsettling. The merchants and shippers of Ys, being free agents, undermine the authority of Roman officials, guilds, laws. Men disappear from the stations of life to which they were born. They reappear in traffic that goes unregulated, untaxed, yet scarcely troubles itself to be clandestine. This year Ysans began acquiring substantial amounts of Hivernian gold. It flows about, uncoined, driving the Emperor's money into total worthlessness, thereby making people mutter that perhaps they have no need of an Emperor at all. No, I tell you the authorities cannot indefinitely permit the life of the region to go on outside their control. They dare not.'

Gratillonius decided to make no mention of his own irregularities. Some Roman officials must have some peripheral awareness of them; but to investigate would take those persons out of comfortable routine, into forests, heaths, slums, barbarian camps. Why force them to that? It could only make difficulties for all concerned – most of all for Rome, because the damned stupid government was not itself doing what was plainly necessary for survival.

'They certainly hold religion against us,' he growled. 'But we have a church and pastor. We persecute nobody.'

'I hear that Honorius is devout,' Apuleius said. 'When he grows up, he may transform weakness into zeal.'

'Maximus once threatened to invade Ys.'

'He fell. Stilicho is more formidable.'

Apuleius took his friend by the arm. 'I don't mean to perturb you,' he went on. 'I only give you an early warning. You have time to prepare and take preventive steps. I've promised you to serve as your advocate with influential men. I believe we can forestall an order for your recall, because that would risk Armorica falling into chaos, a crisis which Stilicho surely regards as unnecessary at this juncture. But you must do your part. You must be more circumspect. You must forbid smuggling, and curb the most blatant of it. You – ' Apuleius stopped.

'What?' asked Gratillonius.

'It would help mightily if you accepted the Faith and worked for the conversion of Ys.'

'I'm sorry. That's impossible.'

'I know.. How often I've prayed to God that He lift the scales from your eyes. It's heretical of me, but I suspect that the knowledge you were burning in hell would diminish my joy in Heaven, should I be found worthy of going there.'

Gratillonius reined in a reply. As he had told Corentinus in their generally amicable arguments, he didn't think an eternity of torment was the proper punishment for an incorrect opinion, and saw no righteousness in a God Who did. Corentinus retorted that mere mortals had no business passing judgement on the Almighty; what did they understand?

Apuleius brightened. 'Enough,' he said. 'You have the gist of what I wanted to tell you. Think it over, sleep on it, and tomorrow we'll talk further. Let's simply be ourselves until then. Look, there's the villa ahead.'

They walked on. Security from attack and revival of trade had drawn workers out of inland refuges. Maximus's veterans had additionally eased the labour shortage. Agriculture was again thriving around Aquilo, not in the form of latifundia but as sharecropping and even some freeholds. No longer neglected, the land surrounding the Apuleian manor house, which stood near the northwest corner of the cleared section with the forest at its back – this land showed neat fields, sleek livestock, buildings

340

refurbished and permanently in use. At the house itself, whitewashed walls, glazed windows, red tile roof called back to Gratillonius his father's. But here the owner was no curial between the millstones, he was a senator, the closest thing to a free man that Roman law recognized.

The children saw who approached and burst from within, to dash down the garden path and be hugged. Only six, Salomon outpaced his sister regardless. Big for his age, he was coming to resemble his father, though Apuleius must have been a quieter boy. The parents had explained to Gratillonius that they named him after a king of the ancient Jews in hopes that this would cause God to let him live. That had happened, but thereafter Rovinda continued to suffer stillbirths and infant deaths.

Verania followed. At ten she was well-made if rather small. She had her father's hazel eyes, her mother's light-brown hair, and a countenance blending the comelinesses in both. Near to Gratillonius, she abruptly blushed and became very polite, her greeting barely audible through the wind.

'Well, well!' he said. 'How good to see you two again. I'll spare you any remarks about how you've grown since last. We're doing nicely in Ys. I've much to tell you about that. For a start, here're a couple of little things from there for you.'

He squatted on the gravel and opened the package. Its contents were modest, because Apuleius frowned on ostentation. However, they drew a shout from Salomon, a soft cry from Verania. He got a Roman sword and sheath, scaled to his size. 'A copy of my old military piece. Someday, I think, you'll lead men too.' She received a portable harp, exquisitely carved. 'From Hivernia. I know you're musical. Among the Scoti, some of their poets and bards are women.'

341

Worship looked back at him, until Salomon sprang up. 'I know what we've got for you!' he crowed.

'Hush,' said Verania. 'Wait till father's ready.'

Apuleius laughed. 'Why wait? Here we are. Before we step indoors and have a cup of something, let's go see.' He linked his arm with Gratillonius's. 'You've been so generous to us over the years, so helpful, that we'd like to make some slight return.'

Salomon capered and hallooed. Verania walked on the other side of the prefect, not quite touching him, her glance bent downward.

The stable was dim, warm, smelling sweetly of hay and pungently of manure. Apuleius halted at one stall. From within, a stallion colt looked alertly out. Gratillonius would learn that he had overestimated the age, about six months, because it was so large – a splendid creature, sorrel with a white star, of the tall kind that bore cataphracts to battle.

'This is yours to take back with you,' Apuleius said.

'By Hercules, but you're generous!' Gratillonius marvelled.

'Well, as a matter of fact, my interest in breeding this sort began when you told me how your father's been trying the same in Britannia. I think we're having some success. Favonius is our best thus far. I suspect he'll prove the best possible. You're a horseman. We want you to have him.'

'Thank you so much.' Gratillonius reached over the bars, stroked mane and head, cupped his hand around the muzzle. How soft it was. 'I'll raise him right, and – and when I ride him here in future, help yourself to his stud services. Favonius, did you say?'

'Our name for him. You can change it if you like. It's a

342

rather literary word, meaning the west wind that brings the springtime.'

'Oh, it's fine. I'll keep it.'

Apuleius smiled in the duskiness. 'May he bear you to a springtime of your own.'

XVI

1

Tiberius Metellus Carsa was of Cadurcic descent, but his family had long dwelt in Burdigala and mingled its blood with others that pulsed in the city. Its men took to the sea, and he himself inherited the rank of captain after he was trained and a position had opened up. For some years he carried freight between the ports of Aquitania and as far as northern Hispania. At last he encountered pirates. Many such had taken advantage of the strife between Theodosius and Arbogast, and not all were immediately suppressed after the Empire was pacified.

With Carsa in this battle was his oldest son Aulus, born to the trade and, at age fourteen, making his first real sea voyage. The boy acquitted himself well. He was expert with the sling. Though he had not grown into his full strength, from the cabin top he wrought havoc, certainly braining one man and disabling several. Meanwhile his father led a spirited defence at the rail. The upshot was that the reavers took heavy losses and fled before their vessel should be boarded.

That incident decided the owners to put Carsa on the Armorican run.

Those waters were tricky, but the human hazard had much diminished in the decade or so since Ys emerged from isolation. True, lately the barbarians had again been grieving Britannia. However, Ys kept them at arm's length; and now that he had disposed of his rival, the

344

praetorian prefect of the East, Stilicho was dispatching an expeditionary force against them.

Therefore, when shipping season began next year, Carsa sailed the seven-hundred-ton *Livia* down the Garumna and north-northwest over the gulf. His cargo was mostly wine and olive oil, his destination Ys. With him went Aulus.

It was a rough passage, winds often foul, taking a full ten days because the captain was cautious. 'I'd rather arrive late in Ys than early in hell,' he said. 'Although I've heard churchmen declare there is a great deal of hell already in that town.'

Young Aulus scarcely heard. He was staring ahead. Wonder stood before him.

The day was chill and gusty, casting saltiness off the whitecaps on to his lips. Waves brawled green, here and there darkened by kelp, bursting white over rocks. Afar lay an island, its flatness broken by a single turreted building. Fowl rode the water and wheeled overhead, hundredfold, crying through wind and surf, gulls, terns, guillemots, puffins, cormorants. Seals frolicked about or basked on skerries. *Livia* rocked forward under shortened sail, the master peering now at the reefs and now at the periplus fluttering in his grasp, men at the sides ready to fend off if need be. This cape had a grim reputation. It did not seem to trouble the vessels, mostly fishermen, that were in sight; but Roman mariners supposed Ys had a pact with the demons its people worshipped.

The city lay ahead. Its wall bowed out into the sea whose queen it was, filling the space between two looming promontories, the hue of dark roses, up and up to a frieze of fabulous creatures and thereafter battlements and turrets. Farther back, higher still, spires pierced heaven, glass agleam, until the roofs flared into fantastical shapes.

345

As tidal flow commenced the gate was slowly closing. The harbour beyond, docks, warehouses, ships, boats, life, seemed to Aulus a paradise about to be denied him.

Out of the basin hastened four longboats. Shouts went back and forth. Lines snaked downward, were caught and made fast. The Romans struck sail. The Ysans bent to their oars and towed the ship in. Aulus gasped as he passed the sheer, copper-green doors.

In a daze of delight, he watched the tugmen warp *Livia* into a slip and collect their pay; a robed official come up the gangplank, accompanied by two guards in armour unlike any elsewhere, and confer with his father; the crew snug things down for the stay in port and, impatiently, shoulder their bags; the captain at last, at last grant shore leave!

Among the longshoremen, hawkers, whores, strolling entertainers, curious spectators who thronged the dock, were runners from various inns, each trying to outsing the others in praise of his place. They all knew some Latin. Tiberius grinned. 'Let's hope our poor devils don't get fleeced too badly,' he said to his son. 'We'll be here for several days. If we're to ply this route regularly, we need to familiarize ourselves with the port.'

'Where'll we stay, you and I?' Aulus asked breathlessly.

'A respectable hostel. I have directions. Get our baggage and we'll go.'

On their way, the Carsae found much – everything – to stare at. Nothing, not even those things the Romans had built, was quite like home; always the proportions and the artwork were subtly altered into something elongated and sleek, swirling and surging. The city throbbed and clamoured with activity. Most Ysans appeared prosperous. It showed more in bright garments and jewellery than on bodies, except that folk were bathed and well-groomed.

They tended to be lean, energetic, but basically dignified. Many resembled the aborigines and Celts who had been among their ancestors, but often the Phoenician heritage revealed itself in hawk face or dark complexion. Men usually had close-trimmed beards and hair drawn into a queue; some wore tunics, some jacket and trousers, a few robes. Women's tresses were set according to fancy, from high-piled coiffure to free flow beneath a headband. They generally wore long-sleeved, broad-belted gowns that gave ample freedom of movement, and they walked as boldly as men. The Carsae had heard their rights and liberties were essentially equal. Servants, too, were free agents working for pay, slavery being banned in Ys – an almost exact reversal of Roman practice.

Like the city it stood in, the hostel was clean and well-furnished. In the room that father and son got, a fresco depicted a ship at sea and, sky-tall and beautiful, a woman in a blue cloak whose hand upheld a star above the mast.

'Pagans,' Tiberius muttered. 'Damned souls. Licentious too, I hear. But they have a Christian church somewhere.'

'We, we must deal with them . . . mustn't we?' asked Aulus. 'They can't be *wicked*. Not if – ' He waved an awkward hand at the view in the window. 'Not if they made this.'

'Oh, we'll mind our manners, you and I. The trade's too profitable. Also, we've got much to learn, and there'll be pleasures as well. Only be sure to keep your soul steady as she goes. I'm told the Armoricans have stories like ours, about sirens who lure seamen on to the rocks. Well, even inside wall and gate, the reefs of hell are underneath us.'

Some of the food set before them in the common room was curious, all was delicious – marinated mussels, leeks cooked in chicken broth, plaice lightly fried with thyme

347

and watercress, white bread wherein hazelnuts had been baked, sweet butter, blue-veined cheese, honeycake, and a dry, herbal-flavoured mead that sang on the tongue. The serving wench, about Aulus's age, gave him glances and smiles that caused his father to frown.

However, Tiberius responded gladly when a messenger appeared, a boy whose red tunic had embroidered upon the breast a golden wheel. 'Captain Carsa?' he asked. His Latin had a peculiar construction. 'I am from King Gratillonius. Ever is he desirous of making strangers welcome and hearing from them about the larger world. Therefore is word of them always borne to him. He will be glad to receive you this very eventide.'

'Why, why, of course!' Tiberius exclaimed. 'But I'm just a merchant skipper.'

'One new to us, sir. Let me say as well that a ship of ours returned from Hivernia on the morning tide, and its chief passengers will likewise be at the palace.'

Tiberius glanced at Aulus, saw strickenness, and cleared his throat. 'Um, this is my son – '

'I understand, sir. He is invited too.'

Joy kindled a beacon.

The two put on their best clothes and went with the messenger for a guide. Along the way he pointed out sights till Aulus's head whirled.

Four men flanked the entrance gate of the royal grounds, two in Ysan battle array, two in Roman. Beyond, labyrinthine paths among flowerbeds, hedges, topiaries, bowers seemed to create more room than was possible. The palace was of modest size, but the pride was boundless. Its side walls bore scenes of wild beasts in the forest. A bronze boar and bear guarded the main stair-case. Above a copper roof swelled a dome, whereon the image of an eagle spread wings whose gilt blazed against sundown.

Passing through an anteroom, the visitors came into a chamber great and marble-pillared, frescoed with pictures of the four seasons, floor mosaic of a chariot race. Clerestory windows were duskening, but oil lamps and wax candles gave lavish light. Servants glided about refilling winecups and offering titbits of food. Flute and harp trilled in a corner.

Only a few persons were on hand, none elaborately clad. Seated in chairs as if presiding over an occasion of state, they nonetheless appeared quite at ease. A big auburn-haired man with rugged features lifted his arm as the new guests entered. 'Greeting,' he said. His Latin was plain-spoken, with a South Britannic overtone. 'I'm Gaius Valerius Gratillonius, centurion in the Second, prefect of Rome, and – ' he smiled – 'King of Ys. I'd like to hear whatever you care to tell and try to answer your questions, but feel free to mingle with people. We'll have a lantern-bearer to take you back.'

He introduced the others. Two were female, two of his notorious nine wives. They conveyed no sense of being more than handsome middle-aged ladies – until they joined the conversation as outspokenly and intelligently as any man. A couple of male Ysans were present, an old scholar and the head of a mercantile house. A fairly young Redonian – lean, tough-looking with his fork beard and scarred cheek – was one of those in from Hivernia; Aulus caught his name at once, Rufinus, because it had been famous last year as somebody else's. With him was a fellow not much older than Aulus, defiantly attired in a Scotic kilt and a saffron-dyed shirt secured at the throat by a penannular brooch.

'Sit down,' Gratillonius urged. 'Drink. You aren't on

349

stage. This isn't the Symposium, eh, Bodilis? Tell me, Captain Carsa, how was your voyage?'

He had a gift for putting company at ease: though Aulus suspected that when he administered a tongue-lashing, lightning sizzled blue. Before long, individuals were freely at converse with whomever they chose. Gratillonius drew Tiberius out about happenings in the South. Since Aulus already knew that, he shortly found himself off in a corner with Tommaltach.

That was the Scotian. His Latin was still somewhat broken, but had a musical lilt to it. Despite his having done battle in his home island, despite his being pagan and unlettered, his liveliness ranged so widely that Aulus felt like a child again. Yet Tommaltach did not patronize him.

– 'Ah, you could do well among the girls of Ys, Carsa,' he laughed. His glance probed. Aulus's frame was filling out into sturdiness; his countenance was broad, blunt-nosed, regular, beneath curly dark-brown hair. 'Can you get away? The hunting's better with two. I'm not talking of some copper-a-tumble whore, you understand; not but what such aren't usually well worth it in Ys. I mean lusty servant women, hoping to marry someday but meanwhile ready for fun if they like you. They're apt to saunter the streets in pairs – '

The Roman wished his face would not heat.

'You could be staying over a while,' Tommaltach said, 'between two calls your ship makes. My friend Rufinus would take care of arrangements. Sure, and he's a good-hearted man. Your dad should be happy, if you ask him right.' Seriously: 'It's more than pleasure this would be. It's an e-du-ca-tion. The learning, the folk from everywhere, the marvels, the magic – '

He broke off, turned, and stared. Silence fell upon the

350

room. The girl who had entered, already more than half-woman, was so beautiful.

In white raiment, garland of apple blossoms on the loose amber-coloured hair, she flowed over the floor to Gratillonius. She murmured huskily in Ysan, then, observing the company, changed to excellent Latin: 'Why, father, you didn't tell me you expected guests. I could have left my Temple duties earlier.'

The King beamed. 'I didn't know you meant to spend the night here, darling. Wasn't it to be with Maldunilis?'

'Oh, she only wants to lie about and eat sweetmeats. I *must* find a place of my own.' The girl checked herself, lifted a hand, and said gravely: 'Welcome, honoured sirs. May the Gods look upon you with kindness.'

'My daughter Dahut,' Gratillonius announced. 'Captain Metellus Carsa, newly from Burdigala. His son . . . Aulus. I don't believe you've met Tommaltach of Mumu, either. You should have, but it never chanced till now.'

Dahut kindled a smile.

Gratillonius laughed. 'Well, why do you wait, little flirt? Go brighten their lives for the young men.'

Dahut lowered her eyes, raised them again, and demurely joined the elders. However, the time was not long before she was in their corner chatting with Tommaltach and the junior Carsa.

2

Summer lay heavy over the land. Westward, cloud masses loomed on the horizon, blue-shadowed white above a sea that shone as if burnished. Ys glittered like a jewel. Grass greened and softened the headlands, save where boulders of ancient stoneworks denied it. The heights leading east bore such wealth of leafage that most of the homes nestled in their folds were hidden. In between, the valley stretched lush and hushed. Warmth baked fragrance out of soil, plants, flowers. Bees droned through clover.

In the courtyard of the Sacred Precinct, two men fought. Wearing full Roman combat armour, they circled warily, probed, defended with shield or sword, sometimes rushed together for a moment's fury. Their hobnails struck sparks from the slate flags. Neither getting past the defence of the other, they broke apart and resumed their stalking. They breathed hard. Sweat runnelled down their faces and stung their eyes. The sun turned the metal they wore into furnaces.

Maeloch the fisher arrived on Processional Way. His stride jarred to a halt. He gaped.

Menservants were watching too, from the porch of the great red house that filled the opposite side of the square. Right and left, its ancillary buildings formed two more boundaries of the courtyard. Black, all but featureless, they radiated that heat which the blood-coloured lodge uttered to vision. The fourth side opened on to the paving of the road. High above roofs, the Wood of the King lifted its crowns, an oakenshaw whose rough circle spanned some seven hundred feet, silence and shadow.

The mightiest of the trees grew at the middle of the courtyard. From the lowest bough of the Challenge Oak hung a round brazen shield, too big and heavy for use. Sunlight dazzled away sight of the wild, bearded visage moulded on it, or the many dents made by the sledge hammer that hung beside.

Blows thudded. They did not rattle or clash. Maeloch eased. Both blades were cased in horsehide.

The slender, more agile man saw himself about to be

forced against the bole. He turned on his heel to slip aside. Suddenly swift, the large man moved at him, not in a leap but in a pivot on widespread, bent legs that kept his footing always firm. His swordpoint slammed at the other's knee and ran up the thigh below the chain mail. The struck man lurched and gasped a Britannic curse.

'Enough, Cynan!' called his opponent. 'If this'd been real, you'd be bleeding to death now.'

'Well done, sir,' panted the other. 'I'm glad you stopped short of my crotch.'

'Ha, never fear. I need my roadpounders entire. Besides, your wife would have my head.'

Cynan limped. 'You did catch me a good one, sir. I'm afraid I can't give you any more worthwhile practice today.'

'I've had plenty as is. Come, let's go inside, get this tin off us, wash up and have a drink.'

Maeloch, whose Latin was scant, had got the drift. His rolling sailor's gait bore him forward. 'My lord King,' he said in Ysan, 'I've sore need to talk with ye.'

Gratillonius removed his helmet. He knew this man, as he did every Ferrier of the Dead. 'I'll hold public court in a few days,' he answered.

The shaggy head shook. 'Can't wait, my lord. Aye, ye're standing your Watch. Never kept ye from handling any business you felt like. And – I also deal with the Gods.'

Gratillonius met the unflinching gaze and smiled. 'A stubborn lot, you fishers. Well, come along, then. Have a beaker while I get clean.'

'I thank ye,' said Maeloch, as he would have replied to an invitation from a fellow seaman.

The three mounted the stairs to the portico. Its columns were carved into images of Taranis and His attributes,

353

wild boar, eagle, thunderbolt, oak tree. Beyond, the massive timbers and shake roof enclosed a feasting hall. Its pillars and wainscots were likewise carved, but hard to make out in the dimness. Age-eaten banners hung from the crossbeams like bats. The fire-trenches in the clay floor lay empty. Nostrils were glad to inhale cool air.

Gratillonius and Cynan stripped and went on into the modernized section for a bath and fresh clothes. Maeloch accepted a goblet of ale and sat down on a bench built into a side. Three men carried the military gear out for cleaning and stowage. A fourth took a feather duster and went about in search of cobwebs.

Maeloch beckoned to him. 'What Queen is here today?' he asked.

The servant halted. 'None, sir.' Unlike his livery, his voice was subdued. A Ferrier of the Dead, in this house of killers, raised too many ghosts.

'Why? He's no weakling, our King. Besides, 'tis plain justice to them, one man with nine wives.'

'The Princess Dahut wanted to dwell here for the three days and nights of this month's Watch. She wanted no grown woman about.'

'Dahut, ye say? What makes the child have such a wish?'

''Tis not for me to guess, sir. But her royal father agreed.'

'Aye, he can deny her naught, I hear. And who'd blame him for that? Where is she now?'

'In the Wood, I believe, sir. She's hours on end in the Wood, both by daylight and moonlight.'

Maeloch frowned. 'That could be dangerous. What if a sacred boar turned ugly? Nay, Grallon yields her too much there.'

'Pray pardon, sir, I must keep on with my work.'

354

Maeloch nodded, leaned back against the smoke-darkened relief of a scene in an ancient tale – the hero Belcar combating the demonic mermaid Quanis – and pondered.

Lightly clad, Gratillonius emerged with Cynan. He clapped his hands. 'Cold mead for two,' he called. 'More ale for our guest if he wishes. Well, Maeloch, what would you of me?'

The seaman had not risen. 'Best we speak under four eyes, my lord,' he replied.

'Hm, you are in a surly mood, nay? Then wait your turn. Sit down, Cynan. I'd like to talk about a couple of things,' Gratillonius said, pointedly, in Latin. 'It was plain, stupid luck that you didn't nail me earlier today with that shield-hooking trick. I've got to overcome my slackness about it. Who can tell what the next challenger will know?'

A man brought the mead, which had been cooled by leaving its bottle in a porous jar full of water. Cynan drank and spoke hurriedly. Despite his centurion's protestations, he soon left.

Gratillonius dismissed the attendants and sat down on the bench beside Maeloch. 'Well?' he asked.

The fisher drew breath. 'This, my lord. We're angry at ye in Scot's Landing, for that ye had poor Usun and Intil flogged. I said I'd bring the grievance. Usun's my shipmate.'

Gratillonius nodded. 'I thought that was the trouble,' he said slowly. ' "Flogging" is the wrong word. Three cuts of an unleaded thong, across those turtle backs, couldn't have hurt much. 'Twas meant for an example, a warning.'

'A disgrace!'

'Nay, now. How often have you decked a man who was

355

unruly or foolish, or triced him up for a few tastes of a rope's end, with no lasting grudges afterwards?'

Maeloch's huge fists knotted on his knees. 'What harm had they done? In this year of poor catches, they took a boat; they fared down the peninsula; they brought back Roman-made wares to sell. But your spies were watching.'

'No spies were needed. Those two flouted the law with no special effort to hide what they were about.'

'What law? We've aye been free traders in Ys, till ye made that bloody decree. Grallon, I'm nay yet your foe. But I warn ye, ye're going astray. Ye whipped two men and took away their goods. Ye had no right.'

Gratillonius sighed. 'Hark, friend. Before Mithras, I wish I'd not had to do it. But they forced me. I'd made it clear as the pool at the Nymphaeum, henceforward our traders into Roman territory must go through the Roman customs. These men did not. Liefer than pay tax, they smuggled Ysan cloth to the Veneti, and took those wares in exchange. Let them count themselves lucky the Romans didn't catch them at it. I punished them for the sake of every lad in Ys who's tempted to try the same. If anyone gets arrested, I can do naught – naught, do you hear? – to save him.'

Some of the bitterness drained out of Maeloch. Pain rose in its stead. 'But why, Grallon?' he whispered harshly. 'After all these years, why feed yon sharks?'

'I did not spell out the reasons as fully as mayhap I should have. My thought was that 'twould stir up too much wrath, too much pride. Some among us might go off and make trouble merely to ease their feelings. And we dare not have that. So I simply declared 'tis high time Ys honour her ancient treaties with Rome, and observe Roman law in Roman lands. The fact is – Think, Maeloch.

356

Shiploads of soldiers are now in Britannia. When they've cleared it of barbarians, if they can, what shall they do next? The Emperor, or rather his guardian Stilicho, is already being urged to crush contumaciously pagan Ys. Naught but our usefulness to Rome keeps us free. We must not provoke Rome further. The Council of Suffetes agreed at equinox.'

Gratillonius laid a hand on the shoulder at his side. 'Bide a while, friend,' he went on, softly. 'I want you to understand, and make your comrades understand, that this is done for their sake.'

He paused before adding: 'Let me say at once, confidentially, I know those are poor men, those two, and confiscation of their cargo means hardship for their families. Well, I cannot let them profit by their misdeed, but . . . between us, surely you and I can work out some quiet way to see them through without undue suffering.'

Maeloch choked. 'What? Grallon, ye *are* a good man.'

A slim form briefly darkened the open doorway. Dahut entered the hall. She seemed to light up its cavernous depths.

'Why, Maeloch,' she cried, 'dear old Maeloch!' and hurried forward to take both his hands. 'Had I but known! You will stay and take supper here, will you not? Say you will!'

Helpless, he must answer, 'Aye, Princess, since 'tis ye who ask.'

Underneath his words rustled a question. What had she been doing in the Wood, why did she want to prowl it, the Wood where someday a stranger was to kill her father?

3

To the Greater Monastery in the Liger valley, near Caesarodunum Turonum, came a pilgrim. Autumn cooled and hazed the air but decked trees in brilliant vestments. The river glided darkling past the huts that clustered on a flat bank. Hemming this in, hills rose nearly sheer, riddled with caves where monks also dwelt. Many were in sight, coarsely clad, roughly tonsured, unwashed. The newcomer had to search before he found one who was not at prayer or meditation but spading a vegetable garden.

'In Christ's holy name, greeting,' he ventured.

'His peace be with you,' replied the monk. He saw a young man, fair-haired, rangy, in tunic, trousers, shoes of stout material though showing hard use. A bedroll and meagre pack of rations were on his back, a wallet for minor objects at his waist, a staff in his hand. Nothing but a curious accent, not quite Britannic, marked him out from countless wanderers.

'Do you seek work?' asked the monk. 'I hear they're short-handed on the Jovianus latifundium.' And they did not inquire as to the antecedents of an able-bodied man. Imperial laws binding folk to the soil had succeeded in displacing thousands of them, as farm after farm went under.

The stranger smiled. 'Not field work, at least not in any earthly fields. Of course, I'll gladly help if my labour is needed. Where may I find your bishop?'

'Holy Martinus? No, son, you've no call to interrupt him at his devotions. We'll put you up for the night, never fear.'

358

'I beg you. This is necessary. He cannot have so entirely forsaken the world that he would refuse to see a kinsman returned from slavery among the heathen.'

Astounded, the monk gave information. The founder and leader of the monastery occupied a single-roomed wattle-and-daub hut, as small and crude as the rest. Its door sagged ajar, to show him prostrate at his prayers. The traveller leaned on his staff and waited.

After about an hour, Martinus emerged. He blinked, for his blue eyes were dimming with age. Thin white hair made an aureole around a face shrivelled and shrunken in on itself. Yet he still moved briskly and spoke vigorously. 'What do you wish, my son?'

'Audience with you, if you will give me that charity,' replied the young man. 'I am Sucat, son of your niece Conchessa and her husband Calpurnius, curial in the Britannic town Banaventa.'

Air soughed in between Martinus's gums. 'Sucat? No, can't be. Sucat perished these . . . seven years ago, was it not, when the Scoti raided along the Sabrina?'

'I did not die, sir. I was borne away captive. Let me prove myself by relating family history. My father was a Silurian who joined the army and rose to centurion's rank. While stationed in Pannonia, he met and married your niece. Upon his discharge, he brought her to his homeland and settled there. He was a pious man, who despite becoming a curial became a deacon as well – '

Martinus cast himself against Sucat and hugged him with surprising force. Tears burst from his eyes. 'God forgive me! Why should I have doubted you? Welcome back, beloved, welcome home!'

He took his visitor into the hut. Virtually its only furniture was a wooden chest and a pair of three-legged stools; but atop the box lay several books. The men sat

359

down. 'Tell me what has happened, I beg you, and how you escaped and, oh, everything,' Martinus exclaimed.

Sucat sighed. 'It's a long story, sir. I was carried away with unfortunates – ah, but how dare I call myself unfortunate when I remember the poor young women? – I came to Ériu, Hivernia. There I fell to the lot of a chieftain in Condacht – well, he took me to his estate in the far west of the island and put me to tending his flocks. For six years I did.'

'You bore it bravely.'

Sucat smiled. 'It was no terrible fate. True, the mountainside was often wet or cold, but God gave me health to endure that. My owner was not cruel by nature, and some other people did me kindnesses from time to time, and often in good weather little children would seek me out in the pasture, to hear me play on a whistle I'd carved or tell stories I remembered from nursery and school – once I'd mastered the language, of course, which has many differences from ours at home. And then, alone under heaven, I found my way back to God. For I confess to having been a light-minded youth, who forgot Him and trod the paths of sin. Now I said a hundred prayers by day and almost as many by night.'

'His mercy is unbounded.'

'I might be there still, for escape across that wild land and the waters beyond looked impossible. But a dream came to me at last, and I knew it was from God and required my obedience. Pursuit never found me. I nearly starved, but always, somehow, there was something to eat in time to keep me from falling. They are so hospitable in Ériu . . . When I could not ask directions, I guessed, and my guesses led me aright. In the end I reached that harbour on the Ulatach shore which my dream had named, and there was a ship loading for Britannia.'

Martinus's military practicality struck through. 'What? I've heard the army is cleaning the barbarians out of Britannia.'

'It is, though I fear, from what I saw, that that's like weeding thistles. Anyhow, peaceful traders aren't forbidden. This cargo was a pack of the great wolfhounds they breed in Ériu. At first the captain spurned me, as ragged and coinless as I was. But I persisted, and God softened his heart.'

'You have gifts of persuasion, it seems.'

Sucat flushed. 'Well, it was another hard journey on the Britannic side, as devastated as the Westlands are, but home I came in the end. My father had gone to his reward – did you know? – but my mother and various kinfolk remain, and made me welcome with hosannahs. They wanted me to stay forever.'

'Why did you not?' Martinus asked.

'I am haunted, reverend father. I cannot forget the people of Ériu – the women who smiled and spoke softly and slipped me a bite of something sweet, the rough comradeliness of men, the innocent children who came to me – even the proud warriors, the majestic druids. It's as if they are all weeping, beseeching, in the night that binds them, crying for the Light.' Sucat swallowed. 'I believe I have a vocation. Because you are my kinsman, and have made this a famous holy place, a school for bishops and missionaries – I beg you, in Christ's name, take me in, teach me, and if I prove worthy, ordain me.'

Martinus was silent a long while. Shadows crept across the floor and lifted in the valley as the sun declined. Finally he murmured: 'I think you're right. I think you're in the hand of God. But we dare not presume to know His will, not without much prayer and thought and austerity. Abide here, dear son, and we'll see what we can do for you. I've a feeling already that a great work awaits you, but you'll be long in preparing for it.' His voice strengthened, rang: 'Yet if I am not mistaken, you'll reach the forefront of ministry; you will be Christ's patrician.'

4

Midwinter rites and festival, together with the Council meeting, went past solstice. On the first midnight after they ended, Forsquilis took Dahut out on to Point Vanis.

The air lay windless and cold. Stars crowded heaven; the River of Tiamat foamed across it ghost-white, ghost-silent. By that light the sentries at Northbridge Gate knew the Athene face whose pallor a cowled cloak framed. They presented arms. Mute, woman and girl passed by, on to the short bridge to the headland.

Huge rocks jutted from the water beneath. An incoming tide roared and snarled among them, dashing itself between wall and cliff, spurting whiteness upwards out of jet. Hoarfrost greyed the earth ahead. To the west, Ocean bore a faint, uneasy shimmer on its raven immensity. A gibbous moon was crawling from the eastern hills.

Where the road from the bridge met Redonian Way, Forsquilis left both and led Dahut northeast across the foreland. The track she followed wound almost too narrow to walk, between tussocks, gorse, dead thistles, boulders. Dahut stumbled. 'I can't see where my feet go,' she complained.

Forsquilis, cat-sure of her own way, answered softly, 'You shall become one with the darkness, I promise you.'

'When? How?'

'Hush. There are those abroad who might hear.' Each word blew forth as a tiny white phantom, instantly lost.

The two went on. The moon crept higher. Stars coruscated. Frost brought leaves forth against shadow. Footfalls and the dry rustle of twigs being brushed were the solitary sounds, until sea-murmur deepened and loudened as the walkers drew near the northern edge.

The destination hove in sight. Centuries of weather had worn down earthen walls which once bulked threefold on the clifftop of a small ness. Grass and brambles had bestormed the fortress, covered it over, crumbled it away with their roots; timbers had rotted and rubble fill washed down into the surf; surely the very dead beneath had yielded their bones to the soil.

Forsquilis stopped before the ruin. Casting back her cloak, she raised arms and chanted, not in Ysan but in the sacred Punic of the Founders: *'Mighty ones, spirits asleep in the depths of time, be not wroth. Awake ye and remember. I, a high priestess of Ishtar, bring unto you Dahut, a virgin who bears fate in her womb. Bid us come into your dreams.'*

It was as if the sea moaned.

The Queen turned to the princess. 'Be not afraid,' she said. 'Where we go tonight, none but the fearless may enter unscathed.'

Dahut straightened. Her hood had fallen off the braids into which her hair was coiled, held by a silver clasp in the form of a snake. Moonlight silvered the right half of her face; the left was in bluish darkness. 'You know I am not afraid,' she replied.

Forsquilis smiled bleakly. 'Aye, well do I know. Of your own free will have you ranged along the borders of the Otherworld, all your brief life; or its creatures have sought you out, but then you never quailed. Ere ever

363

your strange birth, the Gods made you Theirs for some purpose hidden from mortals – and, it may be, from Themselves. Every omen avows it, with never a sign we can clearly read. I have told you how the hope of the Nine has become this: that you, gaining skill in the Old Wisdom that men call witchcraft, may find your way forward to an understanding of your destiny, and make it not terrible but splendid.'

Dahut nodded, wordless.

'It is a heavy load to lay on a young girl,' Forsquilis said. 'Once all the Gallicenae had the gift; but generation by generation, the Power has faded. We can still *sometimes* command the weather, cast a curse, lay a blessing, summon a wanderer, ward off illness or other misfortune, make a death gentle. But Innilis alone has the healer's Touch; I alone can make a Sending or call a demon or lure a God or hear the dead when they speak; and these are fugitive dowers, failing us oftener for each year that slips between our fingers. No longer do the Gallicenae teach a little of the ancient arts to each vestal, all to each new-made Queen. For most, that would be knowledge frightening, troublous, and useless. Give wings to a hare and they will but drag her down, make her easy prey for the wolf.'

'The eagle's wings lift her!' cried Dahut. 'They give her the sky and her quarry.'

'Well spoken. I pray we have judged you aright, and you yourself. 'Twill be years until we can tell. This night is the barest beginning.'

Forsquilis pointed to the earthworks. 'Like most folk, you know this as Lost Castle,' she said. 'You have heard it was built by the earliest Gauls. It is shunned for no single reason – mutterings of bad luck, ghosts, mermaids who slither up from the depths – though I make no doubt you, Dahut, have explored it on your solitary rambles. Did you ever feel a presence here?'

'I am . . . not sure,' the girl whispered.

'Hear what stands in the secret annals, and lock it away in your breast. This was Cargalwen, raised for Targorix, the first of the charioteer kings in our land. Because of a woman, the Old Folk whom he had conquered rose against him. Here on Point Vanis he met them, the sword-hubbed wheels made harvest of them, red rivers twisted down the cliffs to the sea. For a year and a day afterwards, the slain lay where they had fallen, and their decay poisoned the air but enriched the soil. When flesh was gone, Targorix had the skeletons laid out on this tip of land, and said that would be the foundation of his stronghold. Human hands did not make it. His druid Vindomarix sang the dwarfs up from below the world and compelled them.

'Mighty for many years were Cargalwen and its lord. But the curse of the Old Folk hounded him. One by one, his sons died. The last and most promising did when he heard a song under the cliffs. He looked, saw a beautiful woman on a rock by the surf, climbed down to meet her, lost footing and fell to his death. Above in the fortress, they heard her laughter ere she vanished beneath the waves. They risked their necks to bring the body back. Crazed with grief, Targorix vowed he would bury the lad himself, in the heart of Cargalwen. Digging, he uncovered a skeleton. An adder nested in the rib cage. It bit him, and so he perished after hours of anguish, on a night of storm when folk thought they heard his soul shriek as it was ripped away.

'The Osismii took new leaders, who made their seat inland. When the Carthaginians arrived, the stronghold lay abandoned. But the earth, the stones, the waters remember.

'Come.'

Forsquilis took Dahut by the hand and led her across the ditch, through gaps, over remnants, to the inmost circle. 'This will be a long night,' the woman said. 'Dismiss haste from your spirit. We shall be seeking beyond time.'

They sat down cross-legged on the withered grass. Forsquilis turned her face aloft. 'Look on high,' she said. 'See, yonder strides Orion. The Dragon attends the Lodestar. The wheel of heaven is turning, turning, turning. Mount to the Wain, Dahut, enter, be borne down the centuries.'

Vision and soul topple into endless deeps aloft.

The moon climbed higher. The witch crooned. Waves clashed and boomed, but as if very distant.

' – Oneness. All is one and one is all. Dream the dreams they dream who are dead.'

Frost sends slow shudders through earth. Stones toil upward; on nights yet to come, the stars will shine upon them. Seeds asleep wait for springtime. There is a flicker of aurora in the north, a memory of burnings long ago. Surf rumbles like chariot wheels. A breeze rouses, sighs, seeks lips to kiss.

'What does the night say to you? Nay, tell me not, tell yourself. *Eya, eya, baalech ivoni.*'

Tide turned. The moon stood high and small.

Forsquilis rose. 'May the Power be in us,' she said. Dahut did likewise, stiff and dazed.

'Join me in the refrain,' Forsquilis ordered. 'I have taught you.'

'I remember it,' Dahut said. 'Oh, I remember more than ever I knew erenow.'

'Beware. Dwell not overmuch on that which comes

366

from Beyond. But you shall feel the Power this night. Together we will summon the wind.'

The song lifted. Out there on the headland, it was the loneliest sound in the world. But its undertone was the noise of the slowly retreating sea.

The stars turned, the moon mounted. That breeze which had drifted about began to whistle, ever so faintly. It could have been a melody played on a pipe made from a reed. Haziness blurred the western horizon.

Forsquilis danced while she sang beneath the moon. At first the movements of hands and feet and body undulated like low waves. The music loudened, now and then shrill, as if a gull cried. The swiftening breeze fluttered her cloak. Dahut stood aside near a briar bush, her whiteness limned against remnant walls and the sky. At the end of each strophe, she flung forth her lines: ' – *Lords of the elements, Lady of evenstar, Your children evoke you by right of the Blood! –* '

Clouds lifted in the west. The moon dappled their shoulders. The wind could have been a melody played on a pipe made from a dead man's shinbone.

The dance grew violent. Clouds mounted, blotting out constellation after constellation. Moonlight found white-caps. They burst on rocks with roar, whoosh, and hiss. Stars flickered in the wind.

Forsquilis grew still. 'Enough,' she said. Weariness flattened her tones. 'The Gods are vengeful towards those who overreach themselves. We have learned that you are born to the Power. Let us go home.'

Dahut's voice rang wild: 'Nay, let me abide, watch, be here!'

Forsquilis regarded her for a long spell by the wan and waning light. Cloaks flapped and snapped. 'As you will,' Forsquilis said. 'As you must, mayhap.'

She set forth towards Ys. Dahut crouched down into what shelter was to be had. The storm strengthened.

– When it had overrun heaven, when rain and sleet slashed in on a keening gale while the sea tumbled and bellowed against the cliffs, Dahut stood naked, arms wide, face lifted to the blast, and shouted laughter.

– Dawn stole aloft in the wake of the storm, the late dawn of the Black Months, on the Birthday of Mithras. It was a light the hue of ice, above weather still roiling murky over the eastern hills. Elsewhere, streaks of cloud blew thin; the hunchbacked moon seemed to race among them. The waters raged like metal poured out of a cauldron, molten yet somehow winter-cold. Dahut stood on the highest cliff of Point Vanis and chanted:

> 'Green the sea and grey the air,
> Flood come forth and wind arise:
> Green flood, grey flood, windy cloud.
>   All the sea is one.
>
> 'Blackling sea and silver air:
> Clouds churn silver, silver tide,
> Gales across the reefy cloud.
>   All the sea is one.
>
> 'Wracking sea and rushing air,
> Spindrift, skydrift, gale and blast,
> Soar by spray and dive by cloud –
>   All the sea is one.
>
> 'Sea is mine and mine is air,
> Dark of star and wet of moon.
> Wave I fling, I pile the cloud.
>   All that's sea is mine.'

XVII

1

Tommaltach maqq Donngalii returned to Ys with the springtime. Again he came as a partner in a trading venture, and again more for the sake of the visit than for any profit. It fulfilled his wildest dreams when he was received once more at the palace and, there, Princess Dahut offered to show him about the city on her first free day. His heart bounded. That night he lay sleepless.

She guided him to places he had never thought he would enter. A vestal of the first generation had admittance everywhere. Midafternoon found them atop the Water Tower, otherwise reserved for astronomers and philosophers.

Having looked with much respect at the fixed instruments, he let his gaze wander. To one side the city wall curved away beneath this parapet, behind it the blossoming valley. Nestled close was that red-tiled, colonnaded gem called Star House. Not far off, Elven Gardens lifted green and flowery, a chalice for the still more beautiful Temple of Belisama. Other fanes, together with mansions, graced this half of the city. Busy and stately, Lir Way swept down towards the Forum. Towers gleamed into a nearly cloudless heaven. Beyond sea gate and headlands, waters heaved blue and white, past holy Sena to the edge of vision. Sails were out there, and uncounted wings.

His glance went helplessly back to Dahut. She stood at

his side, also looking afar. Air flowed cool, mingling odours of salt and flowers, to press her thin gown against a slenderness more full at bosom and hips than he had seen last year. It ruffled the hair that tumbled over her shoulders. The amber of those waves seemed to take into itself the light spilling from the sun.

He sighed. 'Wonderful, wonderful. If only I could stay.'

She blessed him with a smile. 'You will come back, though,' she said. 'Often.'

He shook his head. His Ysan blundered more than could be accounted for by lack of practice during his months at home. 'The Gods alone know when I can. 'Twas all I could do to get leave for this trip.'

How lightly her fingers passed across his hand, where it gripped the edge of the wall. 'You bespoke this not erenow.'

'I did not, for I wouldn't be spoiling of the joy. But – my father, my tuath have need of me.'

The deep-blue eyes widened. 'Say on.'

'The Romans advance in Britannia. We cannot be sure what they intend. At the very least, pirates who no longer find good pickings there will turn elsewhere. We must guard our shores. Moreover, King Conual, to whom my father is sworn, means to widen his sway. That will likely call for war. I cannot hang back and keep my honour.'

'Oh, poor Tommaltach,' she breathed.

He forced a laugh. 'Why, glory waits for me, and booty, and many a tale to tell afterwards. Will you care to hear my brags?'

'Of course. I will wait so eagerly.'

'I too. Dahut,' he blurted, 'my kinfolk are after me to be marrying. But I'll shy from any such ties – I have hopes – '

Her lashes dipped. 'What mean you?'

370

Hot-faced, he said in a rush, 'I may find a way to settle in Ys. A fighting man or, or a merchant factor, or – something. Rufinus promised he'd help. Dahut, when you are free –'

She smiled anew and reached up to lay fingers over his lips. 'Hush. I've five more years ahead of me.'

'But then – why, Ys might even wish a queen of its own race in Ériu, or –'

Again she silenced him. Her mood darkened. 'Speak not of morrows, I pray you.'

'Why?'

'They're like yonder seas, when a ship comes in whose pilot knows them not. He must pass through, but he cannot tell what reefs wait beneath.' Dahut turned and walked rapidly off. 'Come, let's go down.'

Gloom and echoes filled the circular stairwell inside the tower. Emerging at its base, youth and girl blinked, as if sunlight were an astonishment. Before them lay Star House. A tall man in a plain gown was about to mount its own stairs.

Dahut stiffened, then strode forward. 'What do you want, you raven?' she cried.

Corentinus halted. 'Why, 'tis you, Princess,' he said as mildly as his rough voice allowed. 'What a pleasant surprise. And – aye, the skipper from Hivernia that I've heard about. Welcome, friend.'

Dahut stopped before him. 'Never call us your friends! This place is sacred. How dare you set foot here?'

'Did you not know? There is to be a meeting of the Symposium. Your father has finally won for me an invitation to attend.'

'Why would he do that?'

Corentinus shrugged. 'Well, after ten years I've become somewhat of an institution. And my little flock has grown.

The magnates of Ys must needs take us into their reckonings. The philosophers have wisely decided to exchange ideas with me, seeking mutual understanding, as civilized men ought. I seem to have come early. Wait, and the King will arrive. He's ever glad to see you.'

Dahut's eyes misted. Her lip trembled. 'I don't – want to see him – now,' she gulped. 'Come, Tommaltach.'

She led the Scotian off. Corentinus stared sadly after them.

2

Wonder burst over Aulus Metellus Carsa.

Not only did his father agree, after much argument, that he could remain in Ys until the last voyage back to Burdigala in autumn: his term began shortly before midsummer, when festivities were fountaining. True, the captain gave his son into the care of the chorepiscopus, who was to see that the lad led a sober and godly life, pursuing proper studies and being introduced to just such aspects of the city as would be helpful to know about when developing commercial relations further. However, Corentinus knew what it was like to be young. Besides, one could not build goodwill for the firm if one refused invitations from Ysans who were interested in meeting this Roman – some of which invitations came from the very palace – could one?

And then Dahut asked him to be her steersman!

That happened in the course of the merrymaking which followed the solstice rites. It went on for days. After the Council adjourned, King Gratillonius was free to offer his distinguished guest, Apuleius Vero, his full attention.

Not that entertainment had been lacking. On this, his first visit to Ys, the tribune of Aquilo confessed himself bewildered by the endless marvels offered him. Some were of the Roman kind, banquets, games and races and athletic exhibitions in the amphitheatre, performances of music and dance and drama in the odeion; but he exclaimed that everything was finer than he had encountered anywhere else, free of coarseness and brutality, yet tinged with a strangeness that freshened it like a sea wind. Other things he beheld were altogether alien. Certain of them he could admire artistically if not spiritually, such as the pagan temples and processions; certain he must deplore, such as men and women dancing together, or the general boldness of females, or the frequent hostility to Christ. But into much he could enter wholeheartedly – library, observatory, creativeness newly reawakened and breaking free of ancient canons, the Symposium, long private conversations with scholars or the learned Queen Bodilis, whipcrack wit, a sense of pridefulness and hope even among the lowliest, a feeling that the horizon was no longer a boundary.

When he told Gratillonius, the King replied, 'Thanks. You don't see the underside of things. But never mind; you can guess what that's like. I'll tell you my troubles later, because maybe we can help each other. Now, though, let's enjoy ourselves. We've earned it.'

'Have you something special in mind?' Apuleius inquired.

Gratillonius nodded. 'I've decided to revive an old custom. It lay fallow a long time because of pirates and the like, but once it was a big event of the season and there's no reason it can't be again. I mean the yacht race.'

Traditionally it had gone from the marine station to Garomagus and back, using boats of a single class. Today both terminals lay in ruins, and such pleasure craft as existed in Ys were wildly varied. Gratillonius had devised new rules. Participants would meet outside the sea gate, on the morning ebb. They would round Point Vanis and steer into Roman Bay. The murdered town would be too melancholy a rendezvous, but a short way past it, where the land bent abruptly north, was a fine broad bench. Small vessels could hug the shore; larger ones must stand farther out before turning east, a distance set by hull length and number of oars available; but those could only be used if it proved impossible to sail.

The balancing was crude. Gratillonius did not pretend that this would be a real contest in seamanship. To emphasize that it was simply sport, he sent people ahead to make a feast ready on the beach. The winning crew would receive their wreaths there and everyone would join in celebration before starting homeward.

'Will you be my steersman?' Dahut asked Carsa at the palace, in her fluent Latin.

'What?' he exclaimed, staggered. 'Won't you go with your father?'

She tossed her head. 'He won't compete, just preside. Anyhow, in that ship of his, with the high bulwarks, with crew babbling and bumbling, I never feel truly near the sea. He's given me my own boat; but he still forbids me to singlehand it.' Candlelight glowed on her countenance, in her eyes. Harp and flute lilted around her voice. 'He knows you for a skilful sailor. If I ask him in the right words, he'll agree.'

That night Carsa lay sleepless.

3

The boat was a twenty-foot currach on the Scotic model,
nimble and seaworthy, light enough for two men to row
or one to scull. A small deck forward covered a stowage
space and gave on a miniature figurehead, a gilt swan,
wings outspread as if straining to be free. Otherwise the
leather-clad hull was open, save for a pair of thwarts. The
mast had been stepped but was still bare.

The day was lucent, the swells gentle beneath a northwest breeze. Vessels danced. Shouts and trumpet call
mingled with the cries of the kittiwakes. Carsa accepted a
tow from the royal yacht, which was rowed at the beginning, until safely out to sea. What he bore was immeas-
urably precious. Nevertheless, once he had cast loose and
hoisted the azure-and-argent-striped sail, he had hard
navigation. Often he must grip a sheet in either hand
while his knees wedged against the tiller to control the
steering oar. He gloried in it, for Dahut praised him.

After he turned the promontory, his task became much
easier. Poled out, the sail bellied to the wind. The rudder
felt like a live, responsive animal as he wielded it to
maintain the proper heading. With shallow draught, a
currach could scarcely point up, but on a reach such as
this it surged along, lee rail low, parallel to a coast which
grew gradually less rugged. Water hissed by, swirled in
wake, murmured enormously all around. It was blue,
blue-green, violet, snowy-foamed. Leather throbbed,
frame and lashings creaked, rigging thrummed. A vast
curve of land rimmed most of the world, distance-hazed.
Boats and small ships filled its embrace. Afar in the west

bobbed the dark hulls and drab sails of fishermen at their labour. Seafowl skimmed past. The air blew keen.

Dahut sat on the thwart immediately forward of Carsa. A rough gown and hooded cloak wrapped her. She looked out at him, radiant. 'I'm still surprised your father permits this, my lady,' he ventured. 'It's not without danger.'

'Usually I must have two men with me,' she answered, 'but today we've a whale-pod around us, and I persuaded him to let me . . . travel light, in hopes of winning.' She grinned. 'Fear not. We'll get another tow on the return trip.'

'If we should capsize – '

Her glance ignored the floats kept against that chance. 'I swim like a seal,' she said haughtily. 'I am of the sea.' Concern flitted across her face. 'You do swim? I never thought to ask.'

He nodded. 'These are chilly waters for learning how.'

'I was born to them.'

He sensed that this was no matter to pursue and fell silent, content to have her in his sight.

She said hardly anything more herself. Instead, she fell to staring outward, sometimes into the distances, sometimes into the deeps. Her vivacity had left her. He could not tell what was rising in its place.

Time streamed past on the wind. The racers laid Ysan land abaft and entered Roman Bay.

Though Carsa used every trick of seamanship that was his, it became clear this craft would not arrive first at the goal. He nerved himself to say it. 'I'm sorry, my lady. We should be among the earlier ones.' Dahut shrugged. Her gaze stayed remote.

Now he made out the remnant of Garomagus. An islet guarded the mouth of a stream emptying into the bight. Behind it were roofless walls and gaping doorways. The view east, dead ahead, was more comforting, buildings strewn toylike. He could not be sure, though, which were inhabited, and certainly the signs of civilization were few; woods had overrun much of the land. It came to him that most of the clearing and ploughing must be reclamation after King Gratillonius had given peace to these parts.

He pointed. 'Look!' he cried. 'The beach we want. The smoke of the cookfires.'

Dahut threw back her cowl – light flared over braided hair – and cocked her head. Was she listening to the waves?

'The wind's fallen,' Carsa went on after a while, in search of talk. 'That northern headland blocks it. However, we'll have enough to make our goal.' Several craft were already clustered there. The larger had dropped anchor and employed tenders to bring their people ashore, the smaller were aground.

Dahut shook herself. She regarded him where he stood in the stern, as if across miles or through sea depths. 'Don't.' Her voice was faint, but he heard her clearly.

Startled, he let his hand slip on the tiller. The boat yawed, the sail slatted. 'What?'

Dahut turned from him to peer starboard. Her finger lifted. 'Go yonder,' she said.

'To Garomagus?' He was appalled. 'No, that's ruins. I can't take you there.'

She rose, felinely balanced. While she lacked her full growth, the cloak flapped about her shoulders as if she would take wing, and command flared forth cold as northern lights, in the language of Ys: 'Obey! Lir speaks!'

He looked around. No help was in sight. The racers were veering away from him, ardent for landing. Laggards toiled too far aft. Nobody heeded this low little vessel.

The King doubtless would have, but his yacht was at the destination.

'Christ help me,' he pleaded. 'I must not bring you into d-danger, Princess.'

She scorned the Name. 'I have heard Lir in the wind,' she told him. 'There is no danger. There is someone I must meet. Steer, or be forever my enemy.'

He surrendered, inwardly cursing his weakness. 'If you will have it thus,' he said in her speech. 'We cannot stay long. They'll wonder what's happened to you and come searching.'

Her slight smile laved his spirit. 'We'll join them in good time. And I'll remember your service, Carsa.' Then he shuddered a bit, for she added, 'The Gods will remember.'

Lest he grow afraid, he devoted himself to sailing. The change of course astounded him, so easily it went; he could not account for it. And how peculiar also, he thought, that nobody whatsoever noticed the currach go astray.

To slip in past the isle looked too risky. Besides, he couldn't expect to find a useable wharf. He grounded on the beach just east. Its shoreline turned north, an out-thrust of land hiding it from the Ysans beyond. Having struck the sail, he sprang forward, down on to the sand, and dragged the boat higher. Thereupon he gave Dahut his arm for her disembarkation. She had no real need of that.

Her visage was white, her eyes enormous, she shivered and spoke unevenly: 'Wait here. I'll soon be back.'

'No,' he protested, falling unawares into Latin, 'I can't let you go alone. I won't. What is it you're after?'

'I know not,' she whispered. 'I have been called.' Her utterance rose to a yell. She stabbed two fingers at him.

'Abide! Let me go by myself! I lay on you the gess that you not follow, by the power of Belisama, Taranis, and almighty Lir!'

Whirling about, she ran off, over the dunes, through the harsh grass that bordered them, past the snags of a defensive wall, in among the houses. She was gone. A cormorant flew black overhead.

Mechanically, Carsa reached for the anchor rode and made the currach secure. What else could he do?

What else? It struck him in a hammerblow. She had forgotten that he was no pagan, to cower before the demons she called Gods or heed a word she had merely, childishly laid on him. He was a Roman. Anybody might skulk hereabouts. He *would* follow, and be ready to defend her. He wished he had brought his sling. However, a knife was at his belt, and he got the boathook.

Of course, chances were that this place was quite deserted, apart from ghosts and devils. Best would be that she never know of his disobedience. He'd stay cautious . . . A haze had begun to dim the day. Wind had swung west and blew louder, colder. He summoned up courage to move forward.

Her trail was clear. Dust and sand had drifted into the streets to take footprints; plants grew to be bruised; her tread had splintered potsherds and displaced brickbats, as his did. He was vaguely glad that tracking kept his mind off what surrounded him. Weather had long since bleached the stains of fire and blood, but likewise colours, every human trace. Lichen was patiently gnawing walls which enclosed vacancy.

He found her at the mouth of the stream. It was an abrupt sight, as he came around a building. A few yards away, she knelt on a patch of silver-grey grass, limned athwart the islet beyond. He crammed himself back against the gritty wall and peered with a single eye. Sounds reached him above the shrilling of wind, mutter of brook and bay, half-heard rolling of Ocean.

She knelt before a seal that had crawled out of the water. Its coat shimmered golden-dark. Her arms were around its neck, her face pressed to its head, hidden from him. He heard her weep. He heard the seal hum, a deep plangency he had not known such a creature could make. A flipper reached to stroke Dahut's locks.

Christ have mercy, to this had the dream-voice called her, she who began the day so blithe. Carsa's knuckles whitened on the boathook shaft. Almost, he dashed to attack the soulless thing and save Dahut.

But she began to sing too. Her tone came thin and small; he was not sure how he made it out through wind and tide and the mewing of the kittiwakes. Somehow he knew that she was turning into Ysan words, for her own understanding, as well as she could in the middle of grief, the song that the seal sang.

'Harken, my darling. Hear me through.
Little I have to tell.
Now at the last I come to you,
To bid you for aye farewell.

'Hear what I say ere I depart,
That which I think you ween.
You were the child beneath my heart.
When I was your father's Queen.

'Torn from my side one winter night
Out in a wrathful sea,
You are the child whose fate takes flight
Beyond what is given me.

'Kiss me, my sea-child, ere we part
As it was long foreseen.
He that shall rip away my heart
Came down from the North yestre'en.'

Carsa stole off. At the boat, he prayed to Christ.
Presently Dahut returned. Beneath the cowl, her face was
blank, a visor. As empty was the voice wherein she told
him to launch her craft and bring them to the feast.

4

Osprey had fared under oars to the nets placed out the
day before. Those having been tended, the smack sailed
back, trawling. Her course brought her past Goat Foreland and across the mouth of Roman Bay. Heaven had
drawn a veil across earlier brightness, the sun had gone
wan and the air mordant. Then wind, stiffening, swung
around until it blew almost straight out of the west.

Maeloch swore. Water chopped grey-green. Whitecaps
began to star it. Land lay shadowy at the eastern horizon
but rose and grew closer as it bent west; even across five
or so leagues he made out the cliffs of Point Vanis, which
he must round. Spraddle-legged against the rolling of his
deck, he growled, 'We'll nay be free of another haul at
the sweeps, seems.' A fisher captain took his turn on the
benches.

A crewman laughed. 'Well, nor will yon fine
yachtsmen.'

'Ah, they've hirelings to sweat for 'em,' said another.

'Belay that,' Maeloch ordered. 'Be ye rabble for Nagon
Demari to rant at? The Queens, the King, the Suffetes,

381

they're as much Ys as ye and me . . . We'll try how far we can beat upwind ere we run out of sea room.'

The men moved towards the sheets to haul the sail around. He lifted a hand. 'Nay, hold a moment.' He went to the port rail and squinted. A swimmer had come in sight, outbound from the bay.

'Seal,' declared a sailor. 'I'll fetch my sling and give him a taste.' The animals were sacred, but they had to be discouraged from raiding fishnets.

'Not that 'un,' Maeloch answered. 'I know her. D'ye see the golden sheen in her pelt? She's the pet of Princess Dahut.' Recalling certain things he had witnessed, he drew the Hammer sign of protection with his forefinger, furtively, lest others notice and go uneasy. He himself did not feel threatened, but this was an uncanny beast.

The seal came alongside. She lifted her upper body out of the waves. Her gaze met Maeloch's and lingered for heartbeats. How soft those eyes were.

She swam onward, falling aft of the boat, heading into the boundlessness of Ocean.

'*Fin ho!*' bawled a man.

Maeloch ran to the starboard side and leaned out. Breath whistled in between his teeth. He knew that high black triangle, seldom though its bearers came this far south. 'Orca,' he muttered.

The killer whale veered. Maeloch realized where it was aimed. Did the seal? She swam on as if blind. Not that she could escape that rush – 'To oars!' Maeloch shouted. 'Bring us around! Ye, Donan, get my harpoon!'

Water foamed with speed. The black shape broke surface. Flukes drove it forward faster than Maeloch knew his craft could ever move. He glimpsed its belly, white as snow, white as death.

It struck. He seemed to feel the shock in his own guts.

The mighty jaws sheered and closed. Hunter and prey plunged under.

'Belay,' Maeloch said dully. 'We'll nay see either of them again.'

Blood coloured the waves, so broad a stain that he could hope the seal had died instantly.

'Stand by to come about,' Maeloch said. 'We're going home.'

It tore from him, a croak: 'How shall I tell the little princess?'

5

'Follow her,' Bodilis urged.

Gratillonius hesitated. 'She'd fain be alone. I've seen her thus erenow.'

Forsquilis shook her head. 'Something terrible happened this day. I know not what, but I heard ghosts wailing in the wind.'

'Never mind that,' said Fennalis. 'I can tell when a girl needs her daddy. *Go*, you lout!'

Gratillonius reached decision, nodded, and hastened down the gangplank. Dahut had already passed between two warehouses and disappeared.

The Roman youth Carsa stood forlorn on the dock, staring in that direction. His throat worked. He had debarked at her heels, obviously offering – begging – to accompany her. She dismissed him with a chopping gesture and some or other word that crushed him. Earlier, she had quite neglected him, first at the beach when they joined the rest, afterwards aboard the royal yacht when her currach was towed. But then, she had shunned everybody, giving the shortest of answers if directly spoken to, sitting at the trestle table with food untasted before her or wandering off by herself down the strand. The change from her cheeriness of the morning was like a fall into an abyss. It had spoiled the revel for Gratillonius; he must force himself to be jovial.

True, Dahut had always been a being as moody as Armorican weather. The small girl would flare into furies, the maiden would descend into gloom, suddenly, without any cause comprehensible by him. Her mirth and charm returned equally fast. Yet he had never hitherto watched anything like this. He thought that under a rawhide-tight self-control, anguish devoured her. Why?

Such of the Gallicenae as were in the party had withdrawn to the cabin on the way back and conferred. When the ship came to rest in the harbour basin, they had given him their counsel.

He brushed past Carsa – might have to interrogate that boy, but later, later – and those persons ashore who hailed him. Few tried. Ys had learned to let King Grallon be when he strode along iron-faced. Emerging on the street, he looked left and right. Which way? At eventide, folk off to their homes or their pleasures, the quarter was nearly vacant. He couldn't ask if anyone had seen a desolate lass in outdoor garb go by.

Wait. He did not really know his eldest daughter. No one did. She mingled easily when she chose, but always remained private to the point of secretiveness. However . . . she would not have headed left to Skippers' Market and Lir way, nor struck off into the maze of old streets ahead. Wounded, she would seek solitude. Gratillonius turned right.

Dusk welled up inside the city wall. Foul wind and heavy seas had slowed the passage home. Hurrying along the Ropewalk, Gratillonius glimpsed vessels under construction in the now silent shipyard. Their unplanked ribs might have been the skeletons of whales. At the end he swung right again, to the stairs leading on to the top of the rampart, and mounted them.

His heart stumbled. He had guessed truly. Yonder she was.

She seemed tiny below the Raven Tower. Fragments of mist blew above, blurring sight of its battlements. The lower stones glowed with sunset light. Wind had dropped to a whisper, still sharply cold. Ocean ran strong, bursting and booming where it struck, purple-dark in its outer reaches. There fog banks roiled and moved landward. Sometimes they hid the sinking sun, sometimes its rays struck level through a rift. They turned the vapours gold, amber, sulphur, and cast long unrestful shadows over the waves.

Dahut leaned forth between two merlons, clutching them, to gaze down at furious surf and minute beach between the wall and the upthrust of Cape Rach. The noise rolled hollowly around her.

She heard Gratillonius approach and looked to see who did. Her eyes appeared to fill the countenance that was, O Mithras, like Dahilis's. He halted before her. Words were difficult to find. 'I want to help you. Please let me try.'

Her lips moved once or twice before she got out: 'You can't. Nobody can.' He could barely hear her through the sea-thunder.

'Oh, now, be not so sure of that.' He smiled, put arms akimbo, rocked on his heels, anything that might make his talk more reassuring. 'I'm your old Papa, remember? Your first friend, who – ' his voice cracked – 'who loves you.'

Her glance drifted from him, back to the violence below.

Anger stirred. He knew it was at his own powerlessness, and allowed it only to put metal into his tone, as when he the centurion wanted to know about some trouble among the soldiers. 'Dahut. Hear me. You must answer. What happened? Your companion missed his proper landing and the two of you came belated to the feast. They were teasing him about it, and he took it glumly. Did he do aught untoward while you were alone?'

When she made no response, Gratillonius added: 'If I must brace him to get the truth, so be it. I'll do whatever proves necessary. For I am the King of Ys.'

Then she whirled to confront him. He saw horror on her. 'Nay, oh, nay, father! Carsa's been – courteous, helpful – He knows naught, I swear, naught!'

'I wonder about that. I wonder greatly. He's a sailor boy. He should not have made a stupid mistake in steering. He should not have been shaken to his roots merely because you fell into a bad mood. Aye, best that Carsa and I have a little talk.'

'Father – ' He saw her fight not to weep. 'S-stay your hand. I swear to you – by my mother – nothing unlawful happened. I swear it.'

He softened his words again: 'I'll believe you, sweetling. Yet something has shattered you today. You cannot leave me in the dark. I *am* the King of Ys; and they say you bear our destiny; but 'tis enough that you are my child by Dahilis, Dahilis that I loved beyond all the world, and still love.'

He held out his arms. Blindly, she came into them. He hugged her close. Her cheek lay against his breast. His hand stroked her slimness, over and over. He murmured, and slowly her shuddering eased.

386

'Come,' he said at last, 'let's go out where we can be by ourselves.'

A few others had been astroll on the wall, and there were the marines at the tower. None had ventured nigh, and Gratillonius and Dahut had ignored them, but he knew what probing pierced the misty glow. He took her hand – it nestled in his like a weary bird – and led her by the guards, on past the war engines in their kennels, to the sea gate.

There they must stop, unless they would descend to the warder's walk. Fog smoked in, ever thicker, hooding them from view beyond a few paces. Its yellow grew furnace-hot to westward, where an unseen sun poured forth a final extravagance of light; but the breeze nipped keenly. Below them, at their backs, the harbour glimmered out of murk. At their feet, surf smashed in a smother of white. To the side, surges went to and fro between the doors, sucking and sobbing.

Dahut stared outward. 'We can't see Sena,' she said raggedly.

'Nay, of course not.' He picked his way forward, word by word. 'Would you fain?'

She nodded. 'That . . . is where I was born, and – mother – '

'I've told you before, and I will again, never blame yourself, darling. She died blessing you. I'm sure she did, blessing you as ever I've since done myself.'

'I know. I knew. Until today -- '

He waited.

She looked up at him. 'Where do the dead go after they must leave us?'

'What?' He was surprised. 'Oh, folk have many different beliefs. You, a vestal, you must be more learned than I am about what the wisest in Ys think.'

She shook her head. 'They only say the Gods apportion our dooms. 'Tis not what I meant. Father, sometimes the dead come back. They are born anew so they can – watch over us – But what happens to them when they die again?'

He called to mind eerie rumours that had reached him over the years. Chill shot along his back and out to his fingertips. 'That seal who comes to you – '

'She died. A beast killed her.'

'How do you know?' he mumbled.

'*She* knew. She told me. I think the Gods saw that – if she stayed – she'd keep me from – from – I know not what, from something They may want of me – Oh, father, where is she now?'

Dahut cast herself back into the arms of Gratillonius. The tears broke loose. She clawed against him and screamed.

He gripped her and endured.

At length, still an animal hurt and terrified, gone to earth in his bosom, at length she could plead, 'Help me, father. Leave me not. Be with me always.'

'I will, . . . daughter of Dahilis.' He dared inquire no further. Belike he never would, nor she say any more. Yet he felt within himself the strength he had reached for.

'Promise!'

'I do.' Gratillonius looked above her tousled head. The sun must have gone under, for hues had drained from the fog and twilight was rapidly thickening. Wind cut through, though, and he spied the battlements of the Raven Tower clear against uneasy heaven, afire with the last radiance of the Unconquered. In a crypt beneath lay his holy of holies. The strength rose higher, defiant of the cruel Gods of Ys.

'I promise,' he said. 'I will never forsake you, Dahut, beloved, never deny you. By Mithras I swear.'

They sought home together.

Notes

Although we hope our story explains itself, it may raise a few questions in the minds of some readers, while others may wish to know a little more about the period. These notes are intended for them.

1

Chairs: In the ancient world these were usually reserved for persons of status. Ordinary folk sat on stools, benches, or the floor.

Augustus: At this time there was more than one Roman Emperor. The senior of two was titled 'Augustus', his colleague and heir apparent 'Caesar'. Usually both the Western and Eastern parts of the Empire had such a double monarchy. (Occasionally a given Augustus had two or more Caesars, each responsible for a part of his domains.) Hence the name 'Tetrarchy'. Evidently Maximus's designation as Augustus amounted to recognition that the Empire had now split into three coequal realms, *de facto* if not quite *de jure*. St Ambrose, bishop of Milan, had played a leading role in persuading him to settle for that, rather than trying to take over the entire West. In 387 he would break the agreement and invade Italy.

Augusta Treverorum: Trier (Trèves).

Early this year: Maximus made his terms with Valentinian

and Theodosius late in 384 or early in 385; the date is uncertain, like the dates of many events in this era.

Africa: North Africa, exclusive of Egypt and Ethiopia.

Illyricum: A Roman diocese (major administrative division) occupying, approximately, most of the territory now comprising Yugoslavia and Greece.

Lugdunum: Lyons.

Burdigala: Bordeaux.

Sena: Île de Sein.

Sign of the Ram, etc.: Precessing, the vernal equinox moved from Aries to Pisces about the time of Christ, and by the fourth century was well within the latter. To populations obsessed with astrology, this had an obscure but apocalyptic significance. It may in some degree have aided the initial spread of the Christian religion and (together with the ICHTHYS acronym) influenced the adoption of the fish as a symbol of Christ.

Gallia: Gaul.

Pagans in high Roman office: Symmachus is best known from this time, but there were numerous others, despite Christianity being now the state religion and attempts made to proscribe all the rest.

Empire: The Roman state still called itself a republic, but had of course long ceased to be any such thing. Nobody took the fiction seriously. So, to avoid confusing modern readers, we have our characters speak the word which was actually in their minds.

Italian Mediolanum: Milan. Several cities bore that name.

Ambrosius: Today known as St Ambrose.

(Gallia) Lugdunensis: A province of Gaul, comprising most of what is now northern and a fair portion of central France.

(Gallia) Aquitania: A province of Gaul, bounded approxi-

mately by the Atlantic Ocean and the Garonne and Loire Rivers.

Osismii: A tribe occupying the western end of Brittany, hence the immediate neighbours of Ys.

Ahriman: The supreme lord of evil in the Mithraic religion.

II

Tuba: In the Roman world, this was a long, straight trumpet, used especially by the military for commanding, signalling, setting cadence, etc.

Pontus: A Roman diocese, comprising Anatolia.

Hispania: A Roman diocese, comprising what are now Spain and Portugal.

Caledonia: A loose term, referring more or less to what is now Scotland. Cf. the notes to *Roma Mater*.

Condate Redonum: Rennes.

Liger: The River Loire.

Juliomagus: Angers.

Namnetes: A tribe occupying the right bank of the Loire from the seashore to its confluence with the Mayenne.

Caesarodunum Turonum: Tours. At this time, those parts of city names that designated local tribes were increasingly displacing those parts the Romans had bestowed. Thus they often became the ancestors of the present-day names.

Laeti: Barbarians allowed to settle within the Empire on condition that they give it allegiance – a proviso observed only loosely, at best.

Jerkin: No such garment is attested until a much later

date, but something of the kind must have been in use long before.

Gesoriacum: Boulogne.

Redones: A tribe occupying the area around Rennes.

Maedraeacum: Médréac, a village near which we once spent a pleasant week in a *gîte*. The reconstruction of the ancient name is entirely conjectural, as is the history. However, many such communities did originate as latifundia.

Last Day: Chiliasm was rampant in this era. About 380, St Martin of Tours told a disciple that the Antichrist had been born. Countless people, high and low, educated and ignorant, were finding their own portents of the imminent end of the world. Like numerous other features of late West Roman society, this one looks rather familiar to an inhabitant of the late twentieth century.

Organization of the Bacaudae (also spelled *Bagaudae*): Little is recorded about this. A couple of chronicles mention an 'emperor', though that word (Latin *imperator*) may there simply have its original meaning of 'commander'. Since the Bacaudae persisted for a long time and occasionally won pitched battles, they must have had more structure than, say, the medieval Jacquerie. But we can scarcely compare them to modern guerrillas; they lacked both a formalized ideology and the assistance of powerful foreign states. Our guess is that, as more and more individuals fled from an oppressive civilization and then perforce turned about to prey on it, they necessarily and almost blindly developed primitive institutions and a moralistic rationalization of their actions.

Hand to arm: The Roman equivalent of the later handshake.

III

Martinus: Today known as St Martin of Tours.

The appearance of St Martin: At this time there were not yet any particular vestments or other distinguishing marks for the clergy. Indeed, most still earned their livelihoods in ordinary ways and preached in their spare time; many were married; some of the married, when the husband had been ordained, vowed sexual abstention, but not all did by any means. Likewise, tonsures for cenobites were neither standardized nor universal. The kind adopted by St Martin, which he may have originated, became that of the Celtic Church, eventually superseded by the Roman form with which we today are more familiar. Martin's looks and traits are described by his disciple and biographer Sulpicius Severus.

Martin's elevation to bishop: This story, given us by Sulpicius, is not as incredible as it looks. Ecclesiastical procedures were often *ad hoc*, especially in the provinces, and there are well-attested cases of laymen being called to the episcopate and only then receiving baptism. A full bishop had so much secular importance that ordinary people sometimes demanded a voice in the choosing of him.

Pannonia: A Roman province occupying an area now shared by parts of Hungary, Austria, and Czechoslovakia. Its inhabitants at the time were largely, if not exclusively, Celtic.

Avela (or *Abula*): Ávila.

Ossanuba: Faro, Portugal.

Manicheanism: A religion which was, like Mithraism, of

393

Iranian origin, but if anything more of a threat to Christianity, since it incorporated important elements of the latter. Throughout the centuries, under one name or another, it has been a recurrent heresy. Among other deviations, it attributes creative powers to Satan.

Gates of Trier: In Roman Imperial times there were four of these, of which the Porta Nigra survives as a ruin. Its name is medieval; originally it was not blackened by centuries of smoke.

Mosella: The River Moselle (or Mosel).

Rhenus: The River Rhine.

Bonna: Bonn.

Juthungi: A Germanic tribe living near Raetia.

Raetia (or *Rhaetia*): A Roman province covering, approximately, what is now Bavaria.

Basilica: Originally this word meant an administrative centre, civil or military.

The fate of the Priscillianists: Much is uncertain about events surrounding this trial, the historical importance of which includes the fact that it is the first recorded persecution of Christians by other Christians. The dates and the very year are debatable. We have chosen the 385 favoured by most scholars and assumed that, because so much had been going on before, the trial took place rather late in that year. Some accounts say the heretics were burned, but it seems likelier that they were beheaded; the stake did not come into vogue until the Middle Ages.

Fortifications: Legionaries on campaign had normally dug a trench and erected an earthwork around every camp, then levelled these upon leaving to keep an enemy from taking them over. By the late fourth century this cannot have been common practice, for the old-style legion was on the way out. We assume that it lasted later in Britain than elsewhere.

Lugdunum (or *Lugudunum*): Lyons. Several other cities bore this name.

Vienna: Vienne. (Wien in Austria, Vienna to speakers of English, was then Vindobona.) Remnants of a Mithraeum, such as are not found in Lyons, suggested that the cult persisted there, though by the time of Gratillonius's visit it had been driven into a private home.

Rhodanus: The River Rhône.

Circus: A space with tiers of seats on three sides, divided lengthwise by a barrier, for races, games, and shows.

Asiatic: By 'Asia' the Romans meant what we now call 'Asia Minor' or 'the Near East'.

The Mithraeum in Vienne: As the model for this hypothetical last survivor, we have chosen some that have been excavated in Ostia.

Tauroctony: A depiction of Mithras slaying the primordial Bull.

Burdigala: Bordeaux.

Rhetoric: Occasionally one sees Classical schools of rhetoric, such as the great one at Bordeaux, referred to as universities. This is anachronistic, but only mildly so. Rhetoric, the study of persuasive argument, embraced not just oratory, but languages, logic, history, literature, and much else. Thus a mastery of it amounted to a liberal education.

Garumna: The River Garonne.

Paulinus: Ausonius's grandson grew up into the kind of life that the old man envisioned, but it was shattered by the arrival of the Visigoths and other calamities.

Duranius: The River Dordogne.

V

Mumu: Munster. The boundaries were probably less definite than in later times. Its association with women, musicians, and magic was ancient, and persisted into the Middle Ages.

Ériu: Ireland.

Children of Danu: Best known by a later name, the Tuatha Dé Danaan. According to legend, this race, the tuaths (only approximately equivalent to tribes; see the notes to *Roma Mater*) descended from the goddess Danu, held Ireland before the Milesians arrived from Spain. Overcome by the invaders, they retreated to the *síd*, mounds and hills whose interiors they made their dwellings. They themselves became the fairy folk. Most modern commentators think they are a Christian euhemerization of the pagan gods, and doubtless there is much truth in this view. However, the tradition of a war between them and the newcomers is so basic to Irish mythology that it must have some foundation in fact. Successive Celtic peoples did enter, taking land by force of arms. Our guess is that one or more of the earlier peoples, to whom their conquerors attributed magical powers, became conflated with the old gods, but that this had not yet happened at the time of our story.

Children of Ír and Éber: Later called the Milesians; tradition makes them the last invaders of Ireland before the Vikings.

The Mountain of Fair Women: Now Slievenamon, south-west of Cashel.

Síd (or *sídh*): Singular of *sídhe*. Both are pronounced, approximately, 'shee'.

Condacht: Connaught.

Qóiqet Lagini: Leinster.

Mide: A realm carved out of Connaught and Leinster, centred on Tara.

The Ulati: The people of Ulster (*Qóiqet nUlat*). It should be remembered that the boundaries of all these territories were vague, and generally not identical with those of the modern provinces.

Trade between Munster and the Romans: This has been archaeologically proved.

Christianity: The histories indicate that there was already an established and growing body of Christians in Munster, if not elsewhere in Ireland. For one thing, Palladius was sent to minister to them; and other bishops are mentioned, together with Irish clergymen serving on the Continent – all before the mission of St Patrick.

Conual Corcc (today usually rendered as *Conall Corc*): His dates are still more uncertain than Niall's, and the stories about him that have come down to us are even more confused and contradictory. In both cases, we have tried to put together versions that make some logical sense.

Fostering: Children in ancient Ireland, at least among the upper classes, more often than not were raised in other homes than their parents'. The ties thus created between families were as sacred as those of blood kinship.

Alba: The early Irish name for what is now, more or less, Scotland. Sometimes 'Alba' also included England and Wales. The name 'Scotland' comes from its heavy colonization by Scoti, i.e., people from Ireland – just as Armorica was to become Brittany (Breizh, in its own language) after immigrants from Britain took it over. At the time of our story, the Scotic settlement amounted largely to an extension, into what is now Argyll, of the kingdom of Dál Riata, in what is now northern Antrim. (Some authorities put its founding as late as 500 A.D., but the event would have become possible soon after the Romans abandoned the Antonine Wall towards the end of the second century, and a date in the middle fourth century is consistent with other assumptions we have made for story purposes.) However, a king from Mide, adventuring in Alba, could well have defeated a Pictish leader and imposed an alliance in which the latter was a junior partner.

The ogamm (today *ogham*) *shield*: This is evidently a Celtic form of an ancient and widespread story. Quite possibly the Vikings, in their day, brought it back to Denmark from Ireland. 'Hamlet' – 'Amleth(us)' in Saxo Grammaticus, Shakespeare's ultimate source – is not a name otherwise found; one scholar has suggested that it may be a Scandinavian reading of the Gaelic spelling of the Nordic 'Olaf'! Ogham was a very primitive and limited form of writing, so to alter it would not have been difficult.

Ordovices and Silures: Tribes inhabiting what is now Wales.

VI

Éndae Qennsalach: Perhaps historical, perhaps not. The second half of his name refers to his ancestry.

Founding of Mide: This is the legendary version. See the notes to *Roma Mater*.

Origin of the Bóruma: This is also a legend, of course, but one which people of Niall's time may well have believed. The tribute itself and its evil consequences are historical fact.

Niall's warefare: The sources say nothing specific; but given our story assumptions, campaigns like these are plausible.

Ruirthech: The River Liffey. Then it seems to have marked the northern frontier of Leinster.

Chariots: Roman tactics had long since made the military chariot obsolete, but it persisted in Ireland, where it did not have to face well-drilled infantry and cavalry, until past our time. As for other equipment, see the notes to *Roma Mater*.

Niall's two queens: Not only concubinage but polygyny was accepted in ancient Ireland, even after the conversion to Christianity. (For a while canon law decreed that a *priest* could have only one wife!) The chronicles say that Niall had fourteen sons by two wives, whom we suppose to have been more or less contemporaneous. Surely he had daughters too, and children by other women.

Nobles and tenants: For a brief description of the classes *flaith*, *soer-céli*, and *doer-céli*, see the notes to *Roma Mater*.

Combat tactics: Like the equipment, these too were little changed in Ireland from the old Celtic forms.

Lifting a knee: Stools and tables were very low. To rise when a visitor appeared was a token of full respect. Short of this, though still polite, was to raise a knee, as if about to get up.

Verse: Like Nordic skalds of a later date, early Irish poets used intricate forms, yet were expected to be able to compose within those forms on a moment's notice. Our rendition here is a much simplified version of one scheme. Each stanza, expressing a complete thought, consists of four seven-syllabled lines. Besides the alliteration and rhyme, it is required that end-words of the second and fourth lines have one more syllable than those of the first and third. Oral skill such as this is entirely possible and historically attested. The poet naturally had to have an innate gift together with long and arduous training.

Satire: The Celtic peoples were great believers in word magic. Well into Christian times, satirists were dreaded in Ireland. To a modern mind, it is not implausible that they could bring on psychosomatic disorders, even wasting illness. Our story supposes their powers went beyond that.

VII

Odita: The River Odet. (Our Latin name is conjectural.) The distances mentioned have been rounded off, as they would be in the mind of any ordinary traveller. It should be noted that this stream was deeper then than it is now, when impoundments in the watershed have diminished its sources.

Stegir: The River Steir. (This is also conjectural on our part.)

Aquilo: Locmaria, now a district at the south end of Quimper. While the existence of Roman Aquilo is attested, our history and description of it are still more conjecture.

Mons Ferruginus: Mont Frugy. More conjecture, this time based on the fact that there is iron ore in the area.

Durocotorum: Rheims.

Apuleius Vero: The ancient tripartite system of nomenclature had long since broken down. Some people still employed it, but others, in the upper classes, did not. 'Vero' is a hypothetical Gallo-Roman name commemorating the family's most important connection of that kind. 'Apuleius', the old *gens* name, now went from father to eldest son, much as the same given and middle names may pass through several generations in our own era. Upon succeeding to the paternal estate, this Apuleius dropped whatever other names he had borne, if any. In this as in several more significant respects, he typified a man of his time, place, and station in life. More provincial and thus more conservative, the Gratillonii of Britain clung to traditional usages.

The Duke of the Armorican Tract: The Roman military official in charge of defence of the entire area. (This is a shortened version of the actual title, such as we suppose people employed in everyday speech.) Armorica was, in fact, considered a military district, not a political entity. Ravages along the coasts indicate that at this time the Duke's efforts were concentrated in the east and the interior of the peninsula. This was doubtless because resources were limited and, terrible though the depredations of pirates often were, they seemed less of a threat than a possible Germanic invasion overland. Gaul had already suffered the latter, again and again, and sometimes the Romans had managed only barely and slowly to drive the barbarians back. Under such circumstances, the Duke might be glad to delegate authority in the west to some competent leader. Our idea that this particular Duke was covertly opposed to Maximus is a guess – nothing is known for certain – but not unreasonable.

Troops: Increasingly, locally recruited soldiers were providing garrisons such as here described. Not being attached to any legion, they were known as *numeri* or *cunei* rather than auxiliaries. Civilian men, *limitanei*, were being made into reservists. These processes had gone much further in the Eastern half of the Empire than they had, as yet, in the West.

The Pulcher villa: Baths, such as would have belonged to a substantial estate, have been excavated at Poulker (near Benodet). The form of this place name is unusual in Brittany. However, we only venture a guess as to its possible origin.

The defences of Aquilo: Our idea of what these may have amounted to is based on the lack of archaeological evidence for anything else. Actually, the Gallic wall was a good, solid structure.

Corentinus: Known in France at the present day as St Corentin. His historicity is uncertain, but there are many legends about him, including that of the miracle of the fish and his later career as the first bishop of Quimper. For reasons discussed in the Afterword to the last of these volumes, we have conflated him with the equally enigmatic figure of St Guénolé.

Smoke: As we remarked in the notes to *Roma Mater*, primitive Celtic dwellings neither needed nor had vent holes for smoke. It filtered out through the thatch, killing vermin along the way.

Pictavum: Poitiers.

Pomoerium: The space kept clear just inside and outside a defensive wall.

Consecration of the Mithraeum: Our description of this draws in part on our imaginations, but largely on the ideas of such authorities as Cumont, Stewardson, and Saunders.

Pater and Heliodromos: Father and Runner (or Courier) of the Sun, the first and second degrees of a Mithraic congregation. Although knowledge of this religion is, today, fragmentary, what we do possess shows its many resemblances to Christianity, not only in belief but in liturgy, organization, and requirements laid upon the faithful.

VIII

Lugdunensis Tertia: The Roman province comprising northwestern France.

Church buildings: Most were quite small. The cathedral in Tours may have been the size of a fairly large present-day house.

Samarobriva: Amiens.

St Martin as a military physician: This is not in the chronicles, but some modern biographers think it is probable.

Exorcists: In this era, such priests were not specifically charged with driving out demons, but simply with the supervision of the energumens and similar duties.

The service: Obviously this was very different from today's ritual. It varied from place to place; what we have sketched was the so-called Gallic Mass. Strictly speaking,

403

though, the Mass was the Communion service, reserved for the baptized.

Biblical texts: Respectively Amos xviii, 8, I Corinthians ii, 4, and Matthew xviii, 8.

Martin and the bishops: His refusal to attend any synods after the Priscillian affair is attested.

Greater Monastery: Majus Monasterium, which probably is the origin of the place name 'Marmoutier', although some scholars derive it from 'Martin'.

Chorepiscopus: The powers granted priests in the early Church were very limited. A chorepiscopus, 'country bishop', ranked above them but below a full bishop. He had most of the powers later given a parish priest, but not all. See the notes to *Roma Mater*.

Paenula: A poncho-like outer garment. From everyday garb of this period and later derived the priestly vestments of the Church. The paenula became the chasuble.

Cernunnos: An ancient Gallic god.

IX

Sarmatian: What people the Classical geographers meant by this name is obscure, and evidently varied over the centuries. To Corentinus, we suppose, the word would designate one of those Slavic tribes that were drifting into what is now Poland and Prussia as the Germanic inhabitants moved elsewhere.

Suebian Sea: The Baltic (*Mare Suebicum*).

Cimbrian Chersonese: Jutland. The Heruls, whom tradition says once inhabited the adjacent islands, had by now migrated south, and the Danes were moving in from what is now Sweden. Jutes and Angles were still at home, although soon many of them would be among the invaders of Britain.

Franks: This word (*Franci*) was a generic Roman term for Germanic tribes originating north of the River Main and along the North Sea. Moving into Gaul, they eventually gave that name to the entire country of France. Our account of their pagan religious practices draws on descriptions from other times and places; but it seems plausible to us. Whatever the details, we have scarcely exaggerated the brutality of the Franks. It was notorious. Even after they had become Christian, the history of the early Merovingians is a catalogue of horrors.

Cataphract: A heavy cavalryman.

Aquileia: Near present-day Trieste.

Death of Maximus and Victor: Authorities disagree on the precise date and manner of this, but it occurred in the summer of 388.

X

The defeat of Maximus: According to one source, only two Romans died at Aquileia, Maximus and Victor. This implies that both armies were composed entirely of barbarian mercenaries, which seems to us unlikely in the extreme. Surely Maximus, at least, would have needed legionaries to drive Valentinian out of Italy, and then, lacking effective cavalry such as Theodosius possessed, would have brought them to meet the latter.

Maximus's veterans: There is a tradition that they were settled in Armorica, and some modern historians consider it plausible. If this did happen, then doubtless the involuntary colonists included certain of the troops Maximus

405

had left behind in Gaul, though probably only those whose loyalty to the re-established Imperium of the West was very questionable.

The gravestone: Roman epitaphs, especially when military, were generally short and employed abbreviations. Expanded and translated, this one reads TO QUINTUS JUNIUS EPPILLUS / OPTIO (deputy) IN THE SECOND LEGION AUGUSTA / HIS FELLOW SOLDIERS MADE THIS.

XI

Thracia: Thrace, occupying approximately what are now the northeastern end of Greece, the northwestern end of Turkey, and southern Bulgaria.

Saxons in Britain: There is good evidence for some colonization, as well as piracy, by these barbarians as early as the later fourth century. Be that as it may, Stilicho had hard fights against them.

Sabrina: The River Severn.

Silures: The British tribe inhabiting what is now, more or less, Glamorganshire and Monmouth.

Sucat (or *Succat*): Birth name of St Patrick. As nearly as possible, we follow traditional accounts of him, including that interpretation of them which makes the year of his capture, rather than his birth, 389. It must be added that a number of modern scholars have called into question all the dates and other details of his story; some actually challenge his historicity. His appearance before Niall is our own idea. Even tradition does not make clear where he passed his time of servitude. Somewhat arbitrarily, we adopt the suggestion that it was in County Mayo.

Temir: Tara.

Cú Culanni: Today better known as Cuchulainn, the greatest hero of the Ulster cycle. His king, Conchobar, was said by medieval writers to have died of fury at hearing that Christ had been crucified, though he himself was a pagan. This at least gives some hint at the time that tradition assigned to these sagas.

Emain Macha: The ancient seat of the supreme Ulster kings, near present-day Armagh. The Red Branch (more accurately, but hardly ever, rendered as Royal Branch) was the lodge where their chief warriors met.

Fifth: For the ancient division of Ireland into five parts, autonomous if not exactly nation-states, see the notes to *Roma Mater*.

Qóiqet nUlat: the Fifth of the Ulati people.

Cruthini and Firi Bolg: There were Picts (whom the Irish called Cruthini) in Ireland as well as in Scotland-to-be – and, for that matter, in northern Gaul. As we have noted earlier, they were not at all the dwarfs of modern folklore, nor backward with respect to the Gaels; however, they were a distinct people. The Firi Bolg were, in legend, the first colonists of Ireland, subjugated by the invading Children of Danu. Perhaps this tale embodies a dim folk memory of an aboriginal population whom the first wave or waves of incoming Celts overran and intermarried with. If so, pride of ancestry persisted well into historical times; and to this day, there do appear to be at least two racial types native to the country.

Conduct of the Ulati: Tradition does not say that the upper classes in Ulster were especially oppressive. However, the Uí Néill seem to have had little difficulty in keeping the Aregésla (or Airgialla), about whom more later, a puppet power. This has given some modern writers the idea that a malcontent population was present in the first place – a suggestion we have followed. Granted, at worst the yoke would have been far lighter than that upon the peoples of the Roman Empire or, for that matter, virtually everybody today. The Irish aristocrats were not saints or libertarians, but they lacked the apparatus available to organize governments.

Starving: Among the early Irish, a man who had a grievance against one more powerful, and could not otherwise get redress, often sat down at the door of the latter and fasted. If this did not shame the second party into making a settlement, then he too was expected to deny himself food, and it became an endurance contest.

Sinand: The River Shannon. The territory we have described Niall as taking includes present-day County Cavan and part of Monaghan. Of course, our depiction of events is purely conjectural, and some modern scholars deny that it could have happened this way at all.

Mag Slecht: The 'Plain of Prostrations', in County Cavan, where stood the idols of Cromb Cróche (or Crom Cruach) and his twelve attendants. The chronicles say these were the most powerful and revered gods in Ireland until St Patrick overthrew them.

The lunar eclipse: This took place on 13 July 390 (Gregorian calendar).

The comet of 390: It is recorded as having been visible from 22 August to 17 September (Gregorian dates). The magnitude is not known, but it was presumably conspicuous.

Polaris: Prior to the development of elevators, locations in a tall building were less desirable the farther up they were. Structures of this height were forbidden in Rome as being too hazardous, but we suppose the Ysans had more confidence in their architects, and knew how to make self-bracing frameworks.

Corentinus's sermon: Few if any Christians of this period denied the reality of pagan gods. Sometimes they were considered to be mere euhemerizations, but oftener demons or, at best, beings with certain powers and perhaps without evil intentions, to whom it was nevertheless wrong to pay divine honours.

XII

Lúgnassat (later *Lugnasad*): A harvest festival taking its name from the god Lúg. In Christian times it occurred on 1 August. The English know it as Lammas, though that name has another derivation. Lacking the Roman calendar, the pagan Celts must have set the date some other way; we guess that the moon helped determine it.

Fairs: The ancient Irish held a number of such events, at various localities each year. Religious as well as secular, they were open to all.

Cromb Cróche and the death of Domnuald: Our description of the sanctuary and the ceremonies that took place there is conjectural, though based on the chronicles, on local traditions in the area said to have held it, and on similar things in other milieus. Domnuald and his fate are imaginary, but the story does go that the slaying of a son of his made Niall ready to kill the hostages he had from the folk of the murderers.

Éricc (later *eraic*): Akin to the Teutonic weregild, a payment to an injured party or his heirs, the amount depending on the actual harm done and the possible provocation.

Honour price: Unlike the Germanic peoples, the Irish made some effort to equalize justice between rich and poor. A man of rank, who owed an éricc, must pay in addition an amount of goods which increased with his social standing.

Clón Tarui: Now Clontarf, a district of Dublin.

Tallten: Now Teltown, on the River Blackwater in County Meath. Our description of the size and importance of the fair (*óenach*) there is not exaggerated; like its counterparts, it continued for centuries after Ireland became Christian, so reliable records exist. That an eponymous goddess should have been buried at the site is not unique. For example, though the Nordic god Baldr died in the early days of the world, he seems to have had a cult.

The Dagdae (later *Dagda*): A god especially wise. His well is our invention.

Mag Mell: The Plain of Honey, one of the paradises that Celtic myth located afar in the western ocean. Sometimes the name was applied to all of them together. The Celts do not appear to have had any clear or consistent ideas about an afterlife. There are mentions of favoured persons whose souls were borne west to abide a while before returning and being reincarnated. Probably the most usual supposition was that the dead inhabited their graves, coming out to spook around on the eves of Beltene and Samain.

Irish arts and crafts: The glorious works that remain to us prove that, for all its violence and technological backwardness, this society had as keen a sense for beauty as ever the Greeks did.

Expulsion of the Irish from Wales: This is attested.

Eóganachta: The royal family, or rather set of families claiming a common ancestor, in Munster.

Tanist: The heir apparent of an Irish king, chosen well beforehand. It was doubtless done in the hope of an orderly succession. Any man with royal blood and no

410

physical impairment, whether born in or out of wedlock, could become king if he had the power to enforce his claim. This could easily lead to war between rival pretenders. The laws and institutions of Rome had decayed so far that the Empire must needs invent something of the kind for itself, the Caesar associated with the Augustus.

Nath Í: Tradition says that this nephew of Niall succeeded him. The medieval account of his career creates so many chronological problems that several modern scholars have decided he must be purely fictional and that Niall – if he himself ever lived – should be dated a generation later than he is in the chronicles. It may be; or it may not. Given all the uncertainties, we have felt free to stay with the tradition, which better fits our story, and to put in modifications or new material of our own. The contradictions in the sources *could* mainly be due to their authors, drawing on oral history handed down for lifetimes, getting different persons and their acts confused with each other.

The Walls of the Ulati: Known as the Black Pig's Dyke, remnants of ancient fortifications – earthen walls and fosses – occur approximately along the southern boundary of Ulster. They may have been raised in imitation of Roman works, or they may be older than that. They were probably not a continuous line of defence, but rather a set of strongpoints for controlling movement along the main routes of travel. Elsewhere, forest, bog, and other natural obstacles would have sufficiently hindered invaders or retreating cattle rustlers.

Commandments and prohibitions laid on royal persons: Those mentioned here are in the annals. A taboo applying to an individual or a class of people was known as a *gess* (later *geas*), plural *gessa*.

The redemption of the hostages: This is in the tradition, though it does not state where they were from. We have

411

put the incident just after Lúgnassat, partly so we could describe a little of the fair, partly because the chronicles say that the Rock of Cashel was revealed 'when the leaves were yellow', which must have been in autumn.

Darioritum: Vannes.

Tambilis and Gratillonius: Most peoples, including our own until recent times, have considered a girl of sixteen to be nubile.

Veneti: A tribe in southern Brittany. Under the Empire, tribes had no independence and their identities gradually eroded, but they did constitute units of local government, not totally unlike American states.

XIII

The Síd Drommen (or *Sídhe-Druimm*): This is one of several names the great rock originally bore. They all suggest the supernatural.

The finding of Cashel: We have tried to synthesize the legends, omitting Christian elements that the chroniclers inserted. There are enough pagan ones. Swine were anciently associated with the dead, which may be why kings could not own them. The yew, one of the three trees the Irish held sacred (together with the hazel and the rowan), was a patron of the Eóganachta; the name of their ancester, Eógan, means 'yew'. At his ceremony of accession, a new king always stood on a flagstone (*lecc*).

The career of Conual: It is not known when or how Cashel and the kingdom that grew from it were actually founded. We have followed tradition as far as possible, including parts that some modern scholars hold to be purely mythical. For example, Byrne considers Conual's second wife,

412

Ámend, a humanized sun goddess, daughter of the lightning (Bolg). That may be. Yet it seems quite plausible that Conual made a political marriage, and that his early successes were in large part due to the awe inspired by the seemingly supernatural circumstances of his advent – circumstances that may have been accidental or may have been engineered, but that he, who had been exposed to Roman civilization, was quick to take advantage of. Some authorities suggest that he was a Christian. We suppose not, if only because the chronicles declare that his grandson was the first king of Cashel to take the Faith, and the tale of that baptism by St Patrick is too delightful to give up willingly. Hardly any historian disputes that a Roman-style fortress was erected on the outcrop sometime in the late fourth or early fifth century; that the name Cassel, later Caisel, now Cashel, derives from Latin *castellum*, meaning such a stronghold; and that from this nucleus developed the kingdom of Munster. Eventually deeded to the Church, the rock became an important ecclesiastical site.

Aregésla (later *Airgialla*): Occupying, approximately, what are now Counties Monaghan, Cavan, and Leitrim, this kingdom does appear to have been established as a puppet of Niall or his sons. Our account of the founding is conjectural. Giving local chieftains authority over the rites of Mag Slecht would not have debarred the kings of Tara from that ready access to Crom Cruach which the legend of St Patrick says they had.

Niall of the Nine Hostages: By this name is the ancestor of the Uí Néill dynasties known to history. Just when or how he got the sobriquet is unknown. At any given time, any king of importance surely held more than nine individual hostages. Hence the reference must be to some who were especially significant. According to one chronicle, Niall had them from each of the Fifths of Ireland, and four from Britain; according to another, besides the five Irish, they were from Scotland (the Picts), the Britons, the Saxons, and the Franks. This makes little or no sense. For once we go along with modern commentators and suppose that the nine were of the Aregésla, whose establishment as subordinate allies marked a turning point in the destiny of the Uí Néill.

The hallowing of the newborn: There is no reason why a healthy woman who has given birth should not get up and walk about, at least for fairly short distances, a few hours later.

Niall Náegéslach (later *Nóigiallach*): Niall of the Nine Hostages. It is our conjecture that he took advantage of Stilicho's departure to ravage Britain and so assert his power in the face of Conual Corcc's spectacular successes. It squares with the tradition. Certainly Scotic raids increased about this time.

The Loígis: Presumably this set of tribes gave their name to present-day County Laoighis; but the sources indicate that they held the western frontiers of Leinster as far down as the sea.

Ossraige: A kingdom occupying the western parts of what are now Counties Laoighis and Kilkenny. Apparently it had a subordinate relation to the Leinster high kings, somewhat like that of the Aregésla to the Uí Néill.

The origin of the Lagini: We repeat the legends.

Dún Alinni: Near present-day Kildare.

Fomóri: A legendary race who harassed the Firi Bolg in ancient times and whom the children of Danu expelled.

Eochaid's raid: This, and its aftermath, are traditional tales, though of course we have filled in many details as best we could.

XIV

Menstrual pad: Today's convenient sanitary napkins and tampons are quite a recent development, but people have always had the problem to cope with as best they could, and we may suppose the upper-class Ysan women had arrangements available to them that were better than most.

Vervain: Now more commonly known as verbena. Both the Romans and the Gauls credited it with numerous wonderful properties.

Irish gold: The country was rich in this metal, though in the course of centuries the sources would be exhausted.

Praetorian prefect: For some discussion of this high office, see the notes to *Roma Mater*.

Salomon: A form of the name closer to the original than 'Solomon' and still common on the Continent. The early Church made little use of the Old Testament, except for a few lyrical and prophetic parts, so it is natural that Gratillonius would be ignorant of ancient Jewish history, while a scholarly sort like Apuleius could be well versed in it.

XV

Carsa: Another conjectural family name. We fancy that it could relate to Carsac, a village in the Dordogne where we have spent pleasant days.

Cadurci: A Gallic tribe inhabiting the Dordogne.

Burdigala: Bordeaux.

Garumna: The River Garonne.

The Armorican run: Archaeological evidence shows that commerce was still going on between southern France and Brittany.

The shipping season: In the ancient world, this was generally from April through October. The virtual cessation of maritime traffic in the winter was less for fear of storms – most ships were quite seaworthy – than because weather made navigation difficult.

Tonnage: Mediterranean grain ships had burdens of up to 1200 tons. Ocean-going vessels were doubtless smaller, but not too much so. A typical merchantman is described in *Roma Mater*.

Speed: Merchantmen could do four or five knots under good conditions. They could point up to the wind to a limited extent and lie hove to, after a fashion, when that was the prudent thing to do.

Periplus: A set of sailing directions for a given route, describing landmarks, hazards, etc. Maps were so crude as to be virtually useless to navigators.

Clerestory: Not Roman; but we suppose there was some Egyptian influence on Ysan architecture.

Sucat and Martin: Again we are forced to select from among the often contradictory stories about St Patrick; but we have invented essentially nothing. He may actually have been an Armorican rather than a Briton, and he may have been born as late as 389. However, this would probably rule out the kinship to St Martin which tradition gives him, and certainly the story that he became a disciple of the latter. His career after escape from captivity is obscure in the extreme. The reconstruction that we employ has him come to Marmoutier in 396, seeking holy

416

orders, and live there until the bishop's death, after which he went south to pursue his studies and devotions.

Banaventa (or *Bannauenta* or other variants): Mentioned in Patrick's *Confessions* (which some modern scholars consider spurious), this may have been Daventry, but may also have been one of three places in Glamorganshire called Banwent; we assume the latter. It is described as the home of his mother's parents, whom he was visiting when the raiders struck, but this does not seem to square with the claim that she was Martin's niece, so we follow the school of thought that makes Banaventa his father's and his own dwelling place.

Sucat's future: He spent many years on the Continent. Legend declares that Pope Celestine, in consecrating him for his mission, gave him the new name Patricius – now Patrick. There is reason to think he may have assumed it himself and, indeed, even consecrated himself a bishop. The traditional date for his return to Ireland is 432, for his death 461. Thus he, like Martin, had a long life, active until the very end.

XVI

Garomagus: Our conjectural name for a Roman town that, archaeology has revealed, existed on the site of present-day Douarnenez. In fact, the entire littoral of the bay there was reasonably populous and prosperous in the heyday of the Empire. Local tradition makes the city Douarnenez the seat of legendary King Mark, and the islet bears the name of his nephew Tristan. This suggests that the area has ancient magical associations.

Roman Bay: Baie de Douarnenez. This is the Ysan name; what the Romans called it is not known.

Goat Foreland: Cap de la Chèvre. We are supposing that a name Gallic or even older has kept the same meaning though languages have changed – unless the identity is coincidental.

Geographical Glossary

These equivalents are for the most part only approximations. For further details, see the Notes.

Africa: North Africa, exclusive of Egypt and Ethiopia.
Alba: Scotic name of what is now Scotland, sometimes including England.
Aquileia: Near present-day Trieste.
Aquilo: Locmaria, now a district at the south end of Quimper.
Aquitania: See *Gallia Aquitania*.
Aregésla: Counties Monaghan, Cavan, and Leitrim in Ireland.
Armorica: Brittany.
Asia: Asia Minor.
Augusta Treverorum: Trier.
Avela: Ávila.
Banaventa: Banwent (?).
Bonna: Bonn.
Britannia: The Roman part of Britain, essentially England and Wales.
Burdigala: Bordeaux.
Caesarodunum Turonum: Tours.
Caledonia: Roman name of Scotland.
Cape Rach: Pointe du Raz (hypothetical).
Cassel: Cashel.
Castellum: Original form of 'Cassel'.
Cimbrian Chersonese: Jutland.
Clón Tarui: Clontarf, now a district of Dublin.

Condacht: Connaught.

Condate Redonum: Rennes.

Darioritum: Vannes.

Dún Alinni: Near present-day Kildare.

Duranius: The River Dordogne.

Durocotorum: Rheims.

Ériu: Ireland.

Gallia: Gaul, including France and parts of Belgium, Germany, and Switzerland.

Gallia Aquitania: A province of Gaul, bounded approximately by the Atlantic Ocean and the Garonne and Loire Rivers.

Gallia Lugdunensis: A province of Gaul, comprising most of what is now northern and a fair portion of central France.

Garomagus: A town at or near present-day Douarnenez (hypothetical).

Garumna: The River Garonne.

Gesoriacum: Boulogne.

Gobaean Promontory (*Promontorium Gobaeum*): Cap Sizun.

Goat Foreland: Cap de la Chèvre (hypothetical).

Hispania: Spain and Portugal.

Hivernia: Roman name of Ireland.

Illyricum: A Roman diocese (major administrative division) occupying, approximately, most of what is now Yugoslavia and Greece.

Juliomagus: Angers.

Liger: The River Loire.

Lugdunensis: See *Gallia Lugdunensis*.

Lugdunensis Tertia: The Roman province comprising northwestern France.

Lugdunum: Lyons.

Maedraeacum: Médréac (hypothetical).

Mag Slecht: A pagan sanctuary in County Cavan, Ireland.

Mediolanum: Milan.

Mide: A realm occupying present-day Counties Meath, Westmeath, and Longford, with parts of Kildare and Offaly, Ireland.

Mons Ferruginus: Mont Frugy (hypothetical).

Mosella: The River Moselle (or Mosel).

Mumu: Munster.

Odita: The River Odet (hypothetical).

Ossanuba: Faro, Portugal.

Ossraige: A realm occupying the western parts of Counties Laoighis and Kilkenny, Ireland.

Pannonia: A Roman province occupying parts of Hungary, Austria, and Czechoslovakia.

Pictavum: Poitiers.

Point Vanis: Pointe du Van (hypothetical).

Pontus: A Roman diocese comprising Anatolia.

Portus Namnetum: Nantes (in part).

Qóiqet Lagini: Leinster (in part).

Qóiqet nUlat: Ulster.

Raetia (or *Rhaetia*): A Roman province occupying, approximately, Bavaria.

Redonum: See *Condate Redonum*.

Rhenus: The River Rhine.

Rhodanus: The River Rhône.

Roman Bay: Baie de Douarnenez (hypothetical).

Ruirthech: The River Liffey.

Sabrina: The River Severn.

Samarobriva: Amiens.

Sena: Île de Sein.

Sinand: The River Shannon.

Stegir: The River Steir (hypothetical).

Suebian Sea (Mare Suebicum): The Baltic Sea.

Tallten: Teltown in County Meath, Ireland.

Temir: Tara.

Thracia: Thrace, occupying approximately the north-eastern end of Greece, the northwestern end of Turkey, and a part of Bulgaria.

Treverorum: See *Augusta Treverorum*.

Vienna: Vienne.

Ys: City-state at the far end of the Gobaean Promontory (legendary).

Dramatis Personae

Where characters are fictional or legendary, their names are in Roman lower case; where historical (in the opinion of most authorities), in Roman capitals; where of doubtful or debatable historicity, in italics. When a full name has not appeared in the text, it is generally not here either, for it was of no great importance even to the bearer.

Adminius: A legionary from Londinium in Britannia, second in command (deputy) of Gratillonius's detachment in Ys.

Adruval Tyri: Sea Lord of Ys, head of the navy and marines.

Aed: A tuathal king in Munster.

AETHBE: A wife of Niall (name conjectural).

Amair: Youngest daughter of Fennalis, by Hoel.

AMBROSIUS: Bishop of Milan, today known as St Ambrose.

Ámend: Second wife of Conual Corcc.

Antonia: Second daughter of Guilvilis and Gratillonius.

Apuleius Vero: A senator in Aquilo and tribune of the city.

Arator: A Gallo-Roman prelate.

ARBOGAST: A Frankish general in the Roman army.

ARCADIUS, FLAVIUS: A son of Theodosius and his successor as Augustus of the East.

Arel: Father of Donnerch.

Audris: Daughter of Innilis by Hoel.

Augustina: Daughter of Vindilis and Gratillonius.

AUSONIUS, DECIMUS MAGNUS: Gallo-Roman poet, scholar, teacher, and sometime Imperial officer.

Avonis: Sister of Herun, eventually wife of Adminius.

Belcar: A legendary Ysan hero.

Bodilis: A Queen of Ys.

Boia: A daughter of Lanarvilis and Hoel.

Bolce Ben-bretnach: Mother of Conual Corcc.

Bomatin Kusuri: A Suffete of Ys, a sea captain and Mariner delegate to the Council.

Breccan: Eldest son of Niall, killed in battle at Ys.

Breifa: A female servant of Bodilis.

Brennilis: Leader of the Gallicenae at the time of Julius and Augustus Caesàr, responsible for the building of the sea wall and gate.

Budic: A legionary in Gratillonius's detachment, of the Coritanean tribe in Britain.

CALVINUS: An agent of Maximus's secret police.

CALPURNIUS: Father of Sucat.

Camilla: Third daughter of Guilvilis and Gratillonius.

Carenn: Mother of Niall.

Carsa, Aulus Metellus: A young Gallo-Roman seaman from Burdigala.

Carsa, Tiberius Metellus: A Gallo-Roman sea captain, father of the above.

Cathual: Charioteer to Niall.

Childeric: A son of Merowech.

Clothair: A Frank settled in the Redonic canton.

Colconor: Former King of Ys, slain by Gratillonius.

CONUAL CORCC MAQQ LUGTHACI: Founder of the kingdom of Cashel.

CONCHESSA: Niece of Martinus and mother of Sucat.

Corentinus: A holy man, known today as St Corentin.

Coriran: A swineherd in Munster.

Cotta: A Mithraist in Vienne.

Craumthan maqq Fidaci: Brother of Mongfind, at one time King at Tara.

CUNEDAG: A prince of the Votadini, settled in Wales.

Cynan: A legionary in Gratillonius's detachment, of the Demetaic tribe in Britain, and a convert to Mithraism.

Dahilis: A former Queen of Ys, mother of Dahut by Gratillonius.

Dahut: Daughter of Dahilis and Gratillonius.

DAMASUS: Pope, 366–384.

Dardriu: A swineherd in Munster.

DELPHINUS: Late friend of Ausonius.

Domnuald: A son of Niall.

Donan: A member of Maeloch's crew.

Donnerch: A carter in Ys.

Drusus, Publius Flavius: A centurion of the Sixth and friend of Gratillonius; later a settler in Armorica.

Elissa: Birth name of Lanarvilis.

Éndae Qennsalach: Supreme King in Leinster.

Eochaid: A son of Éndae.

Eppillus, Quintus Junius: A legionary in Gratillonius's detachment, his deputy at the time, killed in battle at Ys.

Esmunin Sironai: Chief astrologer in Ys.

Estar: (1) Birth name of Dahilis. (2) Second daughter of Tambilis and Gratillonius.

Eucherius: Former chorepiscopus in Ys.

EUGENIUS: Briefly Augustus of the West, as a puppet of Arbogast.

Evar: A maidservant of Innilis.

Favonius: Gratillonius's favourite horse.

Féchra: A late half-brother of Niall.

Fedelmm: A witch, fostermother of Conual Corcc.

FELIX: A clergyman who became bishop of Trier.

Fennalis: A Queen of Ys.

Fland Dub maqq Ninnedo: Murderer of Domnuald.

Florus: A Gallo-Roman merchant.

Forsquilis: A Queen of Ys.

Fredegond: A son of Merowech.

Gaetulius: A former King of Ys.

GRATIANUS, FLAVIUS: Co-Emperor of the West with Valentinianus; defeated by Maximus and murdered.

Gratillonius, Gaius Valerius: A Romano-Briton of the Belgic tribe, centurion in the Second Legion Augusta, sent by Maximus to be the Roman prefect in Ys and caused by the Gallicenae to become its King.

Gratillonius, Marcus Valerius: Father of the above.

Guilvilis: A Queen of Ys.

Hannon Baltisi: Lir Captain in Ys.

Herun Taniti: An officer in the Ysan navy.

Hoel: A former King of Ys.

Hornach: An Osismian who would be King.

HONORIUS, FLAVIUS: A son of Theodosius, by him made Augustus of the West.

Innilis: A Queen of Ys.

Intil: An Ysan fisherman.

Ita: Late sister of Rufinus.

ITHACIUS: Bishop of Faro.

Jonan: A labourer in Ys.

Julia: Daughter of Lanarvilis and Gratillonius.

JULIANUS, FLAVIUS CLAUDIUS: Today known as Julian the apostate, this Emperor (361–363) tried to revive paganism under auspices of the state.

Kadrach: A cooper in Ys.

Keban: A prostitute in Ys, later Budic's wife.

Kerna: Second daughter of Bodilis by Hoel.

Laidchenn maqq Barchedo: An ollam poet in Niall's retinue.

Lanarvilis: A Queen of Ys.

Lugthach maqq Aillelo: A king in Munster, father of Conual Corcc.

Maclavius: A legionary in Gratillonius's detachment and fellow Mithraist.

Maeloch: An Ysan fisher captain and Ferrier of the Dead.

Maldunilis: A Queen of Ys.

MARIA: Daughter of Stilicho, who became wife of Honorius.

MARTINUS: Bishop of Tours and founder of the monastery at Marmoutier; today known as St Martin of Tours.

MAXIMUS, MAGNUS CLEMENS: Commander of Roman forces in Britain, who later forcibly took power as co-Emperor.

Mella: A servant and medical assistant of Innilis.

Merowech: A leader of the Frankish laeti around Redonum.

Mílchu: Owner of Sucat when the latter was a slave.

Miraine: A daughter of Lanarvilis by Hoel.

Moethaire of the Corco Óchae: Father of Fedelmm.

Mongfind: Stepmother of Niall, said to have been a witch.

Nagon Demari: A Suffete and the Labour Councillor in Ys.

Nath Í: Nephew and tanist of Niall.

Nemeta: Daughter of Forsquilis and Gratillonius.

NIALL MAQQ ECHACH, later known as NIALL OF THE NINE HOSTAGES: King at Tara, overlord of Mide in Ireland.

Oengus Bolg: A king in Munster, father of Ámend.

PATRICIUS: An advocate in the service of Maximus.

PAULINUS: A grandson of Ausonius.

PRISCILLIANUS: Heretical bishop of Ávila.

Quanis: A demonic mermaid in Ysan legend.

Quinipilis: A Queen of Ys.

Rovinda: Wife of Apuleius Vero.

Rufinus: A Redonic Bacauda, later Gratillonius's henchman.

RUFINUS: Praetorian prefect of Arcadius, overthrown by Stilicho.

Runa: Daughter of Vindilis by Hoel.

Salomon: Son of Apuleius Vero and Rovinda.

Sasai: First daughter of Guilvilis and Gratillonius.

Semuramat: (1) Third daughter of Bodilis by Hoel; later known as Tambilis. (2) First daughter of her and Gratillonius.

SERENA: Wife of Stilicho.

Sicorus: The large landowner at Maedraeacum.

Silis: A prostitute in Ys.

Soren Cartagi: Speaker for Taranis in Ys, Timberman delegate to the Council.

STILICHO, FLAVIUS: A powerful Roman general.

SUCAT (or SUCCAT): Birth name of St Patrick.

Syrus, Lucas Orgetuorig: Mithraic Father in Vienne.

Talavair: First daughter of Bodilis by Hoel.

Tambilis: A Queen of Ys, daughter of Bodilis and Hoel.

Targorix: An early Celtic king.

THEODOSIUS, FLAVIUS: Today known as the Great; Augustus of the East, eventually, briefly, sole Roman Emperor.

Theuderich: A son of Merowech.

Tigernach: A son of Laidchenn.

Tommaltach maqq Donngalii: A young man from Munster.

Torna Éces: Great poet in Ireland who fostered both Niall and Conual and who taught Laidchenn.

Tóthual the Desired: Founder of Mide.

Uail maqq Carbri: A henchman of Niall.

Una: Daughter of Bodilis and Gratillonius.

Usan: An Ysan fisherman, Maeloch's mate on *Osprey*.

Utican the Wanderer: An Ysan poet.

VALENTINIANUS, FLAVIUS: Co-Emperor of the West.

Valeria: Fourth daughter of Guilvilis and Gratillonius.

Verania: Daughter of Apuleius Vero and Rovinda.

Verica: A legionary in Gratillonius's detachment and fellow Mithraist.

VICTOR: A son of Maximus.

Vindilis: A Queen of Ys.

Vindomarix: Druid to Targorix.

Witch-Hanai: An Ysan poet.

Wulfgar: A former King of Ys.

Zisa: First daughter of Maldunilis and Gratillonius.